Alexis

*To Doreen & Tony
Enjoy Eliza's journey*

by

Pamela J Fulton

Pamela J. Fulton

DOREEN DENNY
01237-478316

Order this book online at www.trafford.com/07-1639
or email orders@trafford.com

Most Trafford titles are also available at major online book retailers.

© Copyright 2008 Pamela J. Fulton.

All rights reserved. No part of this publication may be reproduced, stored in a retrieval system, or transmitted, in any form or by any means, electronic, mechanical, photocopying, recording, or otherwise, without the written prior permission of the author.

Note for Librarians: A cataloguing record for this book is available from Library and Archives Canada at www.collectionscanada.ca/amicus/index-e.html

Printed in Victoria, BC, Canada.

ISBN: 978-1-4251-4024-3

We at Trafford believe that it is the responsibility of us all, as both individuals and corporations, to make choices that are environmentally and socially sound. You, in turn, are supporting this responsible conduct each time you purchase a Trafford book, or make use of our publishing services. To find out how you are helping, please visit www.trafford.com/responsiblepublishing.html

Our mission is to efficiently provide the world's finest, most comprehensive book publishing service, enabling every author to experience success. To find out how to publish your book, your way, and have it available worldwide, visit us online at www.trafford.com/10510

 www.trafford.com

North America & international
toll-free: 1 888 232 4444 (USA & Canada)
phone: 250 383 6864 ♦ fax: 250 383 6804 ♦ email: info@trafford.com

The United Kingdom & Europe
phone: +44 (0)1865 722 113 ♦ local rate: 0845 230 9601
facsimile: +44 (0)1865 722 868 ♦ email: info.uk@trafford.com

10 9 8 7 6 5 4 3 2

BOOK I

THE WEST COUNTRY

CHAPTER 1

ALL BECAUSE OF TESS

"...two persons were walking rapidly ...One of the pair was Angel Clare, the other a tall budding creature - half girl, half woman - a spiritualised image of Tess, slighter than she, but with the same beautiful eyes - Clare's sister-in-law, Liza-Lu. Their pale faces seem to have shrunk to half their natural size. They moved on hand in hand ..." Thomas Hardy — *Tess of the D'Urbervilles*.

— Mr Clare, what shall we do now?

Angel Clare, erstwhile dairyman, failed independent farmer and now instant widower, turns his hollow eyes on his sister-in-law.

— We must be strong. We must be strong for Tess' sake. That's what she wanted.

Each time he grits out the word *strong* he unconsciously squeezes her hand. Unconscious to him but not to Liza-Lu who is very aware of her hand being in his grip ever since they'd left the gallows. The longest time, in fact the first time, her hand has been in any man's grip. At mention of her sister's name, her throat tightens.

— I can't believe it. I can't believe poor Tess is gone, like *that*.

Tears begin to swell her sight until she has to stop walking. She feels Clare's arm across her back in a fumbling familiar gesture to comfort her, to help her cope.

— You know, Liza-Lu, that Tessie tried to spare you her anguish. You are, were, so dear to her, being next in age. It was too much for your mother and the younger ones to visit her in prison. Tess feared it might be too much for you, too. She killed that fellow, D'Urberville; stabbed him in desperation for my sake. She told me she did it because of what we nearly had, might have had, but lost. It's all my fault.

He swallows hard.

— Tess said to me, 'I forgive you, Angel.' Forgave *me*! When it was *I* who doubted *her*. It was I who went off to South America to forget her and too late realized she was not duplicitous, as I'd imagined. Just a simple country girl, trusting and doubting; and I let her down.

Now it's Liza-Lu's turn to become the comforter. They fall against one another in their sorrow. For the first time the awful reality of their loss sweeps over them as they pause there sobbing, tears falling on the unfeeling stones of the high street. Unwilling witnesses.

From the western gate of the town they move on, still hand in hand, towards the treeless hill with the monument on top. Clare helps pull her up the steep grassy slope until they stand, surveying the tiled rooftops of the freestone houses. Gusts of wind under her wide-brimmed hat send Liza-Lu's auburn hair dancing around her heart-shaped face, obscuring her vision as suddenly as it reveals her innocent violet gaze: Tess' eyes. Clare looks at her now in the early sun of that July morning as if he is aware of her for the first time as a person and not as an appendage of Tess. She is tall, slender, no, willowy; and despite her uncertainty in the midst of this crisis she exhibits an air of confidence that he'd never perceived in Tess. He indicates a spot for them to sit down on the grass and releases her hand. Liza-Lu half sits, half leans against the marble base of the monument.

— Why not sit on the grass with me?

— It's damp; and besides, I might stain my skirts.

They are silent a while as if they are both weighed down by the same thought.

— You know, Liza-Lu, in those few days Tess and I had together before she was taken into custody on Salisbury Plain, we had the deepest and most serious discussions about life, and death, and the future. Tess had very clear ideas about the future for us, you and me, I mean. I think she somehow thought she could make it up to me by having you fill her place in our relationship so that the two people she loved the most would be together, and would find the happiness that eluded her.

Liza-Lu nods. *Tess always shared her innermost thoughts with me but I'm not going to reveal them to you, Mr Angel Clare, at this point in time. I barely know you although I know a lot about you, spilled into my youthful ears over the last three years from my poor sister's twice-broken heart. I know you only from Tess' perspective: a fair-haired knight training as a gentleman farmer at*

Alexis 7

the same place where she was employed as a dairymaid. How you wooed her in the meadows and were going to educate her up and take her away from tenant farms and contract work forever. And how you played the harp so magically, of all things! She told me how you two married very quietly, without any family from either side present, then you abandoned her on your wedding night in a fit of high principle after insisting you both bare your deepest regrets, your deepest secrets.

She told me you confessed to visiting a brothel in London which had shocked her no end but as you were now married she had no other option but to forgive you. Then she felt free to tell you about the big impediment she had tried and tried to bring up in conversation with you before the wedding but opportunities kept slipping by. At last she was able to tell you about Alec D'Urberville, a wealthy young squire who took advantage of her late one night when she was lost coming home from the Trantridge Fair; and how she tried to distance herself from him; how he was unaware he was the father of her child (poor little thing died within the year), used her for fun then dropped her. I pleaded with her to tell you before the wedding, and she tried to tell you. Oh, she tried! And when the truth, which had been eating her up, was at last torn from her, you, Angel Clare, spurned her, implying that the same act you were involved with in London made Tess (in your eyes) practically married to the man who compromised her. You even took back the set of heirloom diamond jewellery you'd given her, the one your godmother sent as a wedding present.

This is the Angel Clare I know. You sent Tess back to Mother but Tess couldn't face us, and left, only to be claimed again by that same miscreant young upstart, D'Urberville himself. 'I should have listened to you, Liza-Lu, I should have listened!'

Oh yes, I know about you. I was only sixteen at the beginning of all this and from all she told me I learned of her extremely bumpy rite of passage from innocent girlhood into the cold, hard, jaded world of men: a path that I, Liza-Lu Durbeyfield, am determined to avoid at all costs. Sweet nothings lead only to babies and promises. I really loved Tess, and looked up to her but maybe being born beautiful has its drawbacks. When I look in the looking glass I see very similar features, the same unusual violet eyes; and although my hair is auburn, gold in the sunlight, we have the same rosebud lips and milky white skin.

All these memories flash through her mind in a moment.

— I barely know you, Mr Clare. And now, so soon after, are you propositioning me?

All through her reverie he is watching her.

— She told me she'd discussed her thoughts with you, as well.

— We had no secrets, Tess and I. She told me everything because I didn't judge. Listened, but I didn't judge.

She turns and looks pointedly at him, prompting him to explain.

— I didn't judge her either. Well, perhaps I did. I didn't mean to. I was very young then, immature. Although it's only months in time it feels like eons in experience. You don't know how much I've learned since those days when I had my high standards, high ideals. You've no idea how it hit me when I heard that confession from my innocent (or so I thought) bride. I couldn't think straight. I had my family, my reputation, to protect. I had to get away to clear my head. That's why I left; I arranged for Tess to draw money when I was gone; and I also believed her to be at your place. When I returned (and I nearly didn't make it), I found her missing, gone. You know the story how I tracked her down in Sandbourne, only it was too late. They were living as man and wife but she still loved me. She killed him in despair after I knocked on the door and she sent me away; left him there and followed after me. Then we had those few days together hiding out in rapture until the hue and cry caught up with us.

CHAPTER 2

Proposal

Liza-Lu looks over the roofs to St Catherine's Hill behind the town, and beyond to the up and downlands shorn by grazing sheep, a series of tranquil rolling hills she tries to use to calm her rising disquietude. *'I will lift up mine eyes unto the hills, from whence cometh my help.'*

— On Salisbury Plain Tess talked of you before they found her and took her away. She was concerned about the future, not her own, but mine and yours; and she asked me to watch over you, Liza-Lu. She begged and implored me, if I should lose her, to marry you, as you are the only one she would want to share me with; and for me to train you, and teach you, and mould you so you could be my helpmeet in life, something I was unable to complete with her.

I remember her pleadings, too, when I visited her in the prison. Somehow, I couldn't bring myself to promise her anything. I wasn't even able to grant a dying woman's wish. I felt numb, out of control, as if the world were pushing me along in her dreams. Now, I again feel independence slipping away. I'm too caught up in the vortex Tess left behind.

—I have no logical reason to deny her this last wish but I don't know you at all, Mr Clare. All this love you profess for my sister is like a fountain that you have suppressed, and now you are directing it at me.

— I admit it sounds hasty but it's not an ill-conceived plan. You have all her attributes, and more. You are indeed very pleasing to the eye; you did well in school, Tess told me, and reached Standard Six before she did, well enough in fact to become the teacher's assistant; you are sheltered, live at home, and are malleable, as Tess mentioned. Above all, you are young, a virgin, and have not been toyed with by men.

She levels her violet eyes at him.

— I think you've been around cattle auctions a little too much, Mr Clare. You have this all worked out down to the fine detail.

— I've considered all things from my perspective.

— Have you considered them from *my* perspective? You sound like you're following a blueprint without taking my feelings into account. Maybe I'm not as malleable as you imagine. I may be young and naive in many ways but I'm not your inner image of Tess.

— Oh, I don't mean to sound manipulating. Forgive me for being so forthright. I thought you might come to see this in the same light as Tess and I did. If you would agree to such an arrangement, it would work out perfectly for both of us. You don't have any prospects, I hope?

— You can set your mind to rest on that score. However, I do have ambitions. You seem to overlook the fact that I'm an individual with hopes and aspirations in life that are not the products of either your or Tess' imaginations.

— She always said you were the more practical one. You are more free-spoken, too.

— I've seen the results of hasty decisions that brought nothing but grief to those who made them. I, too, long for an exciting, romantic life. It seems, though, to have brought Tess more heartache than joy. That turned me practical in short order. Tess is, was, always a hopeful dreamer, and superstitious too. Father was a dreamer but she takes, took, after Mother in the other respect; very impressionable. All Mother wanted for her was a fine gentleman to take her away; and look where it got her. And you, you never visited our house but once.

— It was not for lack of wanting. I admit I was too lofty in my ideals about a perfect wife. Consequently I was flung so low when things went against me. Now I'm older and have had time to see the balance. That is why I now understand that a reasoned union, not an impassioned one, such as between yourself and myself, would work in this topsy-turvy world. I'm a gentleman farmer with a small inheritance and I can provide you with a comfortable living, a servant even, maybe two: one for the farm and one for the house. My father is the Vicar at Emminster which you probably already know, and my two older brothers are in the church. I would be honoured if you would be my wife. I could provide you with an abundance of literature to read which would broaden your experience, and marriage would provide you with instant security.

— But I enjoy teaching children. Maybe someday I'll become a governess. If I marry you, I'll have to abandon that dream, and I'm still only eighteen years old.

— Wouldn't you, in the long run, still want the security of a husband and family? By marrying me, you could eliminate that uncertain middle step.

— But I don't love you!

— Can't you see that's a blessing? Look what love did to Tess. Look what it's done to me: nearly destroyed me both physically and mentally. At first I, too, protested Tess' pleading. After all, you are my sister-in-law; but she pointed out that many men around your village married sisters-in-law. It's not illegal. It's not even incestuous.

— I cannot give you an answer right away, Mr Clare.

— Angel.

— I will have to think it over. Balance it. You may well be right. At least an impassionate proposal allows us to weigh the pros and cons. I've heard arranged marriages often work, grow warm with time, even become intimate. Marriage is often no more than an alliance with another man's property. Land I mean. Let me take a look at you. Take off your hat!

She turns to him, face-on, as they are about the same height, and scrutinizes his features: fair to golden hair naturally tightly-curled (real ringlets if it were any longer) and parted in the middle; a delicate rectangular face and soft blue eyes. *He seems almost vulnerable.* Thin white lips on a small, compressed mouth.

— You will think on it, Liza-Lu? May I call on you at your mother's, Rose Cottage isn't it, for my answer?

— What! No courting? No walking out together? No flowers? No sweets in crinkly paper left behind to remind me of you? Just a proposal and an answer?

— You're not a sweet-nothings person, Liza-Lu. You said you were the practical one. Would it make a difference if I did come courting?

She looks him straight in the eye, and blinks, as if thinking right through him.

— I'll have to think on it. Come by my mother's the last Sunday of the month and I'll give you an answer. I don't wish to pursue this conversation for the rest of the way home.

The two figures turn and walk together rapidly away from the town under the now mid-morning sun, two straw hats deep in their own thoughts.

CHAPTER 3

Rose Cottage

Rose Cottage, Liza-Lu's most recent home, is the very same cottage where Tess had been appointed to look after old Mrs D'Urberville's fowls in the days when Tess first encountered Alec D'Urberville. It's a thatched cottage, very old, old enough for ivy to get a firm footing on the stone walls and rugged chimney, its dark, shining green keeping the stones cool during the summer. The old cottage is part of the The Slopes estate the D'Urbervilles bought before they built the new manor house. Mrs D'Urberville, who had a passion for fowls, exotic and domestic, had used the lower floor of the cottage as a hen house. Surrounding the rectangular building is a rectangular fortress-like brick-walled 'garden' which has been allowed to decay into a sandy bare wasteland during the avian occupation. When the destitute Durbeyfields were deposited there by Alec they named it 'Rose Cottage" because of the derelict climbing roses on the garden wall, whose only entrance is through a wooden gate.

Downstairs consists of two rooms, a kitchen with a stone hearth belonging to the ample chimney on the left of the central entrance, and another larger room on the right, a living room *cum* parlour. A door at the rear provides a nice breeze-way in summer and a glacial alley in winter, and leads back to the rubbish tip and outhouse. The central staircase leads up from the entrance to four small half-storey bedrooms with sloping ceilings under the gables. Widow Joan Durbeyfield shares one of the front rooms with her youngest, Charlie, aged five. Abraham, who is next to Liza-Lu in age and still in school, and John, seven, share a back room, as do Hope, eleven, and Modesty, nine. Liza-Lu, now being the eldest and the odd man out, as it were, has the luxury of the other front room to herself, sparsely furnished though it is. A black iron bedstead and a hope chest at the foot; a row of hooks along one wall; a plain little dresser without a mirror that she'd shared with Tess (one their father had brought home on the cart years ago when he was 'trading'); and a shelf above her bed; the sum total of her furniture.

The old lady, Mrs D'Urberville, had died some months before Mr Alec brought the Durbeyfield family to Rose Cottage after he had "found" Tess again. Tess said Mrs D'Urberville was blind, and a little off the beam. It was Tess' job to take the birds up to the manor house daily, and Mrs D'Urberville would pet them on her lap and talk to them as if they were old friends. When she went, so did her fowls; Alec saw to that. He'd left Rose Cottage untouched when his mother died and there was a terrible mess to clean up both in the enclosure and in the lower floors as the hens had the run of the downstairs. At least he had taken care of their family when Tess went off to live with him, and he provided them with free rent of the cottage. He declined living by himself in the new manor house his parents had built; and now the Durbeyfields' tenure is up in the air again as the need to put something down on paper had not occurred to Alec. Now the bailiff had come and given Joan Durbeyfield notice: pay the back rent and vacate by the end of the month.

Joan doesn't have the money for the rent. Tall and wiry with red hair (that's where Liza-Lu gets it from) and fair skin that goes to freckles in the sun, she barely makes enough from the washing and mending she takes in to give all seven mouths enough to fill their bellies. Everything is scrounged. She knits the children's pullovers and stockings from unbleached wool, seconds, from a nearby mill, and spends almost as much time separating the burrs from the wool as she does constructing the garments. Liza-Lu helps with the needlework but it's not steady employment. They have been there only a few months, not enough time to build up a clientele, and now they face eviction again.

*Mother sees me as the family's only way out of poverty. Because of his love of Tess, Angel Clare promised he'd marry me, as well as take care of my whole family (ergo, pay the rent for Rose Cottage, plus keep). If I spurn his offer now, I'll wreck all our chances. I feel like an animal herded into a narrower and narrower pen, trapped. I don't think I'm a selfish person but I can't help thinking: What if Tess had not the scruples she did, and had **not** told Angel about D'Urberville and the baby? Why hadn't she kept her mouth shut? Mother often wonders about this out loud, wails it: 'Tess could have been the wife of a gentleman farmer!' Now I feel I'm being coerced into the very same role, same laid-out mould.*

— I feel like I'm being pushed into this, by you, Mother, by circumstances, by Angel, by Tess! Am I a fool to pass up such an offer? I have nothing to bring to such a marriage except my similarity to Tess, my eyes, skin, youth, naivete; perhaps a little less gullible than Tess, and I have more schooling. I haven't even thought of marriage before. Well, like all my friends, I've dreamed of a knight in shining armour who'll carry me off into the sunset, when I'm ready to be swept off my feet but this knight is not the one I'd imagined. He's coming too soon, and I'm not ready. It's as if it's all been decided ahead of time and is out of my hands. What say do I have, except 'yes' or 'no'? It's as if I've been signed, sealed, and delivered.

— What! Pass up a chance like this? It's a golden opportunity, my girl. Your future is presented to you on a tray. [She was going to say 'a silver platter' but decided a tray was more the level of a farmer's wife.] He's begging you, Liza-Lu, and he does seem to be a very nice man.

She looks at her daughter coyly.

— You've only met him once, Mother!

— Well, to me he seemed a very nice man. He's taken Tess' fate very hard. I think it would be nice to have the same son-in-law twice.

— Oh, Mother, there you go again, romanticising. This is my future, my life, we're talking about, my fate: about what is to become of *me*.

— You really are simple-brained, my girl. Now that Mr Alec is dead and we're no longer under his patronage, we have to move from Rose Cottage or find a way to stay here. And you are our way of staying here. You'll have to put those governess notions right out of your head or else you, my girl, being the eldest, will have to get your hands dirty and hire yourself out around here to help support your family. Abraham will have to leave school and find work, or else become apprenticed. If he does that there'll be no money coming in and the young'uns will have to leave school to help me with the washing; *unless* you accept Mr Angel Clare's very kind offer. He swore to Tess he'd look after us, and this is his way of keeping his promise.

— Are you saying that I am a bargaining chip, a way for him to ease his conscience? You really want me to say 'yes', don't you?

— Now, now, Liza-Lu, I don't mean to influence you in any way. I just want to lay out the way things are, from a mother's point of view. He's not *that* bad. Strikes a fair figure; and he has prospects, Liza-Lu, prospects.

— The way I see it unfolding is you expect me to marry for convenience, not love.

— You can learn to love him. People do, all the time; kings and queens and the heads of Europe. It's like a bargain, a deal, a mutually satisfying arrangement. He's not disagreeable to look at – the fair curly hair, the mustache; dresses well; comes from a very good family; and a grammar school education, no less. Reads a lot of books, he told me: that's fairly harmless. Serious sort of fella. You might get to love him yet.

Mother's subtly applying the pressure. I can feel it being laid down layer by layer, heavier and heavier. Liza-Lu: the saviour of the Durbeyfield family. There go my dreams over the horizon. Shakespeare writes, 'To thine own self be true' but I can't be true to myself. They won't let me. I don't want to go through with this but Mother, for all her narrow-mindedness, has seen this as the only practical solution. I must get my practicality from her. Father and Tess were the dreamers, and the dreamers are both gone. It's now up to Mother and me to raise the family. I've always wanted to be a governess and follow in Jane Eyre's footsteps to shape little minds and teach the three Rs and singing; and read them adventures about other countries, and poetry. Those hopes are now only a dream, a dream that is disappearing fast. If I marry Mr Clare, my chances of a career are at an end and I'll never meet my Mr Rochester.

— If I could become a governess, I'd get my room and board and I could send the rest of my wages to you.

— It's a pipe dream, Liza-Lu, only a pipe dream. You're not a qualified governess, and I haven't the money to send you to be trained up as one. It's the here and now that's got to be taken care of, here and now. The best way out of our troubles here and now is for you to take Mr Clare up on his offer smart quick before he thinks better of it and changes his mind. Right now, your duty is to your family.

Powerless. Numb. Mother's right, though. I'm all out of arguments.

CHAPTER 4

A STUDY OF MATRIMONY

To get away from the oppressive atmosphere, Liza-Lu leaves the room and goes upstairs to think it through rationally, to decide. Taking down her *Book of Common Prayer* from amongst others on the shelf above her head, she lies prone on the bed looking for the section on marriage. *I'll review this section in detail, even though it's fairly familiar. After all, these are the words I'll be swearing to God to keep. Couples get married regularly during Sunday service but those vows belong to them, certainly not to the congregation. These words have only skimmed through my head, until now. Until now!*

She deliberately flips through the onion skin pages until she comes to "Solemnization of Matrimony', and solemn and serious it is. 'If any of you know cause or just impediment, why these two persons should not be joined in Holy Matrimony, ye are to declare it.' She remembers her heroine, Jane Eyre, and shivers. *There's always a chance that could happen. However, Mr Clare is a bona fide widower and I'm a spinster, and we are not blood relatives.* 'Holy Matrimony …is not to be enterprised, nor taken in hand, unadvisedly, lightly, or wantonly …' *Unadvisedly. Who can I turn to for advice? Mother is obviously biassed, and Hope and Modesty are too young to be confidants. My girlhood friends? I left them behind in Marlot. I don't know the local vicar: we haven't been here long enough. I could have spoken to our old one, Parson Tringham, the family historian who told Father that our surname, Durbeyfield, is a mashed up form of the name D'Urberville, a noble family that came over from France with William the Conqueror in 1066 and settled in Kingsbere, south of here. It was Mother's insistence on Tess pursuing a relationship with the D'Urbervilles of Trantridge that directly led to her early death. I can remember Mother urging Tess to claim kinship in order to better* herself. **Better** herself! Look where it got her. D'Urberville, Durbeyfield. They sound similar if slurred or spoken through closed teeth. Some clerk or census taker in the past wrote down what he thought he heard, and changed history. In the flourish of a pen a new surname was born. Mother and Father were quite convinced of our nobility but I have yet to see any good heaped on our family because of it. I'm getting away from my task here.

I'll just have to be my own adviser. I'm certainly not considering the subject of marriage lightly, or wantonly; probably less wantonly than other young women. The 'want' is more Mr Clare's persistence. 'Holy Matrimony was ordained for the mutual society, help, and comfort, that the one ought to have for the other, both in prosperity and adversity.' *Angel Clare is promising me a comfortable life but I'd better remind him about 'adversity'. Poor Tess was in a mess of adversity, yet he abandoned her.*

The husband promises to 'love', 'comfort', 'honour' and 'keep' me in sickness and in health, and 'forsaking all other'. I have to promise to 'obey' and 'serve' him as well as all the rest. I don't know about the 'obey' part. I don't want to be controlled by someone else, to be subservient and only do what he allows me to do. If I marry now, I can't take a position or work at all as it will look as if my husband cannot afford to keep me, or cannot control me. Oh, what am I going to do?

'Who giveth this woman ...?' Who indeed? Father being dead, could Mother 'give me away'? Give me away, as if she didn't want me any more, get rid of me. If I marry, I want to be the one to make the choice to step up beside a man because **I** decided to go through life with him, not be 'given away'. Still, I suppose I'll have to be. Maybe Abraham could hand me into bondage. He's fifteen now. Is there a minimum age for the head of the household? Twenty-one perhaps? What's next?

She runs her finger zig-zag down the page under each of the lines. 'To have and to hold.' *I like that phrase. To have and to hold Mr Angel Clare. It's repeated down here: he promises to have and hold me. It might be nice to be held close. I remember how he held my hand after we left the prison for the last time.* 'For better for worse, for richer for poorer, in sickness and in health, to love and to cherish ...' *I remember those words; they're kind of sing-songy. I'd have no problems promising that. Interesting how 'love' and 'cherish' come last of all. If I decide to take up his offer, even though 'love' and 'cherish* **are** *last, they would likely grow and become more important. I think it would be nice to be cherished; like an old servant, or a dog, or a favourite grandmother.*

The tough one is having to promise to obey. *Very difficult. Maybe if I swallow hard when I say it, it won't be so bad.* 'Obey' is followed by '*'til death do us* part'. *That's a long time to obey: from eighteen until death; but Mr Clare doesn't seem too demanding or domineering, just serious. Maybe even depressed.*

The man says, 'I plight thee my troth.' *What is 'troth'? I have to say.* 'I give you my troth.' *That's probably what it means: the man plights, and the woman gives. Is that an equal exchange? Or does she come off second best again?*

Here's an interesting section. The man says, 'with my Body I thee worship, and with all my worldly Goods I thee endow.' *That might equal things out. Mother's always said,* 'marriage is give and take' *Now here comes the thunderous line,* 'those whom God hath joined together let no man put asunder'! *Alec D'Urberville, the man who sundered Tess and Angel's marriage, was stabbed through the heart! With him gone, the D'Urberville influence on the Durbeyfields is also gone forever.*

I wonder how that affected Mr Clare when he resolved to carry out Tess' dying wish? I think he really means to keep his promise this time. All things considered, I could probably bring myself to be tender toward him.

She snaps the prayer book closed and puts it back. *It's been a good idea to weigh the pros and cons without being caught up in a giddy romance. Those girlfriends back in Marlot who were infatuated over their very ordinary swains appeared to have their heads in the clouds, and never seemed to face matrimony with common sense, soberly considered. Instead they were all giggly and smug-looking:* 'We've got our man. Where's yours?'

Liza-Lu returns to the living room and finds Joan darning in a corner by the window, squinting in the fading light.

— Mother? I think I might accept Mr Clare's proposal. He's not unpleasant to look at, as you say; maybe a little morose but what can you expect after what he's been through? I might even be able to brighten him up a bit. I'm sure the man can smile. I think I would make a good farmer's wife. I can't milk but I could learn if I had to. I'm organized; I like to get up early; I like baking, and I can cook. Furthermore, he's said he'll look after you and the children. That's quite a lot of baggage to go along with a bride, and no dowry.

— Oh, Liza-Lu! You're a good, good girl! You're going to save the family *and* get quite a prize into the bargain. I know how you set your heart on being a governess ….

— Hush, Mother, I would have had to go away and get training, and we've no money for that. I accept that now. He's even promised to school me up in literature: 'finish' me, no less.

— You don't want to be wasting your time on literature. You'll be too busy making babies and sewing and knitting and running the household.

— I'm too young for babies, Mother.

— Nonsense, my girl. Why, on your marriage night you'll have to do your duty.

— My duty? What do you mean?

— Why, every man has the right to roger his wife.

— What?

— You know, put his thing inside you. Men call it Roger and use their wives when they feel like it.

That must be what 'to have and to hold' means; or maybe, 'with my body I thee worship'. What am I getting myself into?

— What if I don't feel like it?

— For better, for worse!

— How is it done? How often do they do it?

— Oh girl, you ask too many questions. You'll find out soon enough. It's one of your wifely duties.

Sobered by this information, Liza-Lu is thinking: *What other wifely duties are there I don't know about? Changing my status is now on an entirely different footing. 'Roger the wife.' I always wanted my knight in shining armour to carry me away but I never thought about what happens afterwards.*

— It doesn't hurt. Much. You'll get used to it. He's been through a lot, Liza-Lu. He'll be tender with you, and I'm sure he'll be a lot lighter-hearted when you see him again, you mark my words.

Liza-Lu pulls a flat little smile.

— Then he can woo you proper.

— Maybe you're right. I'll just have to wait and see what changes a month can make. Mother, please don't take this on as a Crusade; or push me any further *(like you did with Tess)*. Just let it unfold. Please.

— Orright, orright. Now get started on them spuds. They won't peel theirselves, you know. You've lots of time to mull this over come the end of the month.

CHAPTER 5

Angel Comes Courting

The end of the month arrives, and with it Mr Angel Clare, courting a Miss Durbeyfield for the second time.

Liza-Lu comes into the house, murmuring. She's been sitting out in the garden in the narrow early afternoon shade of the wall, and the air is perfumed by a thousand petals. She's been reading a book of Wordsworth and marvelling at his choice and scarcity of words on paper and how they can produce such a profound effect on the reader of them. Comes into the house murmuring, 'she is in her grave, and oh, the difference to me'.

— Busy yourself, Liza-Lu. Look who's coming through the gate.

— Mrs Durbeyfield? I believe we have already met. I'm Angel Clare.

— Why Mr Clare, you don't look a bit different from when I seen you last.

Angel is wearing a mustard-coloured waistcoat under a light brown suit, with his jacket open, and must have plucked one of the pink rambling roses from the wall as he passed. It protrudes through the buttonhole of his jacket. He removes his boater.

— Liza-Lu will take that for you. Come in, Mr Clare, come right in. Of course, you know Liza-Lu.

Liza-Lu comes forward and extends her hand. He takes it as if to shake it but brings it to his lips instead where he holds it for some time, looking at her.

— My dear Liza-Lu, I'm very happy to see you again. He swallows, realizing just how beautiful Liza-Lu has become with that deep auburn hair and those eyes, whose effect on him she is yet unaware of.

— Mr Clare, Angel, I'm very pleased to see you *(looking so happy; but I can't say that)* again, too.

She takes his hat.

— Won't you come into the parlour?

She leads the way, hanging his hat on a hook in the hall on the way in.

— Do sit down. Can we offer you a cool drink?

— That would be very nice, thank you. I walked from Trantridge Cross where the coach dropped me. The summers seem to be getting hotter year by year.

Liza-Lu pours out three raspberry cordials and brings them over on a wooden tray, with a sprig of mint in each. Angel takes his and drains half of it, evidence of his thirst. She offers one to her mother who intends to chaperone this auspicious meeting from a chair in the corner. Joan likes corners: they are comfortable and she can survey the developing scene in its entirety. She is determined to keep tighter control of this liaison than she did with her eldest daughter. Lacking tact, she blurts out,

— Mr Clare, Liza-Lu's been thinking over your offer. We've been waiting for you to come and lay your plans on the table. I understand you're willing to keep us on here at Rose Cottage?

— Mother! *Don't be so direct or you'll drive him away, although he seems more amused by her bluntness, even if a little startled.*

— I want to do what's right by Liza-Lu, Mrs Durbeyfield. I realize that by taking her to be my wife, I take you all; and I'm quite prepared to do that. My plan is to buy a small farm here in the West Country, a model farm they call them, mixed farm; you know, a mixture of crops and animals. Then, if the corn gets the rust or the chickens get wheezy I'll only take a partial loss. Living out the old proverb: not putting all your eggs in one basket.

— That's a very wise move, Mr Clare.

Joan is now seeing the saviour in a more realistic light, and liking more and more of what she sees.

— It's so very kind of you to keep us on here at Rose Cottage. You don't know how indebted we are to you. Children! Come in and meet Mr Clare.

The younger children, all clustered around the door, don't need inviting. They spill into the room with a rush. Abraham is the only one absent.

— Hope, Modesty, say 'How-de-do' to Mr Clare.

The girls shyly come up to Angel and he shakes their hands seriously.

— Hello, Hope.

The eleven year old looks briefly into his face with solemn eyes, then drops them.

— And you're Modesty.

It so happens Modesty doesn't quite live up to her name. She has wild tomboyish hair and brown eyes set in a perfectly round face.

— How-de-do, Mr Clare. Are you going to take Liza-Lu away, too?

Angel smiles at her.

— That all depends on Liza-Lu.

Young John is next to be presented. He stops toe to toe with Angel and salutes.

— Hello, Mr Clare.

— How do you do, Sir.

— I'm going to be a soldier when I grow up.

— Well, I hope you save the country, John.

— Don't worry. It's in the bag.

Angel has now met the younger brood, all except Little Charlie, the five year old. He has great big blue eyes and curly red hair, and stands very quietly, staring intently at Angel.

— You're not a angel. You haven't any wings.

The whole room erupts into laughter.

— Angel is my name, not what I am. I don't know why my parents settled on such a name.

Joan is more than happy to see the easy interaction between her hoped-for again son-in-law and her children. If only Liza-Lu keeps her side of the bargain! She calls Hope and Modesty over to her.

— Would you two girls go and make the tea now? And be careful with the boiling water. You can put the scones on the table, Modesty. Liza-Lu, why don't you take Angel out and show him the garden while the girls are getting the tea ready?

She gestures with her eyes towards the door.

At twenty-eight Angel is ten years older than Liza-Lu, his fair tightly-curled hair receding at the temples. He holds the door as he and Liza-Lu step into the 'garden'. Liza-Lu explains.

— Since we've been here Mother has tried to grow a few vegetables to add to the pot, beans, carrots and the like, and a few herbs: free vegetables. Otherwise, it's just the climbing roses.

— It looks like I've come at the right time for the roses; and you, Liza-Lu, are the sweetest bud of all.

He says this, casually, as they stroll away from the house walking shoulder to shoulder. *I can feel his rough coat against my arm.* When they reach the

gate that leads out of the walled enclosure, he puts his hand on the latch.

— We can't go through there, Angel. We'll be out of sight of the house.

— That's just the point. There are too many eyes boring into us.

He opens the gate and motions her to pass through into the shade of the tall pines and ash trees that form a visual barrier between Rose Cottage and the red brick manor house, and when they're both through, he leans against the cool brick wall.

— Have you an answer for me, Liza-Lu? You know that's why I came today, the last of the month, as promised.

— Well, Mr Clare, Angel, I've thought things through very seriously and have concluded that we could make a marriage work.

— Tess was very proud of how your family is descended from the original D'Urberville family down our way at Kingsbere.

— Mother and Father had her convinced she was almost nobility but what's the use of putting on airs, even if it's true, when there's no money to ennoble us?

— I'm afraid I'm the one who told her the legend of the D'Urberville coach. Hundreds of years ago a terrible crime was committed in the family coach. Now, when a true D'Urberville descendant hears the sound of coach wheels, or sees the coach, disaster or death is immanent.

— I've heard that story too, but I don't believe it. Tess was like Mother, very superstitious. You know how superstitious Mother is: crossed knives, wearing green, black cats, ladders. She even has a book of dreams that tells you what your dreams mean: what it means if you dream of spiders or royalty, and what will happen in your life: *The Book of Fate*. Tess swallowed that coach story hook, line and sinker. To me it's as fairy-taleish as 'The Princess and the Pea'.

— You seem noble to me, Liza-Lu and despite your pecuniary situation I feel I am not marrying down, but up.

— I feel the same way, Angel. I think we'll be very compatible.

He takes her hands, both hands, in his.

He's standing so close. Now he's pulling me, gently, towards him. I'm closer to him than I've ever been to any man. What's he waiting for? What's going to happen next? His face is so close, square. And his wavy hair; and pale blue eyes so intent. I think he's attracted to me. Will you cherish me and keep me, Angel Clare? Stop looking at me. What is happening?

Angel steps forward until they are bosom to bosom. He lets go of her hands and reaches up, running his through her glowing hair.

— In that case, Miss Durbeyfield, I think we should consider ourselves engaged.

He's leaning even closer. He's kissing me on the lips! What am I supposed to do? I'll just stand still and let this first kiss happen. His moustache is tickly, hairy.

— Let us go and tell your family, then we can work out arrangements for the wedding. You've made me a happy man, Liza-Lu and I promise I won't let you down. I'll really try to be a good husband, and provide for you and your family.

So this is love. It's not exactly exhilarating; but it's secure.

Angel and Liza-Lu go back through the gate and over to Rose Cottage, he with a proprietary arm around her waist. Hands and faces are plastered against the windows of the parlour and kitchen that look onto the garden, and as they near the cottage Joan hurries out.

— You accepted him, Liza-Lu? Yes, oh yes. Yes!

She hugs Liza-Lu, and then hugs Angel.

— You two come in and have some tea now and tell us all about it. And Mr Clare, Angel, you can tell us all about yourself and your plans for our Liza-Lu.

After feasting heartily on the freshly-baked country scones and jam, and refreshing himself with good strong tea, Joan sends the younger children, who are now beginning to tire of the novelty of the stranger, out to play; and directs Hope and Modesty to do the washing up.

— Tell us about yourself, Angel.

Joan is interested in background: past, present and future.

— My parents live in Emminster, where I grew up and where my father is currently the vicar; but he comes from Harrowford, further west. I'm the youngest of three boys, by far the youngest. My two older brothers, Felix and Cuthbert were both sent up to Cambridge to be educated. One is a curate, and the other soon will be. I was educated at Harrowford Grammar School and I was more interested in nature and the land than in theology. I enjoyed my studies while I was there (I was a boarder) but I was more interested in practical learning than theoretical learning. When I finished school, Father sent me to the Royal Agricultural College. Afterwards I arranged with Mr Crick at Talbothay's Dairy (you may have heard Tess speak of him) to study dairying with him, as part of gaining practical knowledge of that industry. As you know, that's where I first met Tess. After our, um, misunderstanding, I used part of the money Father set aside in lieu of a

Cambridge education to go to Brazil, in South America, where they were opening up new country to encourage immigrants; farmers, that is. I no sooner landed there and started to clear my allotment when I developed a fever, carried by the bite of a mosquito they tell me, and became too weak and sick to carry on. I didn't even have the strength to rise from my cot. The doctors here say I was lucky to get out and back to England in one piece. I still get attacks of chills and fever.

As for Tess, you know how I repented of leaving her in haste, and how I found her again, only to learn she'd given up on me and gone to live with that D'Urberville as his wife. When I turned up unexpectedly at their lodgings, I think the shock was too much for her. 'Too late! Too late!' she said; and went upstairs and stabbed him through the heart with a kitchen knife. Then it was her turn to be remorseful; but she was right: it was too late and she received the Crown's punishment for her crime. I thought I could never love again (and he steals a coy look at Liza-Lu) but you Durbeyfields seem to have an attraction for me, and here I've come today to claim Liza-Lu as my bride.

With this he turns and beams at Liza-Lu. Joan is all for pinning this dreamer down. Only down to earth reality brings concrete results.

— Where do you intend to settle, Angel?

— I'm presently looking for a mixed farm around Emminster. There are a couple that I'm interested in and I hope to finalize arrangements within a month or two. We can stay at my parents' until then. Meanwhile, I need your permission, Mrs Durbeyfield …

— Mother. Call me Mother Durbeyfield. If I'm to call you Angel, you must call me Mother. — Mother Durbeyfield, I need your permission to marry Liza-Lu by licence. My father wishes to marry us at the vicarage, and I've asked my very best and oldest friend from my grammar school days to be my groomsman.

He looks at Liza-Lu and smiles again.

— I felt certain you'd say 'Yes', Liza-Lu, so I started on the arrangements.

A disappointed look crosses Joan's very readable face.

— Emminster? I can't possibly make it all the way to Emminster. I can't leave the children; neither can they travel all that way, not with all the moving about we've done lately. I don't want to unsettle them any more.

— That's all right, Mother. It is I who am marrying Angel, not you. When would you like me to come, Angel?

— I was planning on us going back together, today.

— Today!

Liza-Lu's mouth falls open. *Today! Life is moving very quickly: a first kiss, a new fiancé, and now, today! Well…why not?*

— I've ordered the trap to come by at four o'clock. It connects with the southern coach at Trantridge at five. You've only got an hour.

— If I'm going with you today I'd better get my belongings together. It's a good thing I started a hope chest. I've crocheted some doilies, and embroidered two table cloths and napkins myself. My other things will fit in if I squash them down.

— That's my clever girl.

He watches approvingly as Liza-Lu hurries upstairs.

— We'll stay at the vicarage, Mother Durbeyfield, until I purchase my property. I'll continue to pay the rent here until the middle of next month so you will not want for a roof over your heads. I've spoken with the bailiff who wants all tenants off the property by then. I take it the estate's in a bit of a shambles as Alec D'Urberville was an only child and didn't have a will.

— We have to move again?

— You won't have to worry. I've been looking around Emminster and I've found a cottage a few streets from the vicarage that I can rent for you, a little roomier than this one. It's called 'Linden'; you'll know why when you see it. You'll be close to Liza-Lu until I buy my farm.

— Angel, you are very kind. A guardian angel, that's what you are, and I thank you.

Just then Abraham comes in.

— Tea in the parlour? Scones and jam? Or rather, remnants of scones and jam. What's the big occasion?

He stops when he sees Angel.

— Abraham, this is going to be your new brother-in-law, Angel Clare. He's going to look after us.

— Oh, hello. Are there any more scones in the kitchen? I'm starving.

CHAPTER 6

The Emminster Vicarage

The coach groans as its brakes grind and hold, winding its way down Emminster Hill to the town at the bottom nestled among slightly lesser hills, with the red church tower rising as if to compete with the neighbouring hill tops. Liza-Lu and Angel sit next to each other, riding backwards thigh to thigh, holding hands, slowly lurching and bumping one another left and right as the coach winds down the only hill in the region that requires resting the horses three times on the way up. The windows are let down, owing to the exceptionally fine weather, and Liza-Lu's eyes dart this way and that, soaking up the unfamiliar country, until the lurching stops.

Angel feels so proud, bringing his bride home. He squeezes her hand and smiles at her then jumps out to assist her down the step. He identifies her trunk and arranges for it to be delivered. Picking up her bag, he ushers her up the street, past the church and churchyard to the vicarage next door. His mother has heard the coach arrive and is at the verandah railing watching for him.

— Mother! I've brought her home!

He gently pushes Liza-Lu up the steps.

— Mother, I'd like you to meet Miss Liza-Lu Durbeyfield who has graciously accepted my proposal of marriage. Liza-Lu, this is my mother.

Liza-Lu gives a little curtsey.

— How do you do, Mrs Clare.

— Why, she's just a child. How do you do, my dear. Come on inside. Angel, take her up to Felix' old room. You can wash up, dear, then we can have supper as soon as the Reverend gets back from his parish visits. It wasn't too dusty for you, was it, on the coach?

— Oh no. It was very pleasant, thank you.

She's not a bad old thing. Angel told me his mother is quite judgmental, probably because he never took Tess to meet them before or after he married her. I can understand why the old lady (and she does seem to be quite old) was disappointed at not being at the wedding, or even meeting her first daughter-in-law. I'm going to be as good and thoughtful a daughter-in-law as I can be. What's more, I really like older people.

Liza-Lu pours some water into the basin and uses the lavender soap Mrs Clare has put on the wash stand. It's fresh field smell rises in the warm water. She catches sight of herself in the mirror and whispers to her image.

— I'm going to be a bride in a couple of days. Will I look any different after?

She dabs her face and dries her hands on the embroidered linen towel then pins her thick hair to one side of her face, pulls and smooths her dress, and goes downstairs.

The Reverend James Clare's narrow face can be seen coming purposefully and thoughtfully from right to left just above the trimmed privet hedge, and turns in at the gate, a slightly stooped man in his sixties who carries his head forward on his neck, probably due to years of peering at text in dim light. He notices the trunk on the verandah and goes in through the screen door.

— Oh, ho! The bride has arrived! Where is everyone?

— We're in here, Father.

Angel jumps up and meets his father at the parlour doors, a real parlour this one, used for formal occasions, the front room.

— This girl must be very special to be given a parlour welcome. You must be Liza-Lu. Welcome to the Emminster Vicarage. I seem to have held up your supper. My, my, look at the time. Is it ready, Mrs Clare?

— It's always ready for you, James.

Mrs Clare explains to Liza-Lu that the evening meal is always a cold one, on account of their never knowing exactly what time they will be eating, owing to their parish duties. Tonight there is cold meat pie and slices of cold roast beef, garden salad vegetables, especially tomatoes which Mr Clare carefully tends in the raised garden beds out the back; bread, cheese, and a cold apple tart. Old Lina, their help, lays the table every day before leaving, and all Mrs Clare has to do is boil the water for tea. The old gentleman senses Liza-Lu's unease in this new situation and tries to make her feel at home.

— Angel tells us you're from up north?

— Not the north of the country but north of here. I was born and raised in Marlot, in Blackmore Vale but now our family, my mother and younger brothers and sisters, live between Trantridge Cross and Chaseborough.

— Will your mother be coming to the wedding?

— Alas, no. You see, my little brothers and sisters range in age from nearly sixteen down to five so Mother has to stay home with them.

— We're planning a very simple but nice ceremony, and Mrs Clare (he always refers to his wife in this way) has arranged to have a catered luncheon here afterwards.

— That is very kind of you, Mr and Mrs Clare. You don't have to put yourselves to any trouble on my account.

— Nonsense. This is the first family wedding we've had here.

James Clare looks at his soon to be daughter-in-law and likes her immensely. Young, demure, polite, she has all the Christian virtues and will make a good little wife for Angel, who needs to settle down. His life has been in turmoil. He's been in the newspapers, and so soon, too, after coming home sick from South America. James has never seen him look so settled, and this red-haired practical girl looks just the kind to make him do it.

— Are you planning on taking this lass away on a little holiday, Angel?

— Yes, Father. I'm rather hoping we can get to the west coast for a few days. They say that high summer's the best time for hiking those coastal tracks beyond the moors.

Liza-Lu's eyes open wide. *That's the first I've heard about this.*

— The west coast. You mean the sea? I've never seen the sea. Oh, Angel, really?

Her violet eyes always deepen and sparkle when she's excited.

— Really?

— I was going to keep it a surprise but then I thought anticipation might make it more appealing. Jack and Mary Turville are coming up from the West Country tomorrow by train and we can return with them the following day as far as Millcroft, where they are staying with Mary's parents, and then we'll continue on to Exeter by train and then to Barnstaple by coach. I told you, didn't I Father, Jack will be standing up with me?

— Yes, yes. Is he home for good?

— I'm not sure. We'll find out tomorrow.

The next day, the day before the wedding, Angel leaves to meet the eastbound coach from Chalk Newton at the Inn, leaving Liza-Lu alone at the vicarage. The senior Clares have left together to visit sick parishioners, taking a large basket of freshly-baked rolls with them. Liza-Lu visually explores the downstairs of the vicarage, her new home until Angel decides on his farm. She tries out the sofa and the other chairs, and looks at the pictures on the walls up close. Some are pastoral sketches such as 'Bringing Them Home' - sheep coming down a road through the woods followed by a shepherd with his dog. Some are sombre portraits in dark carved frames; a bald man with frizzy whiskers; and a couple, the man standing with his hand along the back of the chair, and an austere old woman seated. *No doubt my new relatives.* She turns her head sideways and reads the gilt-embossed book titles behind the glass doors of the cabinet: *The History of the Decline and Fall of the Roman Empire*, Edward Gibbon; *Shakespeare: The Complete Works*; *Great Expectations*, Charles Dickens, until her neck gets stiff, trying to get a feel for the Clares.

Clare. I will be a Clare tomorrow. A few words, the stroke of a pen, and my name will be erased forever, no longer a Durbeyfield. I will never write it, never sign, Eliza Louisa Durbeyfield, again. I remember at home when I was young, if any stray pieces of paper came my way I would practise writing my name, my signature, giving an artistic flourish to the capitals, especially capital 'D'. Now I'll have to make do with the very ordinary capital 'C'. Liza-Lu Clare. Liza-Lu Clare. It sounds too young, not a married lady's name. Eliza Clare. That sounds much more dignified. Eliza. That's what Mother calls me when she's vexed with me: 'I'll have no more of that, thank you, Eliza'. Now that I'm about to step into a new life, a new role, maybe I should have a more suitable name to go with it. Lifting her head high, she approaches one of the portraits.

— How do you do. My name is Eliza, Eliza Clare.

It's not just writing my new surname, I will have to give up **feeling** *a Durbeyfield. Mother and Tess were convinced that the Durbyfield name is a derivation of D'Urberville. They said I should be proud to carry it. Even Angel is convinced we have roots in a grand family, and now, tomorrow, I have to change it. Strange thing about Angel. He feels special marrying a D'Urberville yet it was a D'Urberville who destroyed his life. I'm like a free-standing cardboard character with a Durbeyfield/D'Urberville girl painted on one side and a Clare on the other. Do I just switch them round at the stroke of eleven tomorrow morning? Or am I both sides?*

She sits there, in one of the wing chairs, rough tapestry, with only the measured 'clonk clonk' of the pendulum clock as company, slowing down her thoughts. *I'm marrying into his family more than he's marrying into mine. I will become Mrs Clare, will be expected to live with my new in-laws. I will gain a father, a man of the cloth, no less; as well as two brothers-in-law, also* men of the cloth. And what does Mrs Clare expect of me? Help with parish relief, church suppers, arranging flowers in the church each Saturday and removing them on Mondays? Teach Sunday School? Knit and sew for charity? Become a younger version of the elder Mrs Clare? No! No! It's not that I don't want to help. I just don't want to be pressed into 'the vicar's daughter-in-law' mould. However, on the other side of the coin there is a certain amount of social status to be had by marrying Angel. Last night at supper Angel and his parents were totally at home with table manners and etiquette that I was never taught other than, 'Let the boys eat first', and 'Don't talk with your mouth full'. Unconsciously, this family knows exactly which fork or spoon to use with what dish. They all have little cloths to dab their lips and wipe the corners of their mouths with. Not once do they use their knuckle or their sleeve. They don't butter bread in their hands but use a small plate on the left with a special knife just for buttering. They don't reach across the table for items they want. Instead, they cock their head on one side, and say 'Would you please pass the butter?' and 'May I have the salt cellar please?' I may seem shy and hesitant to them but I'm taking it all in and following their every move. This is the world I'm marrying into.

I've been watching Angel at mealtimes, too. He's looking very pleased with himself. I think he's happy that his parents accept me. He refers to me as if he already owns me: 'my bride', and 'my little wife'. I'm as tall as he is, for goodness sake. He's taken over even the smallest details of the arrangements for tomorrow. He arranged for this friend and his wife (they should be getting here soon) to be witnesses. Never thought of consulting me. Now he's arranged a wedding trip without asking me. Of course, I'm thrilled to be going to the coast; but he could have asked me first. Maybe he needs to feel manly, in charge.

On walking through to the dining room she notices the silver-legged salt and pepper containers on their little silver tray on the sideboard ('crewet' they'd called it). The other bowls and dishes are laid out on the dark mahogany, all set on lace doilies so as not to scratch the wood. As she runs her hand over the polished surface she hears the gate click and footsteps clumping across the verandah, and goes back out into the parlour.

— Liza-Lu! Liza-Lu, where are you? I've brought our guests.

Angel and Jack put the bags down in the hall and follow her voice into the parlour.

— Liza-Lu, I'd like you to meet my long-time and oldest friend, Jack Turville. Jack, this is Liza-Lu Durbeyfield, soon to be Mrs Angel Clare. Isn't she beautiful?

Liza-Lu puts out her hand to be greeted by the firmest friendliest grip and looks up into the strongest blue eyes she has ever seen. He is tall and broad-shouldered, with a square sun-tanned face and a shock of straw-coloured hair parted against the fashion, on the side. He gives her a grin, and her hand an extra shake, and those startling blue eyes crinkle with boyish energy.

— How do you do, Liza-Lu. It's a great honour to be a witness at your wedding. We've come all the way from Millcroft just to meet you. Allow me to present my wife, Mary.

Oh, goodness. Head: stop reeling! Feet: stay on the ground! Face: smile! Say something! My hand is in yours. My fate is in your hand. Close your mouth. It's hanging open.

— Mary, this is Liza-Lu.

Mary Turville, who is behind her husband, moves forward between Jack and Angel and gives Liza-Lu a hug, kissing her on the cheek. She is slight, almost thin, with an oval face and the kindest eyes.

— My dear Liza-Lu, I'm so happy to meet you. When we got Angel's telegram we knew you'd be special. We wouldn't have missed your wedding for anything.

What a kind and warm welcome! What a lovely person she is; but I can still feel the shock of Jack's handshake. It's gone all through me from top to toe. What a firm, clean-shaven jaw he has. There's something in the way he looks; and he's still smiling.

— I hope we can become fast friends.

Covering her confusion by playing the hostess, Liza-Lu shows them up to the other spare room, Angel's brother Cuthbert's old bedroom. She then goes downstairs and sets out some light refreshments. Afterwards, Angel suggests they all go for a walk and they decide to climb Emminster Hill, as Jack hasn't visited the town before.

— The best view of the town and the layout of the countryside is from the top. Why don't you girls walk up the road that follows the lesser slope and old Jack and I will attack the steep side from the bottom?

They set off in the late afternoon, Liza-Lu wearing a wide-brimmed hat with a violet ribbon that matches her eyes. Mary carries a parasol against the glare; Jack is bare-headed while Angel wears his usual boater. The two friends stride ahead and disappear through a hedge at the base of the hill, catching up on each other's doings while Mary and Liza-Lu take their time, especially on the steeper parts.

— You live in Millcroft, do you?

Dark haired, and with an animated face, Mary pants a little as she replies.

— Oh no. We're just visiting my parents. My mother is very poorly so we decided to come home for a visit.

— Do you live far from her?

— We live in Australia.

— Australia! You *have* come a long way.

— We decided to bring our little girl home so she could meet her grandparents, my parents that is. It's meant everything to Mother so I'm glad we did, even though it's such a long way to come. Polly's only four and probably won't remember them very well. I don't know how much longer my mum has. The doctor says it's her heart. She may live quite a while but she could go at any time.

The girls rest more frequently as they near the top and when they reach it they find Angel has scouted out the best view and has spread a blanket that he brought with him on the grass.

— What kept you? You had the easy way up.

From their vantage point they can see the town and the river below them, and the hills receding in the west.

— It really is quite a beautiful evening.

Liza-Lu takes off her hat and shakes her hair.

— You won't be able to do that after tomorrow. You'll be an old married lady and will have to wear your hair up.

— I don't have any hairpins. I might just have to break with tradition.

The hills are turning purple in the lessening light and the clear pale sky in the west is tinged with pink and orange. Jack takes a deep breath from a faint breeze that blows over the miniature daisies.

— 'It is a beauteous evening, calm and free'.

That's one of my favourite poets!

— That's Wordsworth, isn't it?

— You know Wordsworth?

Those piercing eyes are fixed on me! He's quoting again. Is he referring to me?

— 'A violet by a mossy stone
Half hidden from the eye
Fair as a star, when only one
Is shining in the sky.'

Mary smiles.

— It's Angel who should be commenting on your eyes.

Don't keep looking at him. He's noticed my eyes. I hope nobody noticed me looking at him. That shiver wasn't noticeable, was it? I have a feeling, a very certain feeling, that we are meant to be together but he's a married man, and quite content by the look of it; and tomorrow I'm marrying his best friend. The die is cast, or was cast when he married Mary. It will be cast again tomorrow, and that's two casts against me as far as Jack is concerned. Strange that I don't shiver when I look at Angel. This time tomorrow I'll be his wife. Maybe I'll acquire feelings like those in time; or maybe it's because Jack feels so secure in his marriage he can afford a little banter.

— Do you like any other poets, Liza-Lu?

— Oh yes. Browning and Keats, 'The Rubáiyát' …, Coleridge, Hardy. Their words are always running through my head. They have a meaning for everything I do, the words I mean, like colour gives meaning to a black and white sketch. I think the poems we are forced to memorize in school act as anchors, and give our lives extra meaning.

— I didn't realize I was marrying a philosopher.

— Not a philosopher, Angel, just a practical thinker.

— Jack's been telling me about Australia, Liza-Lu.

— Yes, Mary told me they are home on a visit.

— Have you been in contact with your father, Jack?

— No, and I don't expect to.

He gives Liza-Lu a rueful smile.

— My father disowned me. According to him, I'm the black sheep of the family. Five years ago he sent me packing. He's a funny man, the Squire. By 'funny' I mean incomprehensible. Even though my older brother is set to inherit the estate, I was the one who was always interested in the land while he wanted travel and adventure. I was always hanging about the Mews, the farmhands' and tradesmen's village of cottages on the estate. I wanted to learn all I could from them about the dairy side of things, the different crops, the sheep, and all I could from the blacksmith, shearers and thatchers. My mother was an invalid. I'm told she was sick the whole length of her confinement with me. I was born prematurely, only weighed two pounds, and slept in a butter box close by the fire all the first winter, so they tell me. They fed me on fresh cow's milk, still warm.

Angel chips in.

— You've certainly made up for it since, Jack. You have wrestler's arms. Ever since we were first at school together you were the strongest boy in the form.

— It must have been that awful brown bread and apricot jam at recess.

— It sounds delicious.

— Delicious to you, maybe, Liza-Lu, but not day in, day out, year after year. I haven't touched an apricot or any of its by-products since I left school.

— That's understandable, Jack. Tell me, how did you and Mary meet?

Mary looks up at Jack, and smiles.

— I'm another of his father's disappointments. He wanted Jack to marry a daughter of the landed gentry in those parts; not a particular one, just one from the same social class. Jack and Angel both attended the same agricultural college in Millcroft, where I'm from, and we met at a church supper. I was a seamstress, an honourable enough job but one which falls far below the Squire's standards or qualifications for a daughter-in-law. When Jack left the college and went home filled with new ideas about crop rotation, hardier varieties of seeds, new milking techniques …

Jack continues his list of sins.

— …new methods of thatching *and* a prospective bride, the Squire hit the roof: 'The old ways always served the family well enough. I've seen these young upstarts, college-trained young fellas, seen them make mistakes and get burned. Over and over I've seen it. There'll be no fancy modern changes on the Turville estate. It's going to stay just as it is. I don't need your new ideas. If you're so keen to try them, I suggest you do so elsewhere. It's time for you to go out into the world and make your own way. As for this young seamstress you're interested in — completely unacceptable. You needn't bother bringing her here.' That's what made me marry Mary (and he looks at her fondly), and what drove me to go to New South Wales.

— New South Wales, that's on the east coast of Australia, isn't it?

— Yes. It's the most populous state with the biggest, the original city, Sydney. We live about sixty miles south of Sydney in the coastal region known as the Illawarra, a native word that means 'between the mountains and the sea'.

— There's a string of towns running down along the coast, with mountains behind; and a lot of coal in the mountains, mining. We live in the biggest, fastest growing town in the area, Wollongong. It's pronounced 'Woolen' as in blankets, 'gong' - Wollongong. I know how to say it but I don't know the native meaning of it.

Meanwhile, the sky has crimsoned and the evening is getting deeper.

— I don't recall such vivid skies or such an excellent string of dry weather.

— It must be due to a volcanic eruption in some country far away.

— What makes you say that, Liza-Lu?

— I read it somewhere. The dust from the volcano goes high up into the sky and is carried round the world by the winds so when the sun sets here it shines through the dust and gives us these pink and red and orange skies.

Angel looks closely at Liza-Lu: he is marrying a veritable encyclopaedia. They lazily stand up and brush their clothes while he folds the rug, then each man takes his girl's hand and they descend the hill.

The big day is here at last. Liza-Lu opens her eyes. *This is my day of destiny. My wedding day! Am I marrying the right man? Is there someone else out there, someone not already married, who is meant for me? What if I pledge my troth to Angel and afterwards meet Mr Right, the man of my dreams? Or is Angel my Mr Right and I don't recognize how fortunate I am? Should I have weighed things over more, and waited to give him my answer? Can I change my mind or is it too late? Too late to get out of it and run away? I should have gone last night; but all the arrangements are made here, and I'd be letting everybody down. What would Mother say, if I did? Angel's friends have come all this way.* She takes a deep breath when she thinks of Jack; and lets out a sigh when she sees Mary in her mind's eye. *Mary's as good and faithful a wife as any man could want.*

I can't imagine my future being exciting, or even romantic, but it won't be that unpleasant either. Dull, plodding, monotonous: just look at any couple's life a few months after the wedding. Things and people settle down into a routine. Isn't that what everyone aspires to? Then children come along and keep you there.

There's a timid knock.

— Liza-Lu?

It's Mary. She pops her head around the door.

— I thought you might like some help in getting ready: your hair, your dress. Look! I picked you a bouquet from the garden.

She holds out a beautiful posy wrapped in white cut-out paper, and tied with pink and yellow ribbons.

— I didn't know what your colour scheme is. I think of pink and yellow as warm happy colours, like you, so I picked as many pink and yellow flowers as I could find.

— Mary, thank you. They're lovely. Actually, I'm thinking of wearing a cream dress for the wedding that can double as a going away dress, with a tan travelling cloak and hat, and boots to match. What do you think?

She shows Mary the garments hanging on the back of the door to get the wrinkles out.

— Why Liza-Lu, they're perfect, and the cream will look beautiful with your hair. It's such a rich lustre and so thick compared to my thin lanks. How are you planning to wear it?

The two of them discuss purely women's issues as Liza-Lu prepares to go down for breakfast.

— You can't go down for breakfast. Not today. It's bad luck for the groom to see his bride on their wedding day. I'll bring up a tray and we can sit on the bed and eat breakfast in style.

Mary disappears then Liza-Lu hears her slower steps coming up the stairs again. She has certainly loaded up their tray: boiled eggs, piles of thick brown toast, tea, sugar, milk, butter and marmalade. They settle the tray in the middle of the bed and Liza-Lu sits cross-legged at the head in her camisole and pantaloons with a pillow behind her. Mary unfastens her jacket and skirt and removes them, laying them over the back of a chair. She carefully climbs onto the foot of the bed so as not to upset the tray, and puts the other pillow between her back and the brass footings.

— Let's tuck in first; then we can talk.

When they are licking the last marmalade from their upper lips, Mary asks.

— Do you have 'something old, something new, something borrowed and something blue' to wear?

— No, I forgot. It was all so rushed.

— Well, let's think. Old: something old. Maybe Mrs Clare has something old you can wear. If she does, that could also count as 'something borrowed'. Do you have anything new?

— My dress and cloak are almost new but I've worn them before.

— That won't do. Let me think. I know! I brought different coloured ribbons with me that I tied your posy with. What if I make a little blue bow for you to pin on your cami? That will cover the 'new' and the 'blue'; and you'll be all set.

Mary is very pleased with the solution, and Liza-Lu, too; and grateful to have such a nice new friend.

— Thank you for thinking of these things, Mary. What else might I have overlooked? Do you know if Angel bought a ring?

— I'm sure he has.

— And the train tickets?

— Jack says he's very organized, Liza-Lu. One thing you might want to consider is taking a hamper with you. You'll be on the train well into the evening and when you're at the coast you may want to go for picnics.

— What a good idea. We can pack it with the remains of the wedding luncheon.

Mary slides off the bed, gets dressed and gathers up the breakfast remains.

— Close the door. I'll be back.

Liza-Lu goes over to the window and looks down from Felix's room, soon to be her married chamber, the largest of the boys' bedrooms; a front room, he being the eldest. His view is over a corner of the front garden, what can be seen of it through a large tree planted near the corner of the house. *It's going to be a little strange living in a house that isn't really **my** house. I wonder if the Clares will let me pick whatever flowers I want, or, for that matter, plant whatever I want; or are they possessive about their house and garden?*

Mary is back in no time.

— Look what *I've* got! I asked Mrs Clare if she had anything old that you could borrow, and she brought out this.

She is holding out a long case with three tiny spring hinges. Liza-Lu opens the lid, and there, on maroon velvet, lies an exquisitely-jointed silver bracelet.

— It hardly looks worn.

— Mrs Clare said she'd tell you about it later. You can borrow it for the ceremony.

— Isn't it lovely? Would you do up the clasp for me, Mary?

— Yes, and we'd better start getting you ready. It's getting on towards eleven. How do you want to wear your hair, Liza-Lu?

— Well, I'm not quite a matron yet. I think I'll wear it free-flowing or maybe sweep it up over my forehead, and pin it back with a flower. What do you think? Or wear a ribbon; or a garland of flowers over the top?

— Or in a loop around the back; but that would take too long to prepare. I think a large white bloom on one side where you pin it back would look best. Now let's get your corset on good and tight and get you into this dress. Nice bustle! And the leg of mutton sleeves suit your figure.

There! Oh, that does look nice. Have a look in the glass. It sits very nice across your bust; no wrinkles.

Once again Mary runs down and out into the garden, and Liza-Lu can see her dashing from plant to plant to find the best specimen for her hair. She comes back up, panting.

— Final arrangements down below. They're setting up the parlour. Mrs Clare is putting vases of flowers in the parlour and on the dining room table. Angel is pacing up and down but there's no sign of Mr Clare. Look what I found for your hair - a white peony, half-open. Smell! Isn't that heavenly? Only the white ones have a perfume like that. The darker they are, the less perfume they have. The deep purple ones have no smell at all.

The clock downstairs chimes a quarter to the hour. *The eleventh hour. Only fifteen minutes of freedom.*

Wake up! They're waiting for you to speak.

— I, Eliza Louisa Durbeyfield, take thee, Angel James Clare ….

Now they are kneeling on the floor of the parlour, on the sofa cushions, hand in hand, heads bowed, with the Reverend James Clare's surplice brushing their foreheads as he goes through the prayers. The congregation, consisting of Mrs Clare and Jack and Mary Turville, say 'Amen' at the appropriate places. Now a ring, a plain gold ring; the crash of a dropped platter and a giggle from the kitchen; a hug from Mary; a peck on the cheek from Mrs Clare, and a genuine embrace from the Reverend James.

— Welcome to the family, Liza-Lu.

— Thank you, Mr Clare.

— No 'Mr Clares'. You are now our daughter, by law. You must call me Father, or Father Clare.

— I like 'Father Clare'.

— And you can call Mrs Clare 'Mother Clare'. Isn't that correct, Mrs Clare?

— Yes James, it is.

— I, too, have a new name I want to be called by. Now that I've achieved a new status, I wish to be called by my whole first name, Eliza, not my childish name.

They all look at her. *That made them stop and take notice.*

— But Liza-Lu …

— No, Angel. Liza-Lu has grown up and become a married lady. It's Eliza from now on.

— Welcome to the family, Eliza.

— Why, thank you, Father Clare. Thank you, everyone.

The tinkle of a bell announces that Old Lina and the church ladies have the luncheon ready, and they move into the dining room and sit down to the wedding breakfast. There is corned silverside, sausage rolls and ham, steamed cabbage and hot new potatoes, cold asparagus, and warm freshly-baked bread. For dessert there's a magnificent trifle made with three different jellies and topped with whipped cream: a splendid lunch indeed. Even Mrs Clare seems relaxed, and smiles a little, caught up in the good humour and chatter. Angel had told Eliza he wanted a little wine to toast his bride but his parents had always been very strict in that department. 'No liquor in this house'. Now Mr Clare claps his hands.

— Bring in the good ladies from the kitchen.

Three women wearing large aprons and perspiration moustaches reluctantly come into the room and line up in front of the sideboard. Angel rises to his feet.

— Ladies, my bride and I would like to thank you from the bottom of our hearts for the truly delicious repast which you have so generously prepared and served to us today.

With those words the whole table applauds. The women smile with pleasure and hurry back to the kitchen but not before stealing a good look at the beautiful young bride.

— What time does your train leave, my son?

— Four fifteen, Mother. We'll have to be at Chalk Newton station by four.

— Eliza, dear, you know the name 'Eliza' really does suit you better than the old one, I was going to tell you about the bracelet I lent you. It was given to me by the Reverend as an engagement present. It is far too ostentatious for a vicar's wife and I couldn't, in good conscience, wear it among the parishioners. It looks very nice on you, dear, and I want you to keep it as a gift from the Reverend and me.

Eliza blushes — partly from pleasure and partly from finding herself the centre of conversation.

— Thank you, Mother Clare. It's the first bracelet I ever had.

CHAPTER 7

Jack's Illawarra

The Reverend Clare now turns to his other guests.

— Angel tells me you've done very well for yourself, Jack, in New South Wales.

— Yes, I have. Going there allowed me to prosper beyond my wildest dreams. It was only a few years ago we went out. I started as a cedar cutter in the Illawarra district south of Sydney. Everyone was after red cedar: the single, sparse, isolated specimens deep in the gullies of the rainforest. It was the most sought-after wood, good for boards and building, lasts for ever, very valuable; but becoming scarcer and scarcer. Everyone was after it. In the early days they were bringing out eighty thousand feet a month; but I must be boring you.

— No, no, go on, my boy. It's very interesting.

— It was dangerous work, too, getting the trees down and out, and hard work cutting them up. They were often sixty to ninety feet tall, or long, after they were on the ground. We would cut a pit under the whole length of the tree, and support it on stays. One of us would get down in the pit, take one end of the saw, and saw upwards; while another would stand above, and saw downwards. The up-cutter has the worse time of it as he not only has to push upwards but he gets covered with saw dust. Very hard work; but very good pay. We sawed it into planks, avoiding the centre as it was too soft. Then we'd have to carry or drag the planks to a pick-up spot where they were loaded onto bullock drays and taken either down to the coast or up to the road on the top of the escarpment. There's a very steep escarpment running parallel to the coast behind what is sometimes a very narrow coastal plain; and this escarpment is interrupted by mountains and hills that run right into the sea.

— It's very attractive country. There are pockets of cabbage palms and huge tree ferns, and you've never heard such birds! There's one they call the Laughing Jackass which sounds just like a person laughing, 'Kook-kook-kook-kook-ha-ha-ha-ha-ha.

— Mary's right but it's not very attractive when you're risking life and limb. There are lots of accidents on the steep ground. Frequently, trees that fall and should lie still, slip and skid, and there are many injuries like crushed limbs, broken backs, and gashes when saws slip. Men who cut cedar for a living are pale as ghosts because the trees have such an immense canopy and the jungle is so thick, no sunlight ever reaches the ground. In the beginning I was in that for a while, for the money. Then I began to buy tracts of forest. Bit by bit I hired my own crews, and cut other species of trees as well. The towns and villages along the coast are really going ahead. There are a lot of immigrants, mostly from here and Ireland, and they all need houses, schools, shops, hotels, churches. I send the excess wood from my timber lands to the coast, and then to Sydney by ship. That's how I became a timber merchant.

— It's a wonderful place to get ahead. Jack was fortunate to have a general farming background. That's how he became interested in his new venture.

— What's that, Jack?

— I had a look at the whole Illawarra coastal strip.

— 'The land between the mountains and the sea.'

— Good memory, Eliza. The town of Wollongong more or less divides the Illawarra north and south. The north is mostly given over to mining, coal. Coal is king; very plentiful. It crops out in veins running right into the sea from deep under the mountains. Coalcliff, Bulli, Mt Keira and Mt Kembla behind Wollongong are all full of coal, and there are little coal trains running from the collieries in the hills down to jetties on the beaches where they load the coal onto ships. South of Wollongong, however, is a different scene, mostly lush dairy country around Unanderra, and Kiama and Gerringong on the coast. Near Jamberoo is a spectacular waterfall discovered recently that flows over the edge of the escarpment into deep jungle; and from the top of Saddleback Mountain you can see a quilt of different greens, dairy and mixed crops, running along the coast. Curving white beaches separate the green from the deep blue sea. In this area there are many creameries and cheese factories as dairying is the biggest industry on the south coast, Bodalla being especially famous for its tangy strong cheese. And you know me and dairying! I invested in a little creamery, and now the railway's been extended to Wollongong we can get our milk, cream and butter daily to the Sydney markets without it going rancid, ice it down. We also provide local delivery with a horse and cart.

— Jack and I eventually bought a house in Wollongong. He calls the town 'the hub of the south' but it's really only half a hub as the town's on the coast. We're on Cliff Road, right above North Wollongong Beach, and the house is called Seafoam for obvious reasons. That's where our little Polly was born.

Angel has been following his friend's descriptions with growing interest. Jack is very enthusiastic.

— You should really consider New South Wales, Angel. Now *there's* a place where an aspiring farmer can let his head go. For starters, you don't have to worry about winter. It can be a bit shivery but it never freezes, never falls much below forty-five at the coldest, maybe a little frost in the morning in the hollows. You can grow crops all year round, and cows don't need barns, just lean-to's where they're milked. Sheep don't have to be kept inside, and chickens (they call them 'chooks' over there) can be raised outside with just a bit of corrugated iron over a pen. We have pumpkins climbing over the roof of ours.

— I never thought I'd be harvesting pumpkins from the roof of a chook house; it's cheaper than the market. There's an old Irishwoman called Granny Anderson who lives in a slab hut on the side of Bulli Mountain who has only one cow and a hive of bees. She comes to the market every Saturday morning and sells butter, honey and honeycomb.

— Anyone who's willing to do a lick of work can make a go of it out there. It's a wide-open opportunity, Angel, and they're begging for immigrants. Only way for the place to get ahead; and the climate's a lot more equable than Brazil. Yes, I tell you, Wollongong is a coming town.

At the mention of Brazil, Angel shudders; not only because he remembers his delirious sojourn there that had drained him so, but the thrill of a totally unexpected possibility: New South Wales! Illawarra. Wollongong. It's hard just to get the tongue around these lilting names.

— You wouldn't go away again so soon, Angel, not after being so ill?

His mother is genuinely worried about her youngest son.

— Don't you worry, Mrs Clare. The boy will do what he thinks is right for him and his little bride.

Up to this point Eliza has been fascinated, listening to Jack and Mary describe their home on the other side of the world. *What's Angel up to? If he's having a sudden change in thinking, then it involves me as well. Any decision of his dictates the direction my life will take, for haven't I just taken the oath to obey him?*

— Tell me more about the Illawarra, Jack.

Angel asks questions about the crops, the soil, rainfall, local industries, the economy and prospects in general. Mary chats to Eliza about town life,

— You'd love the beach, Eliza. I take Polly down every day (we live on the cliff top; there are steps) to play on the edge of the waves. We dig big holes in the sand, big enough for both of us to fit in; make sandcastles with a little bucket and spade; or go for walks around the rock pools at low tide.

She stares at the opposite wall seeing all this, seeing her young daughter frolicking on the beach; then snaps back to reality.

— We have to get that hamper packed with the left-overs. The coach leaves for the train in a little over an hour.

They've all been so engrossed in the conversation they've almost forgotten the time. The sky has darkened and there are distant rumblings. Mrs Clare looks tense.

— A stormy wedding day forebodes a stormy marriage.

The Reverend intercedes.

— Don't be ridiculous, Mrs Clare. Keep those maudlin thoughts to yourself. Why, it's nothing more than a fresh beginning. *Tempus fugit.* You youngsters had better go and pack up.

— It seems that you've only just arrived and now you're leaving so soon. We've hardly had a chance to get to know you, Eliza.

— We'll be back from our trip in a few days, Mother. Then we'll all get to know Eliza, and she us.

CHAPTER 8

West to Exeter

They just make it onto the coach with their bags as the first big drops of rain plop down on the roof. Angel calls from the window.

— Hurry home, Father! No need to stay and wave us off; you'll only get drenched. We'll see you next week.

It's five miles down Crimmercronk Lane to the station at Chalk Newton. Eliza is excited about her first train trip, straining to catch the first glimpse of it down the track in the distance. First she sees the light, and as the engine gets larger and larger she can hear the bell. She is not prepared for the surge of noise as the engine and carriages rush past on the glistening rails and pull up with a metallic screech of metal against metal amid bursts of steam; and she backs up, spreading her hands against the waiting room wall. Angel admonishes her.

— Don't be silly, Eliza. It won't eat you. It runs on rails, you know. Come and get on. It won't wait forever.

Once on the train they stash their luggage in the overhead racks and soon they are speeding west, deeper into the storm. They are sitting opposite each other: Jack with Mary, Angel with Eliza in a polished wood compartment with tall windows. Now the rain is beating against the windows, obscuring any view.

— It's a poor start to your wedding trip, and your first train journey, Eliza. You can't see a thing.

— The storm will soon be over. It's coming from the west so we'll be through it twice as quickly as if we'd stayed still in one place; and there's plenty of afternoon left.

The rain brings back memories for Angel of the tropical downpours in

South America. A look of anguish comes over his face. He seems to be really struggling with his past.

— This reminds me of Brazil except there the rain is steamy, and the incredible humidity doesn't cool things down like storms are supposed to.

Mary reaches over and touches him on the knee. She says sympathetically.

— Tell us about it, Angel.

— You might have noticed that I've lost a lot of weight since you saw me last, Jack. I feel like I've been through a physical and emotional nightmare. You know I truly loved my first wife, Tess. She was a dairymaid at Talbothay's Dairy where I was learning the trade from Mr Crick. She embodied all that was young, fresh, country and pure; but she didn't tell me about an indiscretion she was involved in until *after* we were married, in fact, the very night we were married. Then, I'm afraid, my upbringing caught up with me. What would my parents say about marrying beneath my social class? My high standards had been compromised. I'd been tricked into marrying a fallen woman! She had to be taught a lesson. I couldn't cope with the thought of married life on that basis, so I left her and sent her home to her mother while I put some distance between us in order to take stock of the mess I'd got myself into. Were my parents right? Or is the love of a woman all that a man needs?

I took myself off to Brazil on the spur of the moment to try out my new farming skills. I'd thought previously of buying a farm in either England or the colonies but if I did I'd still have to face British laws and social conventions. When I saw the advertisement for land in Brazil, available on very reasonable terms for immigrants, I saw my way out of the situation. The planting season was at hand. It was 'now or never'. So I went.

Once I arrived, I found the land I'd been so quick to purchase (sight unseen) was bordered by a vast mosquito-ridden swamp. True, it was *potentially* good agricultural land once you cut down the trees, de-stumped the ground, and installed proper drainage. This was necessary to drain away the excess from floods during the wet season; and yes, the temperature is such that there is a year round growing season but all this clearing of the land seems to have changed the weather patterns and the soils. The original impression given to me of a reward of vast rich fields like England's would take generations of work. I didn't realize until I arrived on my 'estate' that it would take all of the eight hundred years that it had in England to create those 'pastures green', if not longer.

Granted, I arrived there as prepared as I could be, with a variety of English seeds: maize, corn, oats and barley. I spent three days travelling to the new 'lands of opportunity' to find nothing but trees. I set up my tent by the river (the advertisement had assured me of 'a good water supply'), and within twenty-four hours was suffering from diarrhoea. I had to fell enough trees so sunlight could reach the crops, lopping off the limbs and burning them in piles. The trunks I left where they lay, and the stumps where they stood. I tried to get the trees falling in the same direction so I could eventually sow the seeds in the thin tracts between them.

The air was always full of smoke, as this frantic settlement pattern was happening all around me. The others were also burning their ground and stumps, so I decided to burn mine as well — make it easier for the grubbing hoe. For breakfast, dinner, and supper I had the same flat pancake of flour, salt and water fried in pork fat, washed down with sugary tea. Those were the only rations I'd taken with me as I was told the country abounded in fresh fruit and vegetables, and that meat could be bought for a song at the weekly markets. It was true: these commodities *were* available in plenty in the settled areas but not in the back stumps where I was, at least three days' walk across unbroken terrain.

I was so anxious to get the seed in the ground that I worked from dawn until sunset as much as my strength would allow. My hands were blistered, then bloody, then calloused from daily use of the axe, and my muscles stretched and aching from the constant chopping, grubbing, bending and lifting. I was getting weaker by the day, and losing weight but had to toil on in the humid heat. I kept repeating to myself that preparation is nine tenths of the job. Once the crops were in I could relax the gruelling schedule I'd set myself.

The rains came early that year and were both a blessing and a curse. On the plus side they softened the ground which, with the burned surface, made it easier to break up and would hasten germination. On the negative side, the rain never fell gently. It pelted down from the heavens often washing the seed right out of the ground, sending runnels of water between the rows and making a quagmire of the exposed ground. Rivulets ran into the river turning it muddy; and I could never get dry. I worked all day in wet boots, and preferred working naked to the waist and to the cloudy sky than have a wet shirt sticking to me.

At night I lay on a canvas ground sheet but the damp seeped up through it; and I found it difficult to keep even a small fire alight to cook my food. I drank muddy water; I washed in muddy water; and with the moisture came the insects, mosquitoes in particular. I found the best way to prevent them biting me at night was to cover my exposed skin with mud which would dry somewhat. Still, I was covered in bites when I woke up. It was during the long spells of darkness (and near the equator night falls abruptly at six) that I tried to remain civilized. I kept a few books and my writing materials in an oilskin pouch so the damp would not affect them; and I would bring out the books, a Bible, a Farmers Almanac and others, and try to decipher them by firelight but I could only do this for a short time before my eyes lost their focus.

I would spend the rest of the night musing about Tess, my present circumstances, and Fate in general. Had I been too harsh on this maid, who professed to have loved only me? Have I been too harsh on myself, getting on my high horse and insisting on everyone meeting my high principles? I know now it was my social background that spoke and acted for me when I spurned Tess. I thought her confession about Alec D'Urberville was something a vicar's son could not accept, even though I professed to be a modern and forward thinker. I have to admit that it hit me where it shocked me most. Yet, as I lay there in Brazil, mulling these things over and over, I thought to myself: Look where my actions have brought me.

Here I am, a gentleman living in muck, toiling physically in the draining heat from dawn until dusk, with all my book learning useless to me, and all the social graces of my class inappropriate in such a setting. I spurned love, and look where it got me. And what of her? She isn't suffering as much as me. I left her plenty well-off for her well being; and I imagined her back home working at Talbothay's Dairy. How was I to know her circumstances had changed for the worse? I had no idea of the outcome and agonies my righteous decision had on her. Deep down I wanted to believe she loved me; and I was glad I hadn't brought her out to *that*. Maybe I'd been too harsh, too impulsive. Maybe I would take her back if things improved on the land.

I was hotter than usual one night, and I imagined Tess was there with me. I looked at the fire and I saw her wearing the diamonds I gave her as a wedding present. They glinted in the firelight the same as they did that night. 'Tess! Tess!' I cried, groping for a cup of tepid water; but she didn't hear me. They say that's when the fever took my mind and my body.

It was written up later. I have the clipping here somewhere. I left everything behind in Brazil. They had to bring me out for medical attention. Here it is: "His eyes…were gazing…on a limitless expanse of country from the back of a mule which was bearing him from the interior of the South-American Continent towards the coast. His experiences of this strange land had been sad. The severe illness from which he had suffered shortly after his arrival had never wholly left him, and he had by degrees almost decided to relinquish his hope of farming here."

Recalling this angst, Angel cannot stop tears from running down his cheeks. Mary is visibly saddened by this account of his failed venture and his obviously failed health.
— Oh, poor Angel!
Eliza's heart sinks. *Belly up in Brazil; and I've just got married to a man who cries! For better or worse. How much worse can it get?*
Mary makes a valiant attempt to try and brighten the mood. She changes the subject.
— Jack, tell Angel and Eliza about your early morning swims on North Wollongong Beach. This is a good story but he couldn't tell it in front of your parents. It's a bit risqué.
— In the course of my business I came to know various merchants in Wollongong, and just down from the *Illawarra Mercury* office on Crown Street, Jimmy Dean, the tailor, lives with his family above his shop. He often stands out on the footpath with his hands in his pockets, well-dressed little fellow, always on the lookout to drum up business. A few doors down from him is Puckey the chemist who has a huge blue bottle, glass bottle, in his window, obviously his way of attracting business. He doesn't live above the shop but lives with his wife and daughter in the bush opposite Stuart Park across Fairy Creek. There's a little wooden footbridge over the creek and a sluice gate at the bottom of Puckey's estate to control the flow of the creek as it empties out to sea across the beach at Stuart Park.
— Too much detail. Get on with the story, Jack. You're digressing.
— Sorry about that. Puckey and Jimmy Dean get up early and routinely go bathing in the surf early in the morning, and since I got to know them they invited me to join them. It's just across the street and down the steps for me. They have further to walk. There's never anyone around; just the sun coming up across the water, the crashing foaming waves, and three naked men stretched flat out with toes and hands pointed, like cigars, catching the breakers right up onto the sand if we're lucky. Invigorating! We towel off as the heat from the sun becomes stronger, and after dressing we carry our boots and socks up into the dry sandy grasses above the high water mark until the sand dries on our feet and can be easily brushed off. Then, on with our boots and off to our respective businesses.
— No one ever sees you?
— No, it's too early. Later in the day women bring children down to the

beach to play, and there a quite a few people who wade in the sea in their neck-to-knee swimming costumes.

— When Jack says 'wade' he means standing in hip-deep water waiting to be carried in by the next big wave which often breaks over your head. The sea is never smooth or calm. You can't swim as we know it here. The waves are so strong they knock you off your feet. The trick is to 'catch' the waves.

— Can you do it, Mary?

—No, I'm too timid. Jack can.

— You just have to know when to jump up and flatten out so the curling wave carries you forward in a big rush.

Angel raises his eyebrows.

— It sounds very exciting.

— Nothing like a morning swim to clear the head.

— Talk about clearing. Look! There's even a glimmer of sun.

Eliza is able to see more and more of the green rolling country as they clickety-clack westward. *The train is much smoother than a coach, and faster too*. Mary leans forward and takes Eliza's hand.

— Eliza, I'm really glad to know you. Our stop is coming up next and we aren't likely to see one another again before we return to New South Wales.

— Thank you for everything, Mary; and for being so helpful with the wedding. It's been wonderful to have you for a friend.

The two girls stand up and hug one another.

— Angel, think seriously about what I've said. I think you would do very well on the south coast.

— I will, Jack. First though I'm going to check out a couple of farms in the West Country. I've written to the owners and I'll be visiting them on this trip.

The brakes go on. Jack takes down their bags and they stand near the door as the train slows to a stop. 'All aboard', calls the conductor leaning out from a door on the train and lowering a red cloth in his hand. The train chugs and begins to move forward.

— Mama! Mama! Daddy!

Eliza catches a glimpse of a blond-haired moppet breaking from an older man's grip and jumping into her father's arms as they pass. Polly.

CHAPTER 9

THE WEDDING TOUR

By the time Eliza and Angel pull into Exeter, it's dusk, and they are thoroughly weary of their journey which had been a novelty only a few hours before. Eliza carries her portmanteau, Angel a suitcase, and they each take a handle of the wicker hamper between them.

— This was a really good idea, Eliza. I'm sure it's too late for dinner at the hotel.

They enter the Railway Hotel. Angel registers and asks for the best room they have.

— Would the bridal suite be all right, Sir?

— That will do perfectly, thank you.

He turns to Eliza and whispers.

— Nothing but the best for the Clares.

That's right. I'm Mrs Clare. Mrs Clare. Mrs Clare. Mrs Clare. Eliza Clare. It still feels strange.

Their suite consists of a bedroom, dressing room, washroom, and a large lounge with a fireplace.

— The fire is set, Sir. Would you like me to light it?

— It's August, the middle of summer.

— The nights can get chilly around here, Sir.

— Very well, then. I take it it's too late for dinner?

— I'm afraid so, Sir.

— Could you send up a big pot of tea, then?

— I'm sure that can be arranged. I've turned the bed down. Will that be all, Sir?

The lounge doors open onto a wide wooden verandah. Eliza peers over the verandah railing into the still-busy street below and gives a little shiver. The evenings do get chilly. She goes in and finds Angel unpacking the hamper. He spears a thick slice of the fresh bread with the fireplace fork and, squatting down, holds it over the flames.

— I had an idea. Hot toast will go down very well with our supper.

— Do you take milk and sugar, Angel?

— Sugar only; no milk. I learned to drink it black in Brazil from necessity.

Why does he have to keep mentioning Brazil?

They bring their plates and cups of tea to the couch, which is set at an angle to the fire, and sit next to each other staring into the flames. Angel turns to look at Eliza and how the flames turn her hair a burnished red. He cups the nape of her neck with his hand and feels her thick lustrous hair.

— My little wife is very lovely. I have something for you.

From the table he retrieves a box.

— My godmother gave me these jewels for my bride. Tess had them briefly but they went back into the safety deposit box. Now they are rightfully yours.

He hands her the box.

— Go on, open it. They're yours.

She lifts the lid and immediately sees the brilliants sparkle in the firelight.

— Here, let me clasp on the pendant. There are earings as well. These jewels are symbolic to me, the bestower. First, as a failed husband, for I set Tess too high on a pedestal. I realize that now. We are all human and fall short of the ideal in many ways. These heirlooms are now yours, Eliza. In a way they are a prize for virginity, for purity, for that is what you are.

— Did you say 'price' or 'prize'?

— Prize. Reward. 'Who can find a virtuous woman? For her price is far above rubies …Her children arise up, and call her blessed; her husband also, and he praiseth her.'

— That's from "Proverbs". I've read it too, often; and try to live by it.

— I know so very little about you, Eliza. You're such a vibrant beauty I can imagine all sorts of young swains from the village wanting to walk out with you.

Eliza smiles.

— No young swains. Remember, my life too has been in upheaval the last couple of years: Father dying, Tess gone, the family uprooted from Marlot to Rose Cottage. No time for shilly-shallying around door posts.

— I knew I'd picked a winner. Tess was right: you'll be very good for me, and I promise I'll be very good to you. Not many people get a second chance at being a good husband but I've seen the error of my ways. No more running away from my responsibilities.

— You are wonderful to take the financial worry from my poor mother.

— It's nothing, Liza-Lu, er Eliza, I mean. When Tess and I were married we agreed to bare our pasts to each other. I think I know your past (no swains) but I want you to know my lowest point.

— It's not necessary, Angel. From now on we move forward as man and wife.

— It's important to me, Eliza. I had to tell Tess, and I have to tell you, too, before we can start our life together with a clean slate, a *tabula rasa*. When I was having doubts about my life before I proposed to Tess I went up to London and in a fit of despair, debauched myself for two days in one of those, um, houses where they keep, um, certain kinds of women. That is the lowest, the worst thing, I've ever done and I want your forgiveness.

— You don't need my forgiveness, Angel. I understand that men need to get their experience from somewhere.

— Oh my dear, you've taken a great load off my back. Now there is nothing standing between us, and I promise to be as kind and gentle, and good and faithful a husband as I can be.

He undoes the clasp on the pendant and puts it and its companions back in their velvet resting places. He then takes off his coat and loosens his tie. He draws Eliza to him and starts to unfasten her bodice.

— How do these things come off?

— It's not time for bed yet, Angel. We haven't tidied up the supper things

He leads her across to the bedroom.

— It's time for bed; but not for sleeping. This is our marriage night, Eliza.

*This is all new to me. So this is what a man is like when he's 'in passion'. He's so quick to lose himself in the moment, and at the same time so vulnerable. He doesn't realize I'm awake, and thinking. He's not even aware that **I** am here! I could never reach these heights of ecstasy. I can't breathe; he's pushing me down. And it hurts. Oh! It hurts!*

— Oh! Oh!

— You feel it too, dear?

— I ...I ...

The four poster rocks and the mattress springs squeak rhythmically.

Is this what happens every time? All this panting and heavy breathing, then,

— Aaaah!

Is it over? He's rolling off me. I can breathe again. Is he asleep? So soon? This is it? Does it get any better? Or is this the worse in 'for better or worse'? This must be my 'duty'. Am I to expect to be squashed every night? Once a week? Once in a month of Sundays? Take it or leave it - I could really leave it to once in a month of Sundays.

The next morning there is not a word from Angel about last night, about what to her was a life-changing experience. *When I came down to breakfast I could feel everybody's eyes on me, the new bride. They all know what we were doing up there last night, every one of them; but do they know how I feel? I feel like Eve must have felt when she learned the last secret.*

Angel's in very high spirits.

— Eat up. We're leaving for Barnstaple on the ten o'clock coach up the Exe valley.

— Are we going to Exmoor? That's Lorna Doone country.

— Near the edge of it. I'm going to look at a farm near Oakford, where the coach stops. You can rest there and we'll take the afternoon coach west to Swimbridge where I'm meeting the second farmer

— I could come with you.

— No, no. We'll be walking through fields and barns. You'll get your skirts all dirty; and besides, you don't know anything about farming.

Eliza has a pleasant lunch in the pub at Oakford, midway down the hill, and then it's on to Swimbridge where they follow a river all the way into the village.

— What a pretty setting! Look how close the hills come down to the road, and it's all so green. What sort of farm are you going to look at, Angel?

— A mixed farm, mainly wheat and oats; and sheep, by the look of those hills, hundreds of them. You can hear their bleating quite loudly from down here.

They meet the jolly round-faced farmer at the Swimbridge Arms who insists on 'bringing the little lady' along. He takes them a mile or so northwest up a lane so narrow the hedgerows swish against the cart on both sides to a whitewashed thatched cottage.

— I'd like 'ee to meet the missus.

'The missus', who would be in her mid-thirties, puts the kettle on so she and Eliza can socialize while the men go out and discuss farming details.

— I'm Eliza Clare.

— Pleased to meet you. I'm Sally Gaydon. Are you staying here tonight?

— No, I believe we're staying in Barnstaple. Gaydon? That's one of my mother's ancestors. We might be related. We're on our wedding tour, actually. We're going to do some walking, and I want to see the sea.

— The sea? I haven't seen it myself, although I'm in for weeks and weeks of seeing nothing else.

— What do you mean?

— The reason Jimmy's selling up the place is we are emigrating to Australia.

— You're not!

— Yes, we are. We're booked on the *Nimrod* out of Plymouth the middle of next month. Jimmy's brother and his wife, and her sister and husband went out two years ago and are now doing very well. We have nothing to hold us here so we're joining them in New South Wales.

— That's where our friends live. It seems everyone's on the move.

— Do you take milk and sugar? The milk here in the West Country is very creamy. This part of the world is famous for its clotted cream. Here's some to put on your scones.

The men come back, and *they* are talking about New South Wales as well.

— I'll let you know about the farm, Mr Gaydon. Of course, I'll have to think it over.

They thank their hosts, and Jimmy takes them back to the inn to wait for their coach which isn't scheduled to leave until five o'clock. That will allow Eliza time to visit the Swimbridge churchyard to look for names of some of her ancestors. Her mother's side of the family originated in Swimbridge and hereabouts. She has a list with her of the nearby locations and the names of the ancestors associated with them — three families from Barnstaple, thirteen surnames connected to Bishops Tawton, three more from Chittlehampton, and five from Landkey where they are going to pass through without stopping. *I'll just have to wave to them in the graveyard as I go by.*

There are more old family names scattered around in Charles, Georgeham, North Molton, Shirwell and Tavistock but Eliza's mission this afternoon is to try and locate those of her forebears buried in St James churchyard right here in Swimbridge. They enter under the large stone arch across the road from the inn.

— Look, right here, a Gaydon.

— I think we'll find the earliest tombstones closest to the church. They really look old, don't they, some of them?

— Let me see your list.

— I have it in alphabetical order. Some of the families go back twelve generations. It's strange. I feel rooted here, as if I've always known the place. Have you decided when you're going to buy the farm?

— I'm going to wait until after our holiday, when we're back in Emminster. Keep my head clear and not be clouded by the rush of the moment. By the look of this list we'll be wandering through here for hours.

He reads the names out loud as they spread apart.

— Bowden, Cowel, Davies, Dowell, Dowman, Fry, Gaydon, Gould, Lewis, Moore, Rode, Slade, Smalden, Snowe, Squire, Stribling, Westacott, Yeo, Zeale. It's a noble thing your mother did, collecting her family history.

— It's Grandpa Stribling's people who are all buried here. He made out the list of names. Just think, Angel, if even one of these people had not lived, I wouldn't exist. I owe my very being to all of them.

— Here's one: John Cowel, died 1726. His wife, Joanne Snowe died 1692. Here's a Gaydon. Maybe you're related to Jimmy. Alexander Gaydon died 1792. His wife, Dorothy Westacott died 1799. Their son, Alexander, died 1798, only six years after his father, aged 31 years.

— I've found a Richard Moore, died 1576, and his daughter Joanne Goule, died 1648, wife of Ambrose Goule who also died 1648. Maybe there was a plague or fever as they both died in the same year. I think that's supposed to be Gould. It just goes to show how the same name can be spelled differently, just like Durbeyfield and D'Urberville. Here's a Gould; and here's a Goole, Richard, died 1595. That's the earliest name I have. And they're all my ancestors.

— Eliza, I hear the coach coming. We have to run back to the inn to get our bags.

— You hear coach wheels, do you? You might be a D'Urberville, too, and not know it. I wish we had more time.

They come to a panting stop at the inn at the same time as the coach horses, and they go in to retrieve their luggage.

— At least I know my ancestors are resting in a very pretty village.

And she silently gives them a farewell nod as they pass the churchyard.

— Barnstaple tonight and then the coast tomorrow, Eliza.

The more she sees of the West Country, the more Eliza likes it: the deeply wooded ravines, here called 'combes', a suffix added to many place names; the lush hillsides divided by lines of rounded hedges; and roads lined by hedges often so high you can't see any views out the coach windows.

Tonight is a repeat of last night, my wedding night: Angel acting normally until bedtime when he again becomes all worked up, rolling on top of me, nearly *suffocating me, jerking and breathing loudly, afterwards falling immediately into a limp, exhausted sleep; leaving me gasping in the dark. Is this what married life consists of every night? He's polite and courteous during the day, treating me more like a cousin than a wife. How **is** a wife supposed to act towards a husband? This is not something taught in schools. It ought to be. Most of the population ends up marrying. Do they all go in as blind as I did? Is it 'on the job training' generation after generation? I don't feel a real partner. I feel sort of used. Mother never told me what to expect, except for that one conversation we had, and now I remember her murmuring to Angel, 'Be gentle with her'. If this is gentle, I'm not looking forward to the rest of my nights.*

As usual, Angel appears quite normal in the morning, even chipper.

— Wake up, Eliza, we need to get an early start. Today, the coast!

He is standing looking out the window, doing his deep-breathing exercises, bringing his arms together across his chest on the outbreath, then spreading them wide as he inhales through his nose.

— We're taking the narrow gauge Barnstaple and Lynton Railway to Lynton where we can do some cliff walks.

— How do you know all this, Angel? Have you been here before?

— I wrote to the Chambers of Commerce in Barnstaple, Lynton and Ilfracombe and they sent me all the literature on what to do and see in the area; the walks, the beaches, and where to stay. These are the cream visitor destinations in the West Country. There's a big theatre here in Barnstaple, the Theatre Royal, as well as another good one in Ilfracombe. We'll have to find out what's playing.

— I've never been to a theatre. I'd really love to go.

— I'll inquire.

They board the narrow-gauge railway that runs the twenty or so miles across the hills to Lynton on the coast, taking only one suitcase, and the hamper which the hotel had filled for them, and now they are pulling into the station. Eliza reads the platform sign: 'Lynton and Lynmouth' but there is no sign of any town or habitation nearby. They follow the other passengers out of the station and down a path that turns a corner at the end. When they turn the corner, there, way down below them, is Lynton, perched high on the side of the hill. Beyond the village are three strips of blue: the sky, the distant curving green-blue coastline, and the deep blue sea. They are not at the shore at all; they are not even in Lynton. Angel reads his literature as they stand at the top of a sweep of very steep wooded hills that plunge into the sea below.

— 'From the railway station there is a path that descends four hundred feet to Lynton which is situated approximately halfway down the hill. From Lynton you descend to the village of Lynmouth at the bottom of the cliff, five hundred feet below in the water-powered Lynton-Lynmouth Lift Railway'. Imagine, you can't see it from here, Eliza, but Lynmouth is nine hundred feet below us!

— Look how blue the sea is!

— First, let's find lodgings, and then we can take some of the walks this place is famous for. They say it's quite the holiday spot although Ilfracombe is *the* place to stay.

They walk down to Lynton with the hamper between them bumping against their legs. Eliza is beginning to feel the hamper is aptly named. Angel finds a pleasant front room at the Seaview Inn and after transferring half the contents of the hamper into his knapsack, he seeks out the innkeeper for maps of scenic walks and places to see. On returning, he tells Eliza.

— There are a number of walks we can take: cliff walks, or the Valley of the Rocks, or Watersmeet where the East Lynn and Hoars Oak rivers join to flow into the ocean.

— Watersmeet sounds nice.

— We can do that tomorrow. I want to see the Valley of the Rocks. It says, 'Turn left out the front door and follow the road about half a mile westward until it drops down into the Valley of the Rocks'.

They set out. Although the sun is shining, the air is cool and humid, and full of birds' chortles and twitterings. It smells different, too. As they make their way along, Eliza notices the ground is covered with low bushes all growing close together, their tiny purple flowers giving a mauve tinge to the hills which are dotted with clumps of yellow gorse. They stop where a side path leads steeply downhill. Angel consults his literature. 'The path drops into the Valley of the Rocks. Walk down to Castle Rock, the largest rock in the valley'. He looks up and points.

— That must be it over there.

Eliza sweeps her eyes over the scene below her. Through a gorge in the coastal ridge of hills she can see the sea, and scattered about the gorge are mighty wind-weathered rocks.

— Look at the shape of them. And there are some of the goats you mentioned, Angel. Let's go down.

— It says here one is named 'Rugged Jack'. If we walk out to the coast we can get to Lynmouth by the lower cliff walk. Let's do it. We can then go back up to Lynton on the Cliff Railway.

— You'll not get me on that thing. I'll climb up.

— There's nothing to it. Let's get going. We can eat our lunch on the rocks, by the sea.

He strides off and Eliza has to scramble to keep up, or rather, down, with him. After descending for about fifteen minutes they find themselves in the valley, towered over by rocks, as they make their way to the cleft in the hills. As they get nearer they hear a dull roaring noise; and the nearer they get, the louder and louder the sound until they come over the rise and face the full force and noise of the incoming tide as it meets the land. It takes Eliza's breath away. Wave after wave crashes against the rocks, breaking into white foam that runs up the rocks only to be sucked back into the sea to start the onslaught again. Never stopping; never slowing; always coming.

— High tide.

Angel knows about these things but Eliza still stands in wonderment.

All the time I've been alive; all of my family before me; ever since the world began, these waves have come ashore day and night, forever. She watches them smash themselves against the cliffs, recede, and smash themselves again. She feels herself holding her breath, like you do in a storm, waiting for the thunderclap. 'Roll on, thou deep and dark blue ocean, roll.'

— Up here!

Angel calls from a spot he's found on the ridge. They sit down amongst the heather and open their lunch; roast beef sandwiches, and ones filled with local tangy cheese; jam turnovers; an apple; a pear; and two jars of local cider. Although by now she is very hungry, Eliza is too enthralled by the vistas to the left, to the right, and beneath her feet to eat anything. She can't fill her eyes enough with the precipitous cliffs and the blue sea and the gulls rising and wheeling, screeching into the wind which blows in with the tide. Angel is full of facts.

— You see that line of land across the water in the distance? That's Wales. And it says in my literature that Shelley holidayed here, and compared these hills to Switzerland. Wordsworth, your favourite poet …

— One of my favourites.

— …and Coleridge also visited Lynton and Lynmouth, and they are supposed to have inspired him to write "The Ancient Mariner".

— 'Merrily did we drop
Below the Kirk, below the hill
Below the lighthouse top.'

That's certainly the case, with Lynton above and Lynmouth below.

They spend a lazy afternoon on the ridge in the warm Devon sun just savouring the presence of the sea. Eliza looks over the local map Angel brought with him from the Inn.

— Angel, let's walk the cliff path towards Combe Martin and return along the coastal path.

— Are you sure you can handle it? You aren't used to a lot of walking.

— Of course I'm sure. I took note of your advice and wore my thick socks and boots.

— Very well. Let's go.

— It also mentions the Hangman Hills walk. I don't know whether I'd want to try that one or not.

They walk down a tree-lined combe or ravine following a stream until it runs into Lee Bay with cliffs and steep slopes on both sides of them. Clambering over boulders and shingle they reach the sand and notice the tide has begun to recede, exposing large rock pools. Eliza takes off her boots and hose, lifts up her skirts, and pampers her hot feet in the refreshing water.

— Taste it.

— What do you mean, Angel?

— Taste the water.

She bends down, cups her hands and brings the cool water to her lips, then her mouth puckers because the taste is so shocking.

— Ugh! It's salty!

— The whole ocean's salty. Undrinkable.

— Well, my toes can't taste and they find it very salubrious. Why don't you come in for a paddle?

— My feet might swell and I may not be able to get my boots back on.

They retrace their steps up the combe and find the shore path that leads around the headland to Lynmouth.

— It looks like someone pulled a giant plug and all the water's drained away. Look at the boats. They're lying on their sides, dry-anchored in the sand. The whole ocean floor is bare, like the parting of the Red Sea.

— Twice a day, every day. Two high tides, two low.

— It's amazing that these things happen while most people go about their daily lives, oblivious.

Eliza is now leading the way, almost leaping ahead. The sea air invigorates her; but Angel is lagging.

— Come on, Angel, you with all your hiking experience!

— I'm so tired. I don't understand it.

The shore path rounds the last blind turn and before them is Lynmouth at the bottom of the cliff. The high hills run sheer down into the sea as far as they can see along the coast. The tide is really on the wane and the bottom of the pebbly bay is entirely exposed to old stone houses tightly wedged in a single line between the bottom of the cliff and the beach. Fishing boats lie resting on their sides anchored to chains that are stretched across the sand between the narrow harbour walls. Angel is visibly lagging now, even on the level path.

— We can stop in Lynmouth for tea, and you can rest, Angel.

— That's not a bad idea. There's an inn here I read about that used to be a smugglers' lair.

— Sounds perfect.

They have their snack looking out across the bay and they can hear the seagulls crying, even from inside.

— Did that little break give you the energy to walk back up to Lynton?

— I'm afraid not, Eliza. I'm getting really achey and shivery like I did in Brazil, and I'm developing the worst headache. They told me I would get bouts of it from time to time. I hope it's not as bad as the first time, though. Anyway, from now on I have you to look after me. I couldn't make that walk if you paid me a hundred pounds. We'll take the Cliff Railway.

— I don't want to go on it, Angel. I don't like heights. I'd rather walk.

— Well, I am *not* walking. I don't feel well. We'll take the lift railway, as I said.

— You take it, Angel, and I'll walk up.

— Don't be ridiculous. What would people say if we arrived back at the Inn separately? We're going up on the railway and that's that. You're my wife now, and you'll do as I say.

*Why is he chiding me like this? Has he no regard for my feelings? I'm terrified of heights, and enclosed spaces. Those little boxes going up and down the hill: I can't bear it. Maybe he's testy because he's coming down with something. If we arrive back at our lodgings at different times he could always tell them why. I don't even mind being made fun of: 'My wife is afraid of heights, ha ha.' Better to be the butt of a light joke than to ride up in **that** thing. Surely he could show a little consideration; but I don't think he will.*

They leave the inn and turn toward the cliff where the two cars on the railway are passing one another vertically. Angel is reading from his pamphlet again.

— 'The Lynton and Lynmouth Lift Company was formed in 1888

and is based on water powered lifts used in mines. Each of the two cars carries a 700 gallon tank below the passenger level. The tank is filled from a continually running stream in Lynton at the top of the cliff. The lower driver releases the water from the tank so that gravity ….' He keeps on reading about its length, gradient, and other details as Eliza watches the two cars going in opposite directions. Their car descends nearer and nearer. She swallows hard. It stops gently on the buffer at the lower station.

— I can't go up in that. I'll walk.

— Nonsense. Get in the car!

Maybe his illness is making him irritable. He hands their tickets to the conductor and crowds her on from behind. Most of the passengers, including Angel, move toward the windows on the outward-facing side to get the best view of the spectacle before them as they are lifted backwards up the steep cliff. Eliza finds a position at the rear of the car. She puts her head down, closes her eyes and clenches her hands. *I can't hear anything except 'Bang', 'bang', 'bang', 'bang', the beating of my heart in my head, and the gulls screeling. I'm being lifted up, up to heaven; not 'mine eyes unto the hills' but my heart, up through my head and out. It's going to let go and we'll all be killed.* 'Oooh, aaah. Isn't it beautiful?' *No, it's not beautiful. It's not beautiful until it stops. Please stop. Stop. Hurry up and stop. It's slowing down! There's the bump.*

They're at the top. She's the first off.

— There, that wasn't so bad now, was it, Eliza?

A passenger, a girl about her own age, says, 'This ride has been the highlight of my life. It's just breath-taking.' *Breath-taking it certainly is.*

Back at Seaview Inn, Angel's chills become worse and he is shaking all over. Eliza goes down to the desk and asks for an extra blanket for him, even though it's summer; and she also orders some soup to warm him up. By the time the soup arrives his teeth are chattering so much and his hands shaking so much she has to feed it to him. He complains of a splitting headache, and is becoming very petulant.

— I think you ought to see a doctor, Angel.

— No, no, I'm all right. It's exactly how it started in Brazil. The fever will come next. I'll be all right in the morning.

In the small hours of the morning he begins moaning and shifting around in bed. He throws off the blankets and claws at his nightshirt; and he calls out. Not for her: he calls for Tess. Eliza feels his forehead. It's burning hot, and his nightshirt and bedclothes are soaked with sweat.

— Angel, Angel! Are you all right?

He doesn't answer. Cannot answer? He murmurs and mutters, and moves his head back and forth; very restless. *I'm all alone, responsible for him. What is the best thing to do? Is this the worst it gets? How am I going to get some fluid into him? Oh, I wish it were light. What if he remains like this for days? Who is to pay the bill? He insists he's the head of the household and handles all the money matters to spare me from worrying about it. Now, here he is, delirious, and I can't access his account or draw any money from the bank. It's still dark: it's not even four o'clock. He's sick. He's really sick; he's burning up. He needs a doctor. If I obey him and don't call a doctor, what if he should die? Then I would be accused of negligence. He really needs a doctor.*

She puts her travelling cloak over her shoulders, lets herself out and goes downstairs to find the innkeeper's room.

The doctor has the story from a very worried Eliza, and when he takes his first look at Angel, he says, 'Ah', and nods his head.

— I've seen it often, Mrs Clare, that's one good thing. We have quite a few visitors to Lynton who have contracted this disease in the tropics. Your husband was quite right. It is a recurrent fever, all due to the bite of a tiny mosquito. And it's not catching, unless you, too, were bitten by the same mosquito that carries it from person to person. There's very little that can be done but when he's in this sweating stage you can bathe him with tepid water and a sponge. That will cool him down. He may be quite sick for a few days and then the chills and fever will leave him, until next time. I also noticed he's a little jaundiced, yellow.

— Yes, his mother has also noticed that since he came home from Brazil.

— Ah, Brazil!

— I'm sorry to have brought you out in the middle of the night, Doctor. We are on our wedding trip, and I was worried.

— No, no, my dear, you did the right thing; and now you know how to cope with the chills and the fever. He'll be weak for a few days. Here's my prescription: tender, loving care; good food in small portions; increasing bouts of activity in the fresh air; and plenty of rest in between. Nothing better than the sea air.

Eliza ministers to him in their room at the Seaview Inn for two more days, and when he is over his ordeal Angel goes to settle the bill. He comes back up the room and hits the roof.

— What did you go and get a doctor for? I specifically told you not to.
— I ...

— I specifically said, 'Don't get a doctor', didn't I? I knew what to expect, and now you've put me to this added expense.

— I was afraid you may not live, Angel. You were delirious. The doctor said your brain was very hot.

— What does *he* know? Has *he* been in the tropics? I want you to promise me you won't get any more doctors when I have another of these episodes.

— I'm sorry, Angel. I won't do it again. But just in case something does happen to you, don't you think it would be a good idea for me to have my own bank account?

— Bank account? You don't need a bank account. I'll not discuss this any further. What day is it? We have to move on to Ilfracombe and Barnstaple.

— It's Thursday.

—Thursday! We've lost three whole days.

*Yes, **we** have. Three days of cool sponging, changing bed linen, changing clothes. People have no idea how hard it is to undress and dress an unresponsive body. Three days eating alone in the room; not an hour to go for a walk down to Watersmeet, or Exmoor, or even to the village.*

— You'll just have to accept it, Eliza. There's no time to visit Ilfracombe now. It has to be straight to Barnstaple then back to Emminster.

— You have to make up your mind about the farms, too.

— The farms! I'd forgotten the farms.

— Which one do you think would be a good buy, Angel?

— I haven't really thought about it. I can't make a decision right away, not after what I've just been through.

— You told them you'd let them know by Saturday.

— I know. I know. Don't push me.

He decides to take the narrow gauge train back to Barnstaple the same way they'd come, as going by road would be too bumpy for him, and they arrive back at the hotel in time for midday dinner.

— I'm going down to Reception before dinner to see about some travel information while you freshen up.

Eliza unpacks her few things. *It's good that Angel is interested in things again after being struck down by the fever. He still looks yellow, though, and even more pinched in the face than when we left Emminster only a few days ago. Is that all it's been? I seem to have grown up and got older all in one week - wife, nursemaid, money manager. I wonder, now that Angel's over the fever, will he want to have his way with me every night, or less frequently? I don't look forward to bed time any more and the pain his efforts produce.* **He** *seems* *satisfied enough but it never occurs to him to ask me how **I** feel. Is there anything I could do to make it better? And who could I ask? I know by law that I can't deny him. Maybe the fever has exhausted him. That's one good thing that would come of it.*

— My dear!

He comes in, beaming.

— There are some very interesting things to do in this town with the little time we have left.

— Aren't you supposed to rest, Angel?

— You only have one wedding trip. There's a theatre here, the Theatre Royal, which only re-opened a couple of years ago; quite grand, in fact, Grecian columns and all that. I managed to get two tickets for tonight's performance.

He takes them from his pocket and splays them on the bed.

— *The Pirates of Penzance*! Oh, Angel, *The Pirates of Penzance*! That's famous! Mother used to sing parts of it to us:

> 'Tis better far to live and die
> Under the brave black flag I fly
> Than play a sanctimonious part
> With a pirate head and a pirate heart.'

— You'll have to dress up, Eliza.

— All I have is my wedding dress.

— And the jewels I gave you.

— Yes. A chance to wear them.

— This afternoon, though, we have a choice of venues. We can take the pamphlet with us and discuss it over dinner.

The afternoon sees an apparently happy pair of newlyweds doing the usual rounds of sightseeing. First, it's off to the canopied indoor Pannier Market and Queen Anne statue, and then the long bridge over the Taw River, Barnstaple being a port yet seven miles or so from the sea. They soak up the ancient town, and old it certainly is. Angel happily quotes from his literature as they go along.

— This town was humming even before the Norman invasion. It was a Saxon stronghold, and held off the Danish raiders in the 700s. You remember how Hubba was defeated at Appledore? We learned that in school: "Go, Stranger! Go." Appledore's just over that hill. In 930 A.D.

Barnstaple was granted a charter by Athelstan …it fell to the Normans in 1066 …five ships from Barnstaple fought with Drake against the Armada.' You can almost feel it, can't you, Eliza?

— Yes, I can.

Consulting the map, Eliza discovers they aren't too far from Westward Ho!, a name that had always caught her imagination.

— Angel, do you think we could go? It's our last chance to see the coast.

He looks at his very attractive bride, and smiles.

— We haven't time today. Maybe tomorrow.

They return to the hotel and take an early tea before dressing for the show. This is Eliza's first performance of anything inside a theatre. She's seen singers, mummers and dancers at local country fairs but tonight it's the opera! Angel reminds her it is really an operetta, a lighter musical in English and set, coincidentally, not far down the coast in Cornwall. This makes it more realistic as does the piratical, or rather privateering, history for which the West Country is famous. She piles her auburn hair high on her head like the young matron she is. Her jewels twinkle. Her eyes twinkle. *I feel like I twinkle all over.* Angel smiles approvingly and gives her his arm.

— Shall we to the theatre, Mrs Clare?

— By all means, Mr Clare. Do you have the tickets?

He goes back to the bed to retrieve them and the two of them make their way the short distance by foot from the hotel to the theatre in the heart of old Barnstaple.

— We're upstairs in the dress circle, second row. Nothing but the best for the Clares.

Eliza is entranced. She knows this evening will change her life forever. Old snatches of songs she knows come to life in their context.

> 'Poor wandering one, surely thou hast strayed.
> Can'st thou not find true peace of mind?
> Poor wandering one …'

She alternately cries and laughs at the young lovers' dilemma, the policemen's and pirates' antics, and the awful 'often' and 'orphan' puns. More songs, glorious songs. The whole thing, songs. 'With cat-like tread upon our prey we steal'; the tongue-twisting pomposity of 'I am the very model of a modern Major-General'.

There's an interval half-way through when the lights come up and the audience leaves their seats to drink refreshments down in the side galleries and talk with acquaintances about the show. They, of course, know no one but while Angel stands, Eliza sits on the plush lounge sipping her drink in her gloved hand, absorbing the gowns, the chandeliers, the splendid red carpet: immersed in the hum of the general atmosphere. Bells tinkle; lights dim, and the mass of beautiful people slip back inside for the finale.

Tears roll down her cheeks:

> 'He loves thee, aha,
> Fa-la-la-la; fa-la-la-la …'

And then she is tapping her hand on her knee and nodding as the chorus sings: 'Go ye men to immortality …'

She turns to share the moment with Angel. He is asleep. It really was too much for him, too soon. She claps and claps, and claps, and claps. It is a most amazing night. He's awake now (all that cheering!) She looks at him and smiles.

— This has been the best night of my life!

They spill out onto the brightly lit roadway and walk back to their hotel. Angel unclasps the pendant for her and nods approvingly as she places the ear rings and bracelet alongside it in their box.

— Yes, they really are you.

He yawns as he undresses, and is in bed before her. She brushes her hair 'a hundred times to keep the shine', then puts on her nightdress. She lies beside him, waiting for him to roll over and take his pleasure but he is breathing slowly, deeply, already in an exhausted sleep. She thanks her lucky stars and stays lying on her back looking up at the canopy, imagining it a stage. Pirates and maidens and policemen dance across her mind until she falls into a relaxed sleep, the first time with a smile on her lips since she was married.

— My, my, Eliza! We've overslept, my dear. I'm afraid we've missed breakfast.

— We can breakfast on the sights and sounds from last night's musical feast.

— This is our last day here and we have to make the most of it. Time's a wasting. It was Westward Ho! you wanted to see? There's a coach at eleven. We can get a bite when we get there.

An hour or so later they are gazing at the sea again across a wide ridge of large pebbles, with the sand stretching beyond merging with the low tide. Angel finds a Fish and Chips shop and they take their lunch, wrapped in newspaper, to eat outside. They have to be careful walking on the stones as they roll suddenly under their boots. They are not the kind of pebbles Eliza imagined, small and spherical. On the contrary, the pebbles range from small stones up to those she could put her arms around, worn slippery-smooth just by rubbing against one another. When the young couple reach the hard sand between the pebble ridge and the water, they wander barefoot, hand in hand. *This is more like the wedding trip I was expecting: carefree and happy.* Eliza breaks free, and starts taking large, stealthy steps in the sand much like the pirates did last night, breaking into their song, 'With cat-like tread upon our prey we steal …'; and then she runs along the water's edge, 'Come friends who plough the sea ….'

— I can't get enough of the sea, Angel, now that I've seen it. Do you suppose we could take one of these stones back with us, as a memento of our trip? We could use it as a door stopper.

She bends over, intent on selecting a perfect specimen from the millions that line the upper shore in an arc, flipping first this, and then that one, over.

— This is it! Look! Perfectly round, elliptical. So smooth. Feel it. It's like silk. Cold silk.

She brushes it down her cheek.

— I can use it to cool you down next time you have a fever.

And he laughs. Yes, he laughs as he looks at his young wife clad from neck to nearly ankle in her cotton dress and thinks of the life-size marble sculpture of the discus thrower in the Roman Museum, arched for action, poised to hurl, glistening, naked.

— I agree. It's extremely pleasant here on the coast, although I'm not sure I'd want to be here in a storm at high tide. The man in the fish shop told me the grinding noise from the force of the waves moving these stones over each other can be heard a mile inland; and that's up and over the cliff. This beach reminds me of the one Jack was talking about in Wollongong. I've been thinking, Eliza, seriously thinking about New South Wales. It might be good to have a complete break from the Old Country and try our luck there. Everyone who goes seems to prosper. A lot of people from this part of the world are emigrating.

— What about Mother and the children? I'd be so far away.

— You're married now. You've thrown your lot in with a farmer. I feel poised on the cusp. If I'm going to buy a place, I want to make a totally fresh start. It's not as if we'd be all alone out there. We already know someone established in the colony.

*You want us to move to the **Antipodes**! Most people who go never come back. Well, Jack and Mary came back. It's a long way though it's not impossible. I'd better not mention it.*

— It will be a very good investment of what is left of the inheritance my father set aside, part of which I lost in Brazil. That dairying country south of Wollongong sounds particularly interesting.

Eliza notices a faraway look in his eye, one that she would learn to recognize as Angel's 'dreamer mode'.

— You've really thought this through then?

— Aye. I've asked myself many times: Where do I want to be in five years from now? Not a place, *per se*, but where in life? What do I want to have accomplished? Look at Jack: when he landed in Australia he started out as a labourer, then became an overseer, then a property owner. He's ended up as a timber merchant, well respected in the town. I can see myself, ourselves, starting out owning a farm, dairy and feed crops, then getting into a dairy, maybe several: milk, cream, butter, buttermilk. I tell you, Eliza, there's opportunity there. Opportunity knocks, and I'm going to answer the call!

— When do you propose to go?

— There's really nothing to stop me going as soon as possible; nothing to stop both of us leaving. I'm going to need you, Eliza. I know you're capable. You'll be a great asset in whatever venture I take on.

— That's what I wanted to talk with you about, Angel, about being able to manage things if you are indisposed like you were in Lynton.

— There's no need to worry. I have a line of credit and the bank will honour anything I ask to be covered.

— But it may be different on the other side of the world where they don't know you.

He smiles at her.

— You don't need to worry your pretty head over things that don't concern you. You are my wife and I'll look after you the way the law demands. Right now I have to get back to the hotel and write refusals to those two farmers; and I have to find passage for us to New South Wales. I'll try the shipping agent in Barnstaple.

After he deposits Eliza and her Westward Ho! rock in their room he goes in search of an agent and comes back not long after with some shipping schedules.

— Most of the emigrant ships depart from Liverpool. There are even large posters on the wall in their office advertising for farmers, domestics etc. They'll subsidize us, Eliza. There are three ships leaving Liverpool within the month. Let me see: two bound for Sydney via Melbourne, and one for Melbourne and New Zealand. There's another out of Plymouth, only later. The earliest leaves in three weeks. I think I can get my affairs in order in three weeks.

Eliza seems concerned.

— What about Mother having to move?

— I'll pay for your family's move from Rose Cottage, and the new rent at Linden, you know, the cottage I found in Emminster is paid up for a year. I'll have to arrange for letters of reference from my bank manager to take with me. The bank must have affiliates over there. There's a lot to be done. I'll have to pack my books, technical ones as well, and I'll need to take some of my farming and dairying equipment, small things that will travel: pails and churns and the like. You can't be sure of the quality of goods you'll find over there.

— How long does it take?

— Oh, I should have everything together in two weeks.

— No, I mean how long does it take to get there?

— Let's see here. It departs on …and arrives approximately …oh, about two or three months. There's first, second and third class, and steerage. Only the desperate go steerage. I think the Clares can afford to go second class, don't you?

— It's not too expensive, Angel?

— No, no. Might as well have a little comfort for that length of time. And I must write to Jack to tell him he's done a good selling job! They aren't leaving for another six weeks.

— Are you seriously thinking of finding us a place in the Wollongong area or somewhere else in New South Wales?

— Naturally I'll go where my friend has prospered. It would be foolish to do otherwise. The Illawarra sounds a fertile area, don't you think?

— Yes. They really seem to like it there.

CHAPTER 10

EMIGRANTS

Pack, pack, hurry, hurry. Angel can't wait to get back to Emminster to make arrangements. He will have to ease his parents into the news gently. With all the fuss his mother made after his return from the Brazilian debacle, he wants to assure them that the Australian investment is a reasonable and practical plan. Anyway, Jack filled them in at the wedding breakfast, and the Reverend James seemed interested and impressed with Jack's success. Hopefully, he'll do the same with Angel's proposition.

On the way back in the train he mentions to Eliza.

— I think it best that you spend the next two weeks with your family, for who knows how long it will be before you see them again. I'll come by Rose Cottage and pick you up on my way to Liverpool. That will leave them a week to pack and move to Linden.

It's a great relief to know that Mother and the family are going to be looked after. He's a good man to do that. And it's also good that I'll have a reprieve from the pressure of the nightly marriage ritual. The question remains: Is this a case of history repeating itself? Angel abandoned Tess within a week of marrying her. How will Mother take this? How will the Clares?

Angel continues.

— I think we should leave the necklace and earings in the safety deposit box here in England with the bracelet Mother gave you. Your heirlooms. Anything could happen to them in transit. At least we know they'll be safe here.

— Will I see your parents before we leave?

— Of course. You'll have to stay overnight on the way to your mother's.

I'm glad I'll be seeing his folks again, especially the Reverend James. It seems things are normal, after all. Angel's a little bit self-centred: keeps referring to 'I' instead of 'we'; and I suppose he does have to think for the both of us. He **is** the head of the household. Getting ready to go to New South Wales! Last week I hadn't gone twenty miles from the village where I was born; now I'm planning to cross the world! How does one prepare to migrate? Is food provided for second class passengers or do we have to take supplies and cook our own? Where does the ship stop on the way?

The Clares are exuberant when they walk in the door.

— Here you are. Here you are, home at last! How was your trip?

Trip? I almost entirely forgot about the trip and that yesterday was the highlight of my life.

They have to break the big news, and watch the Clares deflate before their eyes; then the sadness when they realize Eliza is leaving the next day. The Reverend gives her a big hug.

— You come back soon, Missy, do you hear? Maybe the Australian climate will strengthen you, son.

They all go down to the inn next morning to wave Eliza off in the coach. Angel kisses her on the cheek.

— I hope your mother won't be too surprised when she sees you, Eliza; but we didn't have time to write.

Surprised? She'll be beside herself! First Tess, and now me.

Joan's eyes are as big as saucers when Eliza walks into the kitchen.

— Liza-Lu! What you be doin' home? And where's yer husband? Not again, Lord. Not again!

— No Mother, it's not what you think.

— Not what I think? I can see with my own eyes what I think: my newly married daughter sent packing by that good for nothing —

She couldn't think of a word.

— Mother, he hasn't sent me packing, and I haven't left him. Well, in the literal sense he's sent me packing.

— I knew it. I knew it. I feared the worst although I hoped for the best.

—Mother, will you calm down. Look, I am married, Here's my wedding band.

— Ooooh, it's gold.

By now the whole family is gathered in the kitchen, even sixteen year-old Abraham.

— Mother, all of you, I have come home to spend a few days with you before we leave for Australia.

— Australia? Oh, no.

Joan wails again.

— You can't leave me, child. What will become of us? I might never see you again.

— Nothing will happen. Angel has paid up the D'Urberville estate rent, and will pay for your move at the end of the month. He's also paid the rent for the new house in Emminster, Linden, for a year ahead, renewable by the stroke of a pen. He's keeping his end of the bargain, Mother. His friend, Jack Turville, has done very well out there in the timber and dairy business. He was telling us about life in New South Wales. They need new settlers out there, and Angel has found a ship leaving in three weeks. He's staying at his parents' and getting everything together he needs to take. He thought it a good idea if I spend the last two weeks with you. That's all. It won't take *me* that long to get my things together. Then he'll pick me up and we'll have a few days in Liverpool before we sail.

— Are you sure that's all, Liza-Lu?

— Yes, Mother, that's all.

The younger children are full of questions.

— Are there kangaroos hopping down the roads?

— Can you ride them?

— The enormous deadly snakes swallow you whole, don't they?

— When a spider bites you, you're deader than Sleeping Beauty.

— And the whole city is covered with sheep!

— It is not.

— Is too!

— Will you two stop arguing and start peeling those 'taters.

Abraham takes Eliza aside.

— You really want to go?

— Yes, Abe. Now that I'm used to the idea, I'm quite excited.

— Can I go with you, Sis?

— You? What would Mother do without you?

— Same as she did without Pa, and Tess, and you. She'll make out fine, with one less mouth to feed.

— She needs the wages you bring in, Abe, to make ends meet.

— But I want to go, Sis.

— Maybe after we've been there a year or two we could send the fare and bring you out. That would give Mother a bit of time to get on her feet. You are the man of the house now. You'll have to leave at some time in the future. Just give her some time, all right?

He gives her a defeated look and goes out to split wood.

Eliza decides to spend the rest of the time not so much in packing but playing with her little sisters and brothers as a form of farewell. Each night as she tucks them in she sings the songs her mother had sung to her, and she tells them Bible stories, embellishing their dull Sunday School ones with roars of lions in 'Daniel in the Lion's Den' for Little Charlie at seven thirty; and slipping and sliding on imaginary frogs in the 'Exodus' story for Young John at eight. She tries to make it as real as she can. 'Mama! Mama! I'm gonna get m'new boots all wet crossing the Red Sea.' 'Hush, my darling, just make sure they're buttoned up tight, and trust in the Lord.'

Hope and Modesty want Eliza to show them fancy stitches for the samplers they are making at school. Modesty laments.

— I wish my name was shorter, like Meg Spry's. She only has seven letters to cross-stitch while I have eighteen.

— I think you'll be prouder of the finished product, Modesty. Your name will look better, spread out in two rows right across the bottom. Tomorrow I'll teach you how to make French knots.

— Tell us the one about 'The Shoes that were Danced to Pieces'.

— Please, Liza-Lu, and 'The King of the Golden River': East West Wind Esquire.

Eliza smiles as she settles into the old yarns, as the light outside gets dimmer and dimmer.

— Do you remember 'Chimps Parming', Hope?

Hope giggles.

— I was only a baby, Liza-Lu. I couldn't say, 'Prince Charming'; but tell us that one, too.

They practise tongue twisters: 'Round and round the rugged rocks the ragged rascal ran', and 'red leather yellow leather'.

— I have a lolly for the first one who can say, 'the Leith police dismisseth us' correctly, three times in a row without lisping.

Abraham's too old for these distractions as he has many of the heavier chores to do, and is hiring himself out as an agricultural labourer on a day by day basis; but after tea at night he sits in a corner of the kitchen while Eliza sings, and plays games with the younger ones, 'Oranges and Lemons', and 'I Spy'.

— Why do you have to go and leave us, Liza-Lu?

—Well, my darlings, I'm married now, and I have to go with my husband. He was going to buy a farm here in England but he decided to buy a farm on the other side of the world.

— When are you coming back. Liza-Lu?

— I don't know. I promise to come home and see you when Mr Clare makes a good living from his farm. Now hop along up to bed and I'll come and tell you a story.

When she at last comes downstairs she finds her mother sitting in her favourite corner.

— Angel will be here in a couple of days, Mother. Is there anything else that you can think of that I should take with me? I have only the things I took to Emminster when I got married and a few books. I don't have any furniture or furnishings or dishes or anything. No wonder, as the saying goes, 'They landed in the Colony with nothing but the shirts on their backs'.

— I'll miss you when you're gone, Liza-Lu. You're a good girl, and you're a great help with the young ones. Soon, I expect, you'll have young'uns of your own.

— How will I know when I'm going to have a child, Mother?

— Why, Liza-Lu, everyone knows that when you miss a monthly you're in the family way.

— Miss a monthly?

— Why yes, child, didn't you know?

— You never told me.

— Good thing too. What you don't know can't hurt you.

— You said, when you miss a monthly, you're in the family way?

— That's right.

—Mother, mine is late this month. It's never been late before.

— Oh Liza-Lu! That means you're going to have a baby! Oh, this is wonderful. No, it's not. You can't travel in the early stages: you can't go overseas. It will kill the unborn child. You'll have to stay here during your confinement.

— What will Angel think about that?

— It doesn't matter what he thinks about it. No reasonable man would take a young wife in your condition on such a risky voyage. He'll just have to postpone it.

— He can't do that now. He's liquidating everything he has.

— Liquidating? You mean it's driving him to drink?

— No, no. He's turning everything he owns into money, selling it; and he'll be here the day after tomorrow.

— You'll just have to tell him. Confront him

— I can't do that. We've only been married three weeks and a bit.

— If you don't, I'll confront him for you.

Eliza sighs deeply. *In the family way! That's why I feel sick in the mornings. And Angel coming to pick me up in a coach and take me off to the ship, and a new life.*

The day Angel arrives the children are all in school except for little Charlie who is making mud pies in the vegetable garden, and there are only the defiant Joan and Eliza at home. He enters the gate to the enclosure of Rose Cottage for the second time in recent history and crunches across the gravel.

— You stay in the parlour, Liza-Lu. I'll handle this.

Joan opens the door.

— You're right on time, Mr Clare.

— Hello, Mother Durbeyfield. Is my wife all packed?

— Not packed; and not going.

— Not going! Why on earth not?

— Because you, Mr Angel Clare, are going to be a father.

— A father? A baby? So soon?

— It only takes one successful strike, you know, for a woman to fall.

— But I'm all ready to leave.

— You'd better come inside, instead of gaping there on the doorstep. Liza-Lu's in the parlour.

He goes over to where Eliza is standing, and takes both her hands in his.

— Are you really with child, Eliza?

— I'm afraid so. I feel very unwell every morning. Mother says I couldn't possibly travel at this point; not all that way.

— Um. This is very unexpected. You should have been more careful. What am I going to do now?

Careful! I should have been careful? I didn't even know what was happening to me, let alone know how to prevent it.

— We could stay here a year until the child is born, and is able to travel.

— But I want to go now; and I want you to come with me. If I went ahead, I'd miss you too much being separated for that length of time. I've tried that before. How could I work a farm by myself for a year? No, I need you by my side. It's all very, very inconvenient.

He seems vexed, annoyed; and he doesn't seem the least bit pleased or excited about being a father. He hasn't even mentioned it.

At this point Joan prudently breezes into the room: she's been listening at the door and realizes things are sliding out of Eliza's control. There just isn't that feeling of joy in the air that should be, when two love birds have been separated for nearly three weeks.

— What do you think of the news, Angel?

— It's very awkward, having to consider changing plans, especially at the last minute. Very inconvenient.

— I didn't mean that. I mean the baby!

— Oh, the baby. Yes, of course, the baby. Mmmm.

— Like I told Liza-Lu, it would be very dangerous for her to travel, to travel so far, in her condition. No. She'd lose the baby. She can't possibly go with you now.

— What would *you* do, Eliza?

— 'Eliza! Eliza?' What's all this 'Eliza' business? What's wrong with 'Liza-Lu'?

— When I was married, Mother, I felt that I had grown up, and I want to be called by my grown-up name.

— I'll not be calling you 'Eliza', that's for sure. You'll always be Liza-Lu to me.

— I don't mind if you call me that, or the young ones, but 'Eliza' is more a married woman's name. It is to me, at least.

— Please yourself.

Joan glances at Eliza, then at Angel, and shakes her head.

— The ball's in your court now, Mr Angel Clare.

He takes a deep breath and grimaces.

— I suppose, all things considered, I could carry on with the original plan on my own. I'm already halfway to the ship, with all my worldly goods.

*All **his** worldly goods? What about 'All my worldly goods I thee endow'? They're **our** worldly goods, his and mine.*

— I'll write, Angel; and I'll come as soon as Baby is suckling well. By then you'll be on your feet with the farm, and dairy enterprise, no doubt.

He seems to brighten a little.

— I *will* miss you, my dear.

They see him off. Eliza sighs. Joan sighs too, for her own private reasons. Here is daughter number two abandoned by the same man. What is marriage coming to these days?

The children are ecstatic when they come home from school and find Eliza still there.

— Now you can start to read us *A Thousand and One Nights*.

— She won't be around *that* long, Modesty. She'll prob'ly be gone in three hundred and sixty five.

Abraham is also delighted his sister is staying.

— Maybe next year when you go, I can go with you? I want to see the world. There's no future for me here. The only work I can get is farm labour. Mother certainly can't afford to send me to trade school.

— She wouldn't hear of it, Abe, your leaving. She needs you here. Your contribution, small as it may be, helps keep the family together. She'll certainly need you next week for the move to Emminster. You might find more steady work, or a regular job, in the town, *versus* out here in the country. There's always more opportunity and variety in a town. Myself, I would love to help the schoolmistress but they won't take married teachers, married women that is.

— I suppose it must be tough for you too. We're both stuck in a rut.

The move goes well. The sun shines, and Joan is organized. This time she knows where she's going, when she's going, and how she's going. This is a move toward their future, not a futile scrambling for uncertain shelter; and her confidence and contentment filter down through her children. Her new son-in-law has even rented a furnished house, so there are only their personal possessions, which are few, to be loaded onto the wagon.

Toward late afternoon they come down Emminster Hill and into the town, finally finding their new house. Angel had given Joan the key on his way to Liverpool.

— Well, it's aptly named. Look at the size of those trees!

Two huge lindens stand on each side of the gate so thickly inter-branched a mouse hole needed to be cut so people can come and go through the gate. They were obviously planted too close together by an inexperienced shade artist. They give the cottage privacy from the road; in fact, they obscure it completely. It has a central hall plan, with a parlour on one side and a bedroom on the other, in the front. Behind the parlour is a large eat-in kitchen and fireplace, while across the hall from it is a smaller living room, also with a fireplace. In fact, there are fireplaces in the two front rooms as well, each sharing a chimney with the rear rooms. The children run upstairs and report there are four bedrooms under the sloping eaves, each with double beds and a dresser, and mats on the oilcloth flooring. Joan does a quick calculation.

— There's a room for Liza-Lu, one for Abraham, one for the girls, and one for the boys; and I'll take the front bedroom down here. The lady of the house!

It only takes a few days to settle in. First, Eliza pays a visit to the Reverend James and Mrs Clare. They are dumbfounded when they see her.

— I thought you were with Angel?

— Is he here, too?

— No, he went on to Liverpool alone.

— Whatever for? Why aren't you with him?

— I'm in the family way, and Mother said such a journey was not for someone in my condition.

Mrs Clare looks concerned.

— And perfectly right, too.

— Well, we are pleased Eliza. A baby! Think, Mrs Clare, we're going to be grandparents. Isn't that grand?

— He laughs at his feeble joke, and asks.

— Are you staying at Linden as well?

— Yes, it's a very roomy cottage. I plan to follow Angel when the babe is about three months old and suckling well.

— At least we'll have you with us until then. Are you all settled in over at Linden? We'd love you to bring the family here for a visit.

Eliza and her mother accept the invitation. Joan leaves the children at home deliberately so as not to overwhelm the vicarage on first contact, and reciprocates by inviting the Clares to the cottage the following week, which they accept. They know the cottage well as they had visited the previous tenants, parishioners. Then there's school registration for Hope, Modesty and Young John (they start the following Monday). Joan tells Eliza.

— They'll make new friends, and have the advantages of town life.

They are also registered in Sunday School that Sunday, and Little Charlie is registered in the kindergarten run by the church women. The Clares encourage Joan to volunteer in the Ladies' Auxiliary, for by getting to know the other local women she might get more custom in her laundry business. Joan feels settled again. She has not felt this way since John died and they were turfed out of Marlot. The D'Urberville nightmare is at last beginning to fade.

Now that Eliza has a public library at hand she wants to look into the D'Urberville history of the region. Parson Tringham, who had first planted these grandiose ideas in her father's head, had donated his local histories to all the libraries in the county. A couple of days later finds her in the Family History section of the Emminster and District Public Library with a special request for D'Urberville family information. She knows it will upset her mother if she tells her too specifically what she is doing at the library so she tells her she's finding out about Emminster; and she really is, in a roundabout sort of way.

She has a notebook with her, and when the librarian brings out the reference books (two stacks) she sets to work scribbling, and drawing a pedigree chart of the original Norman who came with William the First, Sir Pagan D'Urberville. *Odd name. They **must** have been Christian.* She traces, or rather, copies, Parson Tringham's chart down through Sir Brian D'Urberville to several generations of Sir Johns. *'John' was Father's name.* There are branches of the family all over the county but many of them seem to produce nothing but daughters (and so the name dies out when they marry), while in other branches the males die young. *Here's my surname, Durbeyfield, beginning to creep in and replace the original spelling. This is so exciting. Now, where's the line who settled in Blackmoor Vale, my line?*

*It's an odd feeling: up until now I always felt I lived in the present, which I do, of course; but now I realize that if any of these folks listed here, going way back, had not lived and produced the baby on the next line, then I would not exist. Just one of these people not being born would have thrown a spanner in the works, and I wouldn't be sitting here copying this down. The enormity of chance! And now I'm going to produce another generation of the ancient D'Urbervilles under the Clare name that I can pencil in right **there**.*

She can hear the sound of coach wheels and galloping hoofs. *I must be a true D'Urberville: it's a sign.* Someone is calling her name.

— I'm sorry but we are closing now.

Closing! I've only just sat down. She looks up at the clock. *It can't be! I've just come in. I've been so absorbed in my family history that I've missed dinner, and it's almost time for supper!* She gathers up her papers

— It looks like you'll see me again soon. Thank you for all your help. As you can see, I've found the mother lode.

— Don't mention it. That's what we are here for: anything we can do to help.

Joan opens the door before she reaches it.

— Where have you been? I was getting worried. I waited dinner for you. Eliza gently chides her.

— Mother, I'm a married woman now. I can come and go as I please. I did mean to come home for dinner but I became absorbed in what I was doing in the library.

— Library! You've spent all this time in a library? Emminster must be the most fascinating town in all of England.

— There's a lot of history here.

— You're not getting mixed up with all them old ancestors again, are you?

— Not really.

— 'Cause if you're dredging up all your father's earls and lords, it won't amount to a hill o' beans. We're stuck in this world in quite tight circumstances and they (she turned and jerked her thumb in a southerly direction), all of them marble grandparents lying down Kingsbere can't lift a finger to make our situation one whit better. It's knowing the right people and making the right connections through marriage (and here she nods at Eliza and pulls a wise face) that gets a person ahead; the *only* way for folks like us to get ahead. I don't know why you want to go stirring up the past.

*I remember that vault, underneath the Kingsbere church, the night we started our wanderings after we were evicted from Marlot. I've always thought the name 'Kingsbere' an ironic play on words. 'Kings bier' : the bed of dead kings or lords. Mother's right in a sense. We can gain nothing monetarily from claiming kinship with the remains in the vault. It's just **knowing** we originated in these parts and around the district that gives me a sense of belonging to this part of the world.*

Abraham is lucky. He finds a job as a delivery boy for the local grocer and will have a steady wage coming in to help his mother. Eliza attends a Ladies' Auxiliary meeting with her mother-in-law (Joan stays home, not feeling at ease yet in her new social situation), and picks up a dressmaking order: smocking a new Sunday School frock for one of the parishioners' daughter. She's very good at smocking and knows her finished product will guarantee future work. Every little bit helps.

I wonder how Angel's making out. He'd have sailed by now, heading off to make our future while I stay home carrying our future.

She doesn't have to wait for long before she finds out. A week after they move into Linden she receives a letter, postmarked 'Liverpool'.

'My Dear Eliza,

What a fool I've been. Here I've gone and done it again! Left my bride in order to sail off to a foreign shore. I miss you more than I could ever have imagined. I need you to be with me. You must follow as soon as expedient. I realize now that in your condition you shouldn't travel alone so I have written to Jack Turville to ask him to arrange for your passage on the same ship they'll be returning on. You can't imagine how lonely I've been without you. It's true: absence really does make the heart grow fonder. I can't go on without you (although I'll just have to until I reach New South Wales). This ship sails in the morning, hence the necessity of my writing tonight. Their ship leaves in about five weeks. I know you'll be all right if Jack keeps an eye on you. I've asked him to arrange steerage accommodation for you, for although we are not struggling, we don't want to waste our pennies, do we? You'll no doubt be hearing from him in the near future,

Your loving husband,

Angel.'

She stands rooted in the pathway between the cut in the trees and the front door, staring at the letter in her hand, reading and re-reading it in disbelief. *What about the baby? Both Mother and Mother Clare agree that I shouldn't travel, let alone take a long sea voyage, being in the family way. He never mentions the baby, not once, nor shows any concern for **my** well-being. He's setting out our future in terms of **his** well-being. Just the command that she join him in New South Wales because he's lonely! The coach wheels!*

— Liza-Lu , what's the matter? Is it bad news?

Eliza's chin begins to quiver.

— Is it your husband? Is he killed?

Eliza shakes her head.

— He insists in the letter that I leave for Australia immediately. He misses me.

— Misses you? Is he out of his mind? You can't travel in your condition; it'll kill the baby.

— I fear so myself, Mother. And steerage! With him going second class. It's all too much.

— We'll go and show this to the Clares.

The Reverend James and Mrs Clare are very grave after reading Angel's letter. Mrs Clare seems to understand Angel's point of view better than the others.

— You have to realize, dear, that he's been through a lot and probably wasn't thinking. Of course you shouldn't travel; but he *is* your husband, and your place is by his side.

The Reverend Clare is more moved by Eliza's plight than by his wife's cut and dried solution.

— It's a terrible business. I don't know what to advise you, Eliza. It seems a very ill-conceived plan after what was originally decided. We care as much for the life of our unborn grandchild as you do for your unborn child. Personally, I think you should stay here as planned but Mrs Clare does have a point. What do you want to do?

It seems what I want doesn't matter. It's what is expected of me. What kind of a future would I be forging if I go against my husband's express wishes?

Joan remains adamant.

— She definitely should *not* travel in her condition. She should stay here, safe, and have the baby.

James has an alternate idea.

— Why not wait until you get a note from young Turville? His wife seems to be a sensible little thing. They might be against it, too. Also, there may be no space on the ship. There's no sense in us all getting upset over something that may not come to pass. You ladies go on home and stop worrying.

They go; but Joan cannot stop worrying and fretting, and her protestations grow louder when a letter arrives from Millcroft. She meets Eliza as she comes in the door, waving it. Eliza has been at the library again.

— Here it is. Here's the letter for you from Angel's friend.

Eliza takes it and notices the firm open hand in the address. Her heart jumps. Quickly, she tears it open and scans the contents. She closes her eyes, as if acknowledging her helplessness.

— It looks like I'm leaving on the *Merrie Englande* the middle of next month with the Turvilles. Mary, that's Jack's wife, adds a note at the end. She says, 'I'm so pleased that you'll be travelling with us but I don't understand why Angel left without you.' He didn't tell them!

— Oh, Liza-Lu, I'll never see you again.

— Don't be silly, Mother. I'll come home in a couple of years and show you your new grandchild.

— Oh, the baby!

Eliza can't take any more histrionics and goes upstairs to peruse the details of the letter. She's in turmoil, herself. *I stayed in England, mostly bending to Mother's and the Clares' insistence that travelling will jeopardize my pregnancy. I'm also happy to stay because I still feel awful in the mornings, and sometimes also later into the day. On the other hand, perhaps it looks odd that I separated myself from my husband; yet in the beginning it was Angel who decided, without consulting me, to go to Australia, and more recently to go ahead without me. Am I being unreasonable? Am I being selfish? Are Mother and the Clares over-reacting to old wives tales? I'm only thinking of the child. Is Angel? Or is he just thinking of himself? What should I do in the present, pressing, situation — stay or go? If I put my foot down now, and refuse to* *obey him, what will that mean for the rest of my life, our relationship? If he abandons me, like he did Tess, what will become of Mother and the children? And our baby? It looks like I have no choice. I **have** to sail with the Turvilles.*

A month later she boards the coach at the inn going to the station and climbs aboard with one suitcase, a hatbox and her hope chest which will be designated a 'cabin trunk' during the voyage. Because Angel has purchased a steerage ticket for her she has to carry her own food stores with her which she can prepare in a communal kitchen on board. She has sacks of flour, tea and sugar as well as salt beef and salt fish which she's wrapped in oilcloth; plus root vegetables and dried fruit. These days ships have been taking three to four months port to port, and she had to figure on enough food for a longer, rather than a shorter journey. She calculated the amount of oatmeal she usually has for breakfast (half a cup of dry oats which she soaks overnight in water) and multiplied that by thirty days. That equals fifteen cups a month, times four months, so she had scooped sixty cups of dried oats into a canvas bag and pulled the drawstring tight. That should keep body and soul together until she joins Angel in New South Wales. The food sacks are packed around her feet; and then there are the final farewells and tears. There have been protracted hugs and kisses in the house, down the street, and beside the coach.

— That's funny, Mother, Abe's not here. I thought he was going to try to get some time off to see me away.

— Either he can't get the time or he's sulking. He wants to go with you, Liza-Lu, but I told him I couldn't spare him. He's the main bread winner now.

— Good-bye, Charlie! Good-bye, Johnnie!

The coach lurches forward.

— Don't go, Liza-Lu!

— Come back soon!

— I promise I will, Hope. Bye-bye, Modesty. I'll write to you. Bye, Mother!

And she is on her way.

CHAPTER 11

THE MERRIE ENGLANDE

It takes nearly an hour to reach Chalk Newton where she gets her perishables and non-perishables onto the station platform to wait for the northbound train. She has at least a half-hour to wait and decides to go into the station tea room where she has a pot of tea and a bun with thick pink icing. Then, with a chuffing and a squeal of brakes, the train from Millcroft pulls in, and there is Mary waving a hanky out a carriage window. Jack jumps down and starts loading Eliza's things onto the train.

— How's young Mrs Clare?

— Not as strong as Mr Turville. Thank you, Jack.

— Don't mention it. Here, let me help you on.

He goes to her elbow to help her. *Why am I flustered all of a sudden? He's so close.*

— Thank you but I can manage.

And she swings herself up the steep steps into the corridor of the train.

— Eliza! In here!

Mary is watching for her with her head out the compartment door, and beckons.

— Oh, it's good to see you again, Eliza. I'm so glad you're coming with us.

Eliza says nothing, loading her smaller bags and parcels in the rack overhead. A little girl is dozing in the corner of a seat. Mary smiles at her sleeping cherub.

— It's been a busy day for her and there's still a long way to go.

She puts her hand on Eliza's arm as they sit down opposite each other.

— I want to speak with you before Jack gets back, Eliza. Is everything all right between you and Angel? It's rather unusual to emigrate separately.

— He didn't tell you the reason? Or Jack?

— In his letter he said you'd decided to stay behind.

Looking distressed, Eliza shakes her head.

— I'm pregnant, Mary.

— Ooo-ooh.

Mary sucks in a deep breath. Eliza continues.

— My mother and Angel's parents didn't want me to go with him. I've been sick every morning, and don't feel entirely well at anytime; and they think I'll lose the baby if I travel. I don't know what to think. I wanted to go with Angel but really didn't feel up to it. Then with the pressure from Mother and the concern shown by the Clares, I decided to stay and have the baby in Emminster and follow Angel later. In a very direct letter he posted just before sailing he said I had to come. 'You're my wife', he said, 'and I miss you. Your place is at my side'.

— Oh, Eliza. I do feel for you. You are really caught in a squeeze. At least now you won't be going alone.

— You always have the most comforting words, Mary, and I'm happy to be going out with you.

The moppet in the corner begins to stir.

— Hello, darling. Are you waking up?

A little fist rubs a still closed little eye.

— Mmm-mmm. Are we there yet, Mama?

Mary pats her daughter's arm and rubs her rounded back.

— No, we've only just begun. Sit up Polly. When you're wide awake I'd like you to meet Mummy's friend.

Mary watches her four year-old stretch her arms and bootless legs, and slide more or less upright against her. She still has her eyes closed, and yawns. Thick fair hair (her father's hair) falls across her square-chinned little face as she turns her head back and nestles between her mother's arm and the seat back. She opens her eyes, and looks right into Eliza's. She doesn't move. She stares at her for a long, long time. Eliza smiles; she can't help it. *What a dear little girl!* Polly's eyes smile back.

— So you're awake at last. This is Mummy's friend, Polly. She's coming to Australia with us. You can call her Aunt Eliza. Eliza, this is our daughter, Polly.

— Hello, Polly. Did you have a good rest?

Polly nods, never moving her eyes off Eliza's face. She'd never seen such a face, with skin so white and smooth, and deep golden hair. She decides in her mind that Eliza must be a beautiful fairy.

— This is a big adventure for you, Polly: a ride in the train and then a big ship.

— I been on a big ship before. We came to see Grandma on a big ship.

— So you did! I forgot. You were born in Australia, weren't you?

— Yiss. I'm a little Aussie.

Just then the door opens and Jack comes in.

— Ah, you're awake, my little one.

— Yiss, Daddy. This is Aunty 'Liza. She's coming home with us.

The three adults laugh.

— I managed to get your things stowed in the luggage van, Eliza.

— Thank you, Jack. That's very good of you.

— Well, ladies, shall we make our way to the dining car?

He scoops Polly up in his arms and leads them single file down the swaying passageway. Later that night, when Polly is saying her prayers, 'God bless Mama and Daddy, and Granny and Pop', she adds, ' … and Aunty 'Liza'. Then Mary knows Eliza has made quite an impression on the four year-old.

— Which one's our boat, Daddy?

— Ship, ship. We've been trying to teach her ever since we left, Eliza, the difference between a boat and a ship.

— Our ship, then. Is it that one?

— She's moored at Dock 16: the *Merrie Englande*.

— That's your name, Mama: Mary.

— Here's Dock 11. Can you count to 16 Polly?

— No, Aunty 'Liza but I can count to ten. 1,2,3,4,6,7,9,10!

Eliza's eyes were leaping ahead, counting the ships moored one behind the other. *There it is: the ship that will carry me across the seas to a new land, a new life. Am I doing the right thing by my unborn child, in going? By law I have to obey my husband; but what if Mother and the Clares are right? What if I lose the child? Would it be my fault? Is blind obedience worth it?*

They pull up at the foot of the gangway and Jack helps the driver unload their trunks, bags and boxes.

— What's in all those sacks, Eliza?

— Provisions, Jack.

— They have provisions on board.

— I didn't know that. Nobody told me. I thought steerage passengers had to bring their own food.

— Steerage? You don't have a cabin?

— No. Angel thought he would put the money saved to better use in New South Wales. *He went second class himself. No stinting for him. Mr Clare, gentleman farmer.*

Jack and Mary are met by the purser who calls a steward to take them to their cabin. He then directs Eliza to the steerage section where the poorer assisted emigrants are to spend the better part of the next three months in close proximity. An extra deck, known as the 'tween decks, has been added between the hold and the deck above. The beams are low enough for her to reach up and touch them. The remaining space is again divided into large wooden upper and lower bunks that hold four people. There are two bulkheads dividing the emigrants into the unmarried females aft; those married and with children in the middle; and the single males forward.

The 'tween decks also houses central brick ovens, some tables and trestles, cooking pots, tin cups and the like. On each communal bunk are four blankets, and under each bunk, a slop pail. Because the ceiling is very low and the corners very dark, the air smells stale even before the space has begun to fill up. Eliza sits down on her allotted bunk and bursts into tears.

The *Merrie Englande* sails out of Liverpool fully laden two days later. Parting families throw coloured paper streamers up from the dock, and down over the side from the various decks, making a colourful melange, a random mixed-up twining, no doubt similar to the emotions felt by some of the passengers: some full of excitement and hope; others torn by the knowledge that when those streamers break so will their ties to England. Mothers know they will never see their sons again despite the shouted promises.

Mary is down in the 'tween decks helping Eliza settle into her communal space among the other steerage passengers. She's appalled but says nothing. She, Jack and Polly have a lovely airy cabin with a porthole. Eliza doesn't have much to say, except to thank her friend, and beg her not to come down again. She is both embarrassed and mortified.

— I'm fine, Mary, really. The meals are plain but palatable, and the helpings plentiful.

Mary cautions her.

— Now, Eliza, don't worry if you get a little seasick. Everybody feels under the weather the first few days. Get out from your quartes and get some fresh air up on deck. That cures everything.

And that is where Eliza goes, watching the departure. *A ship of pregnant lives.* They move out into the Irish Sea and the ship begins to dip slightly. Most people have left the rail as the sky is darkening and a squall threatens, when she senses someone at her elbow.

— Hello, Sis.

— Abe! Abraham! What? Where? Shouldn't you be in Emminster?

— I couldn't stand it, Liza. I couldn't stay back there with you going off on the grand adventure.

— It's not a grand adventure for me, believe me. I don't even want to be here.

— Strange, isn't it? You had to be dragged to the ship while I raced to it.

— What's Mother going to do without you, Abe? Did you let her know where you were going? You couldn't possibly have saved up enough as a grocery clerk in so short a time to buy a ticket. How did you get it?

— She doesn't know, actually. Old Joan will do all right. She'll land on her feet; she always does. She's a planner.

— You're not answering my question. Who paid for your passage?

— Well, no one, really. It hasn't been paid for yet.

— What?

She is whispering now.

— You stowed away? But how?

— I got inside one of your boxes and was carried down into the hold. Look, Liza, do you have any food? I'm starving. It's been more than three days and I haven't eaten. I let myself out when all the people were milling about.

— I've come to know some of them now, Abraham, so we can't go and mingle. They'd know you are a new face. Oh, what's to be done? I know. I'll send word for Jack to come down. He'll think of something.

Her brother catches her by the arm as she turns to go.

— Liza-Lu, I haven't eaten in three days, and I'm parched with thirst.

— I thought your speech sounded thick. Stay here out of the way, and I'll go below and get you something.

When she goes down she asks someone to send a message to Mr Turville to meet her on the rear deck. He is there waiting when she arrives with the parcel for Abraham.

— Jack! Thank goodness you're here. Thanks for being so prompt.

Just then half a loaf of bread tumbles out onto the deck from the bundle Eliza is carrying.

— You invited me for a picnic?

— No, no. It's much more serious. Abraham, my brother Abraham, is on the ship. Abe! Abe!

A figure slips into view.

— Abraham, this is Jack Turville, Angel's friend. He's travelling first class with his wife and little girl; lives in Australia.

Abraham shakes Jack's hand. They look steadily at one another. He's a tall boy for sixteen and likes Jack's firm grip. Jack is impressed with Abraham's forthright gaze, like his sister's.

— I think the best thing is to be honest and come clean with the purser right away. Eat up, Abraham, then we'll go up, just the two of us. You wait here, Eliza.

Instead of Jack and Abraham returning, it is Mary who comes to meet her, all excited.

— Who's looking after Polly, Mary?

— Jack is. Isn't he wonderful? He took Abraham straight to the purser who agreed not to prosecute him but to take him on as a hand, and let him work his passage. He's a nice boy, Eliza, and will be a help to you in Australia, I'm sure.

— Hopefully more help than he was to Mother in Emminster.

— Are you sure you're all right, Eliza? You look a little peaky to me.

— I think the ship's motion is making me queasy, on top of already feeling queasy.

Mary gives her a quick hug.

— I must be getting back. Bye for now.

— Bye, Mary, and thank Jack for me, will you?

The ship sails further and further away from the coast, meeting the equinoctial winds as it goes. Eliza prefers to stay up on deck in the cold wind: she isn't the least bit hungry but it's nearly dark, so she goes below. A mixture of warm, stale air hits her like a wall: boiling beef, close bodies, hemp and tar, and the permeating smell of bilge water. She sits on her bunk, perfectly still, for a long time into the night, staring at the floor. She is feeling worse and worse as time goes on, and getting hotter and hotter, hoping against hope that she won't be sick. Then, because she can't help it, she grabs the slop pail and vomits into it.

She retches and heaves the whole night until her ribs ache. Next day she still cannot keep anything down, and can't imagine she has anything else to bring up; but she has. She only has strength to lie on the edge of her bunk, hanging over the edge. Her bunk mates have to climb over her. And she is not alone. Several other passengers are forced to stay below in the worst surroundings, some tending to those who have no one to empty their pails or bring them sips of water as they spew and groan.

I want to get off. I can't go on like this. Oh God, Angel, what have you done to me? This hell is beyond wifely duty. The ancient mariner was right: 'a thousand slimy things lived on, and so did I'. Four days, and I wish I were dead. Let the ship sink; right down to the bottom; and never come up. Please God, let the ship sink and take me with it! Oh, the pains in my belly! Griping pains. They're getting worse than my aching ribs, just like really severe monthly cramps that won't let up. They started during the night and they're getting worse and worse. Oh! Oh!*

One of the other women comments to her.

— What an unfortunate time to have the curse.

Eliza replies weakly.

— Oh, I'm so sorry for you.

— I don't mean me; I mean you.

— Me? I don't have the curse. I'm pregnant.

— Sorry, love, but you're bleeding. Your dress and your bed are all stained.

I'm all hot; and light-headed. I feel like I'm floating. What did she say? I'm bleeding? That's not right. That shouldn't be. Oh! The cramps! Here they come again.

— Are you all right?

— I'll be all right, if only the ship would stay still.

— You don't look too good to me. Are you alone on the ship?

— No, I have friends in first class.

— I think you'd better give me their names and I'll get word to them.

— No, I don't want to bother them.

— I think you'd better and I think you need a doctor.

I'm getting hotter and hotter. Weaker and weaker. Mary! Mary! I'm too weak to think. It's all going dark and ...

This is how Mary finds her, lying unconscious in her own filth and stench, her clothes drenched in blood. She whispers to her senseless friend in terror.

— I'll have you out of here in no time, Eliza. Just hang on a little longer.

Mary races up to the upper deck and finds Jack. She is shaking by this time.

— We have to get the doctor for Eliza. I think she's had a miscarriage. It's frightful down there, Jack. We've got to get her out of there!

— Leave it to me, love.

Eliza awakens in an airy cabin to see Mary anxiously scanning her face.

— Where am I? What time is it? Why am I here?

— You're going to be all right, Eliza. You've been very ill the last two days and Jack arranged for you to have this cabin.

There are tears in Mary's eyes as she speaks, and her voice falls to a whisper as she squeezes Eliza's hand.

— Eliza, I have some very sad news to tell you. You were so sick that you lost your baby. The doctor said he did everything he could to save it but it was too late. Then he had to concentrate on saving *you*. The dreadful seasickness started it. Oh, Eliza, what will Angel say?

Eliza lets this all sink in. *What **will** Angel say? 'I had no idea the voyage would have such an effect on you', or 'It's for the best. Right now I need a strong helpmeet on the farm. A baby would require too much attention'. He'll probably blame me. Maybe it's for the best. God moves in mysterious ways. Maybe there's a reason for having a miscarriage. Is it a punishment? Would life have been too hard for the poor little thing in New South Wales? What other reason could there be? Steerage is no place for nurturing a baby, nor a seasick mother. But the cramps! The awful cramps have gone. Aaaagh.*

She groans.

— What is it, Eliza?

— Nothing, Mary. I'm just glad to be free of the pains. I'm so sleepy. Let me know when I have to go back to my bunk.

— Don't you even think of it. Jack has paid for this cabin for the rest of the way out, as well as for the doctor to attend you as long as you need. We're coming into calmer waters now, entering the Mediterranean. The ship won't be rolling so much.

— Thank the Lord for that.

— The doctor also said you are to stay quiet and rest for the next fortnight, and you are to eat only the lightest food. Look what I have for you. Can I tempt you? Chicken broth and thin strips of toast.

Eliza shakes her head. The mere mention of food turns her stomach. She gasps.

— Not now!

She looks down. She is dressed in a dainty white nightie and is lying in a bunk between ironed sheets that smell so fresh.

— I bathed you, Eliza, with some of my lavender water. We sent your clothes to the laundry; and Jack had your trunk and your provisions brought up here. When you've recovered we'll be able to stroll the deck together, and dine together.

— What will Angel say about all this expense? He'll pay Jack back, of course.
— If you think Jack will take a penny for rescuing his best friend's wife, then you don't know Jack Turville.
But I think I know Angel Clare; and there'll be hell to pay.
— I must go now, Eliza, and look in on Polly.
— Polly. Yes, of course. You've spent too much time on me, Mary.
— No, no, Eliza. It's just that Polly has come down with the measles, like many of the children on board. Two of the little ones have died.
— That's terrible. Is she all right?
— The doctor says she's coming along nicely. She was lucky: she didn't get any of the complications but we have to keep the cabin dark for the next week or two as daylight may affect her eyes. I tell her stories to keep her from getting fidgety.
— Give her my love, Mary, and tell her I'll be along to tell her some new stories as soon as I get stronger.
— God bless you, Eliza.
She stands up, kisses her friend on the forehead and goes out.

The sea becomes calmer and the sun much warmer as the *Merrie Englande* pushes her way east towards Suez. Eliza never quite loses that queasy feeling but she can now take the air on deck, even when it's squalling a little, and eats more nourishing meals. She makes a point of always dropping in to see little Polly who looks forward to the stories Aunty 'Liza makes up about a little girl her own age called Kate (her middle name) who has a magic bear floor mat that can fly her to any country she wishes to see in a night, and back. The bear is her friend and protector, so she can go anywhere in the world fearlessly.
— Aunty 'Liza, are you all better now?
— Yes, darling, I'm a lot better.
— Me too. Mama said we've both been in the wars. I'm better too. I'm allowed outside tomorrow. The doctor said Daddy can take down the blankets from over the windows.
— That's wonderful news. Now you and I can go for walks in the fresh air together. You can see some land from the deck, hills and desert. I'll tell you a story about the wild Berber horsemen.
Jack manages to get word to Abraham about Eliza being so violently seasick, and subsequently losing her baby. He thinks at sixteen Abraham can handle adult news. He's very sorry to learn of his sister's afflictions but as a working

hand he's not allowed in the first class section. Jack arranges for Eliza to meet him in the hold, below the dreaded steerage, on the first calm day. When he sees his sister he notices how much thinner and paler she is. She must have had a long haul. They embrace for a long time.

— I hear you've had quite a time of it, Sis.

— Yes Abe, I've been very unwell. If it wasn't for the Turvilles I doubt I'd be standing here before you; and thank heaven for this smooth stretch. How are you coping with the waves, and the job?

— Job's fine; waves are fine. They don't affect me at all.

— You are indeed a blessed boy.

— My job is to check the cargo in the hold, here, to make sure it doesn't shift in the heavy seas. Things work loose out of the ropes that hold them even though they are firmly cinched in. I also help check the ballast, and see that the pumps are working properly. I'm not supposed to be caught with the passengers so you'd best go now but I'm real glad you're on the mend.

— And I'm glad that you are happy.

— Happy and free!

Eliza and Polly become inseparable. Mary perceives that maybe Polly is filling a void for Eliza: her lost child; or maybe lost opportunities. She doesn't mind sharing her little one, not if it helps her friend recover. She's also glad to have Eliza up on deck with her, for companionship's sake. When Polly is settled in her bunk at night the three adults stroll the deck, Jack with a lady on each arm. *I can feel his manly strength through his light clothing. His very presence is strengthening; his consideration to both Mary and me, something I've not yet seen in Angel. And Mary doesn't seem to mind sharing him. My dear, selfless friend. It's obvious that she and Polly come first in Jack's life. I can only wonder that the Turvilles have opened up their lives, like a break in a circle for me, and then all joined hands again as if I'd always been part of their family.*

Jack comments after dinner one night.

— I wonder how Angel's getting on in New South Wales. He must be there by now. He shouldn't have any trouble procuring a farm.

In the southern hemisphere, at that precise moment, Angel is inking a deal to buy a small dairy farm from a farmer who has become bankrupt, just west of Wollongong on the lower slopes of Mt Keira: lovely rolling, hilly country, green, and mostly cleared to the base of the mountain. There is a milking shed that needs a little work and a homestead that needs a lot more. Patches of forest dot the gullies, as they call them, and a creek runs through the property which can be diverted for a pond. The farmer is a bachelor and has tried to make his living solely from dairying. Angel immediately sees the folly in such a move. Even though the countryside *looks* as if it could sustain only milk cows; he knows that crop rotation and diversification are the only ways for a farm to make a profit. The farmer will be leaving by the end of the month, which is coming up very fast. He's a city chap who thought cows could milk themselves; hadn't realized there was quite so much work to it.

It is only a small herd, Jerseys mainly, seven, but Angel sees great potential. He has walked the perimeter with the farmer and notes the fences are in pretty good shape. He also notes which land faces north, the sunny growing side, and contemplates which crops will do best in their respective eco-niches. He figures he'll have to lay out a little money for some internal fencing as all the pasture is presently open range, and he reaches into his jacket pocket for a small notebook, one of the many objects he carries which weigh his pockets down in the front. He takes a fountain pen from his breast pocket and stops to put down some figures and make some calculations.

He will need to buy a horse and wagon to transport farm supplies, and to take the milk cans to the road for pick-up. He can't help remarking what a good arterial feeder system this part of the world has for the collection of milk for the dairies, as well as for the delivery of goods, and post. During the short time he has been in the Colony he's noticed how communities pull together for their common advancement as well as compete against one another in football matches, sparrow shooting, bicycle races, and other community events. He rides back into Wollongong and returns the rented horse to the livery stables, prioritizing his purchases in his mind.

Jack, Mary, Polly and Eliza stand on the promenade deck as the *Merrie Englande* enters the Canal.

— Here's to Mr DeLessops!

— I can't agree with you more, Jack.

— You feel your old self again, Eliza?

— Just about. I thought before I boarded that I might get a *little* seasick but I never imagined permanent seasickness. This canal is a real respite. Thank you, Jack, for posting my letter to Mother in Port Said. At least she can rest easy about Abraham. I didn't tell her about my being so seasick but I did tell her about losing the baby. I can just hear her: how she will go on.

They ended up being right, didn't they? Maybe it is for the best.

— Look, Aunty 'Liza, there's no grass anywhere. It's all orange sand.

— Very difficult to grow pansies here, Polly.

— They're my favourite flowers. They have little faces. They're friendly flowers. They're like velvet on your cheek, and they smell nice too.

— Well, Mary, my love, let's dine in style tonight and show Eliza the grand effect of the first class dining room. You up to it, Eliza?

— I'm up to anything when the ship is still.

— Can I come down too, Daddy?

— Why not? Can you stay awake that late?

— Yiss.

Her parents exchange glances over her head and smile.

— You can wear your new pink frock and your patent leather shoes.

— I'll pretend I'm the princess who was captured by the Prince of the Barbers. They all wear white nighties and dressing gowns, and ride horses in the desert.

— I think you mean Berbers, Polly.

A few days sailing down the Suez Canal and Red Sea; too few for Eliza. She relishes the smooth waters and hot dry air. It gives her skin a glow. Even Jack notices.

— You are positively glowing with health, Eliza. I think Australia will agree with you. You look a lot better than the miserable waif we rescued from steerage.

— How can I ever repay you, Jack?

— If you mention that again, my girl, Ill send you back down there. We couldn't leave you suffering like that.

The ship begins to sway as the Red Sea opens out into the Indian Ocean. Eliza will not be corrected. 'Pitch' and 'roll' may be nautical terms but to her it sways; and she sways; her eyes sway; her stomach sways; her head sways; but never all in unison. It puts her right off her food. Jack and Mary appear at her cabin door on their way down to the dining room, but always go on alone.

As they head east and south around India's tip the weather becomes more sultry and heavy. Luckily, the sea is calmer. They see many porpoises following the ship as well as leaping and playing beside it which keeps Polly fascinated for hours, watching them. There are also flying fish, and some come right up on deck. Eliza explains to Polly that they go so fast and seem to 'fly' out of the sea because they are being chased by yellowtail tuna looking for lunch. Polly feels sorry for them. They flash so prettily as they flutter through the air only to die, flapping helplessly on the deck.

— Poor fish!

The swells of the Indian Ocean increase as the ship ploughs southward and Eliza spends days at a time without leaving her cabin, with the chamber pot by her side. *Being seasick in first class is a lot more comfortable than in steerage but it's still awful and I can't wait to be off this ship. My first and last sea voyage. I don't know how Angel will accept that, or Mother. Knowing what I do now, why would I ever voluntarily put myself through this again?* Stewards bring her damp towels sprinkled with lemon juice; and change her linen daily. Mary and Jack try to get her to take a few sips of water, lemon soda, soup; but she shakes her head. *I don't feel like taking anything by mouth. Ugh! It makes me shudder. I feel ghastly, and my head throbs.* Finally, it is Polly who coaxes her to try something.

— Aunty 'Liza, won't you try some for me? Just a sip? And another one? Mama says it will make you better.

The only thing that will make me better is dry land, and lots of it. I'd better try a sip just to see her little face brighten. This is definitely my last sea voyage. I will never get on a ship again. Absolutely never. I'll live and die in New South Wales. Oh, to die on terra firma! *That's the first thing I'll tell Angel when I get there. I will be a dutiful wife; I will work my knuckles to the bone but I will never ever go to sea again.*

Out of the Indian Ocean, into the Southern Ocean, through Bass Strait (much calmer) into the Tasman Sea where the *Merrie Englande* lurches, pitches, staggers, undulates, and dips: all those motions which make life miserable for a poor sailor. Eliza continues to suffer but in more genteel surroundings. *It all boils down to this one truth: I will never set foot on a ship again. Whether this constitutes defiance, in Angel's eyes, I cannot fathom, nor do I care. If he's concerned about me one iota, he will never ask me to return to England.*

BOOK II

THE ILLAWARRA

CHAPTER 12

S̲ydney

— Aunty 'Liza! Aunty 'Liza!

Polly rushes into Eliza's cabin.

— Come out on deck, Aunty 'Liza. We're going through the Heads.

The Tasman swells have sent Eliza to her bunk again and she raises herself on an elbow, aware, from the motion, that the ship has turned ninety degrees.

— What heads?

Mary is close on Polly's heels.

— The entrance to Port Jackson, Sydney Harbour. We're here at last!

— Here at last?

— Come and look, Aunty 'Liza. The cliffs are ever so high.

Mary helps her dress.

— No more sea-sickness, Eliza. It's all calm once we pass through the Heads. Come out on deck and see the scenery.

The straight yellow cliffs tower high on their left and their right and the scene ahead is calm and serene. They pass beneath the flagstaff on South Head and the rolling and lurching mercifully cease at last. As they steam past finger after finger of wooded land on both sides running down from ridges into the sea, Eliza notes the crescents of yellow sand between them. Although there are many ships in the roads, the harbour is huge, and can accommodate them all. It is November now, or is it early December? It means little to Eliza, although she realizes the sun has a strength to it she never experienced in England. The greenery is not as green, though, almost blue. The distant trees have a bluish tinge to them. The harbour is blue, deep sparkling blue and by now most of the passengers crowd the decks to catch their first glimpse of their new home. Houses with red roofs begin to appear, and the land on their left seems to be quite built-up. Jack joins them.

— It's come a long way in a hundred years, Sydney. We passed Wollongong on the way up the coast. I suppose you didn't happen to notice, Eliza?

— Enough of your teasing, Jack.

— No, Jack, I didn't. I can't get to land fast enough.

— Mary and I have been talking over what's the best plan of action when we dock. The usual way of getting to Wollongong, sixty miles south, is by water. A regular packet runs but that's out for you. We think it would be a good idea if you, Mary and Polly stay at a hotel in Sydney for a few days while I go down by sea with the cabin baggage. Abraham can come with me and I can introduce him to some people to see if he can find a job. You ladies can pack a small bag each. I'll bring Angel back with me, and then we can proceed down again by train or coach. From what we know the train will be a lot more comfortable even though there are a lot of switchbacks and tunnels to get from the top down to the coast. Bulli Pass can be dangerous in a coach. The brakes are forever failing, and coaches, horses and all go over the side. Well, dear ladies, where do you want to stay? A view of the harbour, perhaps?

— No water for me or Eliza, Jack.

— Very well, we shall penetrate the town. I know just the place.

The biggest town Eliza had ever been in was Barnstaple, on her wedding tour. The closer they come to Sydney, gliding up Port Jackson, the wider her eyes grow. The city looms on their left and the suburbs of the North Shore on their right. Large, substantial stone buildings line the quays where the water looks quite green. The ship is surrounded by ferries and smaller boats as they make their slow way into their dock at Pyrmont. In Darling Harbour they pass one of the numerous wharves that line the shore, and Jack points out a sign.

— There! That's where I'll be catching the Wollongong steamer.

Eliza reads the sign above the wharf: 'Illawarra Steam Navigation Company'.

— The first thing is to get my Three Musketeers settled on dry land, and then I'll transfer all the trunks and bags, as well as your foodstuffs, Eliza, to the steamer.

They have to pass through Customs and Immigration whose officers come on board and set up their paper work and stamps in the main dining room; and have to pass a health inspection as well. All the passengers line up with all their baggage, and are interviewed, their names ticked off, and their goods inspected before they are allowed off the ship. They meet up with Abraham there and Eliza vouches for him. Jack whistles for a carriage on the wharf.

— Abraham, you mind the luggage here. I'll be back as soon as I deposit the party at the hotel.

— You're the boss, Jack.

The horses are tired, and come clomping up slowly to wait for their next customer.

— Where to, Guv'nor?

— Pitt Street. Adams' Hotel, Tattersall's.

— Oh, Jack, are you sure?

— Nothing but the best for my musketeers.

Mary confides to Eliza.

— It's just the best hotel in Sydney, recently refurbished.

— What will Angel say about the cost?

— Don't you worry what old Angel will say. You're our guest, Eliza.

— Yes, and we want you to have a wonderful few days in the greatest city in the antipodes before you wear yourself out running a farm house.

The buildings all seem to be made from a yellowish stone.

— That's Sydney sandstone. Everything here is made of it.

Eliza notices that down near the wharves the houses are smaller and crowded together; and while many of the children go barefoot, boys still wear caps or hats. They drive a few blocks up a steep hill and then they are on the flat, crossing a very busy street, lined with Georgian buildings; then on to Pitt Street where they pull up outside Adams' Tattersall's Hotel.

Jack makes sure they are comfortable in their rooms.

— I'll meet you ladies at four o'clock. We'll go down for afternoon tea and I'll show you the marble bar, Eliza.

— What's that?

— You'll see. Meanwhile, I'll buy young Abraham a set of good clothes.

He returns to the *Merrie Englande* to supervise the transfer of the luggage to the steamer which sails at seven tomorrow morning, then takes Abraham to David Jones to be fitted out with a new set of togs.

For sheer richness, nothing can top Tattersall's: the finest imported woods, marble, chandeliers and stained glass, cut, moulded and carved into inlays and pillars. It's a hum of elegance and the central attraction is the famous curved bar made entirely of polished marble. The mullioned glass doors of the public rooms are curtained in fine lace; potted palms cast leafy shadows on the walls; plenty of gold but not overdone; thick carpets; the rustle of silk skirts; fabulous hats adorned with flowers, feathers and fruit; and a menu that includes the famous Sydney rock oysters, prepared four different ways as part of the savoury selection of their afternoon tea.

— How would you like them, Eliza? Mornay? Kilpatrick? Natural?

She shudders. The very thought of swallowing those slippery little grey things turns her stomach.

— None for me, thank you very much. I'll stick with the cucumber, and watercress sandwiches.

— You should try them, Aunty 'Liza. They're yummy.

She grimaces.

— Polly, for me it's like eating eyeballs. I couldn't do it.

They all laugh from their comfortable chairs at one of the round tables that are set up each afternoon at 3 p.m., with silver bowls of roses or gerberas or waratahs, or whatever flowers are in season, as a centrepiece. Large brass and ceramic pots of cascading fernery sit atop marble half-pillars while waiters move about the tables with their white gloves, deftly pouring tea through silver strainers. Silver platters lined with white napkins hide fresh hot scones; while iced *petit fours* and flaky passionfruit palm leaves are spread out on others. Relaxation. Ambience. The rising and falling waves of conversation.

— I'm having tea, too, Aunty 'Liza. It's mostly milk but it's real tea. I like to test it with my spoon to see how fast my sugar cubes are melting.

— You're quite the little lady, Polly.

The little lady sits up very straight and proud on her knees on the brocade dining chair. Her black patent leather shoes are tucked under her while a wide pink bow in her hair complements her pink taffeta dress with the four tucks in the skirt exactly like her mother's.

— Pass the jam, Mama!

— I beg your pardon?

— *Please* pass the jam, Mama.

Before Jack leaves the following morning, he has a word with Mary.

— Make sure you show Eliza a good time, dear. Do us proud. Poor little thing won't see the big smoke for quite a while if I know old Angel. Heading for penny-pinching times, I fear.

— Don't you worry, Jack. Polly and I will show her the town. When do you expect to get back?

— The steamer will get there this afternoon and then I have to locate him. Probably has a place of his own by now although he may still be staying at our place. Could be three or four days.

— Good-bye, love. I'll see you soon.

He kisses her then sweeps Polly up off the floor.

— You be a good girl for Mummy. And if Aunt Eliza won't eat oysters, see if you can get her to like prawns.

— I will, Daddy. Bye-bye.

Mary is true to her word. Next morning the two young matrons meet up at breakfast in the dining room, hats on, ready to go. Eliza glances down the menu.

— I never knew people ate steak for breakfast. And sausages! And eggs! And tomatoes!

— A working man's breakfast here, Eliza. What part of town do you want to see first? The harbour?

— Mary, by now you should know about me and water. We don't mix. I am determined to never go on it again; and I have no desire to ever go in it, or near it, or sit and gaze at it. Harbours, rivers, beaches, boats of any kind may kindle excitement in the majority but not for me. From now on I'm a land-lubber. 'Land-lubber Eliza'; there's a tongue twister for you, Polly. The only things I consider water good for are tea, washing, and gardens.

Mary leads the way out of Tattersall's, and when they emerge onto Pitt Street she casts her eye up and down the other side of the street looking for something familiar.

— Ah, there it is.

She grasps Polly firmly by the hand.

— Follow me!

They enter what looks like any one of the shops lining Pitt Street except this one is a thoroughfare between two streets, like an indoor lane. Eliza reads 'Strand Arcade' as they enter the terrazzo-tiled walkway. There she stops, looking up and all around. The high narrow passageway stretches before her three stories high, with iron balustrades overhanging the length of the entire second storey on both sides. Bright chandeliers, lit by electricity, hang from the tinted glass roof, and all manner of shops line both sides: ladies' wearing apparel, hats and bonnets, gas lamps and electric lights, intimate little coffee lounges.

— Here we are!

Mary leads them into a shop on the left, a boot and shoe repair place. She unwraps a pair of Polly's boots and hands them to the shop assistant.

— They need to be soled and heeled.

— They'll be ready at three o'clock, Madam.

Mary points to the ceiling, and Eliza's and Polly's eyes follow.

— Watch this.

The shop assistant tucks the docket with the work to be done inside one of the boots, and puts both boots inside a tube. He fits a lid on both ends of the tube and holds the tube up to a round open-ended duct with a diameter just a fraction larger than the tube with the boots in it. There's a sudden sucking rush of air and the tube disappears up the duct. Then they see someone upstairs in the workroom removing the tube and then the boots. The assistant notes their upturned faces, and looks up himself.

— Saves the legs.

As they go on through the arcade to George Street, Polly begs her mother for iced cream.

— Really! Children want everything they see. No, it's too soon after breakfast. Later we'll take Aunt Eliza back to the hotel for some Hokey Pokey.

— Ooh, Hokey Pokey!

They emerge from the Strand Arcade onto the main thoroughfare in Sydney, George Street, which runs from The Rocks down by Circular Quay all the way up past the GPO, Town Hall, St Andrew's Cathedral, and the markets to Railway Square where it seems all the trains, trams, buses and cabs in Sydney converge with the main roads leading west and south out of the city. Eliza stops on the footpath and looks; just looks at the imposing sandstone Georgian buildings, the banks, the GPO with its pillars and large clock on the tower, the horse-drawn single and double-decker omnibuses, the hurrying city folk, the carts, carriages and hansom cabs.

— The biggest city in the southern hemisphere. Half a million people.

— And they're all on this street! It's hard to believe I'm finally here.

— Let's cross over to David Jones. It's a very fine store, the best quality. It has a hydraulic lift with a concertina-type folding cage door. The lift takes you up and down between floors, and a very fancily-dressed doorman operates it, with gloves no less.

— I went in a lift up a cliff in Devon and I was terrified.

— You don't get a feeling of height from this one.

— Sometimes you feel like you've left your tummy behind, don't you, Mama?

Eliza's eyes widen as she walks through the store. She'd never seen such tasteful wares: stained glass; brightly polished copper cooking utensils; the finest linen sheets; and many ready-to-wear items such as suits, frocks, camisoles and corsets; even shoes. There are high counters with chairs set before them where customers are trying on gloves and hats, waited on by the assistants who are all clothed entirely in black. One whole section is devoted to children's ready-to-wear clothing. There's another floor with nothing but beds of all kinds: brass rail, wooden, four-posters and all the bedding to go with them. Another floor displays only furniture; another, Manchester. It is the first true department store in Sydney.

— David Jones has a very large catalogue section as well. We have an account here, and we order from the catalogue in Wollongong. They'll send to anywhere in New South Wales, and they're quick, too.

— Mama, can we go and have iced cream now?

They come out onto George Street again and walk up to King Street, with the ES&A Bank on the corner, re-entering Adams' Hotel and making their way to a smaller room past the marble bar. This one is hushed by red carpets, polished panelled walls with long mirrors, and deeply-padded scooped armchairs which are studded around the top.

Polly whispers.

— Isn't it *sumptuous*, Aunty 'Liza?

— Wherever did you hear a word like that, Polly?

— I don't know; but don't you think it's *sumptuous*?

Eliza looks all around, opens her eyes wide, nods at Polly and whispers back.

— *Very!*

— I have a favourite thing I order every time I come here, and Mama lets me order it all by myself.

The waiter comes over to take their order. He has a long white tablecloth tied around his waist, and a long white napkin draped over his arm. The adults order coffee but Mary says.

— My daughter knows what she wants.

— Yes, Miss, what can I get for you?

— I want some Hokey Pokey iced cream.

— 'Please'

— Please!

— And would you please bring extra spoons? We'll help my daughter finish it off.

— Very good, Ma'am.

— 'Hokey Pokey, penny a lump,
  The more you eat, the more you jump.'

— It's toffee mixed in the iced cream, Eliza, a special toffee made with golden syrup.

They scan Eliza's face as she takes a taste. There's no contest: sumptuous it is.

From there they walk up to Elizabeth Street, which borders a sub-tropical park, to catch a steam tram, as much for the novelty as for the convenience. The tall green spire of St James points heavenward as they wait. Mary explains to Eliza.

— There's quite a network of trams here, and a very frequent schedule. In this part of town, though, they only run along Elizabeth Street.

— Can we go upstairs if it's a double-decker?

— We'll see.

— What a lovely park! It seems to extend for several blocks.

— Hyde Park. There are lots of paths through it. When the tram comes, Polly, I want you to hold Mummy's hand tight and be quick on the running board. We'll ride down to Railway Square. That's where we'll be catching the train for home.

'Home'. Every other reference to home so far had meant England. Now Mary is using it, unconsciously, to mean Wollongong, her Australian home. I wonder how long it takes to feel 'at home' here, and not feel a stranger? The buildings, the vehicles, the clothes, the manners and customs are all familiar; but the landscape, the rocks, the trees and vegetation, even the very air, are all so different, almost startling.

It's an exceptionally smooth ride to Central Station where they alight and wander over to the George Street side, looking in the shop windows as they pass.

— Look, Eliza. This is Orchard's watch and jewellery store. Look at the watches hanging on that little silver tree, and the sign: 'Orchard's. Where the watches grow.' What a catchy display.

— I like that gold bracelet. Isn't it pretty? The scalloped cut-out edges, and it's set with tiny rubies and sapphires all around (the blue stones are sapphires, aren't they?) I suppose I can only dream.

— You have to have dreams, Eliza or you'll never achieve anything. There's the ring that goes with it, like an arc: two small diamonds, two sapphires and a big diamond on top. You don't have an engagement ring, do you? You could ask Angel to buy it for you.

— No, I'd never ask. He's saving to put everything into the farm. I wonder if he's found something by now? It's strange not knowing where you're going to be living, or how. At least *you* have a fair idea of where you'll be in, say, two years time. Me, I cannot imagine.

— You'll know in the next few days when you are re-united with Angel. It can't be that hard for Jack to track him down. He's been staying at our place while he's been looking; and, Eliza dear, you know that you are both very welcome to stay with us as long as you like until you're settled.

Railway Square is very busy but not hurried. Carts, coaches, horses, omnibuses, trams and people all move along, criss-crossing the square. Mary and Eliza try to decide how they will get back down George Street. They prefer a hansom cab, even though it only takes two passengers (Polly could sit on one of their knees); but Polly has her eye on a double-decker omnibus. They climb upstairs to the roof and take their open-air seats, longways to the street, the two rows of passengers sitting back to back.

First they pass Christ Church St Laurence on the corner that forms the square, and head down George Street. 'Down' George Street is really 'up' George Street and the omnibus slows as the horses walk past the hay market. The whole length of the street is lined with buildings, some several storeys high. At the top of the rise on their left they soon come to St Andrew's, then to the Sydney Town Hall next to the Cathedral.

— Look at all those steps!

— They say the pipe organ in the Town Hall is so large, or strong, if they played the lowest note (the biggest pipe), the whole building would fall down.

— No!

The markets come next.

— We'll get off at Market Street. Polly, you hold on tight and come down the stairs between Mummy and Aunt Eliza. I don't want you tumbling into the street.

They walk up to Pitt Street and into Adams' Hotel.

The next couple of days are filled with excursions and chores. They pick up the newly blackened boots in the Strand Arcade ('I like the smell of that shop, Mama'), and return to the 'mirror room' for more Hokey Pokey. Eliza even has one of her own. Polly, true to her childish word, persuades her mother to order a prawn feast for tea at the hotel. Eliza certainly likes these creatures better than slippery oysters which most of the other clientele are devouring with smiles on their faces. Prawns have substance, meat. These, she is informed, are King prawns, two to three inches long, and after she first learns how to take the legs and the shell off, she uses her thumbnail to scrape out the gut tube and then …Mmmmm! Sweet and juicy, with or without the little points of bread and butter. She rinses her fingers in her own cut-glass finger bowl of water with the round of lemon floating on top, and observes Polly who is enjoying her finger bowl almost as much as the prawns.

Next day Mary takes her to an embroidery shop where she picks up some stamped linen table cloths and napkins, and chooses the coloured stranded thread she needs.

— You should try doing some fancy work, Eliza. It passes the time and is useful in the long run. They even have some with Australian plants stamped on them.

— I think I will. Here's a nice one. Not too large.

She asks the assistant.

— What are these flowers?

— They're banksias, Madam. They all have the seed pods, too.

— I don't like the look of the seed pods. They look like evil gnomes. What's this one?

— That's a native fuchsia, Madam. It's a delicate flower and comes in different colours. What shade are you looking for?

They leave with their purchases and enough differently-coloured cotton for smocking, as Mary has to make at least two more dresses and pinafores for Polly who is growing fast. They visit all kinds of specialty shops, one dealing only in chocolates, and Eliza buys some ginger ones. They pass the markets again and Mary buys some strangely-shaped and differently-coloured fruit Eliza has never seen before. Later, they have 'private tastings' in Mary's room. One has yellow speckled skin and smooth sweet yellow flesh with hundreds of shiny black seeds in the centre called a paw paw. The pineapple is knobbly and prickly on the outside but has sweet juicy yellow fruit that sets Eliza's teeth on edge. There's an oval fruit with reddish-yellow skin and black blotches. It has a large pit in the centre and also has slippery orange flesh that drips juice everywhere but tastes, to Eliza, like turpentine. Last, there is a dark purple egg with a thick skin and a membrane inside that tastes like Nirvana. Pity about the little black seeds.

They take a box lunch, packed by Tattersall's, to Mrs Macquarie's Chair down on the wooded foreshores where Eliza begins to appreciate the water again (from a distance). Who could not be impressed with Sydney Harbour? Afterwards, they visit the Museum, see a Punch and Judy show in Hyde Park and, because the basket lunch was so delicious, they take another one next day for a picnic at the beach. They board an express Bondi tram, and to Eliza's surprise, are there in no time. Mary explains.

— There's an expression in Sydney: 'straight through like a Bondi tram'. It's also used as a rude expression after you eat too much tropical fruit!

Sitting on their picnic blanket on the grassy treeless headland they munch on their delicacies watching and listening to the breakers crashing onto the semicircle of Bondi Beach. Of course, Polly has to have a paddle so after lunch they walk down to the sand, take off their boots and stockings, and wade into the frothy ocean holding their skirts above their knees, squealing and jumping. After cooling their feet they sit on the sand to let their legs dry in the summer sun and then have to figure out how to put their stockings back on, discretely, in full public view. They are laughing about this as they re-enter the hotel lobby, their hems still a little soggy and clinging, when two men stand up as they approach.

— Daddy!

Eliza stops. She looks at the other man. *Angel has shrunk since our marriage; how many months before? He's gaunt, yellow, or sunburned; or both. And stooped. He looks worried, almost haunted. And shabby, compared to Jack. I've imagined this meeting so many times in my mind: how I will rush into his open arms; how he will kiss me tenderly; how ....* He comes forward and awkwardly puts his hand on her arm.

— Eliza? Jack told me about the baby. It's for the best. Life's hard out here, especially for a farmer's wife, and you'll need to be working hard.

So this is my welcome; and that is my future. Angel goes on.

— I've found a place west of Wollongong; nice situation; got it for a song.

No embrace. No affection. No longing, you can see it in his face. No missing **me***: just lonely and missing someone, anyone. 'Worse'.*

— That's good. Tell me what the house is like.

— It needs a woman's touch. The previous owner was a bachelor. I've been staying at Jack's and working at the farm site by day: daily milking, you know. We now own a horse and wagon and seven pretty little cows, as well as a golden retriever called, of all things, Rover, who formerly belonged to the bachelor chap but who took a liking to me.

That's all he divulged about her future home.

— Get your things packed, Eliza. We have to move out of this palace.

— Aren't we leaving for Wollongong in the morning?

— We certainly are. I've taken a room at the Grand Hotel in Railway Square.

— But …

— Just run along and get packed, like I told you.

— Will I see you, Mary?

Jack steps in to explain.

— We'll all be leaving together on the nine-thirty train in the morning. Angel and I bought the tickets on the way here. You people are staying with us at Seafoam until Eliza can make the homestead habitable. Then it's the settlers' life for you on the farm.

Angel accompanies her up to her room while she packs, and stands with his back to the fireplace, hands in his pockets, gazing around.

— Look at this place! The ostentation! We can't afford this. And you have some new clothes. Where did you get them?

— When I was sick on board ship. Oh, Angel, I was so sick, dreadfully seasick, and I lost the baby.

She starts to cry. At last she can tell him what happened in detail but he doesn't come over to comfort her; doesn't show any sympathy; doesn't move. He stands by the fireplace tut-tutting, rocking backwards and forwards on the balls of his feet.

— Nobody gets that seasick, Eliza. And why did you let Jack Turville buy you a first class passage? It's a very embarrassing situation you've put me in, very embarrassing. It looks like I can't afford it, and we *can't* afford it, but he won't take any money for it. Says, 'That's what friends are for'. This time, friendship is showing me up. You're showing me up, Eliza, and I don't like it. He probably bought you those clothes, too.

— No, Angel. It was Mary who looked after me. It was she who persuaded him. They couldn't get the blood stains out of my day dress no matter how much they scrubbed. I didn't want to accept them, either. She has a heart of pure gold, Angel.

— Yes, his gold. I want you to get rid of these things they bought you. You'll only wear what I can provide. Leave those things here and only pack what you brought with you.

'Alone, alone, all, all alone …' I wish Angel treated me the way Jack treats Mary. They have a bond, an affinity. You can feel it. Now I understand better what the old saying means: the road to hell is paved with good intentions. Looks like I'm about to start down the road to hell. Angel keeps on.

— It's a terrible thing, Eliza, to be beholden to someone else and not be able to pay them back. I've spent a good part of my savings on this property, and there's a great deal more to be done. The grain crops have to be put in by a certain time. Alone, or even with your help, I don't have the time to plough and plant so I've had to hire it done which saves time but adds extra expense, the labourers and machine hire; but why am I telling you all this? You're only a woman. You wouldn't understand.

— That's my job, as a wife, Angel, to understand, and help carry the burden. That's what marriage is all about. We should share our feelings, our hopes, for richer, for poorer. We haven't had a chance yet in our marriage to work as a partnership. I may never have handled business or money before but I can learn. I might even turn out to be good at it.

— You could be right, Eliza. I haven't been married long enough, to either you or Tess, to let a wife carry part of the burden.

— It's not just the money, Angel. It's the weight of life's events. I really needed you on that ship. In my hour of need I had to depend on your friends. From now on, let's depend on each other, shall we?

He seems to see a glimmer of wisdom in this girl, his wife, and at last comes across the room to face her. He puts his arms around her, and then his shoulders start shaking. They both lay their heads on each other's neck, crying, hugging, and shaking.

Eventually he straightens up, takes up the strapped bag and says.

— Bring your hatbox. Tomorrow our life together will really begin.

As they leave the Grand Hotel on Railway Square next morning to cross over to Central Station, Angel and Eliza pass Orchard's, the jewellers, where the bracelet and ring still lie that caught Eliza's eye. She shyly points them out to Angel, who replies.

—Those trinkets would buy enough fencing for two paddocks, including the posts.

Goodbye Romance. Welcome to Reality.

CHAPTER 13

Points South

The Illawarra train is not heavily patronized today which is a good thing. They choose a compartment with windows that will eventually have a view of the sea, and Eliza establishes herself by the window. Polly, who likes travelling backwards best, sits opposite her, next to her mother and father, while Angel is seated next to Eliza. At first the train moves slowly while it chuffs out of the city, and Eliza catches glimpses of people's backyards abutting the line. She notes their laundry strung between poles; their loos against the back fences; two faces at a window; a morning glory vine; an open door; an eager child waving wildly, and Polly waving back. These backyard blinks that never existed, exist for only a second in time, and now exist for ever. Clackety-clack, clackety-clack, chuff-chuffa, chuff-chuffa, chuffa-chuffa, chuffa-chuffa, getting faster, getting faster. Smaller buildings, space, house, space, house, space, tree, space, house. Suburbs gone and then the bush: thin dry trees flashing past.

— Gum trees. Nothing but gum trees.
— Is that what they are?
— It's flat all the way to Hellensburg, Otford really, where we take on water. Then we start down through the tunnels, switchback tunnels, seven tunnels in seven miles. It's quite a drop from Bald Hill to Stanwell Park. This time last year a local chap, Lawrence Hargrave, tied himself to a chain of box kites on the beach down there at Stanwell Park and was lifted fifteen feet into the air by the wind.
— Wouldn't it be lovely to fly, Aunty 'Liza?
— Who knows? By the time you grow up they might have invented a flying machine.

As the trees blur past and the view from the window takes on a sameness, they turn their interest towards each other until they arrive at Otford. Mary then preps Eliza on the tunnels, especially the long tunnel.

— Wrap yourself well in your cloak, Eliza; and Polly, you too. It will be dark, totally black, for some time. Make sure you cover your faces and breathe slowly. The smoke and soot come in all over us. It's just one of those things to be endured. Progress! Not so long ago one of the twelve-carriage picnic trains that come up from Bulli got stuck in the Otford tunnel. They carry fewer carriages now. It would be a lot more comfortable if the seats were padded but I suppose one can endure a little discomfort for four hours.

Eliza finds it a somewhat unreal sensation: moving through space, downhill, in total darkness, breathing carefully. They don't speak: the previously animated carriage is dark and silent. When at last the welcome daylight glances through the window, Polly complains.

— Mama, my eyes are sore.

The gaseous smell of smoke and soot hangs in the air between them and soaks into their clothes.

— Don't rub your eyes. Blink hard when we come out into the fresh air, love.

— I wonder which of you three girls will see the sea first?

— I will, Daddy! I will!

All heads crane towards the light and there, below, they see a half moon bay between two high fingers of land running out to the sea, and row on row of white surf breaking on a smile of yellow sand. Stanwell Park.

— I saw it first!

— Then you deserve a lolly.

Jack puts his hand in his pocket and brings out a small white paper bag.

— Jelly babies!

— Would you care for one Eliza? Angel?

He opens the bag and they all take one of the little stamped-out jelly people covered in sugar. Some are raspberry; some are lemon; some are aniseed. Polly makes a chimpanzee grin.

— Now your teeth are all black, darling.

— So are Aunty 'Liza's, Mama. She likes the black ones too, don't you? Ooo, here we go again. Cover your head, Aunty 'Liza!

The train enters the next tunnel.

— Now everyone's teeth are black.

Polly giggles at her little joke.

Down and down inside the hills they go, then emerge right on the coast, so close to the sea it seems the rails must be running in the water. In one community the line goes down what had been the main street, and a new road had to be made on the very edge of the ocean. Mountains seamed with coal rise precipitously from the water's edge, and Jack tells them that the road and the line are often blocked by rock falls. The train stops at the aptly named Coalcliff, Clifton, and Coledale stations. The latter settlement is so narrow it doesn't even have room for a strip of sand, only shaly ledges thick with coal which take the full force of the constantly breaking waves.

Austinmer comes next, where the tracks run beside a yellow sandy beach lined by a single row of houses with white picket fences, while the cream and grey sandstone cliff at the northern end of the beach has been sculpted by the weather into a monkey's face. The next settlement is just a little wider, with the only flat space by the water's edge being used for burying their dead. From here on, the hills move a little farther, and a little farther away from the sea, bare except for ring-barked trees that stand like immobile ghosts with their arms in the air.

When they alight briefly at Bulli they can plainly see the edge of an escarpment to the west a thousand feet above them, opening the 'V' of the Illawarra, the land between the mountains and the sea. By the time they pass Woonona there are more signs of town life: churches, schools, gardens and orchards which increase as they near Wollongong station. Mary gives a grateful sigh.

— Home!

*There it is again: Home. Mary, Jack and Polly all feel like they've come home. I wonder when that shift takes place. They've only been away from England five years or so, and now they call Australia 'home'. Does this mental shift have to do with opportunities and monetary advantages? Does it have to do with having a family and a future in the Colony? The word 'home' has emotional connotations. Does coming or going 'home' have more to do with mind-set than with an actual physical location? Or does it have anything to do with knowing you **could** go back to England but don't wish to? Did those people who were sent out as convicts, and who couldn't return to England, regard New South Wales or England as 'home'? The Turvilles certainly regard Wollongong as home. How long will it take me? I've uprooted myself to follow Angel's dream. I've linked my fortune to his; and our future is our fortune. Then there's Mother and the children. Home! England is home for me, for the present, anyway.*

CHAPTER 14

Seafoam

They take two cabs from the station to Cliff Road. Polly is getting very excited now.

— I wonder how Mr Whiskers is? Do you think he's still alive, Mama? We've been away an awful long time.

— You'll find out very soon.

They draw up before Seafoam, a large weatherboard house at the top of a flight of stone steps which lead up to the corner of a shady verandah looking directly over the road and down the cliff to North Wollongong Beach and Stuart Park to the north.

— Oh, Mary! What a beautiful view!

Eliza stands there with her mouth open, gazing north, then south, along the wide sweep of beach.

— Mama, can we go next door and get Mr Whiskers now?

— In a minute, darling. We have to get in the house first.

I can see now why Mary was looking forward to 'going home'. The house is large, airy, bright and open and is surrounded by lawns and gardens with colourful flowers in them. Eliza is astounded by their brightness.

— Those flowers are so vivid when the sun shines on them they almost hurt the eyes.

— Those? Oh, they're pig face. Very common but I'll grant, they *are* colourful. They do very well near the sea: seem to thrive on the salty air.

— The sea air must be healthy for people, too; much better for you than crowded cities.

— It does seem to invigorate people. We always sleep well at night, even on hot nights. Being so near the sea is a great blessing; and, of course, we sleep in the open air, on the verandah, which is a lot cooler as I perspire a lot in my sleep.

— And you're fortunate to have a wrap-around verandah.

— Yes, you forget how fortunate you are but a lot of people here have them. It seems to double the size of the house. We live half inside; half outside.

— Mama, Mama, can we get Mr Whiskers now?

Mary looks over and smiles at Eliza resignedly.

— I suppose it's time to introduce Aunt Eliza to the Harris'.

They go next door. A girl of about ten answers the door.

— Ma! It's the Turvilles. They've come home.

A slim, neat lady with brown hair escaping from its net comes from the rear of the house with two younger children holding onto her skirts. Smiling broadly she gives Mary a gentle hug, and Polly a kiss on the head.

— You made it safely, Mary. Polly, you're so grown-up. I suppose you want to see Mr Whiskers?

— Yes, is he still alive?

— Very much so. Muriel will show you. He's become great friends with the General. Off you go, poppets. Muriel will get you all some cordial.

— Stella, this is my friend Eliza Clare who's come to the Illawarra to help her husband with the dairy farm.

— How do you do, Eliza?

— Very well, thank you. How do you do?

— I've already met your husband; he's been staying next door. How was your trip out from England?

— I will never cross the ocean again.

— That bad?

— Eliza was so seasick; and she lost her baby.

— Oh, I'm so sad to hear it. Come in and sit down. I lost my first as well, and I was on land. There's nothing else to do but carry on. You see my brood: they come when they come. Jack called in when he was down a couple of days ago, so I've done a little cooking to start you off. No, don't protest, Mary. It's just a stew, some bread, sultana scones and a blackberry tart.

— Blackberry tart! I'd quite forgotten. That's one thing the people of the Illawarra have in abundance, Eliza: blackberries. They grow wild on the hillsides and are free for the picking.

— The children and I were out picking yesterday with billycans. You can tell our success by our hands. Look at the scratches!

— Mama! Mama! Mama! Here's Mr Whiskers! Look, Aunty 'Liza.

And Polly thrusts a white mouse at Eliza's bosom.

— Take him! Stroke him!

— No, no, dear. I'm a stranger. He might, um …be frightened of me.

— No he won't. Not Mr Whiskers. He's the tamest white mouse in the whole world!

— Except for the General.

Muriel now comes over and shows the women her pet who looks all around, bright-eyed, twitching his pink nose.

— We made sure Mr Whiskers had lots to eat while Polly was away. Now I think the General will be lonely.

— Put him back in his cage, Polly. We have to be getting home now. What's that in his cage?

Muriel speaks up.

— That's a running wheel Father made for him. He made one for the General as well. They have competitions.

Mary and Eliza make for the door with arms full of food.

— Thank you, Stella, for the lovely surprise for our tea, even though you shouldn't have.

— Don't mention it, Mary. It was my pleasure. I'll see you soon; probably on our knees in the garden. And Eliza, welcome to the Illawarra!

That night at Seafoam the Turvilles, Clares and Durbeyfields are reunited and they make quick work of Stella's blackberry tart. Mary has made a hot runny custard which really brings out the flavour of the berries. They've been discussing Abraham's future. It seems logical he should help Angel and Eliza on the new farm but he points out that he could never get ahead as a farm labourer; also it's messy working for in-laws. Jack has introduced him to a grocer in town, and has also sent him to see a man he knows, the manager of the Mt Keira mine. Abraham takes this opportunity to announce that he can start working coal on Monday.

— The pay's good.

Eliza is suddenly wary for him.

— Do you really want to work as a miner, Abraham? You know the grocery business.

— That's just it. It's too humdrum, and the pay's a lot better in the mine.

— But it's very hard work. Backbreaking. And dangerous, too.

The Turvilles seem to take Abraham's side.

— He's young, and he's strong. They need young fellas like him.

— He can stay with us, Eliza, then you won't have to worry about him. We'll make sure he goes to Church on Sundays, and doesn't stay out too late.

Abraham can see his new independence suddenly sprouting fences.

— Well, as long as you're happy, Abe?

— That suits me fine, Sis; and on weekends I can come out and see you.

Angel, who has been very quiet all evening, suddenly changes the conversation.

— Eliza and I need to get an early start in the morning. We'll drive out to the property so she can assess what we need for the house and what we can do without.

Eliza makes a visual summary of her husband. *He's yellow, definitely yellow; and he's stooped. He seems pre-occupied all the time, anxious.* That night on the verandah he confides to her from the next bed.

— You may judge the homestead to be a little small. After all, it was built by and for a bachelor.

— Good things come in little parcels. We don't need a big house, Angel.

CHAPTER 15

The Farm

At 7 a.m. Angel harnesses the horse and backs him into the wagon.

— Eliza, meet Ned, our mode of transport. He came with the wagon which I need to take the milk cans to the road for pick up. It's not a very fashionable way to travel, nor fast; but it's a very roomy wagon, good for all weathers except rain.

Eliza strokes Ned's nose then climbs up beside Angel. He shakes the reins.

— To Mt Keira! Walk on!

Mt Keira rises up west of the town, flat-topped, with the morning sun on its thickly-treed upper slopes. To the south they can see her twin, Mt Kembla.

— It looks very wooded, Angel.

— The farm's at the base, on the slope. You'll see that the hills are cleared quite a way up as we get closer.

Ned clops in the direction of the mountain which grows imperceptibly larger until they merge with the slopes at its feet, rumbling towards 'home'. The distant cows grow larger; and the blur of green trees up on the hills become individual ones. They hear the creek running; the long low 'moo's; and coming round a bushy corner, Eliza sees the back of the milking shed. Angel extends his arm in a grand gesture.

— There she is!

— The milking shed. Is it far from the house?

— That's not the milking shed. That's the homestead, Eliza.

Her heart sinks.

— That tiny little lean-to is the *house*?

— It's a slab hut, Eliza: the pioneers' homestead. Very serviceable.

— The bachelor farmer actually *lived* in that?

— Of course. It's quite roomy once you're inside. You don't really need more than two rooms.

— What?

— A man eats and sleeps. A room for each is all he needs; and he doesn't need a large sleeping area because he's dead to the world while he's sleeping.

— But I'm not a man. Even where I grew up we didn't have a fancy house but we had more room than this! Oh, Angel!

— You'll feel a lot better once you're inside. I'm sure you'll be able to make it very comfortable. See, the fireplace is at this end with the chimney, the kitchen-living area. It has a window beside the door. Here, let me help you down.

She walks slowly up to the roughly-hewn homestead which is, in reality, nothing more than a single room with a lean-to at the rear.

— Oh, Angel!

— You should be thankful it has a good strong plank floor.

There is no verandah, no porch, no shade. A squared tree trunk does for a step, and she is inside. She stops, looks around, and draws in her breath. It's worse than she could possibly have imagined. She can see daylight through chinks in the walls where the vertical slabs of wood have warped, and don't quite meet anymore; and sky through gaps in the bark roof where the strips don't quite overlap. Even this early in the day she can smell the heat seeping through the walls. A clay brick fireplace on her left, the south, the cooler side, has split wood piled beside it. There is a table constructed from cross cut boards with four saplings for legs, and a large kerosene lamp in the middle of it; a tree stump for a stool, only one. In the fireplace is a trammel with pot hooks and sundry iron pots and pans, as well as stone ledges along the sides for baking.

A large tin wash tub for bathing and a smaller one for dishes lean against one wall under the window, and a crude open dresser with enamel dishes against the other, opposite the fireplace. To the left of the door, there is a shelf with supplies: flour, tea, oatmeal, sugar and the like. In the lean-to on the rear wall is a cot made from saplings and burlap with nails in the wall for hanging clothes.

— Make a list of what we need to make the house livable but watch the spending. I'm going to check on the animals.

The chance to make improvements, *any* improvement, spurs Eliza into thinking constructively rather than reacting in shock to the primitive amenities. *Compared to Adams' Tattersall's Hotel. Don't think of it!* She takes out her notebook and pencil and starts a list: bed and bedding; some sort of divider between 'rooms', a partition, screen or curtain; stove; dining suite: table, four chairs, sideboard; cupboards; verandah; dishes; floor covering; fix walls and roof; window in the 'bedroom' for a cross-breeze; pantry shelving; doormat; curtains; wardrobe and drawers. She keeps scribbling. Angel comes inside again and looks over her shoulder at the list.

— Make another column, and head it 'Income'. Now write, 'sale of milk', 'sale of pigs'.

— Pigs?

— Yes, pigs.

— We have pigs?

— Not yet but I'm buying some piglets to fatten. They eat the skimmed milk that I'll bring home from the creamery. Also add 'sale of eggs'.

— We have chickens, too?

— Soon will, and here they call them chooks, not chickens.

— Probably because of the noise they make.

— I'll build a chicken coop for them and a roosting house; it'll be easier to find the eggs. You're a dressmaker, aren't you? When word gets out we may be able to make some extra money from that. Come outside and I'll show you where I plan to locate things. You're definitely right about the porch or verandah. If we put on a corrugated iron roof we could extend it over the front and support it with two verandah posts. It would certainly cut down on mud being tracked into the house. Here's where I'll build the pig pen. It will need some sort of roof over it, too.

— So close to the house? Pigs smell, you know.

— Hmmm. We could put it out along the driveway. We also need a pump. Pigs need water.

— And we need a vegetable garden. If we had a hand pump near the house instead of a well, it would be a lot more convenient for getting water; and if we put the garden on the down slope we could run water in channels back and forth across the slope.

— Irrigation. Clever girl. You see over there, where the fence posts are lying on the ground? That's where I want to plant some barley and oats for the horse and us, and lucerne for the cows. There they are, under the trees near the creek. They're almost human. They all have names, you know: Flossie, Bessie, Daisy; there's even Matilda, a real Australian name, based on a song. They all walk up and wait near the shed, over there, at four o'clock. Milked twice a day, again at four in the morning. That'll be your job.

— The milking?

— Only the 4 a.m. milking. I'll get up by the time you finish to take the cans to the dairy.

My future's just snapped into focus: daily chores starting at 4 a.m.; cooking; housekeeping; chicken mistress; gardener; and seamstress in my **spare** *time.*

— Let's go in and put that list of yours in order of importance. I've only hired help with the cows for a few more days.

They determine the iron roof is the most important. The verandah can wait. Floor covering is next, either linoleum or black varnish; and because the boards are a little rough in spots, they decide on linoleum. A stove is not *absolutely* necessary for the moment but a bed and bedding are; and there's no need for curtains or an extra window by the weekend. A decent table and chairs are necessary as also are china dishes and cutlery.

— Well, Mrs Clare, now that you've seen the property, it's back to Wollongong to Lance's Emporium.

Lance's has everything; well, almost everything. It's really just a very large general store. Angel goes off in search of wood, wire, and nails while Eliza finds her way to furnishings. She walks longingly past the furnishings and draperies to the furniture. They don't have a big selection on the floor but they do have a David Jones catalogue. The beds in the catalogue are very large and high and would never fit in their slanted nook. However, there is a sturdy, low, double bed frame in the show room that Eliza reserves. She chooses mattress ticking that she can sew and stuff with straw which will be much cooler in this climate; and three sheets for the bed so she can move the top sheet to the bottom each time and have a fresh one for the top. She waits for Angel before deciding on a blanket and they settle on one made from Australian wool. They can buy another when winter comes. She chooses a light brown flecked linoleum that won't show the dirt as much; and picks out a set of willow pattern crockery, including tureens, large and small jugs, and a teapot.

— They don't have any tables and chairs that I like. There's a catalogue, though.

— Let's look in the catalogue, then.

— It's from David Jones. It will be very dear.

— Let's look at it anyway.

— I really like that set. Oh, but look at the price! There are six chairs, two with arms, and a sideboard. Look at the picture, Angel. Carved rosewood. Too many chairs for our little place.

— They could fit in our 'dressing room' on either side of the bed.

— But it's *so* expensive, Angel.

— I want to buy it as a gift to you, Eliza. You came all this way to make a home with me, and all the hope I can offer you is a hut on the hill. Let this be my wedding gift to you.

— You already gave me the family heirlooms, the jewellery.

— You can't *use* them. They're in a safety deposit box in the Emminster bank. You can't use them on a daily basis like you could use this furniture. Sir! Could we place an order, please?

Eliza is overjoyed but cautious. She whispers.

— Are you *sure* we can afford this?

— Yes. I put aside a little for unexpected expenses. By the time we finish these purchases, put on a new roof, build the coop, the pens, the fences, and hire the ploughman to plough and plant the seed, the nest egg will be just about depleted.

Eliza doesn't ask about the previously promised house servant. She anticipates she will be mistress, servant, and all.

Angel drops her at Seafoam then returns to Mt Keira. Mary meets her at the top of the verandah steps where they turn and watch the surf coming in.

— How was your day? You look like you could use a cup of tea.

— Mary, I've aged a hundred years since this morning. The house, if you could call it that, is so small and basic…yet there *is* room for improvement. We've just left Lance's Emporium where we chose a bed and bedding, and I brought this ticking with me. I have to sew a mattress by Monday! Yes, and Angel has ordered the most beautiful dining suite and sideboard from David Jones' catalogue at Lance's. It should be delivered next week, and as soon as I have things fixed up, you'll be our first guests.

Over tea she describes the place in detail. Mary goes and finds a set of brocade curtains that had been there when they moved in.

— There's enough there to make a bedspread as well as a set of curtains for your only window, with enough left over for the second window when you get it.

— Another thing I have to do is get in supplies beyond the basic bachelor subsistence items; things like spices, jam, chutney; a flour serve, a rolling pin, and good cutting knives. I also need soap, scouring brushes …. It looks like we'll mostly be eating stews or spit-roasts as I don't know how to use an open fire for baking.

— You'll learn in time, I'm sure of it. For the time being, I'll get Meg to bake extra bread for you.

— What would I do without you, Mary? And what *will* I do without you? I won't be seeing you much after next week.

Angel doesn't get back to Cliff Road until well after sunset.
— Have you eaten, Angel?
— I'm too tired to eat. I just want to go to bed. Everything that could go wrong, did go wrong.

Fully clothed, he flings himself down on the bed at the other end of the verandah where they are all sitting and falls into an exhausted sleep. Jack looks over at his friend.

— Poor old Angel's worn out. That fever in Brazil certainly weakened his constitution. I suppose I could go out for a few days and help him.
— So could I, Jack. I don't start in the mine until next week. Many hands make light work.
— That would be a great help, Abraham. Thank you, boys!
— Polly and I will make sure you are all well fed. I'll send out a daily picnic basket for the navvies.
— Well, Abe, we volunteers had better get to bed. Are you coming, love?
— I'll sit up with Eliza for a bit, Jack; talk to her while she's sewing.
— In that case, 'Goodnight ladies, goodnight sweet ladies, goodnight, goodnight, goodnight'.

Mary smiles at Eliza.
— Jack is always quoting something from Shakespeare or the poets.

CHAPTER 16

WOLLONGONG

The next few days are very busy. Jack, Abraham and the hired hands are out at Mt Keira helping Angel set up and get the place ship-shape, building, fitting, and receiving equipment. They all tell Eliza to stay out of the way. Her job is to remain in town, finish the mattress cover, bedspread and curtains, and buy the gadgets she'll need. She's forgotten a meat safe and meat grinder, and a separator and butter churn for their own use. She also needs a sewing kit, starch, a clothes line, smoothing irons, another lamp, a large enamel jug, a coir mat — it's endless, the basic things needed to start a home.

This little hut is my new home. Come Monday, I'll be mistress of it. I wonder about the new double bed? Will my wifely duties also include nightly duties now that we'll be in our own place? Angel seems too worn out to do anything but sleep.

— Eliza, get your hat. I'm going to show you Wollongong: the Grand Tour.

The two young women 'do' the town in the buggy with Polly between them. First, south along Cliff Road where Mary points out Brighton Beach within the breakwater, and the rail lines coming in from the Mt Pleasant and Mt Keira mines carrying coal trucks to load the carriers moored in Belmore Basin.

— The trucks empty their coal down chutes into the ships waiting below.

Polly starts counting.

— Eight.

— Eight what's, my love?

— Boats.

— I think there are more than that. Belmore Basin can hold fifteen at a time.

They turn up Harbour Street with the Brighton Hotel on their right.

— Market and Crown are the two main streets with most of the public buildings and shops. We'll drive up Crown Street. There's the Roman Catholic Church, the Post Office, Town Hall, and the *Illawarra Mercury* office. I'll pull up here so you can post that letter to your mother. Watch those piles of manure when you're crossing the street.

— I want to go with Aunty 'Liza.

— No, Polly, you'll get your boots all mucky.

When they resume, she continues with the tour.

— There's the Methodist Church and the Presbyterian Church. There's Puckey's, the chemist, Jack goes swimming with. See the big blue bottle? There's Mr Dean, the tailor.

— Mr Dean! Mr Dean! Hello, Mr Dean!

A short man with whiskers and a totally bald head is standing, dapperly dressed, on the boardwalk, with his hands in his pockets, nodding to passers by. He looks up when he hears the little girl calling his name.

— Oh ho! Look who's home from the far side of the world!

And he waves as they go by.

— He's the one who also goes swimming with Jack and Mr Puckey. Very civic minded: started the ambulance service here. Jack gets his suits made by him. He was a member of the Congregational Church but now he goes to St Michael's, our church. There's another hotel. In the early days Wollongong had twelve hotels. Twelve! Thirsty miners. To get a liquor licence they have to rent rooms as well as provide meals. We'll turn down here. This is Church Street and there's St Michael's where we'll go on Sunday. Will you be able to make it into Church on Sundays?

— I think so. I hope so. It looks like that will be my only outing, except for the market to sell eggs and butter, and vegetables when they start to produce.

— It would be nice if you were able to attend the Saturday afternoon socials. We're having a picnic in Stuart Park this week: that's the park you can see from our place; one side of it on the ocean, the other flanking Fairy Creek. Foot races are very popular for adults as well as for children and there's quite a competition between towns. They even bet on their champs.

— What's that building, Mary?

— That? The Court House.

— A handsome building for a little town.

— Yes. It was built by convicts, as were a number of early buildings in the town. We'll turn down here. Stella's mother runs a boarding house in Bourke Street, see, Farnham? She named it after the place she was born, in England. That reminds me: Stella has a sewing machine, a Wanzer. You know, a table one you turn by hand. That would make short work of your mattress cover. Here we are, back at Seafoam.

Eliza helps Mary and the maid, Meg, prepare tea for the workers who trudge in about seven o'clock. After they wash and sit down to their meal, Jack comments.

— We're lucky we have the most daylight of the whole year to work with. We got a lot done today, and only two casualties: Abe's hands are all blistered up from sawing, and Angel hit his thumbnail with a hammer, splitting it down the middle.

— This is as light as it gets?

— Yes, you'll notice there's not nearly as much twilight as there is in England. It's because Wollongong is closer to the Equator. Seems like where you live is a toss up between light and warmth.

— And if today's any indication, it feels like the summers are a lot hotter and drier than home.

— That's right. The men said they haven't had rain for weeks. The country's getting very dry.

— I hope my well doesn't run dry.

— I think you're all right with the well, Angel, but the creek's only half the size it was in the winter when I was up scouting the mountain for timber. I've seen the changes. You may have to end up pumping water for your animals if the dry continues.

— Pump? We've got a new pump? A hand pump?

Eliza looks expectantly from one face to another. Jack grins.

— Installed today, Mrs Clare, especially for the new mistress of — what are you going to call the place? Every house has to have a name, for the Post Office, and deliveries, and the co-operative.

— I don't know. Clareville? But it's hardly a villa.

— Mt Eliza!

— That sounds very pretentious.

— Angel Heights?

— That's even worse. What about Keira Cottage? Which do you like best, Eliza? We'll leave it up to you.

— I like Keira Cottage.

— Keira Cottage it is, then. Mt Keira Road, Wollongong.

Mary clears the dishes.

— Jack, Angel, Abraham — to bed! Angel, you can't sleep on the table. Eliza, take him to bed.

CHAPTER 17

KEIRA COTTAGE

Two more days of the hardest manual labour Angel has ever done, and then it's Saturday. Eliza accompanies Mary to the market to stock up on supplies for the cottage while the men have a well-earned sleep-in. Then it's off to Stuart Park with baskets of food on their arms, and Eliza and Angel are welcomed as new members of the congregation. Mary and Jack know a lot of people, and they certainly seem to have been missed while they were away, including Polly.

Abraham meets some of the other young men, several of whom he discovers work in the mines, not just the Mt Keira mine. He finds out there are eleven mines in the area, all coal; and coal of the very highest quality, most of it being shipped to Sydney to fuel overseas ships. The remainder of the young men are 'townies', clerks, shop assistants, delivery boys. And there are also some attractive young ladies at the picnic, so time flies for Abe. He is able to show off a bit in a scratch cricket game when he hits a six right into Fairy Creek that flows beside the park. The ball goes 'over the fence'. Luckily, the creek is low and they retrieve the ball easily from among a flock of gulls who rise, squawking, before settling down again on the sandy shallows.

After Church the next day, when they are formally welcomed into the congregation, Angel and Eliza drive out to Keira Cottage with the wagon piled higher than the sideboards. The Turvilles follow some distance behind. The men have really worked hard to surprise Eliza (and Mary too, as this is her first visit to the farm). They turn off the road at a driveway with a crudely carved 'Keira Cottage' nailed to a tree, and drive through the shallow creek and up a hill where the house stands. Eliza opens her eyes wide.

— A verandah! Oh, Angel!

— It was Jack's idea. It was easily added and only took an extra sheet or so of roofing.

— New roof. Oh, I do like the verandah across the front. It changes the place entirely. There's the piggery, and there are the pigs! How many?

— Six to start. See the chicken coop?

— And chickens! I mean, chooks.

— Ten hens, Rhode Island Reds, and a handsome rooster, a Black Orpington. Folks will pay more for brown eggs: they think they're more nutritious. We'll have to keep the sack of wheat in the house so it won't get wet. That's what they eat. That'll be your job, too. And the pigs; and the garden.

They wait for the Turvilles and Abraham to catch up with them, and then Eliza steps onto her new wooden verandah for the first time. *Wide enough for chairs, if we ever get enough time to relax. And tubs of flowers, or herbs; or hanging baskets.* She steps in, onto the new linoleum.

— Doesn't it make a difference? And the dining set came! Look how it gleams! It really is too fancy for a tiny little place like this.

Mary is enjoying her friend's enthusiasm.

— It'll grow with you, Eliza. The bed looks nice. I'll help you stuff the mattress out on the verandah. The boys brought the straw up yesterday.

Eliza puts her head back and looks up at the roof. No daylight. Then she looks over fondly at the boys. Her boys, who have done most of this, are standing in the doorway watching her reaction. She goes up to each one and gives him a hug. Angel pulls away, embarrassed at intimate public attention.

— Watch the thumb!

Abraham gives her arm a brotherly punch; and Jack, so straight and strong. He pats her on the back, all the time smiling broadly.

— Have to start the little lady off on the best foot possible.

— I'll put the kettle on and we'll all have a cup of tea and biscuits that Mary made, and christen the new table; and the new china for that matter.

— When the cows come up at four o'clock you'll have to leave your fancy tea party so that I can teach you how to milk. You're a farmer's wife now, and the job starts in the morning. Jack and Mary, I want to thank you both for your more than generous hospitality, and for taking in my young brother-in-law here.

— You'd do the same for me, old chum, to set me on my feet.

The boys wander off down towards the creek. Mary and Eliza go out onto the verandah.

— Polly! Leave the piggies alone. Come and help Mummy and Aunt Eliza stuff the mattress. That child just adores pigs. I don't understand it.

— You can blame me, Mary. I've been telling her stories about the Wollongong pigs who are rivals with the Bulli pigs. They all have different personalities. The Wollongong pigs like to travel in a double-decker bus, and the Bulli pigs like black jelly babies.

— Oh, Eliza, how do you dream that stuff up? Polly!

— Aunty 'Liza, are these the Wollongong pigs?

— Does one of them have a floppy ear?

— Yiss! He does!

— That must be Uncle Joe.

— Oh, Eliza!

The two young women chuckle as they firm up the mattress by pushing the straw hard into the corners.

Mrs Angel Clare now becomes regimented by nature: up at 3:30 a.m. to get water from the pump for drinking, for the kettle, and for personal ablutions; set the fire and light it for breakfast; start the kettle and the oatmeal, all done so as not to wake the sleeping Angel. Dress, then slip outside to be greeted by Rover who thumps his tail on the verandah floor (also careful not to wake up his master); take the scoured bucket in one hand, and one of the large milk cans in the other, then stagger down to the milking shed; start on Bessie and continue milking down the line of cows; *funny how they arrange themselves in order from the leader down to the lowliest like a cricket team in to bat*; carry the first pail of milk back to the house for their personal use, and on Mondays, Tuesdays, Thursdays and Fridays, several buckets which she will make into butter and sell in town; return to the milking shed with the empty bucket and the other large can; continue milking, her fingers getting weaker as they get tired, until the last of the 'girls' wanders away; pouring the full buckets very carefully into the neck of the cans; plugging them, then rolling them on their round bases to stand like sentinels waiting for Angel to lift them into the cart and drive to the dairy.

By this time it is going on 6 a.m.; put more water on to boil; wake Angel; make the porridge, tea, and the rest of the breakfast; feed Rover; wash up the dishes and scour the milk buckets with hot water, which she seems forever to need; tidy the house; carry fresh water to the chicken coop, and another lot to the pigs halfway down the drive; *I'll have to get a wheelbarrow or my arms will pull right out of their sockets;* take a basket from the house and a scoop of wheat to feed the chooks, scattering the grain and crying, 'Chook!', 'Chook!', 'Chook! Here, chookies!'

Mondays and Thursdays she does the washing in the big tub, with her knuckles rubbing red against the corrugated wash board; no copper or mangle, just screwing the clothes out by hand and pegging them on the new line between the verandah and a nearby gum tree, using a forked tree branch for a clothes prop; clothes dry fast in this dry southern summer weather; Fridays, iron on the old kitchen table, brushing hair off her perspiring face; lifting one iron at a time out of the embers with a pot holder, then spitting on it to test if it's hot enough or too hot, not wanting to scorch the whites; and after that, wash her hair ready for market day, and Church on Sundays; Mondays, Tuesdays, Thursdays and Fridays, churn the milk and make bricks of butter which have to be kept cool somehow; Wednesdays, take Ned to town to sell the eggs and butter to the grocer, and on Saturdays, be in town early for market day to sell the produce there (and vegies, later, when they grow and ripen).

She's very proud of the vegetable garden she dug all by herself, across the hill below the house, and planted as fast as she had the time to add a row. First to go in were potatoes, with carrots, parsnips and beans. Peas, she was told, don't do well in the heat and should be grown in the winter, anyway. 'Finicky things' they said, which was good advice as the last thing she needs to deal with are finicky vegetables. She really wants to plant maize but Angel says it would grow too tall and block the light from the other rows. He should know: he's the one who attended agricultural college. She also has tomatoes and cucumbers, and these all need watering.

As it hasn't rained since they moved in, her brilliant idea of saving rain water from the roof in a barrel that could be let out to irrigate her furrows has come to nothing. Instead, she has to carry water from the pump. In addition to these chores, Angel demands two hot meals a day: he is a working man. Eliza has to plan ahead and get the dinner ready, a stew or roast, for 11:30 a.m. She also planted pumpkins near the chook house, and a new vine to her, passionfruit, to climb the fence. After noon, she makes bran mash for the broody hens, shoos the others away from the nests, and collects the brown eggs.

The days she goes to town to sell her produce and pick up supplies, she has to be home before 4 p.m to put Angel's dinner on and plan a dessert, as he insists on sitting down to tea as soon as he finishes milking the cows. In her spare time she makes the bed; scrubs the floor; saws logs into one and a half foot lengths, splits them further into firewood and carries them inside; after dinner, does the dishes; brings more buckets of water from the pump and puts the big kettle and large pot on to boil for Angel's bath; then gives him the day's receipts and dockets. This is her job description of 'keeping house'; the little time she has left, she sits and does some fancy work or darning but generally she is too exhausted to do anything at all.

After his bath in the big tub, Eliza uses the residual warmth for a little splash of her own before putting on her nightdress, emptying the tub out doors, and setting the oatmeal to soak for breakfast. Some nights she nearly falls asleep sitting on the edge of the bed brushing her hair one hundred times, as she's always done, a routine she is determined not to give up, even though she loses count in the forties or seventies. On nights when she's awake, she glances at her sleeping husband. *How fast the romance has gone out of my life! Since we've settled here on the farm he hasn't made any husbandly advances towards me at night because he's always asleep before me. Sometimes he mutters and tosses in his sleep, calling out so loudly he jerks me awake. By day he's almost totally preoccupied by the cows, the pigs, the crops, the water level in the creek, the weather, the drought, or the heat. He never initiates conversation, only responds to my questions in monosyllables. Even Rover is more sociable!*

Mr Angel Clare rises at six and eats his steaming oatmeal. Summer and winter he's always had oatmeal for breakfast and cannot see any reason to change his habits, even though this is the hottest summer he has ever lived through. Nothing is going to force him to change his eating habits. As a farmer proprietor, he carries the full responsibility of the farm, the animals and their welfare; and is fully aware of the long-term picture which is getting darker and darker before they are fully settled in. By the end of the year the profits of the farm must exceed the expenditures, and he has been bleeding expenditures in setting up Keira Cottage.

He worries about these things constantly, over meals, and when he drives the milk to the co-op. There he meets other dairy farmers who turn up morning after morning with no smiles on their faces. 'It's a poor time to have started up in this business', they tell him. 'There's been a depression coming on for some time now, and we don't know how long the co-op can keep going. Milk prices are the lowest they've been in years. If it wasn't for refrigeration on the trains now, we couldn't get our product to Sydney early and the butter would go rancid. Yer have to look on the bright side.' 'This drought isn't helping any' another tells him. 'It'll affect milk production, and will mean fewer pennies in the jam jar.'

They stand outside the dairy, hands in their pockets, looking at the ground and moving the occasional stick around in the dust with the toe of their boots.

— It's all right for you, Clare, you've also got crops. We're sole dairymen.

— Crops need rain, too; and it's a long time before there are any returns.

— Mmmmm.

They all load their empty cans. Angel loads his, filled with skimmed milk, a waste by-product which the dairy is only too happy to provide him with. He doffs his cap and drives home to fill the troughs for his noisy, inquisitive pigs.

It hasn't rained since they moved to the mountain. The creek is barely running, and that's where the Jerseys spend the hottest part of the day, under the wilting gums. The pasture, which had been green and lush when he bought the place not two months before, is now crisp and turning dun. People talk to him about the summer rains and the Southerly Busters, fierce quick storms that blow up after an exceptionally hot day; but this year is different. He's had to speak with Eliza about the cows.

— You're not getting as much milk out of them as you did in the beginning. Maybe it's your technique. I've told you how Tess used to nuzzle against their flanks. She seemed to almost talk it out of them.

— Well, I'm not Tess. I *was* able to get more milk at first. It's not my technique, Angel. It's the drought; pure and simple.

— Nevertheless, I'll come and watch you in the morning. Better still, I'll watch you milk them this afternoon so I won't have to get up early.

Each day, after feeding the pigs, he walks over his land. '*My* land. All mine! Farmer proprietor.' He'd had to hire two men with a horse to plough to sow the oats and barley in order to get them in the ground in time. Too much for one man. Now, as he walks the fences looking for breaks, he surveys his crops: thin little strands of pale brown no more than four inches high. According to his calculations the stalks should be at least a foot high, and thick and green. 'That means I'll have to continue buying oats for the horse for, let me see, three months, if the crop ever does come in; or maybe I'll have to sell the horse.

Rover accompanies him everywhere, and when Angel stops and leans against the fence, muttering, Rover sits at his feet looking up into his face. Angel ruminates out loud.

— You understand, don't you, boy? You're the only one who understands me, the pressures, the effects of the drought, the money; not being able to buy a stove or a proper house, or even a simple wardrobe to hang my clothes in. At least Eliza (Rover barks when he hears her name) is able to barter the butter and eggs for things we don't have. I suppose I could cut down feeding the chickens wheat and let them roam free. Wheat's expensive since the rust went through here years ago, and has to be brought into the district; but if I don't feed them wheat and bran mash for the setting hens, I won't get the quality or size of egg I'm getting now. If it takes thirty days to hatch a chick, and so many weeks before it's big enough to kill and eat …I was sure I bought enough hens to turn a profit in three months but there's no sign of chickens yet. Maybe the drought has dried up the rooster as well.

He shakes his head.

— 'Don't count your chickens until they're hatched.' How true, how very, very true.

After 'surveying the property' as he calls his daily walk, it's back to the house for a hot dinner and a pipe on the verandah; then, take some buttermilk and bran and mix it for the pigs and carry it down to them; and have to return to the pump for water for their trough. As long as water keeps coming out of the pump, we'll be able to manage. He's shown Eliza how he wants her to harness Ned when she goes to town. He doesn't like her going to town so much, mixing with all the town folk. Too much freedom. 'Her place is here, by my side. I'm going to have to put a stop to that. Once a week to Church is enough gadding about for a farm wife.' At four, he takes a scoured bucket and an empty milk can down to the milking shed where the 'girls' have started gathering in their hierarchical manner, some waiting nearly two hours. If it's a day Eliza goes to town, she's usually back by the time he's started milking, and after she unloads her supplies at the house, she ties Ned and the wagon to the milking shed post. Smells from the kitchen drift over to him as he milks on, dumplings, stew, or suet puddings, and he really works up an appetite, all the time mulling things over in his mind. He is now aware that the girls seem to be getting thinner and that he, now, cannot get as much milk out of them as Eliza can. Dinner at night is his crowning delight: a relaxing cap to an arduous day. He goes to wash up, and relishes sitting down at a freshly-laid table complete with a crisp cloth and napkins.

— Smells delicious. What is it?

— A piece of spit-roasted beef I exchanged for the eggs today.

— Beef? Beef! We can't afford beef, woman. We're struggling.

— I …I thought you'd enjoy it, Angel. We haven't had beef in such a long time.

He hits the roof.

— I work my fingers to the bone all day just to put the basics on the table and you go to town and spend extravagantly. Draining the coffers, that's what you're doing. *I'll go to town from now on and you can do the evening milking as well. You have no idea of the value of money. It's pouring out a lot faster than it's coming in. But why am I wasting my time telling you all this?*

— If you would only tell me the whole situation I could understand and be able to help you.

— Help me? How can you help me? You're just a woman. Squandering my hard-earned cash. I suppose you're squirrelling some away each time to spend on fripperies, eh? I'm the master of the house. I wear the pants and I make the decisions. I couldn't eat this now. I'd choke.

He roughly pushes his untouched dinner across the table, gets up, and goes out on the verandah.

Eliza's heart nearly stops beating. *I feel like my life is swirling in a vortex down a drain. Should **I** continue eating? Should I go out and try to calm him? Should I keep his dinner hot for him? I'm in such a knot, I can't swallow either. What has happened to make him so angry? Is it something **I've** done? I can't think of anything. I already have to juggle far more chores than he does in the course of a day. I feel like saying, 'So you'll be getting dinner, now, will you, while I milk the cows?' but I know when to hold my tongue.* She takes the beef and calls Rover.

— Here, Rover. Someone should enjoy it.

She finishes hers, then takes a bowl of blackberries and cream out to the verandah.

— They're not sweet enough. Bring me some sugar, and bring my tea out here as well.

Later that night at the dining table when she gives him her town receipts, he says.

— Give my shoulders and head a rub, will you? They're so tight. I think I'm getting one of those headaches again, and my body aches all over from head to toe.

She stands behind him and starts to knead his shoulders from the centre out.

— Ooh, agh, oogh.

— Am I hurting you?

— Yes, but keep going. Aagh! It hurts but it feels so good.

Then she works her way up his spine to the base of his skull, rolling her thumbs in double circles. He closes his eyes and gives himself over to this painful bliss.

— Rub hard against the bone, there. It's exquisite, agony.

He puts his own hands against his head, elbows on the table, and while Eliza works his back he digs and rubs his fingers over his eyebrow ridges and over the bumps in his head above them.

— That hard rubbing really helps relieve the tension. I never realized before, Eliza: I have bigger bumps on the left side of my head than on the right. Feel here.

She feels and, sure enough, his skull is not symmetrical.

— Maybe you think more with that side of your hair, Angel.

— Keep on going. Don't stop.

She moves her finger tips in little circles all over his thinning head. *This is the most physical we've been since the first night on our wedding tour.*

— That's enough. Now a good hot soak will wash my troubles away. By the way, I'll be taking the eggs and butter to town from now on.

— What about Mary? And Polly? I won't see them.

— You can see them at Sunday Service. And that's another thing: I don't want you going to the Turville's any more. That Mary puts too many modern ideas in your head.

— But she literally saved my life, Angel.

— Nonsense. You exaggerate. You would have recovered just like all the other seasick passengers.

Eliza is hurt. *He doesn't care about me. Not at all; and now he's taking away my only pleasure, Mary's companionship. And dear little Polly.* She turns away to get the hot water for his bath, tears springing from her eyes. *I'll not let him see he's upset me. I'm a drudge, nothing but an indentured servant. I've done everything he's asked like a dutiful wife should, and now he's taking away the only thing I look forward to. He won't even let me socialize after Church now as he wants me back to cook him a hot dinner. And he thinks **he's** under pressure! There's nowhere I can go; no one I can talk to; no escape. I don't want to burden Mary, and it's no use writing to Mother. I'll just have to go on. There's nothing else to do. As it turns out, it was a good thing I did lose the little babe.*

CHAPTER 18

Downpour

Tonight, like every other night, Angel is in bed asleep before she gets ready for bed. She blows out the light and lies in the hot darkness, too hot for a blanket, and her eyes prickle with unleashed tears. *All I ever wanted was to marry my Prince Charming and settle down happily; and here I am on the other side of the world, living in sham happiness with a man on whom I am totally dependent both for my own welfare and the welfare of my family back home. Angel seems so worried about our financial situation here, I daren't ask him about Mother's rented cottage in Emminster. Just how stable are we all at any given time? How else could I contribute to our recent financial situation? Chop wood? There are plenty of trees for everyone. Work for a wage as a maid, or in a store? If I did that Angel would have to hire another person to do what I do here. Two people. One person wouldn't do what I do for free.*

She falls into a restless sleep. Maybe it's due to the rising humidity but she isn't the only restless sleeper. Just after the moon rises, Angel becomes quite agitated, shudders and jerks several times, then stands up and starts searching for something.

— Where? Where?

— Angel, come back to bed!

— Where? Where?

He keeps walking round the kitchen with one hand out, searching.

— Tess! Tess! Where are you?

Eliza's ears go stiff.

— Gone! Gone! My Tessy, gone!

— Angel?

— Is that you, Tess? Where are you?

— Come back to bed, Angel. Lie down and sleep.
— Oh! Oh!
— There you are. Sleep now.

He curls up in a ball beside her, mumbling incomprehensibly; and falls quiet at last.

By now Eliza feels beads of perspiration around her hair line, and gets out of bed for a drink from the pannikin of water she keeps on the old kitchen table. Suddenly, there's a loud 'Crack!' and a huge flash lights up the tiny cottage inside-out. She sees everything at once, and then, blackness again. The light reverberates on the back of her eyes and it seems she can still see just like day. Then she hears stones on the roof: a relentless, deafening rain of stones on the iron roof. She stands paralysed with fear in the middle of the kitchen. The noise gets worse. It's the loudest noise she's ever heard. Her heart thumps with fright There's another crack and bang: simultaneous lightning and thunder. She is rooted there, shaking. The wind, too. The door blows open and everything flies about the room. Hail stones the size of hens eggs roll across the floor. Rover, whining, beaten down by the hail with his tail between his legs, runs in towards her. Calming him helps calm herself. She kneels down with her arm around him.

— It's just a storm, boy. It takes your breath away but it'll be all right.

She struggles to push the door closed. The loud staccato drumming on the roof turns deeper as hail gives way to rain, rain like she has never experienced in England. Wind drives it through chinks in the walls. The building shakes but holds, and Eliza hears what sounds like waterfalls close by. She thinks of the animals. *If **I'm** scared out of my socks yet have to comfort a trembling dog, man's best friend, how are my poor dumb chooks and pigs faring? And the gentle-eyed little Jerseys? And Ned? It's too dangerous to go out in the middle of the night in the thick of the storm. I'm sure I heard trees snapping, probably struck by lightning; and any lantern would be blown out immediately.*

The intervals between the lightning and thunder begin to increase, indicating the storm is moving away somewhat, and now the rain is falling straight down but still beating on the roof without let-up. Angel sleeps on. Eliza lights a lamp and stirs the fire, then puts another log in the embers. She cannot go back to sleep, not with the sound of splashing, gushing water, and she can now make out the sound of frantic whinnying over the sound of the rain. She goes in and peers at the alarm clock. Nearly three. It won't be dawn until half past four — a quarter to five. Still, she's too nerved up now to get any rest. She gets a cloth and dries Rover who goes and lies in front of the fire. Soon the water boils and she sits in her nightgown on Angel's dining chair sipping hot tea and munching on a piece of bread she's toasted on the fire fork. She gives Rover some, too.

The rain keeps drumming and never lets up. It comes in waves: heavy noise, heavier, then heavy again; months' worth of rain in a few hours. *How can Angel sleep through such a racket? And why did he call out for Tess? In his sleep, does he think **I'm** Tess? And what is he looking for? It's almost symbolic, like Lady Macbeth. Should I tell him what he did and said? Does he really think nothing of me, by night or by day? Now I feel isolated as well as trapped. I'm supposed to be his helpmate but how can I help him? At least the drought has finally broken.*

Rover stretches and yawns with just the faintest sound and Angel is awake and on his feet in no time.

— What's the dog doing inside? And what's all that noise?

— Rain, Angel. 'Good refreshing rain' as the hymn goes. It's been coming down for ages.

— What? I can't hear you.

— A thunder clap woke me up an hour ago, right overhead, and the wind blew the door open and hailstones this big blew in. I think I'd better wait until daylight before I milk the cows. There was a terrible bolt of lightning and a crack. Then it sounded like a tree falling. The rain on the roof comes in waves. It sounds like a coach going over a bridge.

— The D'Urberville coach.

— That's just a myth. It's awfully dark out there.

— Perhaps you're right for once, about the cows. What's that noise of water rushing?

— It must be running off the roof into puddles on the ground. Want an early breakfast?

— Yes. You can make the porridge now. Hello, boy. You were frightened, were you?

The long-haired golden retriever thumps his tail and looks adoringly at his master.

— We don't have anything to keep the rain off when we do go outside. I hope it lets up soon. It can't go on like this too much longer.

The oatmeal plops softly in the pot as they dress in the barest clothes, knowing they'll be soaked to their skin two steps from the door.

— Our boots will be ruined.

— We can't go barefoot. Afterwards I'll stuff them with rags as they dry so they'll keep their shape. The rain's easing up a bit and you can almost see outside. Bring the bucket; I'll help you with the cans. Coming, Rover?

They open the door and step onto the verandah, squinting through the rain in the grey dawn. Puddles and miniature ice dams and running rivulets surround them. A waterfall is cascading off the roof.

— My garden!

The water has cut deep channels through Eliza's vegetable rows, rows that lie flattened by hail.

— Not one plant is standing!

— The crop!

— Let's check the animals first.

Ned is all right, dripping and forlorn; the wagon is half full of ice and overflowing with water.

— I forgot the chickens' feed.

— Chooks, Eliza. I've told you before that here they're called chooks. You'd better go back and get it. I'll go on and check the pigs.

She returns with their wheat and finds a sorry flock, dripping and huddled together as high off the ground as they can perch shaking out their feathers but otherwise unscathed. She slithers her way down the drive and finds a bemused Angel at the pig pen. The pigs are literally swimming in brown icy mud, and loving it!

— One hundred percent. Now for the girls. They haven't come up from the creek like they usually do. We'll have to go and find them.

— Look at the creek, Angel! It's a river!

— Oh my goodness. I hope they haven't been swept away. No, there they are, huddling together under that big gum. Bessie! Flossie! Come, girls!

The cows don't move. A couple are standing and the rest are lying down, all close together for comfort and protection. Rover goes ahead and starts barking at them. Still, they don't make a move.

— Poor little things. They're frozen with fear like I was when the lightning hit. I know just how they feel.

Rover comes bounding back, barking.

— What is it, boy? Cows aren't used to rain; they haven't seen it for so long.

They follow him over to where the Jerseys are, picking their way through the mud and mini lakes that have formed in the hollows. When they get to the cows, the ones lying down are surrouded by ice, the others standing in a foot of it. Angel gives Bessie a smack on the rump.

— Up, girl! You'll get all cold lying there.

— Angel, look at that tree. It's split, right down. The cows — they're still not moving. I think they've been struck by lightning. I think they're all dead.

— They can't be dead. They're just shocked, dazed. Up, Bessie! Flossie! Flossie!

Rover can sense that something is very wrong. He is barking and whining, running from one cow to another, sniffing and nudging them with his nose.

— How do you take a cow's pulse?

— I don't know. Oh God! They can't all be dead, all seven of them.

They push and try to shake the cows' heads; but they are stiff.

— I've never heard of this happening before — cows killed by a thunderbolt. Oh God! I'm ruined! If the crop is anything like the garden, all we have left to make a living from is eggs.

— We've still got the pigs.

— But we can't afford to fatten them.

— Maybe we should check the crop, Angel. It might have survived intact.

The rain is easing now, just misting, and there's enough light to see quite well. They slosh back to the cottage where they discover just how destructive the storm has been, especially the water. Small runnels on the upper slopes have widened into fast running streams and cut and carved out the dry soil. Their fences have all fallen down as the posts have been eroded by swirling eddies.

— The loo — the dunny's gone! Nowhere in sight. Washed clean away.

— You boys did a good job on the pig sty and chook house. They seem very sturdy.

They comfort poor Ned who stands fetlock-deep in water, tethered to a tree stump, then go over to the oats and barley, or what had been the oats and barley. Not a blade of vegetation has survived; instead, just swirls of mud where the crop has struggled for weeks without rain only to be washed away by the one thing that could give it life. Angel falls to his knees, his face as wet with salty tears as with rain. Eliza stands behind him not quite knowing what to do. She decides to be positive.

— We still have the cottage, the chooks, the pigs, Ned, and Rover; and we still have each other.

— Oh, for heaven's sake, can't you see it's hopeless?

He stands up without giving her a glance and heads back to the house, followed by Rover. Eliza surveys the desolation. Trees are blown down on the edge of the pasture, and as the low clouds scatter a little, she catches a glimpse of the mountain. It seems to her there's been a land slip of sorts, or a blow-down higher up. She returns to the cottage and finds Angel changing into dry clothes.

— I'm taking Ned to town. I must see the bank manager.

— Why?

— You leave the finances to me. Only one of us can wear the pants.

— But I don't see why …

He pushes past her, whistles for Rover, and is gone. *Did I really hear the D'Urberville coach? This storm certainly brought disaster on us.* Eliza decides to see to the pigs. She makes a mash out of bran and water instead of skim milk and takes it down to them.

— You can turn your noses up all you like. This is all there is.

Angel and Ned come back up the drive.

— I can't cross the creek, or river as it is now. It's too high and strong. I'll just have to wait until it goes down to get to the road. Now that the rain's stopped, there can't be that much more run-off.

It is two days before Ned can safely ford the creek. Eliza has talked Angel into taking her to town with him. She can sell the eggs, and she wants to find out how Abraham is doing. Angel has relented in his vow, and will now allow her to see Mary and Polly. He's been very moody and untalkative since the storm and has spent much of the last two days walking the property with Rover and muttering to himself. *He seems almost overwhelmed. He won't discuss our immediate predicament or our future. Last night was another emotional night; again, calling out for Tess. Should I tell him what he's doing? Or would that just stir up a can of worms? Should I tell someone? Mary?*

They ride to town in silence. Angel takes the eggs to the grocer's and then drops Eliza at Seafoam. Mary is amazed to learn of the storm damage on the mountain. Wollongong just caught the normal summer storm, the only difference being that Fairy Creek had swollen and they had to open the sluice gates and let it run out across the beach at the edge of Stuart Park. Mr Puckey couldn't get in to work as he lives on the north side of the creek. Other than that, nothing notable in town. The storm had washed away the pier at Bulli but that kind of thing happens regularly. They were lucky: no ships were lost this time as none were loading coal.

— What are you going to do, Eliza?

— I don't know. We can't make a living off eggs as we only have a few hens. Angel won't even talk about it. I have no idea if we are ruined or not.

This is the first time I've let down my guard and confided my feelings about Angel to Mary. Am I being disloyal to him?

— Eliza, how awful for you! Can we help?

— I think that may be part of the problem. His pride. I'm not sure, but I get the feeling he resents the fact that you and Jack always help me, and he can't pay Jack back.

*Well, now it's out. If I've let my guard down a crack I might as well open the floodgates. It's **so** good to be able to share my misgivings; some of them, anyway.*

— It's only money, Eliza, and we have lots to share.

— I understand but Angel doesn't. He told me he doesn't want to be beholden to anybody, and you being our friends gets in the way. Maybe he feels that Jack has been successful and he's been a failure.

— It's not that. It's just pure bad luck.

— To change the subject, Mary, how is Abraham doing?

A shadow comes across Mary's face.

— Well, he's enjoying the work. That's what he says.

— There's something more, isn't there? Is he not well?

— Oh, yes, he's very well. It's just that …I've heard things; and he comes home late for tea; and …

— Where does he go?

— Well, Jack says he goes to the pub after work with the other miners.

— Drinking? Oh, no. Father always liked his wee drop. I hope he doesn't take to the drink like he did.

— I don't know how to tell you this in a kinder way, Eliza, but I fear it's a little more than a wee drop. We can't wake him up in the mornings, and he's often late for his shift, he's such a heavy sleeper: the booze.

— I wish I could see him. I'd try and talk some sense into him.

— Jack's tried to talk to him; even gone to the pub with him but boys will be boys. He's doing men's work now, Eliza, and acting like the other men. Maybe it's his way of fitting in. He's well-liked by his mates.

— They always are, as long as they can afford drinks all round

Angel comes in while they are having afternoon tea on the verandah. He stands with his hands behind his back, looking not at them but out over the ocean.

— It's all settled. I've seen the bank manager. I've sold the farm, liquidated the lot; 'lock, stock, and barrel' as they say.

— You what!

— Sold it, like I said. We'll have to find accommodation here in town. The bank bought the property and the animals, but at a loss to me. A wash out; a total wash out. We're fortunate if we can get out of it with just the clothes on our back.

— What about my dining suite, my wedding present?

— All part of the deal. He gave me a very good price for it too, sight unseen.

Mary is so embarrassed to be an unwilling witness.

— Angel, you and Eliza can stay here until you find lodgings.

— Thank you, Mary, but no. We can't impose on you any more. We'll find a room somewhere.

A room! Keira Cottage seems like a palace in comparison.

— Didn't you say, Mary, that Stella's mother runs a boarding house over on Bourke Street?

— Yes. Why didn't I think of it? We can go and ask her if she has any rooms. Angel? Would that be all right?

— Yes, yes, I'll accompany you.

CHAPTER 19

FARNHAM

It turns out that Farnham has two rooms available, both furnished, a large one in the front with French doors opening onto the verandah and garden, and a smaller cheaper one at the rear. Eliza holds her breath, hoping Angel will take the front one, as he marches back and forth between them, deliberating. He eventually does choose the front room, not for her, but because Rover will be able to sleep on the verandah. *He's more considerate of that dog than he is of me!* The room is amply furnished with a large comfortable bed, a dressing table, a wardrobe, a writing table and chair, and two padded wicker chairs. As well, there are two wooden chairs outside on the verandah. Mrs Edwards, Stella's mother, states what's included in the rent.

— Room and board. Linen and towels changed once a week. Breakfast at eight, dinner at one, tea at six.

Eliza can hardly believe it. *Breakfast at **eight**? That's like the middle of the morning. It'll be **some** compensation for losing my lovely dining suite. Why did he have to sell it? How could he?*

There's no time to lose. It's back to Keira Cottage for the last time to pick up their clothes and a few personal belongings, like the table cloths she had embroidered. *He even sold my willow pattern.* As Ned plods back up the hill, Eliza quizzes Angel. *What have I got to lose? He's sold it all.*

— Why didn't you tell me what you were planning to do?

— I knew you'd go into histrionics if I broached the subject. As head of the house I put us in this situation and it's up to me to pull us out. The bank manager gave me a fair deal. With what I'd already borrowed to buy the place, it was all or nothing. He knows the place has potential for dairying and mixed farming, and the soil's good. It's just a combination of the present depressed prices, the damned drought, and then the storm.

— Angel! You swore!

— Well, who wouldn't? There have been cattle struck down before, he told me, by lightning bolts. I must say, it is bizarre. It's as if all the Fates are conspiring against me.

— Did you *have* to sell the dining suite?

— It was a matter of necessity, Eliza. Cold hard cash is what we need right now. You can't carry a dining suite around with you. 'You can't take it with you'.

He laughs bitterly.

— The bank is sending a man up to look after the animals until a buyer is found, or they can be sold separately. I'll drop Ned off at the bank as soon as I take you back to Farnham. I have to face it: it was a hard life, Eliza. I failed as a farmer. That's the second time I've failed as a farmer. I don't think I have the strength to try again. I'll have to find another line of work. In the meantime, we have enough to live on at Mrs Edwards'. I'm beginning to doubt what Jack said about Australia being the land of opportunity. Maybe we should seriously consider going back home.

Go back home? Not me! Not after what I went through. I'll stay here on parish relief if necessary but I will never, **never***, set foot on a ship again. Should I mention this now or just let his idea die away? Better not bring it to a head. Better to pour oil on troubled waters.*

— You'll find something, I'm sure, Angel, with your knowledge and experience.

— Don't be too sure.

They settle in at Farnham. For Eliza it's a life of luxury. Mrs Edwards is very kind, a widow. Her husband drowned some years back, in Fairy Creek actually, and now she takes in boarders to make a living. They had formerly lived at Woonona and had run the Marlow Bakery, named after where her family came from in Buckinghamshire. Mr Edwards, she tells Eliza over morning tea one day, was a lot like Mr Clare. He was a gentleman, and not used to hard physical labour; and he wrote poetry. The house had been named after Farnham Royal, where she was born. They'd come out in 1863 when her eldest was only seven.

— It was the worst time of my life. I was seasick the whole time.

— So was I! The whole time. I was pregnant, too, and lost the baby on the way.

— Oh, my dear. I'm so sorry.

— No, really, in looking back it was for the best; but you had children to look after.

— Yes, and I had Frederick, Mr Edwards, to help me.

— I had Mary and Jack Turville. I believe they saved my life, the care they gave me. Angel, Mr Clare, was already here.

— They're a very nice young couple. Successful too, and little Polly is such a pet.

— We have quite a bond, Polly and I.

CHAPTER 20

THE MINE

Although Angel doesn't like her being over at Seafoam so much, he can't come up with any legitimate reasons to forbid her so Eliza is able to see more of Mary and Polly. The little girl and her two mentors enjoy going over the road and down the steps to North Wollongong Beach. They take off their boots and stockings, and all three lift up their skirts and paddle in the waves, waves that are finishing their trip across the ocean, running up the beach, their final destination, over toes and ankles, then draining away, leaving hollows around their heels.

— Every seventh wave's a rogue wave, so watch out!

Polly counts and, sure enough, every seventh one is a lot stronger, comes faster, and they have to hurriedly back up the beach, shrieking. The sun is bright this time of year, the waves warm, and the wind blowing from the sea cools their faces. Friends; laughter; relaxation; time stands still; worry is suspended.

Previously Eliza had not been in touch with her brother except at Church on Sundays but now she sees him frequently at the Turvilles', and some nights he comes to tea at Mrs Edwards'. He's a boy no longer: the mine has turned him into a man with his own ideas and his own mates, mainly from underground.

— Tell me about your work in the mine, Abe.

— Well, Sis, it's hard to explain.

— Do you like it?

— Oh, I don't mind the work. It's hard but the pay's good. I work at the weighbridge at the top of the incline to the mine. The men work really hard at the face, those with the picks, mostly married men; and the wheelers who work with the skips.

— Who are they?

— Wheelers are the men who bring their own horse every day, who pull the skips.

— Who are the skips?

— Skips aren't people. That's what they call the carts they fill with the coal. The miners working the seam of coal at the face either use picks or blow up the face, then shovel the coal into the skips which are on wheels. It's pretty dusty, especially when they use explosives. I sometimes help with the shovelling which kicks up its own dust. Sometimes it's a long way into the face. Did you know there are tunnels under Mt Keira a mile or two long? Some are straight; others are twisting. The shafts follow the seam of coal from the outside. If it turns, the tunnel turns. The seam itself can be anything from a foot to several feet thick. And then there's the noises.

— Noises underground?

— Not all the time but sometimes they make you feel uneasy. Thuds and creaking. Noises like that. The tunnels are damp. The roofs and walls are lined with wood that they install as they work back under the mountain following the seam.

Eliza shudders.

— You're *sure* you don't mind it? I certainly wouldn't like working in those conditions.

— Nah. Every job has parts you don't like. The darkness is the worst, for me, anyway. It's always dark in front and behind when you're walking in and out. The only light's the lamp on your head; but as I said, I mostly work at the weighbridge. I feel like we're all brothers in there, and they treat me like one of them.

— So I've heard.

— You mean the pub? We work hard and we drink hard. I'll admit it. It's dangerous work. There was a big explosion in the Bulli mine a few years ago that killed about eighty men underground caused by gas that you can't smell. It goes with the job. That stuff's been trapped under the earth since the ark, and when men hit the coal face with their picks the gas sometimes comes out of the coal and is set off by a spark, either from the explosion, or from our headlamps, or by the lights at the face. We use either kerosene or candles for lighting. Some say the Bulli disaster was caused by smoking. Kerosene's cheap. There's a kerosene works right here in Wollongong. It's made from coal, you know. That's what they use in the street lights. Have you noticed?

— Yes, a sort of eerie glow.

— Well, that's what we use in the mine; only on our heads at the face. At least I get to see daylight on my shift. Some of my mates at the face are bent over for hours or even have to lie down when they're cutting under a seam so it can be blown. I can't complain: at least I have a job. Some of them have been laid off, or have been on strike, for months. A lot of those do-good societies here and up the coast run benefits and collect money, clothes and food for miners' families.

Brother and sister stroll along the beach. It is low tide and they walk on the hard sand way out near the water's edge. Eliza tells Abraham of her current predicament, and how Angel is talking of going home.

— Why would he put you through that? Have you told him?

— Not exactly. He doesn't really understand. He might be lucky enough to find work, if he looks for it.

— I'd put my foot down, if I were you.

— It might just come to that. I can't take another sea voyage.

Eliza writes home to let her mother know her new address, keeping most of the drama out of the letter; and also to assure her that Abraham has a job and is becoming more independent. She also mentions that her new friend, Stella, Mary's neighbour and her new landlady's daughter, has lent her a Wanzer 'A' sewing machine and she is now taking in some dressmaking orders, including drawers and knickers from fine handkerchief lawn and batiste. She describes how hot it is and what frightful storms they have in New South Wales. She ends by writing, 'Angel sends his love'. She knows this is untrue but what a mother-in-law would expect in a letter.

Angel, in fact, is becoming more and more withdrawn. He disappears for hours with Rover on long rambles and can sometimes be seen walking along the beach or on the sandy bluffs on the other side, the north side, of Fairy Creek with his fishing rod. As far as Eliza knows, he's never even looked for work, a 'job' seeming to be beneath his dignity.

One morning after breakfast just after settling down to some serious run and fell seams on a new dress, she hears, or rather first of all feels, a rumble, then the tremendous roar of a blast from the west of town. She, like the rest of Wollongong, doesn't wonder but knows the mine has gone. People are running into the streets, harnessing up their horses and riding pell-mell toward the mountain. Eliza feels sick. Abraham! It's his shift.

She runs into the hall just as a cart pulls up outside. It's Jack and Mary.

— We heard it, too. Get your First Aid supplies, Eliza. Mrs Edwards, can we have as many blankets as you can spare? Where's Angel?

— He's off somewhere with the dog.

— Get in, then. We'll take you up. Thank you, thank you, Mrs Edwards. Now, Eliza, prepare yourself for the worst but hope for the best. Abraham was late leaving for work again today: slept in after a heavy night. Maybe he escaped it. You know what St Paul says: 'Let hope keep you joyful'.

— It's hard to keep joyful after hearing a terrible noise like that.

It seems like half of Wollongong is heading for the tunnel mouth, and more coming: wives and mothers, still with their aprons on; friends and relatives, hurrying along up the dusty incline to the pithead. Jack stops and gives a lift to as many as will fit in the cart.

When they reach the mine they find a lot of boards and iron roofing have been blown off, and lie dangerously jumbled on the ground. The mine manager is stopping people from rushing in to the mine to help. From experience he knows it will not be safe to enter until the ventilation system is checked; and there are injured miners and horses on the outside, and maybe some under the rubble. One wheeler and his pit pony had been bringing out a skip of coal and were still fifty feet from the entrance, inside the mine, and were blown out into the daylight by the blast. The horse had to be shot but the wheeler survived although the whole of his back is singed and blackened. Lucky man.

The mine manager is organizing the local ambulance volunteers in the rubble search above ground before sending rescue teams into the mine. Thick coal dust is still coming out of the black opening.

— Does anyone here know where we could get some white mice. Anyone's children keep them as pets?

Mary steps forward.

— My little girl has a pet white mouse, and so does the child next door.

— Any way we can get them here in a hurry, Ma'am? Do they have cages?

— Oh yes. I can go back right away. I came in the cart.

— I'd appreciate that, Ma'am.

Mary squeezes Eliza's hand.

— Jack will help you look for Abraham. I'm going to get Mr Whiskers and the General. The rescue teams need to carry them for safety. No one can smell or see or taste the gas that lies near the ground in there. It chokes the rescuers before they know it. It's happened before. If the mice die, the rescuers get out quick. If they are still active in their cages, it's safe for the rescuers to proceed. I have to go. I'll be back soon.

She turns the cart and makes her way down the mountain against the human tide making their way up. Jack is helping to lift the beams and roofing, and checking for any survivors. He sees a trouser leg and boot pinned by a beam sticking out from under some roofing.

— Help me! There's someone here.

A team of rescuers starts picking up pieces and throwing them to one side. A man is lying underneath, face down, obviously knocked down by the flying timber.

— One, two, three, heave!

They lift the beam off his leg. The body is very still. Holding him as stiffly as they can, they roll him over.

— Abraham!

— You know this fellow?

— He boards with me. His sister's over there with the women.

Jack kneels down.

— Abraham! Abe! Wake up!

He takes the limp wrist and feels for a pulse.

— I can feel a pulse! He's alive! He must be knocked out. Stretcher! Over here! Gently, now. Watch that leg. He'll need a doctor. Eliza! Eliza! It's Abraham. Stay there. We'll bring him over.

— Is he alive? He's not awake and he isn't moving.

— He's breathing but he's been knocked senseless. They say drink can kill you. In Abraham's case, it saved his life, sleeping in after being out late last night. Don't be too hard on him, Eliza. A beam fell on his leg. If his leg is broken, it's best that the doctor sets it before he wakes up. Doctor! Is there a doctor here yet?

A man with a black Gladstone bag comes hurrying over followed by ambulance volunteers with a blanket and bandages. He pulls Abraham's eyes open and peers in.

— Concussion.

The doctor now examines his head (no actual cut), and proceeds to feel him all over from his head down to his feet. He pays particular attention to the leg that was pinned by the beam, cutting away his trousers, looking at the skin and moving his knee and ankle gently through their range of movement.

— It's not broken but it's severely contused. Ladies, bathe it with iodine and bandage it. Now it's just a case of waiting until he wakes up. He's a very, very lucky young man.

Abraham groans.

— Abe! Abe! It's Liza-Lu. It's me, Sissy. Wake up!

— Aaghh.

His eyes blink, and he sees his sister bending down. She's saying something.

— What? I can't hear. Where? What?

And he tries to sit up.

— Stay there, Abraham. There's been a mine explosion. You've been hurt.

— What? I can't hear you.

She touches his arm to get his attention and points to the mine, making exploding motions with her hands.

— My leg. Oh, my leg!

They gently lift the stretcher and carry him under the shade of a tree, and cover him with the blanket. Eliza makes 'lie still' motions with her hands while Jack goes back to help with the search.

When Mary comes back with the mice in their cages, and the first rescue teams enter the mine, Abraham and three other stretcher patients are lifted into the cart. Jack leaves the search and drives the cart back to Wollongong with Eliza in the back with the patients. They deliver the other three to the hospital which is normally filled with road accident victims, those who have fallen off horses, farmers gored by bulls or those suffering from accidents with scythes, then take Abraham back to Seafoam. He's able to hop on his good leg with someone on either side and they finally get him up the steps and onto the verandah. He indicates his leg is throbbing, and Mary goes off to chip some ice. The doctor is of the old school, wisdom from experience. He's instructed them to pack Abraham's leg in ice several times a day which will take away the pain and the swelling and get him back to normal much faster. He was very specific about this.

— He's to stay off it for a few days but be sure he wiggles his toes and moves his ankle and knee as much as he can tolerate. And don't let him stay in bed too long or he'll lose the use of his leg.

He also explained that the deafness was caused by the loudness of the explosion. His hearing may come back; or like Napoleon's, the damage may be permanent. It's not the loss of his hearing that is upsetting Abraham as much as the possibility of being a cripple.

Angel arrives back at Farnham for dinner only to be informed that Eliza has gone off with Mr and Mrs Turville. He eats his dinner and then goes round to Cliff Road where he finds his brother-in-law the centre of attention.

— Didn't you hear the awful bang, Angel?

— No, I didn't hear anything. I was walking along the beach. All I could hear was the sound of the surf breaking.

Eliza is making a big fuss over Polly whose little square chin hasn't stopped quivering since her mother hurriedly took the mice away earlier in the day. Mrs Harris had been looking after her when her mother had swooped in and carried off Mr Whiskers and the General, and Mrs Harris let her do it!

— You've done a very brave thing, Polly, letting Mr Whiskers go down the mine to save the miners. I'm so proud of you. Mr Whiskers and the General are doing their duty. After dinner, I think you deserve a reward. I'm sure Mummy will let me take you into town and buy you some iced cream. Then we'll stop at Guest's Bakery and get some Neenish tarts. How's that sound?

A little smile breaks through, and Polly nods.

After the meal Abraham puts his hands up to his ears and shakes his head, opening and closing his mouth.

— I think it might be coming back. My ears are full, like I'm hearing under water.

Before Polly and Eliza can leave, a reporter from the *Illawarra Mercury* comes to the house to get a photograph of the littlest helper in the mine rescue operation — Polly. Her picture is in the *Mercury* next day sitting beside Abraham, one of the lucky ones, the walking wounded. She and Muriel are even mentioned in the announcements in Church on Sunday; and to cap it all, Mr Whiskers and the General come through their duty in the mine unscathed.

It takes two days to bring the bodies out of the mine. There are rock falls, dead horses, and bodies. Lots of bodies. Some are almost dismembered and one is found wedged under a skip. Jack's exhausted. Not being a miner, he's volunteered above ground, running a relay of helpers who take the bodies to the Coast Hotel which has the biggest meeting room in the town. The corpses are laid out there as the small mortuary is not able to hold the large volume. The last night, when it's all over, he comes home exhausted and falls asleep before tea, not waking up until noon the following day.

— Jack, I love you; but you'll have to take a bath before you join us for lunch.

— You're right, Mary. How's the patient?

— He's hearing better, and you'd be surprised how good the leg looks. The swelling's down and he's moving it a bit.

— I've never heard of the ice trick before. It certainly works.

At lunch, Abraham announces he's been thinking.

— I've decided to give up black diamonds, Jack, and go back to my old station as a grocer's helper, or maybe get a job at Lance's.

— That's a lot less risky, Abraham.

— Only until I save enough money.

— Save it for what?

— This time I intend to go after gold — Kalgoorlie.

— Western Australia, eh? A lot of chaps from here are trying their luck out there especially in this depression. Good for you, Abraham.

— At least it's above ground.

— Mary's right. It's a lot safer being a gold miner than a coal miner. And a lot more profitable, too, if you find it.

— That too! I can always work as a store clerk out there if my money runs out.

— Too right. I hear it's the store keepers who are the ones making fortunes on the goldfields; not so much the gold panners.

When Eliza pops round to see him, Abraham tells her of his plans, now more or less sanctioned by the Turvilles.

— Now you'll have something to put in Mother's letter. You're always saying there's nothing to tell her.

— And I just wrote home yesterday.

— Seriously, though, what do you think?

— I feel a bit like Banquo in *Macbeth*: 'Not so happy, yet much happier'. I'll be sad to say 'Good-bye' but I'm glad you're happy. No more creakings and thuds inside the earth for you. You must pursue your dream. Men can do that.

— Isn't being here part of your dream, Sis?

— My marrying Angel was more like a deal, Abraham, than a dream. Unlike you, I'm locked in on all sides. You have no restrictions on your movements, so go as soon as you can. I think you'll be able to walk a little tomorrow, holding onto the back of a chair.

CHAPTER 21

Mt Keira

The relentless summer wears on. Still no rain since the downpour that ruined the Clares. There are a couple of dry lightning storms that spark bushfires on the escarpment which teams of men finally beat out. Fairy Creek is so low they have to close the sluice gates on the north side, Puckey's side. Eliza is making a name for herself as a very fine seamstress and has orders from three more ladies. Mary has commissioned a new frock from her for Polly for the Sunday School Anniversary; and Eliza has begun teaching Sunday School, Year One girls which, of course, includes Polly. She has settled into a routine at Farnham: after breakfast she does most of her sewing work before it gets too hot; after dinner she walks around to Cliff Road and spends the afternoon with Mary and Polly. Angel is usually off with Rover; Abraham's at work at the grocer's; and Jack doesn't get home until evening. Mary has a summer cold that's hanging on, a little dry cough.

— You ought to see the doctor about that cough.

— It's nothing, Eliza, just bronchitis. I've had it before. Why don't you take Polly to Stuart Park this afternoon? The walking seems to make me cough more.

— Yes, and I've noticed talking makes you hoarse as well.

— Aunty 'Liza, are you going to Picnic Day?

Mary explains.

— It's official title is the Wollongong Founders' Day Annual Picnic.

— I don't know. Uncle Angel may not want to go, darling.

— But he *has* to go. Everybody goes. We have games and races and an enormous feast under the trees.

Eliza looks over at Mary and raises her eyebrows.

— Every year, on top of Mt Keira. It's always cool and breezy up there no matter how hot it is down below. It's our biggest event of the year. People take up everything they need: trestle tables, streamers strung between trees, the lot. Every family makes up a basket or hamper, and we all share the food and drink laid out on the tables. Most of the people walk up the road while the oldies and the supplies drive up. Run along and get your hat, Polly. Tell me, Eliza, has Angel found anything to do yet?

— I don't think he's even looking, Mary, to tell you the truth. We seem to have become strangers. He keeps almost entirely to himself and doesn't share anything with me, not his hopes, his plans, you know what I mean? And (I haven't told this to anyone else), he's not himself in his sleep. He moans and whimpers and calls out, shouts; but I've never told him.

— I shouldn't, if I were you. That's like a release for his troubles. If you tell him, who knows what he might do? You're not afraid of him, are you?

Polly comes running up with a very strangely-tied hat.

— I tied the bow all by myself. It was easy as winking.

— Well aren't you just the cleverest little girl in Wollongong? Off we go.

— Bye-bye, Mama.

When Eliza gets back to Farnham, Angel is already home, almost as if he's waiting for her. He demands.

— Where have you been?

— I took Polly to Stuart Park. She's such a little …

— You spend entirely too much time at Jack Turville's.

— That's because they're our best friends. Besides, Mary has a cold. That's why I took Polly by myself today.

— He's certainly not *my* best friend. He and he alone is the sole cause of my ruin. My whole life is at loose ends because of him.

— Angel, you can't blame Jack for the drought and the storm.

— Now you're taking *his* side, defending him. I don't want you going over there any more. You're altogether too familiar with him, Eliza. I've seen the way he looks at you. You're *my* wife and you'll spend your time here so I can keep an eye on you.

— But what about Mary? And Polly?

— I'm sure they'll manage to get along without you.

— They've invited us for Christmas!

— Well, I'm not going, and neither are you.

— What will I to tell Mary?

— You'll think of something.

— What about Church activities, and the Picnic?

— We'll limit ourselves to the minimum social interaction with them at public functions. And I don't want them coming here, either.

I've really never thought of Jack as anything but Angel's good and lifelong friend. So Angel thinks Jack notices me? What an absurd notion. Jack has Mary and Polly, and loves them dearly. I love them dearly, too, and wouldn't dream of doing anything to hurt them. Jack's more like a brother to me; and he saved my life! He's done more for me as a friend than Angel has ever done as a husband. Angel must be jealous of Jack! As well, Jack's helped us with the farm and looked after Abraham. In a way he's taken over Angel's responsibilities. Yes, he's jealous of him, and now my first Christmas in New South Wales is ruined.

January in Australia is hot, and the long-awaited day of the Founders' Day Picnic is typical summer — hot enough for cicadas to start droning mid-morning, and for perspiration to begin trickling down your back under a high collar by eleven. Town folk and country folk alike look forward to Picnic Day, a local holiday. The women have been baking for a week. There'll be all kinds of cold meat and sweet pies and tarts, cakes, biscuits, fresh and preserved fruit, jellies, trifles, and cordials: anything that can be packed and is portable. Mrs Edwards has been making fruit buns, iced, with glacé fruit and cherries on top, her specialty. Eliza offers to help.

— Let me think: six boarders and myself. If you can gather up seven of everything we'll need, knives, forks, spoons, glasses, plates, serviettes, rugs to sit on, etc. that would let me concentrate on the food.

Angel is pacing up and down on the verandah, muttering.

— Bloody waste of time. Picnics! I'm going for a walk. I'll see you later.

— Angel, promise me you'll come.

He was morose and moody on the farm. Now there are times, like these, when he sulks, and won't even talk to me.

The whole town makes their way towards the mountain, and the road is clogged with vehicles. There's even a wagon collision where one tried to get past a slower-moving one and clipped the rear end. The other traffic is slowed and has to wind around them. Mrs Edwards has chosen to take her wagon, and drives with Eliza beside her as Angel had not returned by the time they left; the other boarders sit behind, packed in with the hampers, food, rugs, and table cloths, or rather, the food was packed under and around the boarders. They drive up past Keira Cottage but Eliza cannot bring herself to look, then past the entrance to the mine and eventually reach a large relatively clear space before the road to the summit begins. Here people are parking their vehicles and walking up the steep track to make it easier for the horses. Drivers transfer their hampers and boxes to completely fill other wagons and carts that will carry a full load to the top. It's like a staging place for an expedition, a base camp for the assault on Mt Keira a thousand or more feet above them.

The noise of the cicadas is deafening. Their song reverberates so loudly it seems to Eliza it's her ears that are ringing and not the sound on the air all around her. She jumps down, and so do the other passengers. They help transfer more picnic paraphernalia onto Mrs Edwards' wagon before they, too, start the steep climb on foot. Eliza hears a squeal.

— Aunty 'Liza! Aunty 'Liza!

The Turvilles have just reached the drop-off area. Jack slips down.

— It's a great day for the picnic, Eliza.

— It's awfully hot.

— It'll be a lot more pleasant up the top.

— Hello, Polly. How have you been?

— Good. Are you coming up with us?

— No, darling, I'm walking. Mary! Abraham! Lovely day! How's the leg?

— It's coming real well but Jack and Mary won't let me walk up.

— Look what I've got, Aunty Liza!

— What's that, Polly?

Polly opens a shoe box and shows her.

— Oh!

— I've got two Green Grocers, a Yellow Monday and a Black Prince.

— Oh, my goodness. What *are* they?

— They're cicadas. They have prickly legs. Here, let this Green Grocer walk on the back of your hand.

Eliza pulls back and grimaces. Mary interjects.

— They're perfectly harmless, Eliza. All the children collect them at this time of year. It walks very slowly.

Eliza extends her hand tentatively and Polly picks up a green cicada just in front of its wings while it continues to walk in the air, and puts it on Eliza's hand. She draws in a shriek as the three inch long insect slowly walks across, pricking the back of her hand with its six stick-like feet.

— Ah! Take it off!

Mary chuckles.

— The Black Princes are the rarest. They also make the loudest sound.

— I want to go up with Aunty 'Liza.

— No, you and Abraham will drive up with me. You have to save your strength for the races.

— I brought the Hessian bags from the store for the sack races.

— Good for you, Abraham.

— Jack! We're off now. You look after Eliza.

— Righty-oh love. Bye!

— Bye, Daddy. See you up there.

— Well, my girl, I suppose we'd better get going.

Jack has to almost shout. Here in the thick bush at the base of the mountain the cicadas' shrill drone drowns out most other sounds. Eliza wipes her brow with her wrist. She's glad she wore the light hat. She shivers: she can still feel the cicada's feet on her hand. She and Jack fall into stride beside one another on the rutted dirt road that cuts into the flank of the mountain in sharp hairpin bends. Eliza shakes her head as her boots kick up the dust.

— We seem to be going so far in one direction and then so far back in the other. It doesn't seem as if we're getting any higher.

— I know a quicker way but it's a lot steeper.

— You do?

— Yes. I've scouted Mt Keira for timber. We can climb up the face of it and come out on the road near the top but I don't know how you'll do in those skirts.

— I can tuck my waist up a bit. Let's do it, Jack. Anything quicker is better than these long endless bends.

— You're game?

— Game as Ned Kelly.

— In that case, instead of turning at the next bend we'll go straight ahead into the bush and then start the climb.

Eliza is excited by the challenge. Jack leads the way, starting at an uphill angle. It isn't too bad going: they are able to get leverage and pull themselves up by grabbing branches and young tree trunks, carefully placing their feet, one by one, on large protruding rocks, and hauling themselves up. After scrambling up for about twenty minutes, Jack braces his foot against the base of a trunk and waits for Eliza to reach the lower rock, where she pauses.

They have left the full roar of the cicadas below in the dense heat of the bush, and have now reached the big timber — tall gums with smooth grey or orange bark and branching limbs, long leaves waving at their drooping ends, The ground is littered with dry fallen leaves and Eliza can smell the tangy bush smells of eucalyptus, menthol and animals which come on the cooler updrafts; as do the calls of faraway birds which now can be heard distinct from the cicadas. Jack cocks his head to one side.

— Hear them? Bell birds and whip birds:
'And softer than slumber and sweeter than singing
The notes of the bell birds are running and ringing'.
That's from a famous poem by Henry Kendall. Here, let me help you up this big rock. Take my hand. This will be a big jump.

He levers her up to where he is braced but his pull is so powerful she keeps going forward until she bumps into his chest. *The power in that grip! His sheer strength. I feel a jolt going through me.* She takes a step back, nearly losing her balance. He steadies her, still holding her hand.

— Careful, there. Here, lean against this tree and get your breath.

Why don't I pull my hand away? I like him holding it. He's releasing his grip now that I'm steady. Here we are, face to face on the side of this mountain, and his eyes are smiling at me, yet it seems the most normal thing in the world. The warmth of his hand is still creeping up my arm. Now I feel my cheeks getting warm.

She swallows.

— So you really know this mountain like, um, the back of your hand?

She looks down at her small hand compared to his big ones, not used to dainty china teacups, then looks back into those piercing blue eyes. He gently pats the back of her hand, and smiles slowly.

— Like the back of my hand.

*My heart is beating so fast, but not from the climb. There's something in the way he smiles at me. Why do I feel all light and flustery? Because this is what I want; it's what a woman wants, needs: a man's touch and understanding. It feels so right, as if it's meant to be; as if **he** is the one who is meant to have me and hold me, not Angel. I wish Jack would feel the same as I feel; on the other hand I hope he doesn't. I don't want him to overstep the bounds. We're both married and I know he loves Mary and little Polly. Even though my own marriage is a hollow sham, I can't jeopardize their happiness. It's my fault: I agreed to go through with it for Tess' sake. But what a contrast! I could fall into Jack's arms right now, give him the opportunity to kiss me if he wanted to but the consequences would be disastrous. Now he's leaning even closer.*

— Caught your breath yet?

Tears of hopelessness roll down her cheeks.

— I knew it would be too much for you.

— No, no, it isn't that. I just needed a little rest. We must push on.

— Here, give me your hand and I'll help you up the steepest part.

*When he touches me I feel all tingly and excited, hot and jumpy at once but I can't break up a marriage, not **their** marriage. He thrills me but I mustn't let it show. He mustn't know how I feel, nor Mary, or I would be betraying their loyalty. Too many lives are at stake; too many lives would be ruined. At least I've seen what true love is like, even though I can never have it: the way Jack treats Mary, how he puts her first, how he cares.*

— Jack, do you know Angel well?

— Yes. Well, I thought I did. At school we were inseparable. Doesn't say much nowadays, does he?

— I think he dwells on the past a lot. You know the reason I married him was for my sister's sake?

— Your sister?

— Didn't you know Tess was married to Angel before?

— Yes, but I had no idea she was your sister.

— It was all very tragic. Before she died, she made Angel promise to marry me. He came courting, and I was the bargaining chip. If I married him then he would look after my mother and my little brothers and sisters, financially, that is. I did it for my family, really. He's renting a house in Emminster for them. I didn't want to marry him. It was a marriage of convenience on my part but I honestly believed love would grow with time.

— That's too bad. He's a funny fish.

— Now he keeps to himself a lot. The flood really affected him. It didn't entirely destroy him financially although it seems to have destroyed him as a person. It's as if *he's* been wiped out, not the farm. I've tried to tell him, 'Look, we've got each other, and our whole lives ahead of us', but he doesn't seem to listen, just mulls it over and over, keeps dwelling on it.

— If I can do anything to help.

— I think that's part of the problem. He sees you as being so successful, and himself as a failure. I think he even blames you for luring him to New South Wales. I know you didn't; but that's the way he sees it. He's too proud to take any help. I think he's going to pieces, Jack. He won't even talk with the doctor. I have to keep very quiet or he snaps my head off. I've even contemplated the unthinkable — leaving him. I could make my own way as a teacher or governess or even a dressmaker but I'd never make enough to pay the rent on the cottage in Emminster. So that's not an option.

— Poor girl.

They are up very high now.

— Don't look down, Eliza, until I tell you.

— In Devon I was afraid of heights but I'm not afraid with you.

The sheer wall below the flat-topped summit rises almost vertically above them. Jack leads her to a long narrow ledge.

— We'll sit here for a minute to rest. Now you can look.

— Oh! Jack!

She catches her breath.

— Now there's a true bird's eye view for you.

A breeze is rising through the scented trees, cooling as it comes, wafting sweet and pleasant against their faces, warm from the climb. They gaze down on the Illawarra coast, the tiny trees, and the pencil-thin white coastal road winding from left to right below them. The wind also carries the faint low boom of the waves as they break on the strip of sand, wrinkled like bacon rind against the shimmering turquoise sea.

— What a view, Jack! You'd have to go a long way to find something as spectacular as this. Look, you can see Wollongong and the Five Islands.

— And Bulli, too, to the left. We'd best get going. If we follow this ledge it will connect with the summit road, and we still might be amongst the first on top. On to the picnic!

— Daddy! Daddy! Aunty 'Liza! We're going to have the races now.

— I'd better find those sacks Abraham brought.

— They're over there, on Mama's cart.

Eliza hurries over to the judge's table.

— There you are, Mrs Clare. Good. The sacks. And did you bring stockings for the three-legged race?

— Yes, and oranges for the orange race. We can use hats for each team to throw their oranges into.

The official blows his whistle.

— Everyone line up over here for the orange race heats!

The men have been busy setting up the trestle tables, and Mrs Edwards and a few other ladies have brought bed sheets for table cloths. The white sheets blow in the breeze and are quickly loaded down with scores of platters that are placed on them as, one by one, the vehicles are unloaded. Families and groups of friends spread their rugs and blankets on the ground in the shade, and unpack plates and utensils.

Eliza is busy with the races, sometimes holding the strand of wool, the finish line, while at others she is responsible for noting who comes second, presenting them with a red rosette ribbon which she pins on. She's very proud of Polly when she pins her second red one on. Polly finishes her races with one blue ribbon, a first, and the two red ones.

— Go over and show Mummy. Tell her Aunt Eliza said you're a champ.

One of the heats of the orange race has to be re-run. As the participants race back and forth picking up oranges, a familiar figure comes bounding into the race area, carries off one of the evenly-spaced oranges in his mouth, and brings it to Eliza.

— Rover! Here, boy! Put it down, Rover!

— You can be spared now, Mrs Clare. I see your husband has arrived.

Eliza goes over to the road.

— I'm glad to see you're making yourself useful, Eliza.

— Hello, Angel. Did you walk all the way from Wollongong?

— Yes, I enjoy a good walk, although I think Rover's worn out. He's covered four times the distance I have, running into the bush chasing rabbits and other creatures.

— We'll have to go over him for ticks when we get home. They're particularly troublesome for long-haired dogs.

— And hard to find.

— Come and get a drink, Angel. Mrs Edwards' group is over there under the Scribbly Gum.

Angel goes off and joins a group of men smoking. Others have started a game of football but he's not the roughhousing type. *I hope he can talk himself into a job although I think he's convinced himself he's too sick to work. I know he forbade me from seeing the Turvilles but this is a social situation. He can't dictate who I associate with.* She drops down beside Mary on the rug.

— You've been busy ever since you got up here, Eliza.

— I know. I didn't realize how tired I am. I just want to tell you Angel doesn't want me visiting you any more. He . . .

Polly runs over to them.

— What's that you've got, Poll?

— It's a all-day sucker, Mama.

— It's bigger than your face. You'll spoil your lunch.

— No I won't. Are you coming to watch Daddy in the running race?

— No, Mummy's going to rest here. You go over and watch. I'll talk to Aunt Eliza.

Mary starts coughing. Her face is flushed and it seems to Eliza she is thinner than when she last saw her.

— That cold still hanging on, Mary?

She nods, between coughing spasms.

— I think it's because the air's rarer up here, thinner, or maybe it's the bush smells.

She has another coughing spasm and holds a hanky to her mouth. When the coughing subsides, Eliza's heart stops. She notices bright red spots on Mary's hanky.

— Mary, I think you should see a doctor about that cough. Look at your hanky.

— That happens. I think I strain too much when I'm coughing and rupture a little blood vessel. I'm all right. It's the sea air that's the cure. Jack! You're wearing a blue rosette.

— Fifty yard dash, Mary. I'm still the Illawarra champion. Where did Polly go?

— She's with Muriel Harris. Stella's looking after them.

Eliza stands up to go.

— Congratulations, Jack. I think it's almost time for eats. I'd better get back to Mrs Edwards' group. Bye-bye, Mary, we'll talk again, and thanks again for taking such good care of Abraham.

— Don't mention it, my dear.

Eliza walks up and down the trestle tables, selecting the best that Wollongong can provide. Her favourite is the crunchy palm leaf pastries with their passionfruit icing. After she finishes lunch, she goes back for a second palm leaf which crumbles all over her bodice every time she takes a bite. Then she strolls along a cleared path under the long-leafed gums towards a wooden barricade at the edge of the lookout with the word "DANGER' carved in it. Casuarina pines, which give a more open shade, mix with the gums overhead. When she reaches the overlook a blast of cool ocean air sweeps against her face: bracing, compared to the still heat below.

The lighthouse stands out, white against the blue sea, and she can follow the road leading up the mountain. On the left she's able to pick out Stuart Park and Fairy Creek running into the sea. Over to her right is a big body of water, Lake Illawarra. She can hear the sound of whips cracking, the whip birds, and others sounding like bells, and she thinks of Jack.

— Mmmmm.

She leans on the barricade filling her lungs with huge breaths of eucalypt smells. *What a tumultuous day! I can still feel Jack's grip although he's eating picnic lunch with his family. I'm really at peace for the first time because now I know what true love would be like. There's nothing wrong with me loving Jack secretly like I love Mary and Polly. I haven't lost Jack to Mary: I've found him on a different level and can keep him in my heart.* Her inner happiness breaks into a smile and, closing her eyes, she puts her head back so the wind blows her auburn hair off her face, and remembers Wordsworth.

> 'Truths that wake
> To perish never;
> Which neither listlessness, nor mad endeavour,
> Nor man, nor Boy,
> Nor all that is at enmity with joy,
> Can utterly abolish or destroy.'

CHAPTER 22

SOUTHERLY BUSTER

The heat doesn't break. The humidity is awful. For two days after the picnic it is very muggy and close. Eliza's clothes stick to her skin. Everything is warm: the wooden floor, her hair brush, dishes. It's too hot to sew. The material sticks to her fingers, and the needle slips through them. Mrs Edwards makes some chocolate biscuits which melt to the bottom of the jar, and clothes Eliza hangs on the line to dry are just as wet at four in the afternoon when she goes to take them in as when she hung them out. It's no use putting a damp hanky on your forehead or wrists as they are already wet with perspiration. *These Australians drink hot tea to get cool! That only makes me hotter. It's a good thing it's summer holidays. No child could concentrate in school in weather like this.* The only place where it's more bearable is on the beach; not the beach itself, the sand is burning hot but right at the water's edge; and even there, the water is warm.

Everyone is irritable and edgy, and Angel even more so. If he stays in their room, he paces, or drums his fingers on the table, or taps his hand on his thigh and grits his teeth in a restrained way, and feels compelled to walk off his nervous energy in the heat. Eliza fears he'll get sunstroke. Electricity is in the air. You can feel it. Word is the heat will have to break soon. There's never been a hot spell like this before. By three o'clock it's become very still, and the sky in the south has turned purply-black. Eliza is at Mary's having afternoon tea on the verandah with Stella from next door.

— Here comes the storm. Looks like we're in for a biggy. There's forked lightning over Mt Kembla to the south. It won't be long before it hits us.

— A Southerly Buster.

— That's right, Eliza. You're picking up the language.

— You have such extreme weather here in New South Wales. I've never experienced anything like the storm that forced us off the farm.

— 'I love a sunburnt country, a land of sweeping plains,
Of ragged mountain ranges, of droughts and flooding rains.
I love her far horizons; I love her jewelled sea;
Her beauty and her terror, the wide brown land for me.'

— I haven't heard that before, Stella.
— That's "My Country" by Dorothea MacKellar, an Australian poet.
— It's a true description. Look! In the last few minutes, how dark it's become. I just saw a flash over Mt Keira. You can feel the static in the air. You'd better get home, Eliza. I don't like the look of those clouds.
— Yes, I think I'd best be getting back to Farnham, and I have to go into the post office on my way home.
— You'd better go right now if you want to stay dry or the storm will catch up with you.
— Good-bye, ladies, and thanks for the tea, Mary. Bye-bye Polly. It's too hot for a hug, darling; just a little peck on the cheek.

The town of Wollongong closes down early. By four the wind is gusting so fiercely Eliza is nearly lifted off her feet, and by the time she arrives home Mrs Edwards has had to light the lamps.

— Oh, thank goodness you're back. It's not a good time to be outdoors. Mr Clare isn't with you?
— No.
— I hope he has the sense to take shelter. These storms can be very destructive.
— What's that noise — like boulders falling on the roof?
— It's started hailing; big hail, too, by the sound of it. It's a good thing most of my windows are sheltered by verandahs.

There's a loud bang, the sound of shattering glass, and a rush of cool air in the stifling house.

— The front door!

The noise on the roof is now too loud for conversation and Eliza goes to their room. A flash of lightning, followed almost immediately by a crack of thunder, makes her jump. This is followed by lightning and thunder in rapid succession. Suddenly, Angel bursts in from their verandah and a cowering Rover follows. He quickly shuts the door, and Rover shakes hail the size of grapes all over the room. It's impossible to speak, the noise of the hailstones on the iron roof is so loud; almost impossible to think. Eliza pulls the curtain aside a little, and though she flinches every time there's a vivid flash, expecting the almost simultaneous thunder, she can see the hail bouncing high off the lawn which by now is all white. She beckons Angel to come and have a look but he is struggling out of his wet clothes. She gives him a towel to dry off then rubs down Rover who has to be dragged out from under the bed.

— Poor boy. You don't like the noise, do you?

The wind howls in gusts and the clattering noise on the verandah roof turns deeper. As the hail subsides, the wild wind drives heavy rain before it, now impossible to see through in the darkened afternoon. Eliza hears heavy hoof beats and thinks she sees a coach racing up the street. She hears men's shouts and then more hoof beats. *Why would people go out in such a storm? It's not the D'Urberville coach again? So far it's been true to legend: it brought disaster. That must make me a true D'Urberville, whatever implications that might have.* Wave after wave of unrelenting rain sweeps over the wide verandah, even wetting down their window and door. There's a knock on the hall door, the inside door.

— Would you like to come into the parlour? I've made a pot of tea.

— Thank you, Mrs Edwards, we'll be right there.

— You can go if you want to but I'm not going to huddle with a lot of frightened people. Is that letter for me?

— Yes. It's from Emminster.

— You go off and socialize. I'll be content with my news, and Rover.

The dog picks up his ears at the mention of his name.

— He's the best companion I have. You understand me, don't you, boy?

Mrs Edwards has a large teapot with an even larger tea cosy on her round table with one of the starched table cloths Eliza admires. Mrs Edwards did all the fancy work on it herself, cut work, too; and the scalloped edge is daintily crocheted, with serviettes to match. Two of the other boarders have made it home early and are helping themselves to the savouries: Sao biscuits with a slice of peppered tomato; others with cheese.

— Mr Clare not joining us?

— No. He's reading a letter from home. He may come later.

I don't like lying. I've been doing it quite a bit lately — formulating logical excuses for Angel's illogical behaviour. The hot tea is relaxing but Eliza still twitches every time there's a flash, once nearly jumping the teacup clean out of the saucer. Mrs Edwards comments.

— It's not the worst storm we've had since I've been in Wollongong.

Still, it's pretty severe. I lost my husband after a storm just like this back in '86. He was drowned in Fairy Creek. Have some more fruit cake, dear. It's made to be eaten.

How can anyone drown in a creek that's no more than ankle deep? Now the wind increases, and blows the rain horizontally. There's a great sucking moan coming from the front hall from the gaping panels in the front door where the stippled glass had been. Above that, they hear a banging on the door, and a voice, shouting.

— Hullo?! Hullo?!

They follow Mrs Edwards to the door, and through the panels see a man in a sou'wester with water running off him as if he's been under a waterfall. He shouts through the gap.

— There's a flood in the town. The creek's come up suddenly and it's overflowing. It's flooding yards, and in some cases the water's running right through the houses, in one door and out the other. Are there any able men here who can help to rescue people? Trees are down all over the place, and blocking roads. The town's a mess.

— I'll go.

— Me too.

The two boarders who've come home early run to get their Mackintoshes and Wellington boots. The man at the door continues to brief them.

— There's chairs and beds and tables and food and clothing and brooms all swirled up together rushing down the back streets.

— I have two hurricane lamps you can take.

— Good name for them. Thank you, Ma'am.

— I'll go and get my husband.

Eliza runs down the hall to their room.

— Angel! They need you. They need every man ...Angel?

She looks around. He isn't there. Neither is Rover. She opens the verandah door and nearly gets blown back into the room.

— Are you out here, Angel?

There's no sign of him or the dog. Puzzled, she goes back into the hall.

— My husband's gone out again in the storm. I can't understand why.

— He's probably gone to help, Ma'am. Come on, fellas. I have a wagon. It'll be slow going around those fallen trees.

They rumble off. Eliza returns to their room. *Why? Why has he gone out? And in this weather!* The rain has not let up now for about an hour and a half. She notices the wind has died down to gusts, and now the rain is coming straight down. So much rain! And it's still very heavy. Maybe this is the end of the drought, at last. She starts to tidy up the room where Angel has left his wet clothes when she sees a letter on the bed. He is always so fastidious about his mail, so private. She wouldn't dare open his mail, and he always carefully folds his letters after reading them, returning them to their envelopes and putting them on the table in two piles: those he would deal with now and those he would deal with later. *If I happen to nudge the piles when I'm dusting, he accuses me of snooping through his mail when he isn't looking: 'I deal with the bills. You have no interest in going through my mail.' I've even giving up asking after his parents when he receives news from home. 'What's it to you?' he snaps when I inquire. 'I was just asking.' Then he turns on me, accusingly, 'Well, you can stop your prying by not asking.' Talk about isolation! I would have written to them, myself, but he would fly off the handle if he found out. I can't even let Mother know of the sorry state of our marriage as she is likely to mention it to the Clares (knowing Mother and her garrulous tongue). All I've been able to do is to write roundabout general questions in my letters home, such as, 'Have you seen the Clares lately?'*

Now here is a letter postmarked 'Emminster' scattered wide-open on the bed. I mustn't touch it because Angel will think I've read it; but it's so unlike him to be untidy like that, especially in relation to personal post.

She sidles round the end of the bed and brings a table lamp over, holding it above the letter while she tries to read the sloping open handwriting.

' …died peacefully in her sleep, you need have no concern on that score. I know you will grieve the loss of your mother but it is a lot more complicated. There are many things you did not need to know; in fact, you need never have known, and life would have gone on at its regular pace. Circumstances decreed otherwise. You will have to return to England immediately by the first ship. I know you will question my request to return immediately, to interrupt your life so soon after getting on your feet but I beg you to come …' Here the first page finishes.

Eliza looks around furtively lest Angel should return and find her reading his private letter. She quickly lifts the page to read more.

'…home at once. The one thing I had hoped to keep from you is the fact that your mother, as you knew her, was not your real mother, the one who gave birth to you. Your future depends on your knowing your past. I cannot tell you any more in a letter. You *must* come home,

Your loving father,
James Clare.'

Eliza drops the sheet of paper she's holding, and stands stock-still with the lamp in her hand, as it flutters down onto the bed. *Not his real mother?*

And now she's dead. Who was she? And who is, or was, his real mother? And why does it matter?

Oh, my goodness. He must have read this and gone into shock and run out into the storm, Rover with him; the same way he always goes out alone to mull over a problem. He's probably hardly aware of the storm. He's too concentrated on the storm within.

She goes and finds Mrs Edwards.

— My husband's not here, or the dog. I fear he's gone out wandering in the storm. He received some bad news from home.

— Oh, I'm sorry. What happened?

Eliza is quick to cover her slip.

— I don't know exactly. There's a letter on the bed. What should we do?

— There's really nothing you can do except wait until he comes back. It sounds like the storm's beginning to ease up but night's coming on. He knows his way around and he has that lovely retriever with him to keep him out of harm's way. He's come back late before, hasn't he?

— Yes, not at night, though.

— I'll keep his tea hot for him and the kettle on the boil so he can have something nourishing when he gets in. There's really no need to worry.

— Thank you very much, Mrs Edwards.

— I'm getting our tea ready now, even though it's just you and me tonight in the dining room.

The hours tick by: 7 p.m., 8 p.m., 9 p.m. By now Eliza is getting quite anxious. Even Mrs Edwards is a little uneasy. There is no one to go and look for Angel as all the able-bodied men are helping with the rescue and clean-up efforts in town.

— I'm sure he's fallen in with a group of helpers, Eliza. They'll all come in very late, hungry and exhausted. You can help me make up some sandwiches.

It is nearly 1 a.m. when they hear a vehicle pull up and footsteps on the verandah, and all of Mrs Edwards' boarders wearily stump in; all, that is, except Angel Clare.

— Is Mr Clare not with you?

— No, we haven't seen him all night.

— Maybe he's staying with his friends, Eliza.

I know that's not the case. Angel doesn't have any friends, except Jack, and he certainly wouldn't seek refuge there. Also, it's so close to home. Maybe he's twisted his ankle in the dark; maybe a tree fell on him; or maybe he's just really upset and will wander until the sun comes up. If that's the case and we send out a search party, I'll really cop it. 'No news is good news', they say. She moves the letter off the coverlet, opens the window to let the lovely cool air flood the room, and goes to sleep to the sounds of dripping: water off the roof; droplets off the trees — drop, drip, drop, drip, drop, drip, drip ....

CHAPTER 23

THE SEARCH

She wakes with a start. It's morning, a clear, blue, sunny morning. And there is still no Angel. Now she is seriously worried. Mrs Edwards insists she eat breakfast, then she walks over to Cliff Road. Even though Angel would be against it, she only has Jack to turn to for help. When she arrives she finds that Jack hasn't come home yet either. Mary advises.

— It's too early to worry yet, Eliza. It was a terrible storm and the volunteers are still out there. I'm making sandwiches and billies of tea to take to the men cleaning up. You can help me load up.

All this activity helps dispel Eliza's doubts and soon she, Mary and Polly set out on their mercy mission. Trees and telegraph poles are down and there are branches all over the streets. The flooded creek has deposited all kinds of debris and household detritus where the force left it. There is a bicycle wrapped around a post box, shoes against fences, and kitchen chairs upside down in the mud in the middle of the street. The sound of a woman wailing cuts through the air.

They find groups of volunteers, some still using pickaxes to dig channels through front gardens so water can drain out of the houses. Others are clearing debris from the middle of the streets and placing it on the sides so vehicles can pass: tables, branches, a rocking horse, mats, bedding; the list goes on. Whatever once stood in, or filled, the inside of a house is now lying strewn outside it, as if the house has haemorrhaged its contents.

They drive up Crown Street. Some store owners are out early, sweeping up glass and dismantling tattered awnings. A lot have handwritten notices, 'Closed for Business' propped against their doors. On Keira Street they finally find Jack and Abraham.

— You two look exhausted. We've brought you tea and sandwiches.

— Is the house all right, Mary?

— Yes, no structural damage. The beds and table and chairs blew off the verandah and down into the garden, and the garden is ruined; but we're safe, aren't we, Poll?

— I stayed up real late, Daddy. Me and Mama hugged in the kitchen.

Mary looks sheepish.

— She needed comforting.

Everyone laughs.

— You haven't seen Angel, have you, Jack?

— He's not helping with a volunteer group?

— I don't think so. He got some bad news in a letter from home and went out with Rover in the storm early on, and never came home at all last night.

— Umm. I could leave here and go and look for him. How about you, Abe? We've nearly finished. Do you realize that every single window here on Keira Street blew out last night? There's glass everywhere. The rain then blew into the businesses and ruined everything. It was a corker of a storm, wasn't it?

— Can I come with you, Jack?

— I think it's better that you wait at Seafoam with my girls, Eliza. That tea really hits the spot, my love.

He gives Mary a buss on the cheek then he and Abraham take the horse and cart and the rest of the tea and sandwiches, and start off.

— In case we meet old Angel. He'll be starving.

Jack and Abraham return about three in the afternoon. Though they've criss-crossed the town, they've seen no sign of Angel. After checking the hospital, they finally went to the police station to report him missing. The police intend to get up a search party, and told Jack and Abraham to go home and get some sleep. They've now been up for more than thirty hours. It's a good thing the horse knows the way home as they are beginning to nod off as they clop up Cliff Road. When they wearily climb down, Jack apologises.

— We tried our best, Eliza. We looked everywhere.

The two of them fall onto their makeshift beds on the floor in their muddy clothes and are asleep before Mary and Eliza can remove their boots.

A policeman calls round to Seafoam to interview Eliza. He particularly wants to know when she last saw Angel and why he had mysteriously disappeared into the storm. *I don't want to tell him Angel's private business.*

What if he suddenly walks in and finds out the whole town knows about his mother? I could tell him half of it, which is still the truth.

— He received a letter from his father in England informing him his mother had died, and that he should return to England immediately.

— He's probably left for Sydney, Ma'am. He may not be missing at all. He may just be in a hurry to get a ship.

— He didn't take any clothes, or any of his belongings. And his dog is with him.

— Ah! Dog, you say?

— Yes, a long-haired golden retriever called Rover. He goes with him everywhere. I thought if something had happened to Angel, Rover would have come home.

— By 'home' you mean Mrs Edwards', Farnham?

— Yes.

— Is there any particular route the gent takes, like a regular route?

— He often heads up the beach from Stuart Park.

— That's very helpful, Ma'am. We have a party out looking for him now and I'll tell them where to concentrate their search, and look for the dog, too. No need to worry at this stage. The dog might lead us to Mr Clare. We'll also telegraph Sydney to check on all passengers that have bought passage on out-going ships. Don't worry. We'll find him. Are you staying here, or at Farnham?

— I think I should get back to Farnham.

Mary breaks in.

— Nonsense, Eliza. Stay with us until you hear from him. Mrs Edwards can always send word. She knows where you are, and now you do too, Constable.

Around 6 p.m. another policeman comes and informs them Rover has been found sitting on the edge of the rocks at Stuart Park that lead down to Fairy Creek where it crosses the beach to merge with the ocean. Eliza accompanies the policeman to the spot where Rover is sitting, alert and whining. He doesn't move from his position when Eliza arrives, just looks round at her then back over the wide mouth of the creek straight ahead, and whines more. Eliza kneels down beside him and strokes him.

— Rover! What happened! Where is he?

The dog looks across the creek and whines.

— I think he came along here, by the way Rover is acting.

— We'll get a search party up here first thing in the morning. Looks like the creek's gone down a bit.

— Thank you, Officer. I'll be back in the morning too. Come on, Rover. We're going home.

Rover doesn't move; won't budge; just keeps on keenly looking across Fairy Creek to the sand dune on the other side, then out to sea.

Eliza accepts Mary's invitation and spends the night at the Turvilles'. Next morning early, Jack and Abraham are up and dressed and go over to Stuart Park to help with the search. Eliza takes some food for Rover and his water dish. When she arrives, the men have already formed a human chain across Fairy Creek up near the sluice gate which had been opened the night of the storm to let the flooded creek run out across the beach. They link arms and slowly walk down the channel towards the sea, the men on the ends walking on dry land and those in the middle in knee-deep water. By the time they reach the beach, the creek is only a few inches deep. The Chief of Police is directing the search.

— He's not in the creek. You men divide up and search both banks in case he's washed up under the trees.

Rover continues his vigil. He refuses to eat but quickly laps up the water. He looks up at Eliza, back across the creek, and whines.

— I know, boy. We're looking for him.

— You men on the far bank, search the beach and sandhills on your side! We'll do the same over here! You know, Mrs Clare, I think that dog's trying to tell us something. I think he's gazing at the spot where he last saw Mr Clare. I suspect your husband attempted to walk across the creek, as you reported he often did, and didn't reckon on the force of the creek in flood. It would have been at least waist deep.

— Angel couldn't swim; and I think he had trouble with his eyes.

— Then he would have walked into it blind, thinking it was as shallow as usual, and it probably knocked him off his feet. He'd have been carried into the ocean. The surf was real high, too, with the wind up; still is. Look at those dumpers. ('Poor bugger', he thinks to himself, 'he never had a chance'.)

— Won't we find him, um, washed up on the beach somewhere?

The policeman shakes his head.

— Not necessarily. Big sharks down this way.

Eliza pulls away and grimaces.

— There'll be an inquest, Ma'am. And we still have to check the Sydney shipping. If a sweep of the beach comes up empty and he still doesn't come home, we'll call off the search. That dog knows something that we don't. If only it could talk.

Rover sits, and waits on the edge of Fairy Creek where it trickles across the beach amid the seagulls who have already returned to the recently exposed shallows. He lies with his chin on his paws staring into the waves for three days before he can be persuaded to eat. It is Polly who flings her arms around him, looks earnestly into his eyes, and begs.

— Rover, you've got to eat! Here, I brought you a biscuit. Come on, boy, won't you eat it for me?

The dog gives up his vigil and follows the little girl home.

CHAPTER 24

CHOICES

There is no news of Angel. Inquiries in Sydney turn up nothing. It's as if he has disappeared off the face of the earth. The inquest concludes what the police had long suspected: Angel must have been swept out to sea by the swollen Fairy Creek, knocked off his feet by the rush of water and carried over the sandbar into the pounding surf; the remains never having been recovered.

What now? Angel is gone, and there can't even be a funeral. How can there be a funeral and a burial without a body? I feel numb. That's exactly how Mrs Edwards' husband died; the same place. They should put up warning signs. I don't feel sad and I don't feel glad; just numb. I've passed from a non-functioning marriage through a non-marriage to something even worse, widowhood, without the central character, Angel. It's an unreal feeling. I've felt at sea ever since I married him; now I've been officially cast adrift. Was this meant to be? Could I have averted it? Was I a bad wife? Did I cause this? He wasn't there for me so many times. Should I have been there more for him? Now I have to rely more and more on myself, my inner strength — now that he's deemed to be officially missing, gone, not part of this world or my life any more. I can't believe it. Surely he'll come back, appear at any moment, just walk in. Maybe he's escaped and is swimming to South America and will turn up in my life some time in the future.

— Eliza, dear, you must get some rest. You're overwrought. Drink this nice mug of milk cocoa I made for you and go to bed. Tomorrow is another day.

Jack is all practicality. He urges her to see Angel's bank manager and have his account transferred to her. Eliza tells the Turvilles about the real contents of the letter that started the whole thing, which she had withheld from the police. They advise her to read all his other letters to see if they shed any light on the situation. She does, and they don't. One thing she learns is that Angel's parents consistently asked about her and her welfare, as Joan had told them she had lost the baby. Apparently Angel's answers never satisfied them. He never ever mentioned her.

— Poor Father C. He's such a kind man. He seems very determined that Angel should return home. There's some reason he wanted him to go at once. I hate having to write and tell him that he's now lost his son as well as his wife. That's a terrible blow to come by post. Look what it did to Angel. And *how* he died! Awful.

— I think you should go home in his place, Eliza.

— Oh no, Mary. I'm not going back. Ever. I can't. I'd never make it. No, that's definitely out.

She looks at Mary, then at Jack, then Abe. They all look seriously at her, and nod. She shakes her head.

— No. I can't. I just can't. I'll write to Mother. She can break the news to him. She's right on the doorstep.

— That's only half of it, Sis. There's something else the old preacher needed to tell him.

— Why don't *you* go home, Abe? You could carry the news.

— Sis, you're missing the point. He has something to say to Angel that's very important. You've mentioned he looks on you as part of his family, as part of Angel, so he'll need to tell *you*. You are all he has left to remind him of his son.

— I'm very sorry for him but it's not enough to make me go, and that's final.

— Think about it, Eliza.

— There's nothing to think about. I should be getting back to Farnham. Rover! Come on, boy!

Polly is chasing Rover, who is chasing her, in figures of eight all over what remains uncluttered on the lawn. Rover hears his name and barks but doesn't go to Eliza when she calls.

— He wants to play, Aunty 'Liza. Can he stay and play?

She wraps her slender little arms around the dog's neck. He licks her face, all excited.

— Woof!

— Would you like to keep him, Polly?

— Oh Aunty 'Liza, do you mean it?

— It looks like he's your dog now, Polly.

She calls into the English, Scottish & Australian Bank on her way to Farnham, and asks to speak to the manager.
— I know nothing about money.
— You should keep a book, Mrs Clare. At the top of the left hand page write 'Income', that's any money or goods you receive that 'come in', and what they are worth. On the top of the right hand page, write 'Expenditures', which is the money you spend to buy things in stores and items you exchange for other items. Do you understand?
— I - er ...
— You're a dressmaker, you told me.
— Yes.
— When you make a dress, do you always get paid for your work?
— Sometimes; and sometimes, instead of paying me, ladies may give me a pair of boots; or when we were on the farm I'd take eggs to the grocer, who might give me grain to feed the chooks.
— That's my point. The money paid to you is income, and so is the grain you exchanged for the eggs. The money you pay your landlady or the eggs ...
— I'm sorry. I don't understand.
— Let me put it this way, Mrs Clare. You have money coming in and money going out. When you have more money coming in, or saved, you are in a state of credit. This is a state you should always aspire to. That is how you become richer. When you have more money going out than you have coming in, you are in a state of debit. When Mr Clare borrowed money from this bank to buy your late property, the bank lent him the money because he convinced me (I made the decision) that the farm would eventually pay, the money he made from selling the milk and grain would eventually exceed the cost of the farm over several years. This is called a mortgage, a loan of a set amount of money for a set number of years to be paid back to the bank on a monthly basis so that the small monthly payments add up to the full amount of the loan at the end of the payback period, plus some extra money.
— Extra money?
— Yes. It's called 'interest'. Um — it's like a set fee to cover the lender's costs over that time period.
— It sounds very complicated.
— Not really, my dear. When Mr Clare came and asked the bank to

'buy back' the farm so he could have the money (we call it 'liquidating his assets'), I let him have the same value for it. He'd contributed a considerable amount of his savings initially …but in consideration that the economy is in a state of depression I had to make a decision based on the value of the property at a designated time in the future ….

What is he talking about? All these new words. I'm listening as hard as I can but I don't understand what he's talking about. What he's saying and what I'm hearing are on different levels. Until this morning I'd never heard the words 'mortgage', 'interest', 'insolvent', 'creditor'. The bank manager drones on in his teeth-gritting, patronizing way.

— …the upshot being Mr Clare came out ahead, fortunately for him, but only a little ahead. I can transfer his account to yours once probate is granted.

— I don't have a bank account, and what is probate?

— Tch, tch. Dear me. In order to open an account, I have to have proof of identity; a marriage licence, for instance.

— I don't have one.

— Do you know someone who could swear you are who you say you are?

— Mr and Mrs Turville were best man and matron of honour at our wedding.

— Well, that's it. I just need one of them to come and swear to your authenticity on the Bible in my presence. Then we can open an account in your name, issue you some cheques, give you a line of credit …

I don't want to show my ignorance that his words are way over my head again. I'll ask Jack to explain: he's a successful businessman. Fancy! Mrs Eliza Clare issuing cheques!

— You didn't explain that other word, pro …?

— Probate? That's nothing to do with us.

— Oh, I thought you said it was.

— Probate is granted when a will is proved and depends on the assets of the deceased.

— Angel didn't have a will, at least not that I know of. Not here in Australia, anyway. He had some good assets: he attended Harrowford Grammar School; he was a gentleman farmer, and his father is a clergyman of the Church of England.

— By 'assets' I mean monetary assets, what he was worth in monetary terms when he died: what he owned less what he owed. It's a legal thing. The court decides and will grant you the administration of his estate both real and personal. You may have to pay death duties and stamp duty (to the government) but when everything is settled you will become his executrix and we can transfer the moneys in his account to yours, and close his.

Complicated.

— How long will all this take?

— Not more than a few weeks if all goes well.

— Weeks!

— Oh yes. Red tape has a way of taking its own time.

— I'll bring Mr or Mrs Turville with me next time I come, to prove that I'm real.

— It's a formality, Mrs Clare.

— I know. Thank you, you've been very helpful.

— The ES&A Bank is always at your service. Would you like an advance to cover room, board, and sundries? How much do you need?

— I have no idea. My husband always took care of that.

— Well, find out from Mrs Edwards, and when I see you next we can settle on a monthly figure until probate is granted. Good-bye, Mrs Clare.

CHAPTER 25

Decisions

Eliza retraces her steps to Jack and Mary's.

— Eliza, you keep turning up like a bad penny.

— Jack, that's an awful thing to say. We love having you here, Eliza. We want you to think of Seafoam as your second home.

— I do, and I know Jack was just teasing.

She fills them in on the legal and financial developments, and finishes by saying.

— You see, it's going to take weeks, so I couldn't possibly leave Australia even if I want to, which I don't. On the other hand, I can't bring myself to write and post such terrible news.

— You must.

— Not just now. I can't.

— I still think it's best that you return to England as soon as probate is granted. It's the right thing to do.

— Well, that won't be for weeks, so please, stop pressuring me!

Mary gives Jack 'the look', and they drop the subject.

Her friends stop talking about her going home but the subject, once it enters her head, never quite leaves it. *It's all I can think about day and night. It's a thought that I dread — not breaking the news to old Mr Clare, that's inevitable. It's having to face seasickness again for weeks on end. I feel as stubborn and helpless as a child digging in its heels, and shouting, 'I don't want to!' Still, some little, prodding conscience voice, lying low, keeps reminding me, 'You know you have to go'. I have lots of excuses, even reasons, real reasons, why I needn't go back but when I do the washing, or lie in bed at night, I hear it* calmly gathering strength: 'You know you have to go'. When I walk down the street my feet tell me, too, 'You know you have to go', left, right, left, 'you know you have to go'. And in my heart of hearts I know it, as surely as a pregnant woman knows, no matter how much she wants to get out of it, sooner or later she will have to give birth. 'You know you have to go'.

Circumstances help speed the process. Not long after the inquest, probate is granted, it being a straight-forward case. Eliza is declared Angel's widow and legal heir of the deceased, and the money in his bank account is transferred into hers. Jack arranges with the minister at St Michael's to have a memorial service for Angel on Sunday, a funeral still being out of the question, and to consecrate a headstone in the graveyard in his memory. Eliza cannot concentrate during the service. Her mind is too active. *Strange. I don't feel sad for Angel, just a release from the tension between us. The minister is saying all the right words but I don't have the feelings that go with them. Now that Angel's gone I have more responsibilities. I know now how little he had in the bank here. I know nothing about how much he has in the Emminster bank, if anything; and who will pay the rent for Linden, for Mother and the children? I'm the only one who can save them now. I'm the only one who can bring the news to Father Clare and to Mother.* After the service, Eliza goes back to dinner at the Turvilles' and makes the announcement she's been formulating.

— I've decided there's nothing else for it but to go home. I knew you were right all the time. I don't want to go but you're right. I have to go. Oh, but I'm going to miss you Mary, Jack, Polly, Abe, and Australia. I love this land, the eucalypt smells, the lifestyle, the friendliness, the people; even the beach!

— I'll get the shipping news in the morning and find out when the next ships are departing for England.

— Can you also find out which ones are leaving for Western Australia, Jack?

— Abe!

— Yep. I've saved enough for my fare. We could both leave from Sydney at the same time, Sis. It's time for me to seek my fortune.

— Do you really *have* to go, Aunty 'Liza? And when are you coming back?

— I really have to go, Polly. There are people depending on me there. I don't know when I'll be back.

Probably never. Oh Polly, I'm going to miss you like my own. Why do children always cut you to the quick? 'The Lord giveth, and the Lord taketh away': giveth Jack, Mary, and Polly; taketh Angel's life, and now the Turvilles' friendship.

Next morning Jack comes back from the Land and Sea agent's office with news of the immanent departure of the Orient Line's *Orient* on Friday evening. He tells Mary.

— I bought her a ticket. She can pay me the cost of a second class cabin but I bought her a first class ticket, starboard cabin. We'll tell her second class was all sold out.

— Jack, you're a wonderful man. That was the right thing to do. If a person has to suffer seasickness, then she *should* suffer it first class. Good for you.

— I'll show Abraham the schedule. There's a coastal freighter leaving for the west on Saturday. Truth of it is, the *Orient* calls at Albany. Abe could make his way to the goldfields from there.

— In that case, let's do the same thing you did with Eliza. He could share her cabin as far as the west coast. Go and get the ticket. It'll be sad to have them go. I'm really going to miss her, Jack. She's become part of our lives, especially Polly's.

— All these relationships help strengthen us, Mary, and make us better people, even though we have to part.

— I suppose you're right.

That was a frantic week if ever there was one. The Ladies' Auxiliary put on a farewell social for the young widow and her brother at the Church. Eliza is very surprised by the huge turnout, and receives several parting gifts and mementos: serviette rings carved from Illawarra cedar, embroidered hankies, a bottle of sand from North Wollongong Beach, and a set of stereographic views of the town, with a viewer. Also, she hadn't realized just how popular Abraham has become with the young ladies. Two of them seem particularly distressed at his leaving, the young charmer!

The question is: what is to be done with all of Angel's things, his 'personal effects'? His clothes are too small for Abraham or Jack. I'll give them to the Benevolent Society; and I'll donate his farming books to the Mechanics' Institute. I'll keep his poetry books, though, and his gold watch, and his harp. He brought it all the way here and I never heard him play it once. Maybe he was never content with me: Tess said he played it hauntingly. I can't play it but old Mr Clare might like to have something of Angel's. I'll take it back to him. 'A damsel with a dulcimer...'

Eliza is so busy she has to stay up very late for the next two nights finishing up jobs, including a day dress, and a fancy frock for Polly — an extravagant concoction of pale yellow organdy ruffles with balloon sleeves and a yellow satin petticoat to wear underneath. Before she returns the sewing machine to Stella, she makes money belts for herself and Abraham to wear around the waist under clothing but he scorns his. She'd withdrawn all the money in her short-lived account from the bank and now proceeds to fold the notes and slide them into the compartments. She tries it on, and adjusts it, and decides to wear it from there on in, only carrying small amounts in her purse. *It feels good, wearing your money. At least I know where it is at all times. It makes me feel like a woman of substance.*

Mary insists they all go to the photographer's studio to have their portraits taken, with copies for Eliza to take with her, and for Mary to keep. Then there are their last days on the beach together, Mary, Eliza, Polly, and Rover, Eliza acting carefree and silly, as the girl she really is; and Mrs Edwards putting on one of her fabulous afternoon teas at the boarding house on her last day, including a trifle and her special buns. She presents Eliza with a fruitcake that she'd made specially to take on the ship with her and a card with a poem on it, composed by a friend of Mr Edwards.

> The rain is falling on the roof;
> Mt Keira's misty white.
> The timbered range to Bulli Pass
> Is almost out of sight.
> A keen wind sweeps the rain-drenched beach
> Where storm-tossed seagulls throng.
> My mind goes back on memory's wing
> To early Wollongong.

On her last day she packs and is surprised to find she has less than she came with. She gives Mrs Edwards the flat round stone she'd picked up on that Devon beach so long ago to use as a trivet or door stop or whatever she wants to use it for, and spends the evening with Mary. Jack has accompanied Abraham to the pub, his farewell appearance, and is under strict orders to bring him home sober, as Jack and Polly are going up to Sydney with them on the train in the morning. Mary's cough has not improved, so she's staying in Wollongong as the trip up and back would be too tiring.

— Promise me you'll see the doctor about that cough?

Mary gives Eliza a hug.

— As it is your parting request, I shall.

— Now I'll be able to rest easy on my way home on the ship, if I can rest at all. At least this time I don't have to take my own food with me.

— I'm sure you'll be well looked after.

Mary and Jack haven't told Eliza or Abraham about their first class tickets yet but they had seen the schedule. Mary *knows* Eliza will be well looked after, and then some.

— You have lots of ports of call on the way home so you'll have several breaks in the seasickness. That's if you *are* seasick again. It says here the *Orient* has twin screws, whatever difference that makes, and recently the ship made the entire trip in less than six weeks.

Eliza counts up

— There are eight stops between Sydney and London. That's probably at least a day in each place for me to get my land legs back, and the Red Sea will be calm.

— You might be lucky, you never know. You're leaving here at the end of summer and getting to England in the springtime. Lucky you! Daffodils and crocuses, apple and pear blossoms. I love this country but I do miss springtime.

— 'O to be in England, now that April's there'. Browning's "Home Thoughts From Abroad". Let's see: we stop in Melbourne, Adelaide, and Albany where Abraham is getting off; then across the Indian Ocean to Colombo; then up to Suez and Port Said; then Naples — 'See Naples and die'.

— I hope not.

— I might even be able to see Mt Vesuvius. They may run a side trip to Pompeii. I'd love to see the ruins. Then Gibraltar. I may get to see the Barbary apes this time. Then London. Actually, now that I *have* to go I'm sort of looking forward to it.

Eliza spends her last night in Australia at Seafoam, lulled to sleep by the sound of waves breaking, and feels very low next morning when they board the train. *I may never see Mary or Polly or Jack again. My heart still jumps when I think of Jack, and what we never had. Never see him again! Cruel. But life must go on. Mine will go on in England, Abraham's in Western Australia, for now anyway, and the Turvilles' in Wollongong. Lord knows if we'll ever meet again.* She gives Mary a long hug, waves to the well-wishers who've come to see the young widow return home, and puts her arm around Polly who's sitting beside her as the train pulls out. *Good-bye, Illawarra, for ever.*

The *Orient* is moored at Darling Harbour, and they take the trunks and luggage straight there from Central Station. Jack is in charge of arrangements so he has the tickets. Quite a crowd is boarding via the main gangway but Jack tells the driver to pull up at the one nearer the bow.

— Jack, this is the first class gangplank. We'll have to go back.

His eyes twinkle fondly.

— There's no going back for Mrs Angel Clare, or Mr Abraham Durbeyfield. This is our parting gift to you, first class. Very POSH — Starboard Home, and all that. Your cabin's on the shady side once you get to Ceylon.

— Oh, no. We couldn't.

— Too late.

He presents the tickets to the man at the foot of the gangway.

— Welcome aboard!

Abraham whistles when he sees the stateroom, with access to the deck.

— Very swish! There's a bathroom and a lounge room.

— It's a suite, Abraham, and you'll have to be on your best behaviour, and wear your best clothes, and polish your boots for the next few days.

— I don't think I'll have any trouble at all managing that, do you, Jack?

— We want you both to have a good holiday. We still have a few hours left before she sails. Let's go ashore and have a farewell lunch. Where would you like to eat, Eliza?

— Ooh, Daddy, let's go to Adams'.

— It's up to your Aunt Eliza.

— I couldn't think of anywhere better, Polly. It wouldn't be because of the Hokey Pokey?

— Adams' it is, then.

Polly is tickled pink.

— Are we going to have streamers, Daddy?

— Yes, but we'll buy them when we come back.

By five the dock is more than a bustle; it's almost frantic. Friends and relatives mill on the wharf, hang over the rails or tour the luxurious ship. Streamer sellers are making a huge profit. Polly wants at least one of every colour and has to hold them in her skirt as she picks her way up the board-strapped gangplank.

— The rails are beginning to fill up. We'd better get a good pozzy. Let's go up one deck higher.

The ship's band is playing. Half an hour before sailing, stewards go around the ship binging dinner gongs, and calling out, 'All ashore that's going ashore!' and half the people leave the rails to make their way down onto the wharf.

— Let's go, Daddy.

— We can stay a little longer. Look how many streamers have been thrown already.

Jack lifts his daughter up so she can see along the side of the ship over the railing.

— Isn't it beautiful, Aunty 'Liza? The streamers are like paper spider webs that hold the ship to the ground. Now they're playing that song I like, Daddy. What's it called?

— "The Maori Farewell".

— That's it. Here come the gong men again, Daddy. Let's go!

> 'Now is the hour that we must say good-bye.
> Soon I'll be sailing far across the sea.
> When I am gone, oh please remember me …'

At that line, Eliza has tears in her eyes. Jack puts one arm around her and the other around Abraham, and squeezes them tight. Polly clings to all three.

— Bye-bye, darling. You be a really good girl. I love you for ever.

— Bye, Aunty 'Liza. I love you for ever, too.

— Good-bye, Abraham, and keep your eyes open for that big nugget.

— I will, Jack. Thanks for everything. Bye Polly, give Rover a hug from me.

Jack gives Eliza a hug, and a kiss on the cheek.

— Go well, my girl.

She murmurs back.

— Goodbye, Jack.

And then to Polly.

— Stand opposite us when you get down to the wharf so you can catch the streamers.

The last of the visitors straggle off the ship. Eliza and Abraham aim the streamers directly at Jack who catches most of them but sometimes the wind carries them off course. In the end, he and Polly are holding fistfuls of streamer ends, as are the two on the deck above them. Their streamers are so entwined with the hundreds of others they can't be sure that they're holding the same streamer. Eliza drops a couple over the side by mistake. 7 p.m. and the band plays on. The ship's horn blares, and slowly the streamers tighten as five thousand tons slips its berth, and the *Orient* is bound for London. Streamers break; arms wave; people cry to the wind, 'Good-bye!' Familiar faces become too small to recognize. The ship noses down Port Jackson, Sydney Harbour, in the warm dusk as lights wink on in harbourside homes. If she didn't feel so sad about leaving, the sight would elate her. Eliza senses the lift and roll as they meet the Tasman swells, then turn south after passing through the Heads.

BOOK III

HOME

CHAPTER 26

THE ORIENT

Passengers with foresight or those with no one to see them off have already gone to the first sitting for dinner. Abraham now realizes just how hungry he is.

— You have to change for dinner, you know, Abraham.
— Why should I change my clothes to eat dinner?
— All the toffs do it — get dressed up. And we're in first class.
— You're not changing. Aren't you coming?
— No. I'll have something light sent in. You know my tummy.

When he comes back from the dining room he is quite angry.

— They wouldn't even talk to me. Those rich toffs in the dining room ignored me when I told them what I did for a crust. I'll eat with you in future, in here.

Eliza quickly sees that Jack and Mary's gift of a first class passage is an embarrassment not only for her but especially for Abraham. She decides then and there to let Abraham enjoy the perks until he disembarks and then she'll revisit the idea of changing to second class.

The slow rolling motion of a dip, rise, and sideways slip all at once does not make her exactly seasick but it leaves her permanently queasy. She really cannot take any solids, except in port. When the motion stops, the queasiness stops. Simple as that. The ship's doctor tells her it's all in her head. *What does he know? He's not seasick. It's my stomach that's upset, not my head.* She is able to keep down lime juice and finds it very quelling; and the stewards keep her well supplied. Also, Sao biscuits and cheese. *Costing a fortune, and can't eat a thing. What a waste!*

She spends as much time as she can out on deck in the fresh air, sitting, or walking the promenade deck. Mary was right. The weather is considerably better than her outward passage, and the seas calmer. When Abraham disembarks at Albany, Eliza feels very lonely for the first time. What a huge harbour: she had no idea. She makes him promise to send regular notes home, a postcard, anything — just keep in touch.

— I'll try.

— You'd better.

And with a long embrace she bids her younger brother good-bye.

After he becomes a speck on the wharf she returns to her suite and tries to marshal her thoughts. *I feel two different things at once: very much alone. 'Alone, alone, all, all alone, alone on the wide, wide sea ...'; and, like Abraham, very much out of place in first class.*

The *Orient* heads out into the Indian Ocean, working northwest across the Equator. Although she is normally sociable, when she is not up on deck Eliza seeks solace in the first class reading room mainly because there is nobody there. The usual Romantics are on the shelves: Wordsworth, Coleridge, Blake. Tennyson is also there; even Hardy; his poems, that is. He's recently fallen out of favour as a novelist as his realistic themes upset the public, his plots being too racy even for the most modern Victorians. She takes down the Tennyson and it falls open at "Break, Break, Break". *That's exactly how my soul feels right now — broken. I need this forced rest to gather my strength, and plan my future, if anyone **can** plan their future.*

Tears spick from her eyes as she sits in the corner of the reading room, silently sobbing. *The touch of a vanished hand. Jack. Mt Keira.* Her tired body shakes. *I'm not crying for Angel. I should be; but I'm not. I know I'm crying for Jack, for what cannot be, must never be. But oh, if only it **could** have been!* She takes some long deep breaths that end in long deep sighs. *I recognize the healing fingers of time. I must rest, and use this enforced voyage, the next month or so, for soul-searching therapy; weave a solid base from my experiences on which to build the rest of my life. I can start with the words of solace in this room. Now I understand how monks come to self-realization through study and prayer. Personally, I don't get too much from prayer, traditional prayer. Maybe the healing power of prayer is when people are able to get their thoughts out and line them up in front of them. There they can sort them easily, move them around, put them in order, and solve their problems. Ergo: the healing power of prayer. The healing can only come from within.*

She replaces the Tennyson and takes down a volume of Hardy's poetry, and as she reads she feels that Hardy has written these lines just for her, for her alone. *It's so true. He writes about lost love; unrequited love; of one who loves another, hopelessly.* She flicks through the pages and reads "The Division"

> …'O were it but the weather, Dear
> O were it but the miles
> That summed up all our severance,
> There might be room for smiles.
>
> But that thwart thing betwixt us twain,
> Which nothing cleaves or clears,
> Is more than distance, Dear, or rain,
> And longer than the years.'

Oh, Jack! …is more than distance, Dear — and longer than the years. I may never see you again. More tears well up and run down her face. She swallows the internal ones. *I need this realization. I need to see things how they really are. He seems to be writing just for me.*

This man Hardy seems to understand from both sides of the gender. How far can my spirits go down before they rise? How long must they stay down to learn their lessons? Here's another one:

> 'But — after love what comes?
> A scene that lowers
> A few sad vacant hours,
> And then, the curtain.'

She closes the book with finality. *That's lower than I really want to go. After love comes Death? I don't think so. I'm young and resilient.* She takes out the photo of the Turvilles and looks at it fondly. *Certainly I mourn for what might have been but Jack has an obligation to Mary and Polly, and I would not be honourable if I let him abandon them for me. I couldn't live with myself. Fate has taken me away from Jack. What must be, must be. There are a lot of positives working for me: I am now free, free of a loveless marriage, an 'honourable discharge' so to speak; I'm young (too young to be a widow but nevertheless, here I am), with a questionable future, and an unknown inheritance. I have enough money to get home but I don't know how much Angel has in the bank in Emminster and how long it will last to keep a roof over the heads of Mother and the children.*

In New South Wales Angel's money-talk was mostly bravado. He may not have been as rich as he let on so we might have to move again unless I can earn enough to pay the rent. At least I know I can make a living at dressmaking. I'd still like to teach but can't afford the training. Maybe we could all move in with Mr Clare? It's a drastic solution, if Angel has nothing in the bank. As Mother would say, 'Drastic times call for drastic measures'. Why can't this ship go any faster? Now that I'm finding my feet and my own solutions I want to get home and start making my own decisions as soon as possible.

— Well, hello there! What's a beautiful creature like you doing in a stuffy old reading room like this? Allow me to introduce myself. My name is Hugh Morgan.

And mine is Rumpelstiltskin! Now I have to comply with the false banter of the first class elite, which I hate.

— How do you do, Mr Morgan. I'm Eliza Clare.

— *Captain* Morgan, but *you* can call me Hugh.

I'll do no such thing, you glib arrogant peacock.

— I haven't seen you around before. Where has such a fine lady been hiding herself for the last several days?

Stop being so ingratiating!

— I've been very ill, Captain Morgan, and have kept mostly to my state room.

He sits down beside her.

— Hugh. You must call me Hugh. What is that you're reading? Thomas Hardy, eh? Are you a morally advanced lady?

— I find him rather an astute poet. Excuse me. I have to go now.

— Wait! Just a minute. Will I see you at dinner this evening?

— No, I don't believe you will.

Eliza spends the rest of the week trying to avoid the advances of Captain Morgan. *This is my time for spiritual recovery not for leaking my personal history to inquisitive matrons or pushy bachelors like Morgan. What advantage is it to him to flirt and flatter the likes of me? Is he looking for a wife? Why search for one here on the high seas?*

She spends a considerable time on deck, taking in the fresh air, walking and occasionally joining in a game of shuffleboard or deck quoits. She never eats in the dining room: the warm enclosed smell of food and the slow rolling render her incapable of eating, especially when the chandeliers sway back and forth 'with a mazy motion' as Coleridge puts it. She usually has something sent to her suite, and makes a habit, if she feels up to it, of taking afternoon tea on deck in the fresh air and making a meal of it. And here he comes again, like a spider out of the shadows.

— Fancy seeing you here!
— Captain Morgan.
— Fair lady, I beg you to call me Hugh. May I join you?
— I only have tea service for one.
— I don't need any sustenance. Your beauty alone feeds me. Did anyone ever tell you what spell-binding eyes you have?

As this is a rhetorical question, Eliza doesn't bother to answer. In fact, she tries to avoid conversation, even eye contact. *Surely that will rebuff him and his inane observations but it seems to make him more earnest; and he seeks me out all the more.*

— Don't you have any accomplices, I mean acquaintances, on the ship, Captain Morgan, to pass the time with?
— They only help to speed the time. I want to slow it down with you.

Oh, for heaven's sake! He really is becoming annoying. If I were trying to snare a catch, he couldn't be easier; but I'm not. I don't want to be pestered by the likes of him. I just want peace and relaxation. The only way I can get it is to stay in my cabin, and I refuse to do that.

— Look, Captain Morgan, I don't want to appear rude but I'm quite content with my own company. I'm not lonely, and I don't need a companion, especially after what I've been through.

I shouldn't have said that. I shouldn't have said it!

— Dear lady, I had no idea such a bloom could have suffered travails. You can tell me. I'll understand.

Tell him nothing. Don't open up to him. He's just a gold-digger and a bore. Why is he travelling alone from Australia to England? Change the subject and get out of here.

— Are you going to London for business or pleasure, Captain Morgan?

Eliza does converse on general subjects with some of the other first class passengers who seem to specialize in numbing each other with mindless details of their lives and aspirations, eager to surpass one another in possessions and places visited, proud of knowing friends in high places as if they are outbidding one another in the auction of life. *Is this behaviour peculiar to first class? If so, I don't want to be here.* They vie with one another over the number of servants they have in their town and their country houses, the schools their children attend, their clubs, their thoroughbreds; dropping hints, obvious facts, so each can sum the other up, and dish out deference accordingly. They learn very little about this auburn-haired girl with the arresting violet eyes. Eliza, refreshingly, does not play the game. They sense it and despise her for it. She does not appear in a different gown each evening or flaunt a different piece of jewellery at every meal. She is demure, quiet, and well-spoken which some interpret as aloofness but which only adds to her mystery and attractiveness for the Morgans of this world. Is she an heiress travelling incognito? Is she fleeing lovers? Is she really a widow? So young: it seems impossible. Is she really married or just wearing a wedding band? She even thanks the stewards for their kindnesses while her companions disregard their presence entirely. *What am I doing here in first class?*

She goes to see the purser and explains she wishes to share a second class cabin from Colombo on. *Jack paid a princely sum for this ticket, God bless them. First class is really wasted on me and who knows? I may need the money I'll save when I get home. Home! Mmmm. Home.* Her things are moved to a lower inside cabin and she shares the rest of the journey with a jolly middle-aged woman, glad to leave the ephemeral life of first class to those who relish it.

The Red Sea looms ahead, a long stretch of calm. Her second class companions are much more gregarious and more interesting than those in first class, and Eliza is actually enjoying ship board life for the first time. She gets to see Pompeii. When they arrive in Naples she joins a day excursion to the excavated city. Morgan picks her out in the crowd and is by her side like lightning.

— I say, where have you been hiding? I thought you disembarked at Colombo.

She smiles resignedly, and puts up with his flattery for the rest of the day. He even buys her a piece of pumice and pushes it into her hand.

— I want you to have this so you'll remember me, Mystery Woman.

'They never had a chance', she tells her mother later. 'That mountain belched out ash which covered everything feet thick. Only parts of buildings have been dug out and there's a lot more buried underneath the pumice hills; and people, too. The mountain is always there. You turn around and look up, and there it is, Mt Vesuvius: always looming, always there, until it blows again. You know, going there helped me to feel alive, glad to be alive.' To which her mother replies, 'Oh, Liza-Lu, you're too philosophical for me.' She gives her mother the pumice stone. 'And practical, too. It's good for rubbing on callouses.'

By the time the *Orient* passes through the Straits of Gibraltar Eliza, young as she is, has become her own woman. *I've matured beyond my num-*

bered years, I've accepted what life has already thrown at me, and I'm looking at my return with a calm expectation. I hope to have some means, however small, to manage my future and my family's. When I left, I was dependent; now I'm independent, in charge of my own destiny. I'm the one who determines if and how I bend as I face the future, like leaning into a headwind from the bow of a ship. Maybe the prospect of dry land forever under my feet is making me dizzy. Still, I feel confident. As Jack said. 'You've got a tongue in your head. Use it.' Dear practical Jack. When we dock, I'll ask the Hansom driver to take me to the station, and then I'll find the train that goes the closest to Emminster. After that, the coach. One step at a time. From now on, instead of reacting to fate, I'll create it. I'll make my own chances. There's no time for a letter to Mother. If my connections are good, I'll be home before the post. She passes through customs easily, she has so little, then asks a porter to hail a cab.

CHAPTER 27

Return to Emminster

After jostling the five miles down Crimmercronk Lane from Chalk Newton Station, Eliza alights at the Emminster Inn where she leaves her trunks to be collected later, and walks up the street. *It feels so strange. Home. England. Emminster. I don't feel a surge of anything like I thought I would. Home. Maybe 'home' is a place you designate to be your own, then you have to work at loving it.*

She opens the gate to Linden and walks up the path. She knocks and her mother opens the door. Before Joan can close her mouth, Eliza wraps her arms around her mother and starts to cry, the whole stress of the journey finally released.

— Liza-Lu, you've come home! You never let us know. Where's your husband? He didn't leave you, too, my dear, like he did your sister?

— No, Mother. Angel is dead.

— Dead?

— He's dead, Mother. He was drowned in a terrible storm and washed out to sea. He went out in the storm with his dog after reading the letter from Mr Clare telling him about his mother's death.

— Yes, poor soul. He's been looking for Angel to come home. We've been expecting him, not you.

— Did he tell you that Mrs Clare was not Angel's real mother?

— No-ooo. Is that so? You really married a dark horse. Where's your brother? Did he come with you?

Eliza tells her about Abraham's fortune-seeking dreams.

—Well, well. My eldest daughter in her grave, my next a widow, and my eldest son chipping for gold in the desert.

Eliza looks out the front window and sees the red stone Church tower, and suddenly dreads the news she has to share.

— Have a cup of tea first, ducks.

— I can't, Mother. I must go to see Mr Clare and get it over. Put the kettle on. I'll be back soon. I'll bring him over for a cup.

The swing gate to the vicarage squeaks open, and Eliza pauses before stepping up onto the porch. The young season's ivy has not yet taken hold. Then she rings the bell. A chair scrapes back in the study and slow *(old)* footsteps get nearer to the door.

— Why, little missy! What a sight for sore eyes!

She gives her father-in-law a long gentle embrace. He seems frailer, more stooped.

— Where's Angel? He's not with you?

— No, Father Clare. Let's go in and sit down.

— I have a fire in the study. I'll ring for tea.

— Tea is over at Mother's house. I've already invited you.

She glances into the drawing room opposite the study where she was married a hundred years ago in her youth. They sit on the settee, side by side, the fire cheerfully warm on this early spring afternoon.

— Father Clare, I have some terrible news to share with you.

— It's Angel, isn't it?

She can't look at him. She speaks to the fire.

— Yes, he's not with me because he …

— Has crossed over the Great Divide.

— Yes. How do you …?

— It must have been awful for you, losing the babe I mean. Mrs Clare and I sent many prayers your way.

— Oh, Father Clare.

He puts his arm around her and she turns into his shoulder, shaking with sobs. *He has shown me more sympathy in two minutes than Angel ever did.*

— That's over now. I'm sorry, but you'll never have another grandchild by me. Angel drowned; that's what the verdict of the inquest was. He was washed out to sea, and never found.

— Ah, God rest his soul, his poor tortured soul.

— You knew he was tortured?

— He didn't make life easy for himself, and maybe not for you either, dear?

She sniffs again.

— No, life with him was not easy. He never opened up to me, never shared his life. It was self, self, self; but I shouldn't be talking about him like that; not to you, his father.

— He must have received my letter?

— Yes. In fact, he left it open on the bed which was unusual for him. After he went out into the storm with Rover, his dog, I read it. What terrible storms they have over there. It was Rover who led us to the spot where he was washed off his feet, a flooded creek that runs across the beach where he used to walk. Rover sat staring at that spot for three days.

— Poor boy! I didn't mean my news to cause him such distress but, you see, he had to know the truth or part of the truth. You must have read that I told him Mrs Clare was not his natural mother?

— Yes, that's very intriguing. I can imagine what a shock that was, coming in the sentence after you told him about his mother's death. I'm sorry for you, Father Clare. She was your stalwart companion in life.

— Yes, she was, God rest her soul. You're no doubt wondering who Angel's mother really is? Before I tell you, I don't want you to think I had a roving eye or was a philanderer in any way.

— I'd never think that. Were you married before?

— My first wife died in childbirth and I've been faithful to Mrs Clare ever since but that has no bearing on the truth of the matter. You see, Eliza, this is what I had to tell Angel face to face: Mrs Clare was not his natural mother, and I am not his natural father.

Eliza's mouth falls open. She gasps.

— Oh, my! Now I understand why you wanted to tell him in person. But why does it matter? Why did he have to know at all? If you have kept it from him all up through his adult life, why is it so crucial that he knows now?

James Clare smiles: a smile of relief; a smile of someone who knows a lot more, and is about to drop another bombshell. A look comes into his eyes as if to say. 'Are you ready for this?'

— His mother was my sister.

— Ohh.

— Mrs Clare and I agreed to take her child and raise him as our own, providing his mother would not contact him, and leave it to us to raise him with our other two sons so he would never know his origins.

— And she agreed to this?

— Yes, and kept her word. She went on and made another life for herself. She wasn't married when she had him. He was illegitimate, you see.

— Oh.

— We were able to solve two problems with the one solution: make respectable people out of both of them, mother and son My sister kept her word, and we kept ours.

— Then, why did Angel have to know the secret?

— My sister died. She died a few years ago.

— Why not tell him then?

— There was no need at the time. A letter was sent to him here, recently, from her lawyers in London.

The Reverend James goes over to his secretaire and hands Eliza a rather formal envelope addressed to 'Angel Clare, Esquire' from someone called Govett and Bailey.

— You are his legal heir, Eliza?

— Executrix and beneficiary.

— Good, then. Angel's affairs are now finally out of my hands. I'll leave the worry to you.

— This must have been a big strain on you all these years. Did you keep in touch with your sister?

— Only by post. We both kept up our respective ends of the bargain.

— It seems sad when you can't have a loving, even a friendly relationship between brother and sister.

— You're a very understanding girl.

— It's easy with you. I feel like I can tell you anything.

— That's because you're special — my special daughter-in-law. I hope we can stay close.

— We will. You're family now. I'll just open this and then we can go over to Linden for afternoon tea. 'Angel Clare, Esquire. Dear Sir, you are requested to attend these chambers at your earliest convenience. Yours truly, Ernest Bailey, Solicitor.'

— The only way you'll get to the bottom of this is to go up to London. I'll just get my coat. Don't want to keep your good mother waiting.

Joan has made a fresh batch of pumpkin scones; and what a surprise her younger children have when they come home from school to find Liza-Lu pouring the tea.

Next day Eliza writes to the solicitor who sends a missive back, with an appointment at noon the following Monday. She then calls on Angel's bank in Emminster (*my bank, now, I suppose*) who also require proof of identity: birth certificate or marriage certificate. This time the Reverend James in person suffices, although the bank still needs proof of Angel's death before they will give her access to his account or safety deposit box. She discovers there are only enough funds to cover the Linden rental for another three months. He had obviously hoped to augment the account with profits forwarded from New South Wales. In the safety deposit box she finds the bracelet the Clares had given her and the necklace and earings he'd 'given' to both her and Tess on their wedding nights, a present to his bride from his godmother. Could his godmother have been his birth mother posing as his godmother? He'd admitted he didn't know her. *I'll have to ask the Reverend. I now have the added burden of finding accommodation for Mother and the family as of the first of July. There is still always the vicarage option. That way there wouldn't be disruption to the children's schooling.*

Even Little Charlie is in school now. He and Young John are in the Infants' Section, much to John's disgust. Hope is in Standard 7 and quite the serious scholar, while Modesty is involved in everything going in the playground two years behind her sister. Joan has built up a washing clientele; and has a patch of vegetables in the vicarage garden.

CHAPTER 28

A Visit to London

Monday sees Eliza on the early coach to Chalk Newton on the reverse trip down Crimmercronk Lane she had taken only last week, for her appointment. On arriving in London, she discovers she is early, which is far better than being late for Govett and Bailey. She retraces her steps a couple of streets to where she had passed that massive pillared institution, the British Museum, with its swath of green in front bisected by a path; and on the green, spaced at regular intervals, placards commanding. 'Keep Off the Grass'. She goes in and is immediately dwarfed by huge stone busts carved into strong, serene features that once looked down from Egyptian temples on the Nile; and a large flat stone completely covered in carved writing: one message repeated in three languages that was used to break the decipherment of hieroglyphics — the Rosetta stone.

She views white marble carvings of mostly headless men, and men with horses' bodies, shooting arrows at one another, the ones Lord Elgin brought back to England from the Parthenon in Athens; and the base of a pillar from the Areopagus. *That reminds me of one of Thomas Hardy's poems,*

"In the British Museum"

'I know no art, and I only view
A stone from a wall,
But I am thinking that stone has echoed
The voice of Paul.'

Ancient; sobering. Next she passes between two enormous winged lions carved from stone, the entrance to the Assyrian exhibit where she finds a distant scribe has covered the whole surface of a bull-like beast in cuneiform script made up of short and long curved indentations: a vertical message of enormous importance carved for the world to read, now lost to all who gaze upon it.

The time! Goodness! Yes, I still have time. She hurries round to Old Church Lane, number 27, and climbs up the stone steps. The firm of Govett and Bailey is on the second floor and she reads the brass plaque on the large wooden door with the frosted glass panes as she goes in. At the reception desk.

— My name is Eliza Clare. I have an appointment.

— Please take a seat, Mrs Clare. I'll tell Mr Bailey you're here.

Bailey himself? I assumed underlings would attend to such routine affairs as gentlemen farmers' estates.

— Well, well, Mrs Clare. How do you do? My name is Ernest Bailey.

They shake hands

— How do you do, Mr Bailey. I'm Eliza Clare. You know from my note my husband, Angel Clare, died in New South Wales. Drowned, actually. You sent a letter to him at his father's house in Emminster. I have just this week arrived back in England and Mr Clare Senior had saved it for me.

— Yes, yes, my dear. Won't you come into my office?

He holds the door and motions for her to enter before him, and points out a large leather chair facing him across a wide desk.

— I take it that you are Mr Angel Clare's next of kin?

— Yes, I don't have a marriage certificate but I have a letter with me from his father, the Reverend James Clare, who married us. Do you want to see it?

— Yes, please.

She rummages in her purse. While she does so, Bailey continues.

— I also need to know if Mr Angel Clare has any children, any descendants.

— No. I miscarried on the ship on my way to Australia.

— I'm very sorry to hear it. I need to know in order to fulfil the requirements of the will.

She hands him James' letter.

— I didn't know Angel had a will. He never told me; he never told me he had any business with this law firm.

— He didn't, Mrs Clare. It was his late mother who had business with us.

— Mrs Clare had business with you?

— Not Mrs Clare. Mrs Stoke. Mrs Alexis Stoke.

— Oh, his real mother. The Reverend told me when I arrived back that Mrs Clare was not his real mother. His sister was really Angel's mother. Her name was Alexis?

— Yes.

— To think that Angel never knew his real mother's name. I'm sure that learning about her existence was the cause of his death; I'm certain of it.

— Your husband, Angel Clare, is identified in Mrs Stoke's papers, and appears to be the last remaining heir to her estate. I need to verify Mr Clare's death and the fact that he had no issue. Do you have his death certificate with you?

Eliza pushes it across the desk. Bailey rings for assistance, and a young man comes at once from an adjoining room. Bailey says something to him privately and gives him the two documents. He turns back to Eliza.

— He's just going to verify them. He'll be back in a jiffy.

Then, he interlaces his fingers, leans back in his high-back brown leather chair, looks over at Eliza and smiles broadly.

— Mrs Clare, I think you'd better prepare yourself for a very big surprise. Some years ago, when Mrs Simon Stoke filed her will with us, she also left a sealed envelope with instructions that its contents were never to be revealed as long as her only son was living. Her husband had died several years before, leaving her his entire fortune, and a fortune, indeed, it was; as well as his new property in the West Country. He left everything entirely to her, in trust for their only son.

— So Angel was their son?

— No. Please bear with me, Mrs Clare. Their son had a very generous allowance and was notorious for being something of a high liver. After his father died he became more and more in charge but less and less caring of his mother. He 'got' religion, then turned away from it and finally, after his mother died, he left home altogether. It was the housekeeper and gardener who held the place together. Nevertheless, he probably didn't deserve the grisly end that lay in store for him at such a young age. You were probably in the Colonies at the time when Alexander D'Urberville was brutally murdered in the fashionable seaside resort of Sandbourne, stabbed through the heart in a lover's quarrel.

Eliza's mouth falls open and her eyes widen. *Oh, my God! Alec D'Urberville! Tess! Is he related? I can't make head or tail of it. Compose yourself: the lawyer's looking at you.*

— I didn't mean to upset you, Mrs Clare. Maybe I shouldn't have mentioned the details of his death. It was quite sensational — in all the papers. And it wasn't another man who killed him, it was a woman posing as his wife!

— Tess!

— Yes. You've heard of her, then? Her surname was very similar to D'Urberville: Durberfield or Derbyfield or something like that. Beautiful to look at. Must have gazed at the moon too much.

He taps his temple with his finger, and goes on.

— Well, mad or no, they caught up with her in the end, and hanged her for it. The news swept through all the dailies until the trapdoor dropped. After, nothing more was writ nor read as other news consumed the public appetite.

— Poor girl!

— Poor Mr D'Urberville! Mrs Stokes' only child.

— How could his name be D'Urberville if his mother's name was Stoke?

— The name 'D'Urberville' was assumed by his father when he moved down from the north with his family. The Stokes were in no way related to the ancient D'Urberville line at Kingsbere where it gradually died out, the name metamorphosing in the process. Apparently there are a lot of similar names in the area today. The Durberfield girl could well have been a genuine D'Urberville descendant. Mr Stoke (died of apoplexy; we handled his estate as well) added the name to his family name and went by Stoke-D'Urberville. The son, Alexander, who called himself Alec, dropped the Stoke and used just the D'Urberville. Mrs Stoke thought the whole notion was nonsense and kept her official married name.

Eliza is taking time to compose her inner turmoil during Bailey's lengthy explanation, only half listening. *Unbelievable! Alec D'Urberville come back to haunt the family again!*

— What about the sealed envelope?

— Yes, back to the envelope. Mrs Stoke, in her will, left everything to Mr Alec. She also gave us specific instructions that the envelope was never to be opened after her death unless something untoward happened to Mr Alec, resulting in his death which, as I have informed you, it did. We then had the authority to open the envelope, and now let me appraise you of its contents.

He takes the large, legal-size letter from its brown envelope, and begins to read.

— ' …that Angel Clare, my first and base born son, born four months before I married my husband, Simon Stoke, in Greyhampton. It is not necessary in this document to reveal his father's name, only that the child was conceived in love, circumstances forbidding me from revealing to Angel's natural father that I had borne him a son. I gave my golden-haired babe to my brother, James Clare, the vicar at Emminster, to be brought up in the fear of God by him and his wife. I made a solemn pact with my brother that these facts will only come to light in the event that my second born, my legitimate son, Alexander Stoke, also known as D'Urberville, predecease his elder brother. Everything in my will which is the whole of my estate both real and personal not already bequeathed to named individuals, such as stipends to reward long and faithful service, I leave to my son Alexander, his heirs, their assigns etc.

'In the event of his decease, and his having no heirs, all of my estate, both real and personal, I then bequeath to my elder son, Angel Clare: comprising the new manor house near The Chase at Trantridge on a property called The Slopes, the adjoining cottage, out buildings, barn, greenhouses, orchard and land belonging to the farm; the household furniture, bedding, linen, china etc., clothing and jewellery. In addition the trap, phaeton, cabriolet, farm equipment and wagon, pony, horses, cattle and sheep; and last, my investments in the city which are administered by the firm of Govett and Bailey, Old Church Lane, London; the worth of the whole, at this date, amounting to not less than eighty-four thousand pounds.'

Eliza blinks. Twice. She's been listening with her mouth half open as the incredulous facts fall into her ears. *The Slopes? The cottage? Rose Cottage?*

— All this is now Angel's? It's come too late for him to appreciate it.

— Not his, Mrs Clare. All this now belongs to you. And more. This envelope was lodged with us several years ago just after Mr Stoke D'Urberville died. I calculate the estate to be well over one hundred thousand pounds at this time, and growing.

Eliza's mouth keeps opening and closing like a goldfish. *He'll think I'm simple. Get a grip on yourself.* She sits on the edge of her chair and holds out her hands.

— Belongs to me?

— Every bit of it.

It is obvious Mr Ernest Bailey is enjoying breaking this type of news to her. He watches the innocence, the incredulity, and savours the impact of his words as they strike.

— My dear Mrs Clare, you have brought the proof with you, the documents, and I am satisfied that you are indeed his next of kin and therefore, by law, the heir to Mr Angel Clare's estate.

— The pity of it is he couldn't make use of it in his life. Lord knows, he surely needed it.

Despite this dark observation, Bailey cannot prevent himself from beaming.

— Heir to his estate, which was his mother's estate, and is now your estate. You are a very, very wealthy young woman and I strongly advise you to engage an accountant and stock broker forthwith. If you wish, you can continue with the people Mr Alec employed to run his business. I assure you they are very reputable.

— Yes, yes. Of course, Mr Bailey, I'll take your advice. I think I'll need all the advice I can get. Do you have their addresses?

— Most certainly, my dear. Anything I can do to be of assistance. If you invest wisely, you shouldn't want for anything in this life.

Eliza begins gathering up her letter and certificate.

— There's one more thing before you go, Mrs Clare.

The solicitor puts on his spectacles and looks over Alexis' missive one more time. Eliza settles to attention again.

— It often happens, Mrs Clare, that over the years, eccentrics add the odd codicil to their wills; and we are bound to administer the will according to those wishes.

She tenses. *Strings. There are strings attached.* Bailey continues.

— The stipulation is Mr Clare could only inherit the estate if he lived at The Slopes. This property was very special to Mrs Stoke. This means that you, too, to inherit it, must reside there also.

— I don't have any problem with that.

— There is another part of the condition. The other part is somewhat unusual but still within the law.

He leans forward.

— If there are no heirs, and you remarry, or cohabit with any other man, you will forfeit the whole fortune — the house, land, investments and personal estate. Do you understand?

— Yes, but why would anyone impose a condition like that?

— I'm sure she thought the situation would never arise. She wanted her blood line to inherit, Alec's children or, failing that, Angel's children. Nobody knows when the Wheel of Fortune will turn. Today you are certainly on top. If you accept these terms, we can begin to act immediately.

I can see this leading to great opportunities for the family. My young brothers and sisters can get the best education money can buy. Mother will be free of poverty at last. I'm still young but I'll agree to these terms if it means the betterment of my whole family. It means I would have to remain a widow, and I'm willing to do it for them. Yes, I feel strengthened by this decision. She looks up at Bailey.

— I agree, Mr Bailey. I'll sign.

— I have the keys to the new Manor House right here, as well as the keys to the cottage, the gates, etc. Matthew, the groom, has been kept on as outside caretaker; and Mrs Watley as cook and housekeeper for now, as well as Spence, the gardener. They will show you around and acquaint you with the property. If you're happy with their services, you are free to keep them on. The other farm hands were let go after poor Mr Alec passed away …

Poor Mr Alec, indeed!

— …and most of the stock sold off while we were trying to trace Mr Clare. It's entirely up to you if you want to restore the model farm or let the grounds run wild. Mrs Stoke's most valuable jewellery is in a safety deposit box at Barclay's Bank, and here is a letter of introduction to the bank manager and the key to the safety deposit box. Her accountant can better appraise you of all her investments as he worked more closely with her toward the end. She went blind, you know, and was not entirely up to looking after her own affairs. Also, here is the name of her stock broker. I sincerely hope you follow my advice and seek theirs, especially if you haven't wandered these financial paths before.

— I still can hardly believe it, Mr Bailey. It's too much at once. I certainly shall take your advice and contact these individuals.

— Of course, Govett and Bailey will continue to administer the affairs of Mrs Stoke's estate until it's all settled, and will continue to manage your affairs if you wish to retain us.

— I'm sure that will be the best option.

— Will you sign here please, for the keys?

Dumbly she takes the pen, dips it in the inkwell and signs 'Eliza Louisa Clare'. Bailey carefully blots it. She stands up slowly and extends her hand to the solicitor.

— Thank you, Mr Bailey, for all your help. It's been quite a shock. I can hardly believe it.

— It's the kind of shock I rarely have the pleasure of inflicting. Goodbye, Mrs Clare. I'm very happy to have made your acquaintance, and I hope that Govett and Bailey will continue to serve you in the future.

I feel quite giddy with the news. An hour ago I was a struggling widow. Now I can buy and sell every lawyer in this building. She goes down the stairs and out into the street unable to put away the incredulous smile that is keeping her cheeks so tight. *Barclay's Bank; jewellery; The Slopes; Rose Cottage, my old home, now mine; investments; thousands and thousands of pounds! Mine! Mine! When Mother gets by, and feeds and clothes the children on a handful of* *pounds a year, and even a gentleman can support a family of six on a hundred pounds a year, I'll have enough to feed and clothe all the children in England! It can't be true. Alexis. Alexis Clare. We share the same name: my **real** mother-in-law, and I never knew her. Tess did. What did she say about her? She didn't really seem to know much about what was going on; had lots of servants to look after her; something about whistling to birds. Mrs D'Urberville Father Clare's sister! It's too bizarre. Alec D'Urberville's mother. Angel's mother. How much does Mr Clare know? Is there more?*

I'm going home immediately. Those keys and letters can sit there at the bottom of my purse for a few days until I get used to them. She starts thinking again.

*Rich! Well-off; well-to-do; comfortably off (very comfortably off!); prosperous; in the money; in the pink! No need to ever worry again about the price of milk, or corn, or potatoes; and we can afford to eat meat every day. And no more needlework! I'll still sew for pleasure and the 'must do' needlework, like darning; but why should I darn stockings any more when I can afford new ones every day? Mother won't have to take in washing ever again. I wonder what she'll find to do with her time? And I can help the younger children in so many ways. Abraham, too, if he fails up on the goldfields. I'll buy them all luxuries. We'll sleep in satin, not cotton. The girls will wear silk, and I'll get our clothes tailored and made to fit. No more hand-me-downs or thickly-turned hems. No more extra-wide seams on self-made garments that are made to last several seasons as the wearer grows taller or larger. We can now be the givers of hand-me-downs rather than the receivers. Pretty shoes, too. No more button-up boots for the girls. Fine shirts for the boys; milled socks; and soft wool blazers. Frilly petticoats and lace chemises for us girls, real lace; lots and lots of lace; parasols and a variety of cloaks and mantles, maybe even sable in winter. And Mother! Oh, Mother, now I can buy you a house of your own, and we can afford a servant. We'll send the youngsters to school, good schools, stepping stones to the world; maybe even studies beyond school if they show an aptitude. The world is now at Hope's feet: she's an excellent student. At least they won't **have** to leave school early like Tess and me and Abraham. I could go off and train to be a teacher. No, I can't. There's that stipulation in her will about having to live at The Slopes. Maybe it's not my destiny to be a teacher.*

So deep in future planning, she almost goes past her stop. The ride to Emminster in the coach takes the longest time, mainly because she is itching to tell her mother and father-in-law, and find out more about Alexis from the Reverend James.

CHAPTER 29

ELIZA BREAKS THE NEWS

— We're saved, Mother! We're saved!
— What are you talking about, Liza-Lu?
— Mother, I'm rich! Very, very rich.
— Can't be. Angel didn't have *that* kind of money.
— It's not Angel's. Well, it is. It's his mother's.
— His mother was rich?
— Not Mrs Clare. His real mother, I mean. She left everything to him. And Mother, you'll never guess who she was? She was Alec D'Urberville's mother, too!
— What!
— I know! It's unbelievable. After she had Angel, she made an agreement with the Clares for them to raise him as their own son.
— Why would she give him up? A nice young fella like that?
— Because she wasn't married. She would be disgraced.
— You floor me, Liza-Lu. I have to sit down. I can't take all this in standing up. Why did you say she gave Angel to the Clares to raise up?
— She wasn't married. She's Mr Clare's sister. Father Clare said they would raise Angel as their own son, youngest son, if she agreed to keep her distance.
— Then how could she be Alec D'Urberville's mother?
— She married his father in the north just after she gave up Angel.
— I knew them D'Urbervilles were wealthy, *and* related to us. That's what Parson Tringham told your father.
— Well, they weren't.
— Oh yes they were. We Durbeyfields are true D'Urbervilles. That's what he said. You even dug some of that up in your visits to the library. You

214

should know we're related.

— We *are* related to the ancient D'Urberville family. We stem from them; but we are not related to Alec D'Urberville's family.

— How so?

— Alec's father chose the surname D'Urberville when he moved to Trantridge from the North, and he tacked it onto his own name which was Stoke. Alec dropped his former name, Stoke, and adopted the surname D'Urberville.

— Oh, so he wasn't a true D'Urberville?

— No, Mother. You sound a little disappointed.

— I thought the D'Urbervilles were very wealthy.

— It was Mr Stoke, Alec's father, who was wealthy. He left everything to his wife, Alexis, née Clare, the Reverend James' sister. She left everything to Alec but he …died *(poor Tess)*. Alexis left a special envelope at the lawyers that was not to be opened unless Alec was the first of her sons to die.

— Oh, that's why this has just come out now?

— Exactly. They couldn't track Angel down. They really wanted to tell him the news that he was Alexis' last living heir; but as we know, he, too, died prematurely; and now it seems yours truly cops the lot.

— You'll have to improve your colloquialisms, Mrs Clare.

They both laugh and hug. Joan jumps up and swirls her daughter round the room.

— Oh, Liza-Lu, is it really true?

Eliza takes a deep breath.

— It's really true.

— And now it all belongs to you? I just love Rose Cottage, that little cottage Mr Alec let us live in. It's a good omen, Liza-Lu. Just think! It was our Tess what set the whole thing in motion. It really makes you wonder.

Eliza opens her hand.

— What you got there? The keys to the kingdom?

— The keys, Mother, to the manor house at The Slopes, to Rose Cottage, and the gates.

And her face breaks into a huge grin again.

— I must go and tell Mr Clare, and find out more about Alexis.

— What about your dinner?

— Save it for me.

She almost runs to the vicarage where the Reverend James is just sitting down to his meal.

— Stay and have something with me, Eliza. It's awful eating alone.

He calls Old Lina to set a second plate, and Eliza tucks into a cold meat pie while she relates the day's events, peppering him with questions.

— I hope you don't mind me asking you about Alexis. I want to know everything about her. After all, she's my benefactress.

— We grew up west of here where our father was the Headmaster of the Grammar School. It was the boys who were educated then, not the girls. Girls were educated up to the age of about fourteen, and then always expected to leave school and take up sewing, music and the female arts. It was the boys who went on and studied history and Latin and literature. Alexis was a very good scholar and rebelled at being cut off from learning. She read all my text books, Latin, Greek, the lot, and we would even have discussions in Greek in the evening when I would teach her the correct pronunciation. She read all my Shakespeare; even wrote poetry.

— You'd better eat up. She liked birds, didn't she?

— Always loved birds, from as long as I can remember. She had a very calming way with them even though she was headstrong by nature. The most skittish bird, whether wild or domestic, would immediately relax and be still under her touch. Or was it her voice? I don't know. She mesmerised them. Everyone knew Alexis Clare had a passion for birding. She was in charge of our hens; and she'd take long walks, especially by the river banks where the wild birds tend to congregate. Sometimes, on summer mornings, she'd slip out just before dawn to be with the song birds when they woke up, and she would hum and whistle to them. A lady whistling!

— It's a good thing we're having a cold meal. Let me get some more hot water for the tea. What was she like? Look like, I mean.

— She had a long face.

— Like you.

— Yes, but unlike me she had masses of very dark hair, ringlets, which were always escaping from hair pins or nets, or whatever females use. Dark eyes, too. Vivacious, very gregarious; much more so than me. There were just the two us, which was unusual. Our mother died when we were young and Father never remarried. Alexis was of medium height, and her chubby cheeks betrayed her sweet tooth. She could never turn down a candied apple or a chocolate, or a slice of apple-cinnamon pie.

Eliza smiles.

— I can picture her now. You're very good at describing people, Father Clare. What else can you tell me about her?

— Now it's you who isn't eating. You munch while I talk. She always moved quickly, very energetically; 'quick-turned' was how she put it. She was quite carefree in her dress, and very individual in her fashion. She dressed to suit Alexis, not the rest of the family or society. She was really nature's child. I told you she spent a lot of time alone down on the river banks with a book she took with her to identify the different birds by colour as well as by their calls which she learned, to amuse herself. She used to wear trousers whenever she went on rambles in the woods, as her skirts and petticoats consistently became soaked and soiled as she brushed through the damp bracken. Things like that. She was not entirely conventional.

She was practical too, you know, with her hands. She re-wired the hen house and used the left-over chicken wire to build rabbit hutches by covering a light frame of wood on the bottom and sides with the wire mesh, then made a wooden shelter at both ends, and a removable top. The hutches could be pulled over a fresh patch of grass each morning for them to feed on during the day. We also fed them all our peelings. But I'm digressing.

— What did she do for a living?

— She was a governess.

After my own heart!

— When she fell in the family way she moved up north, and after she had Angel, she taught in the Greyhampton Ladies' Academy before she met Stoke and was married. That's about it.

— Angel was born in Greyhampton?

— Yes. Our Aunt Bea, Mother's sister, lived there, and Alexis stayed with her during her confinement. I don't think she even went outside the house the entire time. The only person who knew she was there was the doctor who presided at his birth. Aunt Bea brought Angel directly to us, and when she returned to Greyhampton she helped Alexis find a position at the Academy. Alexis had to earn her own way in the world, and could not have worked if she'd kept Angel. She never had any money until she married Stoke. I don't believe she loved him. She seemed to lose her vitality after she had to give up her love child. She was never really close to Alexander, either. He was like his father who doted on him, by the way, and gave the young fella everything he asked for. Mistake, I call it. He adopted his father's mercenary values, shallow.

— He was very full of himself, and confident, too, wasn't he? That's the impression he made on me when he came to the house one time.

— Yes, cocky. He didn't respect his mother, either. He lorded it over her at The Slopes, especially as she became more and more introspective as time went by. She was losing her sight, too. It's a family thing. She became more and more reclusive and seemed to be in a world of her own; almost an invalid. She did go blind in the end, and the only thing that seemed to give her any enjoyment was her birds. Going back, Stoke, her husband, was a member of the Board of Governors at the Academy. He was much older than Alexis but was smitten by her. I suppose you could call her beautiful. They were married not four months later from Aunt Bea's house, and then she had Alexander. She only had the one child by him. I don't really know why.

— You're Alec's uncle, then?

— Yes, although he never knew it. Alexis promised she would stay away from Angel and not make herself known to him. Things got a bit tricky when her husband decided he wanted to move south, to this very region. Maybe he was thinking of her: that she'd be near her old home. I don't know. Some say he was getting away from a sour business deal (he was in textiles, I think), or union troubles, or some such thing. Alexis and I exchanged the odd letter over the years but we never mentioned Angel specifically, in case Stoke found out. I would write something like 'the boys are all in good health', or some such generality, so she would know Angel was all right. It was Aunt Bea who was his godmother, and who sent the necklace and earings to Angel when he was first married.

— To Tess.

— Yes. I wonder where they are now?

— They're right here in Emminster in the bank, the safety deposit.

— They're yours now, Eliza. Is there anything more you want to know? I think I've told you everything I can about Alexis.

— Do you know who Angel's father was, or is?

— No, I don't. She wouldn't tell me. When she found out she was going to have a baby she came to me (we'd moved here by then), and we worked out the plan for her confinement. That's all I can tell you, dear.

— Thank you for giving me so much information about her, Father Clare. Maybe I could write to the minister at Greyhampton and get a copy of his baptism certificate. It might have his father's name on it.

— It's worth a try.

— I have more of a feel for her now, as if I'm getting to know her. To think that she ended up with all that wealth!

— I've thought of something else, Eliza.

— I always dread it when people say that.

— Nothing dramatic. I haven't thought about her for so long. You remember I told you that she gradually lost her sight?

— Yes.

— It started off with what they call 'tunnel vision'. She couldn't see things on the sides.

— I think Angel must have been getting the same way. He would bump into door frames, and squinted when he was reading. Had to use a magnifying glass. He could only read the heads in the *Illawarra Mercury* without it. Maybe that's why he drowned! He couldn't see anything but right in front of him. He couldn't see how high the creek had risen.

— Poor boy. It sounds a likely explanation. In one of the last letters Alexis wrote while she could still see, she described it was like looking down a tube. Everything to the side faded away. That's why she gave up going for drives in her carriage. She couldn't appreciate the countryside. She could smell it, and feel the sun but she said it wasn't worth going out if she couldn't see the depths of colours and the distant hills. That's one of the reasons she had Stoke build the manor house all on one level. If her eyesight was failing, like our mother's and grandmother's before her, she didn't relish lying on the floor at the bottom of the stairs with a broken hip like Grandma Yandell. The manor house at The Slopes is a house without steps. She even had an aviary built inside the conservatory.

— It seems she had everything money could buy, except love. Poor lady, I feel sorry for her. She lost the man she loved, and the child she loved; and the child she kept ended up having no love or respect for her.

— The vicissitudes of life, my dear. Some fall and some rise. However, it seems that God has showered you with blessings.

— Blessings and responsibilities. It's not enough to *have* a fortune, you have to be able to use it wisely.

— Not only are you blessed, you are also a sensible girl and I know you'll use it wisely. You've already put your family before yourself. When are you going over to take a look at your inheritance? Those keys must be burning a hole in your pocket.

— I'm thinking of hiring a carriage and taking the whole family next weekend. Would you like to come? You've never seen your sister's house, have you?

— No, I haven't seen it. Surely there'll be no room in the carriage.

— Oh, that's nothing. The boys can sit up with the driver. Do come, Father Clare.

— You're really making me feel one of the family, aren't you?

— That's because you are.

And she gives him a kiss on the cheek.

The same evening, after she writes and let's Mrs Watley at The Slopes know to expect seven for afternoon tea on Sunday, she falls to thinking again about her sudden good fortune. *This time last night I was worried about what would happen to us when the rent came due at Linden and how I could make a living in the town. I hardly knew anything about Angel's mother — didn't even know her name. Now, the whole puzzle is almost complete except knowing who Angel's father was, or is, or if he's alive or dead. And does it really matter now? It makes you wonder. Was this all laid out for me, or is it just happenstance, the whim of the gods? All **I** did was to marry Angel in order to support my family. I gave up the chance of true love for a convenient relationship, and received all this as a result; much the same as Alexis did. She did the same thing but ended up empty.* Omar Khayyám might just have a point:

> 'Make the most of what you yet may spend
> Before you, too, into the dust descend.
> Dust into dust, and under dust, to lie
> Sans song, sans wine, sans women, and sans end.'

I must do the most I can, the best I can, with this windfall from heaven. It's hard to know if it's God's will for me or pure chance that has made me, Eliza Louisa Clare, mistress of The Slopes. It still hasn't hit home. I can't believe it.

Before she goes to bed she does the rounds and checks on her sleeping siblings. She whispers.

— Dear little pets. Now I can really be your fairy godmother.

Hugging Joan good-night she goes back to the table and writes first to the vicar at Greyhampton and encloses a donation for the favour if he would look up Angel's baptism. Second, she settles down to write a long letter to Mary and Jack telling them of the momentous events of the last twenty-four hours. She also describes how the crocuses and daffodils are brightening every nook and cranny of an English spring, and sends a whole line of kisses to Polly, as well as a big X to Rover.

CHAPTER 30

The Slopes

It's England, and April is here. God's in his heaven, and all's right with the world. Great lines, those Brownings. Earlier, Joan had said.

— Come on children! Put on your glad rags. We're going to see Liza-Lu's big new house. Hustle, now!

The Durbeyfields and Clares roll through the countryside bright with flowers overflowing tended gardens, and fresh smiles on people's faces as they pass through Trantridge and the new spring-greened Chase until they come to the main gates of The Slopes with their old home, Rose Cottage, behind, and the red brick Manor House hidden by the trees, set in the middle of the sloping hill. Alexis had made sure that the orchard, which was planted around three sides of the house, looked like a natural fruiterie, with the trees not in symmetrical rows. Tree types were also planted seemingly at random, as if an apple, a pear, an almond just happened there, next to a quince or cherry and all agreed to bloom at the same time just to make the humans happy.

The greenhouses are to the left of the manor house as they approach from the oval drive of red pebbles that runs against the front of the house. The architects of the 'new' house had retained as many of the original trees in the oval as they could. There was a huge oak and a very large pine that played their part in the light and shade that fell on the house as the seasons progressed, the oak, especially, allowing warm winter rays into the house yet shading the large mullioned windows in the summer time. Today the oak is leafing out in a light green, leaves that have not yet grown to their full size.

Mrs Watley greets them at the front door. She had heard the hoof beats and wheels crunching on the pebbles. Eliza thinks she looks to be in her fifties. She wears her grey hair in a bun, and has a large apron over her black dress. This gives her an air of quiet competence. She shows them into the large square central hall and then proceeds with a tour of the manor house. The layout is in the shape of a stretched capital H, with the joining-line of the H comprising three rooms: the large square entry hall, a parlour to the left of the main door, a library to the right, and a high glass conservatory behind, separated by another hallway.

The right leg of the H comprises Alexis' suite in front with windows on five sides. At the rear of her bedroom is her sitting room, and behind that, the dining room with one wall forming the glass partition of the conservatory. Behind the dining room is the breakfast room, and at the rear of the right side of the H is the kitchen. The left side of the leg of the H from front to rear are three bedrooms, one of which had been Alec's, followed by a billiard room which also abuts the glass conservatory wall; and behind that are the servants' quarters. The conservatory in the middle of the house opens in the rear to a trellised courtyard covered in vines which Eliza learns later is wisteria. The adults are intensely interested in the tour but the children don't share their enthusiasm.

— I want to see Rose Cottage again.

— Mother will take you over when Mrs Watley finishes showing us the house, John. Just be patient.

Joan, at the head of the delegation, is all oohs and aahs, commenting volubly on every room. James Clare walks with his hands behind his back, looking up and around, and muttering, 'Mm mm' occasionally. The children crowd in next, and Eliza brings up the rear. *My house. I am being shown my house.* She notices all kinds of details not picked up by the others — the angle of the sun at that time of day and how far it reaches into the rooms; the views from the windows; the uniform woodwork; the polished floors and co-ordinated carpet runners; and the warm cream hues of the walls.

The conservatory is very *avant garde* and quite stunning with its internal as well as external glass walls, letting light into nearly all rooms in the house. Its floor is set with stone flags, and large and small tubs of trees some of which touch the glass ceiling panels that can be opened and closed. There is even a banana tree; and oranges hang on a small tree in one corner. There are many tropical plants and two Kentia palms from a remote island in the Pacific Ocean which droop their shredded fronds. An aviary forms a triangle on the right side of the conservatory, and the birds can be seen through the dining room and breakfast room walls. *No doubt Alexis had many enjoyable meals here before her eyesight failed.*

— I took the dust covers off the furniture, Mrs Clare, for your inspection. It's good to see the rooms looking back to normal. We've had Mrs Stoke's rooms shut up since she went, God rest her soul; and Mr Alec's since he too …

— Thank you very much, Mrs Watley, for going to all this trouble for our visit

— Oh, it's nothing, Ma'am. Will you be wishing me to cover it back up or will you be moving in soon?

— I don't know exactly when we'll move. Maybe within the month. Don't bother covering everything again. Mother, here's the key to Rose Cottage. Father Clare, do you want to go with them? It's just out the front door and down through those big trees behind the wall.

— Yes, I must see the famous Rose Cottage. Show me the way, boys. Not too fast, now.

Eliza stands on the porch and watches the young ones skipping and hopping down to see their old haunts, then turns back into the main hall. In the middle of the floor is a square fringed rug. *'Persian rug' immediately comes to mind. I've never seen a Persian rug or carpet but this one, richly woven with red and gold, sums up 'Persian carpet' in my mind.* There are four padded high-backed benches along the walls, one on both sides of the door leading to the parlour and the same opposite, against the library wall.

— I'll just wander around and explore the house further on my own, Mrs Watley.

The parlour is formal, with high plastered ceilings and fancy cornices. It has a cream carpet covered with pink flowers, cream walls, and a deeper shade of pink-flowered chintz covering a settee and chairs, with floor to ceiling dark pink silk curtains held back by cream tassels. A wide mirror reflects the room and the rose garden outside.

When she enters the room on the other side of the main hall, the library, Eliza immediately knows she is home. *I get the feeling it might have been Alexis' favourite room, too.* Two entire walls of small square mullioned windows reach from cornice to baseboard on the front side of the house, with double French doors set between. This room was obviously designed to allow the best light for reading. Eliza goes over and sits down at the large writing desk which is placed so the person sits with their back to the windows, and faces into the room. The walls on her right are lined with bookshelves behind glass and ebony ensconced doors. She goes over to inspect the collection and runs her hands along the volumes — lots of poetry and history, Cook's voyages and Magellan's epic sea journeys, Burton and Speke, and literature: Dickens, Eliot, Shakespeare, the Brontes. *It'll take years just to read them once!* The Romantic poets, Browning, Byron. *Alexis, you're a woman after my own heart.*

As she walks through the dining room she pulls open a drawer in the long dresser. Row on row of silver cutlery, not tin but silver, and polished too, in separate compartments lined with green baize. There are three different-sized forks, three different-sized spoons, two different-sized knives the same shape and other knives with angled blades. As well, there are long-handled spoons, curved-handled spoons, teeny little spoons (for the salt), and others with holes in them. Another drawer reveals serviette rings, wine openers, sugar tongs and other sundries.

Alexis' suite is next, comprising one of the front wings. Windows are a feature of her bedroom with views in five different directions. She opens one of the casements and a warm scented breeze moves the curtains.

> 'It's a warm wind, the west wind, full of birds' cries;
> And I never hear the west wind but tears are in my eyes.
> For it comes from the west lands, the old brown hills,
> And April's in the west wind, and daffodils.'

She smiles as she remembers Masefield's poem and takes a really deep breath before inspecting the room. *I'm standing here in Alexis' private quarters, her 'sanctum sanctorum'. This is where she lived and thought, dozed in the daytime, dreamed; slept and dreamed and woke to live again, her eyesight and mind both slowly falling to pieces. Was she able to see the roses she planted? If she couldn't see them, she'd certainly be able to smell their perfume as they virtually surround Alexis' wing of the building. This woman who kept Angel's secret to herself must have walked these rooms and yearned. Or did she mourn? No one at The Slopes knew of his existence. Maybe this was as close as Alexis dared come to Emminster, hopeful of seeing him by chance some day.*

And if she did, would she recognize him? Or would she see him in every blond boy, youth, and young man who passed? I feel sure it must have gnawed at her. Just thinking of my own lost baby pulls at my heart. It will never run and shout on the village green or dart between parked carts on market day. No wonder Alexis acted strangely: maybe she thought that going blind was God's way of punishing her.

Maybe Angel, in his own disappointment, was right when he reacted to the news I lost the baby when he said, 'It's really a blessing in disguise'. That really cut me to the quick at the time. Not only did he seem not to care about what I'd been through on that awful ship, he didn't show any sorrow that his own child had died. Now I realize that any baby of his would very likely inherit the same affliction that was affecting his own sight, the one that sent his real mother blind. The Lord certainly does work in mysterious ways, or does He? It all comes down to the same old question: Is there an order, a plan, for every single one of us or is everything that happens just wild chance? What-ifs? We respond to the 'what-ifs', and try to make order from the consequences. Maybe the 'mysterious ways' are our own many and varied reactions to those very consequences? If Jack had stayed in England, or never married Mary (dear Mary: a true soul of honour); or if they hadn't convinced Angel to settle in Wollongong.... What if I hadn't obeyed Angel and stayed here? I'll never swear to obey another man; but I don't have to worry. My fate is now dictated by Alexis' will, and lies here at The Slopes. Maybe this is how Alexis felt.

If I had never met Jack, I wouldn't even know what true happiness smelled like. I didn't mean to fall in love with him. It just happened.

— Oh Jack, my Jack!

All the money and all the good fortune in the world can't buy true happiness. I have everything except Jack. Not having him is a bite out of that happiness. Money can buy security and peace of mind for the future, even foolish fun, but true happiness? No.

The old Wheel of Fortune again: chance, up and down. Riches, love, family, possessions, happiness — never all lined up at the same time. From Marlot cottage girl to gentleman farmer's wife, daughter-in-law of a vicar, descendant of the noble D'Urbervilles, and now inheritor of their 'wealth'. If money cannot buy me true happiness, perhaps it can hide the hollowness. Alexis may have felt that way too.

And here I am, right in the centre of Alexis' world.

A four poster hung with heavy damask curtains is cunningly set to receive maximum heat from the fireplace on cold nights. Eliza puts out her hand and feels Alexis' bed, sits on it, and sinks into billowing white coverlets filled with feathers, light and warm. *Soon I'll be sleeping on this.* The polished floor is covered with a large square of carpet, thick, with a rich floral pattern of red, white and black. It really is Persian, but she knows nothing of rugs.

The house hasn't been touched since Alexis died more than two years before. A core staff has been retained to keep it livable for Alec but he had not returned. He'd left home in high derision of his mother, become caught up in a religious revival movement sweeping the area and roamed the countryside preaching love and forgiveness. Unfortunately, he'd not practised his new fanaticism at home. Alexis died before reality and remorse brought him to his senses, and when he finally did return to The Slopes, he found it empty.

Alec didn't realize he missed the old lady; missed sparring verbally with her (she called it arguing); missed her rituals and idiosyncrasies; even missed the fowls, and bullfinches and other birds that filled the aviary with their calls. After he found Tess again (and he was obsessed with her), he could not, in all conscience, take her home, although he did convince her to let Mrs Durbeyfield and the younger children live in Rose Cottage.

Eliza looks around Alexis' bedroom again. The lady did have exquisite taste. From the windows she can see the rose bushes and the two giant trees in the oval lawn; and beyond, the row of pines and ash trees blocking the view of Rose Cottage where she had accepted Angel's proposal. She looks across the rose gardens to Alec's former room in the front, and out the side to the flowering fruit trees in the naturalized orchard.

Alexis' furniture is rich and massive. *And matching! It reminds me of my matching dining suite in little Keira Cottage. I was so proud of that dining suite; then Angel went and sold it without consulting me. His wedding present to me, and he turned it into cash. But here, at The Slopes, everything matches.* The parlour furniture is of the same wood and style as the dining and breakfast rooms: the tables, chairs, sideboards, hutches, serving tables, even the mantles above the different fireplaces match.

Here, in Alexis' bedroom, large rosewood wardrobes, dressing table and chair, wash-stand, chest, drawers, bedstead, bedhead and footboard, the chest, even the posts and canopies gleamed with the same carved curves. The crocheted coverlet, quilts and pillow shams stand out against the wood in clean contrasting white. Eliza can smell their sunshine freshness: they've been aired in the sun.

Mrs Watley has lit a fire to take the sharpness from the Spring air, and the brass handles on all the woodery winks in the flamelight. Eliza reaches towards one of the handles as it invites her to open, but stops. *Although this house now belongs to me, I feel like an intruder, discovering its intimacies. If anyone has a right to open these cupboards and drawers, I do. I'm the only one who has a right to. I inherited them: they're mine. But I still feel like I'm prying, opening up another person's life. Don't be silly, Liza. That's why you're here — to sort out Alexis' belongings. I can't have my bedroom full of another person's things. If I don't deal with these wardrobes and drawers, the chest, and hatboxes piled on top of the wardrobes and lowboys, they'll remain untouched.*

They'll end up covered in cobwebs like Miss Haversham's. She announces to the spirit of the room.

— Alexis, I'm going through your things just like you'd want me to.

She starts with the wardrobes. Alexis must have become stouter as the years passed. The gowns are too large for Eliza, although still very much in fashion. Her practised eye and needlewoman's acumen sums up the situation in a trice. *These dresses would fit me if they were taken in, or fit Mother if the hems were shortened.* She stands on a chair to get the hatboxes down and has a glorious fifteen minutes trying them on in front of the mirror. Next she moves to a chest of drawers; and finally to the dressing table

She sits down on Alexis' tapestry stool in front of the dressing table, facing a large fixed central mirror and two winged ones on the sides. She senses that this was Alexis' favourite place in the room, the heart of The Slopes. Placed on a starched runner are several silver-topped cut-glass perfume bottles with glass stoppers. Two have silver screw tops with tassels. She smells each one in turn. *What a taste in perfume!* A silver brush and comb set lie on an embroidered doily on the right side of the dresser. *Her own handwork?* And a silver-backed mirror with a handle lies face down on the left. Eliza coquettes with the mirrors, playing Alexis. The fire dances off her red-gold hair now worn high atop her lithe neck, and her violet eyes flash in the shadows. She laughs into the mirrors.

— 'Vanity. All is vanity, saith the preacher.'

She opens the top drawer on her right. It slides out easily and quickly. Body powders; different fragrances. 'Magnolia' says one; 'Lavender' another, all lined up on carefully smoothed white tissue paper. Also in the drawer are neat piles of thin, almost diaphanous, handkerchiefs, some with lace corners and some monogrammed with an 'A'. They're of different shades: ecru, salmon, primrose, no doubt to match the gowns. She pulls open other drawers, and turns over Alexis' daily toilette: several caps for day use, hair combs and hair pins, hat pins and scarves, costume jewellery, silk stockings, garter belts, high lace collars, sachets of lavender, and beads; and in the chest of drawers, a whalebone corset, bloomers, pantaloons and petticoats.

Next she reaches down low to the central drawer in front of her. She pulls on the brass handles, shaped like hinged door knockers, but the drawer is stuck. She pulls harder but it remains firm. Then she notices a key hole under the knocker. Alexis must have kept this locked for a reason, but where is the key? Eliza goes to her purse and takes out the keys the solicitor had given her. Even a quick glance shows that none of them is small enough to fit the hidden lock. *Something important, important to Alexis, must be in* that drawer. Another will? I can't bear to think of such a thing. The title deed to the property? Old letters? Her poetry? The Reverend James said she wrote poetry. Jewellery? It's something Alexis didn't mean anyone to find, I feel certain. Where would she keep the key?

She starts looking in the other drawers: more lingerie, a manicure set, and Japanese lacquerware boxes with lids. In a porcelain bowl with a removable shepherdess top, she finds a mixture of foreign coins, gold chains (one with a tiny gold baby in a woven silver basket no larger than her little finger nail: Moses), and some small keys. She eagerly reaches in and extracts five different keys from amongst the other bits and pieces, and places them in the open palm of her left hand. Just then she hears footsteps, and a knock on the door. She swings around, clutching the keys tightly.

— Good afternoon, Missis. They told me I might find you here.

— Mrs Watley. You gave me a start. I was so engrossed.

Mrs Watley glances down at the gowns and hats on the bed.

— I'm glad you've begun to sort out all those clothes. I didn't know what to do with them, and Mr Alec had no inclination to touch them, neither. I imagined they would just muster and mildew away. I came to tell you I've got the afternoon tea ready for you and your family, and it's waiting for you in the parlour right now.

— That's very good of you, Mrs Watley. Thank you. Would you go over to the cottage and inform my mother? I'll be there directly.

The housekeeper gives an approving nod and closes the heavy door noiselessly behind her. Eliza now becomes aware of the little square ends of the keys pressing into her palm, and opens her left hand. Three of the keys are brass with differently shaped heads. Two of the heads are elliptical and smooth while the other is heart-shaped. The other two keys are of a darker metal. She takes the larger of the elliptical heads with its intricate jagged square end, lifts the knocker and tries it in the hidden hole. Too big. She places it on the dresser and next tries the heart-shaped one. It fits the keyhole but turns round and round without unlocking. She puts it up beside the other key and, choosing the last brass key, places it in the lock. It goes in, and when she turns it backwards it turns over easily with a 'click'.

When she pulls on the little knocker, the narrow bottom drawer slides open. The afternoon light has been gradually fading, and the inside of the drawer is quite dark. She lights a candle and moves it to the top edge of the dresser so it will throw as much light as possible into the low drawer in front of her. It doesn't hold anything different from the other drawers. She lifts out several pairs of gloves, long and mid-length, evening and afternoon ones of silk, kid and suede in various colours; utilitarian ones in black and navy; some with scalloped edges; and some open-cut in the Florentine style. *Locked gloves? Why would Alexis lock up her gloves? There must be something more.*

She reaches right into the back, and finds some evening bags: a flat, embroidered silk one with a gold chain handle, one of taffeta, and two beaded ones. She opens each one expectantly. Nothing more than a folded hanky, a mirror, and a penny for good luck. That one must have been a gift. Now she has everything out of the drawer on top of the dresser or in her lap. Nothing left but the lining of tissue paper, folded double thick, shiny side up. *That's everything. Now I have to put all these things back, and afternoon tea getting cold.*

She smooths the tissue out with both hands and feels a slight ridge right in the back. There's a definite ridge under the tissue paper. She slips her nail under the front edge of the lining and gently pulls it out of the drawer, and there, in the back corner, is a piece of dark brown cardboard. She reaches in, takes it out and turns it over. It is dark brown on the other side as well. *Oh, it opens.* She puts both thumbs together and uses her thumb nails to open the flaps. And she stares. *Angel? No.* The world stops. *Jack! It's a picture of Jack. Why in the world would Alexis have a picture of Jack? Was she his mother too? That's too bizarre.* She looks at it closely. *Yes, there are Jack's direct eyes, the strong line of his face and jaw in half profile, his thick, fair wavy hair.* She turns the photograph over again, and discerns a shimmer of dim handwriting against the matte of the cardboard. She holds it nearer the candle, turning it slowly until she can read 'Forever', and underneath that, a large capital 'G'. She hears a scurry of footsteps outside the door before it flies open.

— Liza-Lu! Aren't you coming yet? John and Charlie have eaten half the scones and Mama said your tea is getting stone cold.

Modesty stops in the middle of the room and her eyes fly from the bed to the dresser and back to the bed again, piled high with dresses and hats, gloves and handbags. Her mouth falls open.

— Are these all yours?

— Yes, yes, and lots more, too. I'll have to put these things away after. You can help me. Run and tell Mama I'm coming right away.

Her little sister spins out of the room. Eliza looks closely at Jack's picture again. *'G'?* She holds it against her heart which is beating far too fast for a person cleaning out drawers. Then she drops her chin over it, and takes a deep breath.

— Jack of Hearts. My Jack.

For now, the best place for the photograph is where it has lain for the last who knows how long. She replaces it in the back of the drawer and covers it with the tissue. On standing up she realizes just how hungry she is, and goes out slowly through the dressing room into the hall, shaking her head in disbelief.

CHAPTER 31

Gabriel

Next morning, after the children leave for school, Eliza speaks with Joan.

— It looks like the children will have to be uprooted again, Mother.

— I don't think it'll hurt 'em much, being *up*-rooted. Better than being down-rooted.

— I want them to have the best education. Should we send them off to boarding school, or get a governess, or what?

— Don't worry your head about that just now, Liza-Lu. We'll move first, and they can all go to the Trantridge school until we decide.

— Another thing: they love Rose Cottage.

— They can love it all they like. I, Joan Durbeyfield, intend to live in the Manor House like a lady, and have servants to look after me.

— And that's what I want for you, too, Mother. You've earned it. You can have the front wing opposite mine, the one Alec used. You can decorate it any way you want. The other bedrooms can be shared by the girls and boys. The rooms are a lot larger than they share now; or, we could turn the billiard room into something else.

— Don't worry about arrangements, Liza-Lu. Everything will fall into place, you'll see. What are you going to do with Alec's clothes, and the old lady's things you don't need?

— Father Clare's having a rummage sale next month. I don't expect anything will go to waste. You and I can drive out and have a look at her dresses, and decide if we want to modify any of them, or get new ones. We might have a good laugh trying on the hats. Mother …?

— Mmm?

— I found something yesterday, in a locked drawer, under the lining.

— Ooo, sounds mysterious. A secret?

— Must be. It's a photograph of Jack Turville, Angel's friend, you know, the people I went out with on the ship.

— Why would Angel's mother hide a picture of *him*?

— That's what I'm asking. At first I thought it was Angel, they look so similar; but it wasn't.

— Maybe she's Jack's mother, too?

— That crossed my mind, but how? Someone has written on the back of the photograph 'Forever G'. What do you suppose that means?

— Beats me, Liza-Lu. Maybe the vicar can shed some light on it. Here's the postman. Letter for you from Greyhampton.

Eliza takes the letter and tears it open.

— It's from the vicar at Greyhampton. He says there is no record of Angel's baptism in Greyhampton, and thanks me for my generous donation.

— None? I think you'd better go over and see the Reverend.

— Father Clare, I have some mysteries to clear up. I need more information about Alexis.

— I told you everything I can remember. Did I mention to you she wrote poetry, and had a book, an old ledger, that she copied all her poems into, in red ink?

— Really? I just received a letter from the vicar in Greyhampton. You told me to write and get a copy of Angel's baptism from the parish register to try and find out who Angel's father was. Well, he wasn't baptized in Greyhampton.

— No?

— No. Did you baptize him here?

— No, I thought he was already baptized.

— Poor Angel, he died without ever being baptized. That would have really upset him. Father Clare, I found something very interesting yesterday hidden in one of Alexis' drawers, under lock and key.

— Now that you have my attention, what could it be?

— A photograph of Jack Turville, Angel's friend. Do you suppose your sister was Jack's mother, too?

— I doubt it. I wasn't that close to her but I think she only had the two children.

— There was writing on the back of the picture. It says, 'Forever G'. Who could 'G' be?

— Gabriel.

— Gabriel? Who's Gabriel?

Recognition seems to dawn on James' face.

— Why, Gabriel Turville. Of course!

— Who's he?

— He's young Jack Turville's father. He looks exactly like his father, you know.

— How do you know?

— I saw the likeness immediately when he came here for your wedding.

— No, I mean, how do you know Jack's father?

— Gabriel? We went to school together. Harrowford Grammar. I told you my father was Headmaster.

— Yes, but I didn't know Jack came from Harrowford.

— The Turvilles are the biggest land owners in the county. Gabriel, or 'The Squire', as they call him, lives at the Hall, Harrowford Hall. Very old family. Very influential.

— He's still alive?

— I believe so. I haven't heard to the contrary.

— Maybe it's a photograph of Gabriel, and not of Jack. You said they look alike?

— Spitting image. A chip off the old block.

— Maybe *he* was Angel's father?

— I never thought of that. It's entirely possible. You see, Alexis was governess at Harrowford Hall.

— No!

— Yes. I told you she was a governess.

— I know, but you didn't say where.

— I wonder …. It's entirely possible, you know. Alexis never told anyone who Angel's father was. She left Harrowford and went north before she was showing.

— Why do you suppose she called him 'Angel'? I've never heard of anyone called Angel before.

— In Spain it's quite common. They pronounce it 'Ahn-khel'.

— If Gabriel really is his father, you don't suppose Alexis named him Angel after the Angel Gabriel in the Bible?

— That's exactly the sort of thing she *would* do.

— I'll have to get that picture the next time I'm at The Slopes, and show you. The Reverend James shakes his head.

— The intricacies that people get themselves caught up in! Alexis and

Gabriel ...but he was married and had a family. I don't know what the world is coming to.

— You said you knew him well?

— I did, when we were young. I haven't seen him in years.

— What I'm getting at is — could you give me a letter of introduction, or come with me? I could show him the photograph and ask him if he's Angel's father.

— I suppose I could write a letter, but let's see the photograph first.

CHAPTER 32

DISCOVERING ALEXIS

Eliza once more drives out to her new home. She explains to Mrs Watley she's come to pick up a couple of things, and Mrs Watley kindly has lunch ready at twelve noon. Eliza immediately retrieves the photograph and looks at it very carefully; takes it over to the window and studies it. It's Jack all right, but not quite. Her heart jumps again when she sees it. Little differences give the likeness away like the hair line and the wrinkles around the eyes. She puts it carefully in her purse. *What next?* She glances around and sees some books between bookends on top of the chest of drawers. They seem well-used, as if Alexis had retrieved a few special ones from the library. *Did she read in bed at night? I'm slowly peeling away Alexis' outer layers, getting to know the living, breathing woman.*

She runs her hands and eyes over the small selection. There is a Bible, *The Rubáiyát of Omar Khayyám*, *Wordsworth: The Complete Works*. Next she picks up *The Works of Elizabeth Barrett Browning. All these pages have been turned a lot.* Eliza notices that several lines and stanzas are underlined.

"The Cry of the Children"

'Do ye hear the children weeping,
O my brothers,
'Ere the sorrow comes with years?
They are leaning their young heads against their mothers,
And that cannot stop their tears.
The young lambs are bleating in the meadows.
The young birds are chirping in the nest,

> The young fawns are playing with the shadows.
> The young flowers are blowing towards the west —
> <u>But the young, young children, O my brothers,</u>
> <u>They are weeping bitterly!</u>
> <u>They are weeping in the playtime of the others,</u>
> <u>In the country of the free.</u>

Eliza reads the underlined words again. *Why did Alexis underline those specific lines? Could this be evidence that her husband employed children in his factory in the north? Alexis could have been a key person in his decision to sell up and move south. She would certainly have had* **some** *influence on him. She was also probably very thankful that Angel was getting an alternate upbringing to what he might have, had she kept him. Maybe this very poem influenced her to keep birds and raise lambs at The Slopes. It's also close to the Chase which is full of deer. She may have encouraged Alec in nature's ways by planning this country idyll. But it turned full circle. Tessie was brought low by Alec in those very same trees in the Chase.*

The power of words. Written by one woman years ago, acted on by another, and now making me sad and thoughtful today. What else did Alexis underline? Ah!

> '<u>How do I love thee? Let me count the ways.</u>
> <u>I love thee to the depth and breadth and height</u>
> <u>My soul can reach</u>, when feeling out of sight
> For the ends of Being, and ideal Grace,
> I love thee to the level of every day's
> Most quiet need, by sun and candlelight,
> I love thee freely, as men strive for Right;
> I love thee purely, as they turn from Praise.
> I love thee with the passion put to use
> In my old griefs, and with my childhood faith.
> <u>I love thee with a love I seemed to lose</u>
> With my lost saints — <u>I love thee with the breath,</u>
> <u>Smiles, tears, of all my life!</u> — and, if God choose,
> I shall but love thee better after death.

Tears well up in Eliza's eyes. *A few words can convey so much emotion. My lost love. Alexis' lost love. What we had or might have had. A glimpse of the sunrise, then comes the fog.*

Mmm. What else does she have here? She replaces the Browning and takes up the soft leather-bound Bible. *Sometimes Bibles have a page in the front to record family births, marriages and deaths. Not this one, although it's well-thumbed.* As she flips through it, a page falls open in the *Song of Solomon* and there, almost as a book mark, is a golden ringlet of baby hair. *Angel's hair? Her golden-haired Angel?* This is almost too much for Eliza.

Mrs Watley calls her for lunch. Eliza insists the housekeeper join her for the meal, and plies her with questions about Alexis. Mrs Watley also has questions of her own.

— Do you have any idea, Ma'am, when you and your family might be moving in? It's not that I'm inquisitive; it's just that we have to hire staff, get supplies brought in, get the horses ready — management types of things.

— I had no idea all this had to be co-ordinated. You'll have to help me, Mrs Watley.

— I'll draw up a list of staff and the areas they look after. You can change anything you want. You are, after all, mistress of The Slopes.

— Let's say, then, we'll move on the first of May. Will that give you enough time? It's only a couple of weeks.

— I think so. I'll advertise for a cook, a butler, a scullery maid, and a house maid. Do you or your mother need a personal maid?

— I don't think so. We weren't brought up to it, you know. We can lay out our own clothes, and dress ourselves. Do we need a gardener? What about a shepherd or a farm labourer?

— You're beginning to think like a lady, Ma'am. We need all these people to get the place up and running again. And what about a nanny or a governess?

— You can start looking for a governess. I think my mother will want to double as nanny. She enjoys children.

— I can see that.

— You'd better pack up all of Mr Alec's things for the Church rummage sale. His rooms will be my mother's. I think we may need some more feminine style drapes in there, but she can decide later. We also need to move the two double beds into one of the large rooms for my sisters, and we'll need to buy two more for the boys. I'll have to go to the carriage house to see what we have.

— There's a pony trap, two carriages, and a farm wagon with two draught horses, three for drawing, and a stallion of Mr Alec's.

— I'm thinking of getting ponies for the children to ride and a quieter beast for myself but that's also for later. So it's ship-shape for May the first?

If you can assemble the staff before that, please go ahead. I'll need to have that list and also you'll need to tell me when and how much they are paid.

— Very good, Mrs Clare. I'll do my best to have a cook, housemaid and a groom by the time you arrive.

— I thought the groom had been kept on.

— He left to work in the next parish where his people are from.

Eliza goes back to Alexis' room to continue sorting her belongings. When she removes some boxes from a lowboy shelf, she finds a large ledger in the back with a mottled blue cover. *The one that Father Clare had mentioned?* She opens it. *Yes!* The beginning is in childish handwriting, **her handwriting**, and Eliza sees it firm up and develop an adult slant as the years progress in the pages. Each poem is signed, and in the beginning is dated by her year in school. Her first poem, "The Bellman", ends

'He rings his bell, the time to tell,
So folks will know that all is well.'

Alexis Clare
Stad. 4.

Eliza smiles. An eight year-old. She glances through the book until one poem catches her attention, even though it has no title.

'I came away because you'd best not know
Our love ignited, and within me grows;
And I must bear my punishment and pain
To never look upon your face again.

It was an easy time, an easy birth —
My golden-headed Angel, child of earth.
Since then, this vale of tears I'm wading through,
There's not a moment I don't think of you.'

Oh, that's sad. Poor girl. It makes me think of Jack — 'To never look upon your face again'; *and* 'There's not a moment I don't think of you.' *Alexis! We've a lot in common, you and I. Thank you for this wonderful house. I suppose you forgot all about that ledger as time went by. What's this one?*
"My Angel"
'My darling, I have loved you

> And have kept my promise well
> To shield your name from needless shame,
> My angel Gabriel.
>
> And so I named our little babe;
> 'Twas all that I could do —
> A living memory of your name
> To help remember you.

This is it! Here's proof that Gabriel is Angel's father. 'Forever G.' She never told him. He doesn't know. O, my God! Angel and Jack are brothers! Oh, my goodness. Jack and Angel have the same father. No wonder they look alike. And Jack doesn't know any of this, either. I'll have to take these poems back with me. They're living proof, or dead proof, that Gabriel Turville really is Angel's father; and if Angel was a Turville, we are probably related way back, and if that's the case, I'm probably related to Jack, too!

She can't wait to get home and tell her mother the news, but Joan is hardly interested.

— Don't go getting mixed up with all them old ancestors again, Liza-Lu.

— But Mother, what do you think of the main news, about Angel's father?

— It's not going to bring your husband back, is it? And marriage is what husbands are all about.

Eliza's news has more impact on James.

— Well, my girl, that proves it, doesn't it? That pretty well proves it. Her own handwriting in the old ledger.

Eliza nods.

— Now I *have* to meet the Squire.

— Well, well. Fancy that. Those boys always looked somewhat alike, and young Jack was very like his father at that age, or vice versa. You know what I mean. Tell you what, while you were gone I found some letters that Alexis wrote to me when she first went to Greyhampton. They don't throw any light on our former problem, like the *evidence* does; they're mostly descriptive.

He goes to the writing desk and gives Eliza two envelopes. She opens the first, and recognizes Alexis' hand.

'Dear James,

This is to let you know that I arrived at Aunt Bea's safely. It was wet and drizzling all the way. Greyhampton certainly lives up to its name, up here on the moorland. The blue-grey cobbles glisten in the rain, and the grey stone of the buildings looks darker because of it. The slate roofs, all slate roofs, are an even deeper shiny grey. It hasn't stopped raining since I arrived two days ago. Who knows? When this is all over, maybe I will find true happiness here.

Greyhampton is an industrial city with lots of smoke and factories, entirely different from the West Country. I'm really grateful, James, for your offer. I know it's hard to say it to your face. Thank you. I know you'll bring up my little one in a godly way and give him half a chance in life; more than he would if it stayed with me.

Your loving sister,
Alexis.'

— In the other letter she tells how she became employed and how she met her husband.

— Do you mind if I read it now?

— No, no. Go ahead. They're your letters now, anyway.

'Dear James,

By now you will have had a couple of months to get to know your new little son. I hope he's a good little Angel. No one would ever guess he was my son. His colouring is the opposite of my dark hair. Do give him a kiss from me.

As soon as I was well again, Aunt Bea introduced me to her circle of friends, and I joined the Greyhampton congregation. One of her friends knows the Headmistress at a private girls' school here. With the burgeoning industrial boom, mostly woollen mills, some of the *nouveau riche* in the North want to educate their daughters to the same standard as their sons (and so they should!) A former estate on the outskirts was purchased and converted into the Rose Hill Ladies' Academy. Aunt Bea mentioned that I had worked as a governess, and that Father was Headmaster at Harrowford Grammar, and Lo! Who you know speaks louder than what you know. I was invited up for an interview, and hired then and there as instructor of English and Fine Arts.

And what do you think, James? The Academy has an aviary! It extends the whole length of one wing. They have all kinds of exotic birds strutting imperiously up and down: the usual pea fowl from India with iridescent 'eyes' on their fan-shaped tails. There are a pair of Germains, some Chinese ring-necked pheasants with tiger-striped tails, Malayan crested firebacks, some heavy, waddling, crested Impeyans, and several pairs of Lady Amhersts, the silver mosaic ones, with the unmistakable red eyes and scarlet tail feathers. I couldn't believe it! When I stopped to admire them on the initial tour of the school, they asked me if I was interested in birds. Interested? So now I'm in charge of them.

'Oh, by the way, there's a member of the Board here, a factory owner, who's been giving me the sweet come-ons! Silly old fool. Well, that's about it for now,

From your gainfully employed sister,
Alexis.'

— I'm getting to know your sister better and better.
— Yes, you two would have got along very well. Pushy and headstrong.
— I am not!
— No, not really. Women on their own these days have to be assertive. Maybe Alexis was born several generations too early. You women will have the vote and be running for Parliament next.
— Not just Parliament: Prime Minister!
— Now that you're a land owner, who knows what will happen, eh, daughter?

She gives him a kiss on the cheek.
— Father Clare, you're also ahead of your time.

CHAPTER 33

CONFRONTING THE SQUIRE

The next three days sees Eliza in London meeting with all the recommended people who will assist her in managing Alexis' fortune. The following week, she leaves Emminster early to catch the train west to the station nearest Harrowford. Squire Turville had written that he would be happy to receive the daughter-in-law of his old friend, James Clare.

— Mr Turville? I'm Eliza Clare.

She puts out her hand.

— Gabriel Turville, Mrs Clare. I'm very pleased to know you. Come into the drawing room. Make yourself comfortable. What can it be that brings you to Harrowford?

— Mr Turville …

And those violet eyes look directly into Jack's. *This is unnerving! He looks **exactly** like Jack, just a little older. He has the air of a man sure of his ways, born and bred a country squire used to giving orders and being obeyed.* She swallows, and goes on.

— …I wanted to meet you for two reasons. It's hard for me to know where to begin. They are both sensitive topics, and I couldn't broach them in a letter. Um. I, er, found a photograph of you, at least I think it's you, taken when, um, you were younger, I think. Is this you?

— Why, yes. Where did you find this?

She watches his face.

— I found it in a locked drawer of a dressing table that belonged to Alexis Stoke.

— Alexis, did you say?

— Yes. Alexis Clare, the Reverend James' sister. I believe she was governess to your children.

He takes his pipe out of his mouth, smiles and nods. *Jack's smile.*

— Alexis. Yes, I knew her …quite well, in fact, but how did you come to be going through her dressing table?

— She died, you know, a few years ago.

— I'm sorry to hear it.

— She married a wealthy mill owner who left her very well-off.

— I'm glad she married comfortably but that still doesn't explain how you came to be going through her drawers.

— I'm the heir to her estate, heiress, that is.

— *You* are? How could that be?

— Did you know that when she left Harrowford she was in the family way?

— With child?

— With your child.

— I had no idea. I thought she broke off our …friendship for the sake of my family.

— She was pregnant with your child.

— Oh my.

— She didn't want you to know, and she was successful in that. She did love you, you know. I found two of her poems that explain why she left. She had a baby boy. You knew him — Angel Clare.

— No. Angel is James Clare's son.

— That's what they wanted the world to believe. Father Clare and Alexis made a solemn promise that he would give the baby a chance in life by raising him in the vicarage as his own child if she would agree never to contact her son or reveal that she was his true mother.

— Angel Clare is *my* son? I know he and …another son of mine … looked very much alike when they were at school here, best of friends.

— Jack.

— What? Er, yes, Jack. You've heard of him?

— When I married Angel in Emminster, Jack and his wife Mary were our witnesses.

— Jack was home? When was this?

— Last summer, although it seems eons ago. Mary's mother wasn't well so they brought their little girl home to see her grandmother. She was born in Australia.

— He has a child?

— The dearest little pet. Polly's her name. She's very bright: full of life, and she has the same hair as you and Jack.

— How old is she?

— Now she'd be five.

Gabriel sinks back in his chair.

— You've certainly stirred up some memories, Mrs Clare.

— No, please. You must call me Eliza. After all, I'm your daughter-in-law, too.

— You are sure that Angel Clare is *my* child?

— I copied three of Alexis' poems. Look, you can read them for yourself, and the Reverend James is now convinced of it.

He reads, nodding, saying some of the phrases out loud, 'never look upon your face again', and 'not a moment I don't think of you'.

Gabriel shakes his head, and sighs.

— Dear girl, Alexis. 'Golden-headed Angel' …'to shield my name from shame' …' my angel Gabriel'. It's too bad.

He closes his eyes, and long repressed memories start to surface.

— I copied this one, too. I think it was also written to you. All her poems are numbered. This one's number sixty-nine.

Gabriel reads.

Touch Me

Touch me in the sunshine;
Touch me in the Hall;
Touch me by the orchard gate
Or by the garden wall.
Touch me by the water's edge
Or underneath the moon;
Touch me on the river bank;
Only, touch me soon.

Touch me in the misty dark;
Touch me anywhere;
Touch me as you run your fingers
In and out my hair.

Touch me with your gentle smile;
I'll close my eyes in wonder
And know that our two souls are fused
By silence in the thunder.

> Love's for some, and pain's for some,
> And hell is full of laughter.
> Touch me, while the world's still young:
> There may be no time after.
>
> I'll love you still until I'm old;
> Our secret's safe with me,
> And love you 'til the sun turns cold
> And I have ceased to be.

He rolls his lips together and shakes his head, obviously moved. Eliza gently interjects.

— There's more I have to tell you about Angel.

— What you've already told me is momentous enough: that I have another son.

— Not any more.

— What do you mean? Did something happen to him?

— Yes, in Wollongong, in New South Wales. He drowned in a flooded creek and was washed out to sea. They never found his body.

— Oh, my dear little girl! And my own boy drowned! When did this all happen?

— Only a few months ago, the end of January.

— Where, did you say?

— In Wollongong, in Australia.

— Australia? Angel was in Australia, too?

— I think he was encouraged by Jack's success out there, and after we were married he went out and bought a farm.

— You didn't go with him?

— I went later. I was pregnant, you see, and decided to stay home but he insisted I join him. I was frightfully seasick going out. I don't remember a lot of it. While I was ill I had a miscarriage and lost the baby. Jack and Mary were on the same ship, going home, and if it hadn't been for them, I wouldn't be here telling you this today.

Gabriel looks at her compassionately.

— I'm so sorry, my dear. What a lot of troubles you've had, and so young.

He takes her hand in his large strong brown one *(Jack's hands)*, grips, and shakes it reassuringly.

— I'd really like to know more about Alexis, Squire Turville. I want to discover as much as I can about her.

— I was under a lot of pressure at the time. Ever since Jack's birth my wife, Mary Ann, had been sickly. He was the last, the youngest, my favourite; but a black sheep, a scamp. I did everything for him: sent him to the best grammar school, and on to the Agricultural College. And what was my reward? He did nothing but oppose me.

I must get him off this obviously still prickly subject.

— But what about Alexis?

— Ah, yes. Alexis.

He blinks into the distance.

— Gabriel, my eldest, was boarding at the grammar school, and the two girls, Emma and Julianna, and Jack, were at home. Jack was about three at the time, around that. My golden boy. As I told you, my wife wasn't well, spent most of the time in bed in her shade-drawn room, reclusive. Even had her meals there. She was not around for the children; was not there for me .... I felt quite isolated, estranged. All the upbringing of the children fell to me. There had been a couple of lack-lustre governesses, and then a dark-haired, vivacious, fun-loving young governess came into our lives. She was a breath of fresh air, and totally the opposite to Mary Ann. She exuded strength and health and well-being, and had her own ideas about managing children. They all adored her, with her long black ringlets which she wore free, not up on top of her head. I came to depend on her, not just as a governess but to head the dinner table if I had company, which I often had, as Squire of Harrowford Hall.

He looks over at Eliza with those deep blue Turville eyes.

— You understand how it is? A man gets lonely. At meals, I would be gazing down the table at Alexis, not Mary Ann. Emma and Julianna would sit on one side, and Jack would sit down the other, perched on the giant encyclopaedia beside Alexis. She was so capable with them. She ran and played with them on the lawns. She gave them lots of freedom, and in return they gave her the attention she requested in the schoolroom.

The halls resonated with the rounds she taught them — 'Merrily, merrily, merrily, merrily, life is but a dream'. Alexis taught Jack, even at that tender age, to memorize rhymes. One morning, she brought him before me and Jack recited from memory: never missed a word. Jack would shout out the ditties with relish, and, of course, would get a lot of applause and praise for his efforts. I wanted him to grow up and follow my ways (what father wouldn't?) but he was determined, even as a tiny child. A mind of his own. He'd stand in front of me with his little hands on his hips and say, 'I want to do it *my* way!'

How quickly Gabriel's stories come back to Jack. She pushes on, encouraging Gabriel in his narrative.

— I wish I could have met Alexis. Talking with you and Father Clare, and reading her poetry, and what her housekeeper told me makes me feel close to her. You know what I mean?

— She was easy to get close to. She had that way with her. It was the love the children gave her that made me wish she really was their mother. Whenever she read to them, or told them stories, they would sit, snuggled up to her, and drape their arms around her neck and shoulders. She would hold them close to her heart, or squeeze them when the story reached the climax. Their adoration of her awakened a yearning in me, I suppose, for the touch of companionship that was missing in my life.

I'll never forget that warm autumn day. The leaves had all changed to gold, and had that damp smell to them as if suddenly touched by rain. Normally Alexis wore her governess clothes, with her hems skimming her indoor pumps — large puffed sleeves, high neck collar, cuffs buttoned tight at the wrists, usually in grey, but she often used bright shawls and beads that made her dress more attractive. She also had a habit of dressing in trousers, and slipping out of the house alone to go for contemplative rambles.

I was out for my constitutional on a track through the woods down by the river which was at its lowest that time of year bubbling along slowly in its stony bed, when I heard a lot of scurrying in the dry leaves. I stopped in my walk by the edge of a clearing as the noise got nearer and nearer, when all of a sudden a frantic little rooster shot out of the undergrowth with Alexis, in trousers, in hot pursuit. It ran on its short legs straight for the river then veered on the bank, changing direction by skidding on the fallen leaves. Alexis followed, breaking abruptly into the clearing with her arms sweeping in front of her to prevent the branches from slapping her face. I couldn't help laughing. She stood there, flushed from the chase, with her black hair loose over her shoulders. I was transfixed. I made some inane comment, I don't remember what, and then we were slowly walking towards one another. Her eyes never left mine. I touched those ringlets. I kissed her mouth. We were both hungry: I for what I had been missing, and she for what she had never yet experienced.

Those next few weeks my heart was never so light. I found myself smiling all the time. I had never physically slipped on my marriage vows before (or since), although it had really ceased to be a marriage. I felt reckless whenever Alexis appeared. I would hear her footstep, and my heart would jump. Then I would remember my station and my responsibilities; my place in society; my position as Squire of Harrowford Hall. Married man. Father of four.

Without a word, she was gone. She never even left a note. It was a brief, passionate, intense relationship the likes of which I never experienced before or since. I thought she'd left because the situation was hopeless; and sooner or later someone would have noticed how I looked at her, or she at me. I couldn't pursue her, make inquiries, ask James about her. That would be have been inappropriate. I remember about a week before she left she asked if I had a photograph of myself that she could have. That one there. I wrote 'Forever G.' on the back.

— And that's how I found you. At first, I first thought it was a picture of Angel she had kept, then I was sure it was Jack. It's so much like him.

— Jack looks like that, now, Eliza?

— Like father, like son.

— My dear young lady, you'll have to tell me how you came to marry Angel Clare but before you do — Giles?

An old man-servant appears.

— Giles, we'd like a cup of tea, and buns, or whatever goes with it.

— Very good, Squire.

— But *I* need something stronger.

Gabriel goes over to a glass cabinet and takes out a decanter. Whiskey for me. Would you like some sherry, Eliza?

— A small glass would be nice, thank you, Squire.

She accepts the drink and starts in on the Angel saga. *I trust this country farmer, Master of Harrowford Hall: still tall and broad-shouldered, commanding.* She leaves nothing out. They consume tea, buns and strawberry preserves; she, talking and licking the butter off her fingers; he, intent on the story pouring from this attractive young woman. Tess and Alec D'Urberville (*her* other child; Tess and Angel Clare (*his* child); Angel's well-intentioned but failed farming ventures on two faraway continents; Angel and Eliza; Angel and Jack; Jack and Mary, and Polly (*his* grandchild); Angel's death; Eliza's return: the many faces and facets of love.

She lays everything before the Squire. He's amazed at this young woman, and what she's gone through in the past twelve months. Instead of crushing her, it seems to have matured her.

— Is there more?

— A few other things.

— Then you must stay for lunch.

— No, no. I've taken up most of your morning.

— If there's more, we need to talk longer. I don't know about you, but I can't concentrate if I don't have a full stomach. Can you stay? Will you stay?

— Well, I suppose so. As long as I can get back before dark.

— Done, then. Giles!

And Gabriel gives instructions for lunch.

— Would you like a tour of the house and grounds while Giles gets lunch?

After a tour of the Hall he leads her past the granaries, the blacksmith shop, and stables. He points out his domain, the farm hands' cottages, the town of Harrowford in the valley beyond, the fields of different greens. Eliza is impressed.

— It's like a miniature village.

— It is one, with multitudinous enterprises.

— You run it single-handedly?

— I always have but lately I've been thinking I'd like to sit back on my laurels and not be caught up in the day to day detail.

— You don't have a foreman or manager?

— You can't trust them. It all goes smoothly for a while until they get some notion to change this or that; or they up and leave; or answer you back. Me! Who knows more about farming than all of them put together. The short answer to your question is, there is no one.

— Jack told me you were grooming his brother to take over.

— He did, did he? Well, young Gabriel bought himself a commission in the Navy and left the land for good. You mentioned Jack makes a very good living in New South Wales.

— Very. He's one of the wealthiest businessmen in the Illawarra. He's a timber merchant, and bought into many allied and different businesses: the sawmill, the dairy, the mine (coal); owns most of the gaslight company, and a jam factory; also a bakery, and it was his men who cut the new rock baths in Wollongong.

Gabriel's eyes widen (*Jack's eyes!*)

— So he's made something of himself, has he?

She nods slowly.

— That's what I wanted to ask you, Squire.

— What's that, my dear?

— I know it would mean a lot to Jack if you would contact him. He's very proud of you.

— He's never let me know it.

— He's a man. You're a man. Men don't talk about their feelings to each other. Do you?

— Well, I suppose not.

— And you do have a wonderful little granddaughter.

— Polly. That was my mother's name.

— There you are! And Jack's wife is the loveliest person. A real peacemaker. They're very lucky to have found one another.

— It seems by what you're saying that she's been an influence on him.

— Won't you write to him? Just to make contact?

Gabriel sighs resignedly.

— Has anyone ever been able to refuse those violet eyes of yours, Eliza?

— You'll write?

— Give me his address. I promise I'll drop him a line.

She warms to this strong-willed but vulnerable man. They hear a gong in the distance.

— That's lunch.

Eliza finds Gabriel so easy to talk to. Her morning's revelations lead into ponderings of relationships: in-laws; out-laws; half brothers and sisters; and inheritance. Off Eliza goes again, recounting her ancestor theory of the dispersal of the old D'Urberville name: Durbeyfield, Derbyfield, Durville, Torville. Then why not Turville?

— We might be more distantly related than being modern in-laws.

She is so earnest, interested, absorbed

— My girl, you've turned my whole world upside down in just one day. There's one thing I want you to promise me.

— Yes?

— That you'll come back and see me; fill me in with what's happening in your life. Will you do that?

— My life won't be very interesting from now on. Mostly I'll be at The Slopes. And the family won't be in need any more. That's what Alexis' money has done for me. It's made life secure, peaceful.

— I think that would be impossible for you.

— No, I really mean it. I can relax. I don't have to worry about rents and bailiffs, eating meat only once in a blue moon, or of saving every little scrap of string or paper because it might come in handy later on.

— Now don't forget, Eliza. You are to come whenever you like.

— And you must come and visit us at The Slopes after we move in. You can browse in Alexis' library, and I'll show you the ledger with the poetry, and Angel's baby hair. It isn't your hair, is it? No. It must be his because Alec

D'Urberville had black hair like his mother.

— I will come, you have my word.

— Then, good-bye, Squire. I have so much enjoyed meeting you. Thank you for all the information.

— Cheerio!

After dinner that night, the first thing Eliza does is write to Jack and Mary. She doesn't want to appear to be concentrating on Jack, which she is, so she carefully starts out, as with all her correspondence to them,

'Dear Mary and Jack,

What a momentous day! I went to see your father, Jack. You'll never guess — he is Angel's father too! I have the proof. Isn't that unbelievable? No wonder you two looked alike. You were half-brothers. Your father is an older version of yourself. I found a photograph under the lining of one of Alexis Stoke's drawers. He told me he gave it to her and signed 'Forever G' on the back. Isn't that romantic? They had an *affaire de coeur* but he never knew she was in the family way or that she had a child. Although he knew Angel, he never knew Angel was his son. The sad thing is that Angel never knew who his real mother *or* father were. That's something to be said for the Reverend James' family loyalty.

Anyway, your father is a marvellous man. We really hit it off. He wants me to visit him again at Harrowford Hall (he was telling me stories about when you were little, Jack). I think he's lonely. I told him about you all, especially Polly. He lamented he has no one to run the estate. Your brother left Harrowford and joined the Navy. So now I have two fathers-in-law!

Mother received a letter from Abraham yesterday. He hasn't struck it rich yet. He's found a job in a general store, and says the miners often pay with gold dust or tiny little nuggets. He's bought a claim, and after work and on weekends he pans and fossicks for gold. He says he likes the desert; says he can think more clearly where there are fewer trees!

How's the weather there? No more storms, I hope. Here, spring is giving way to early summer. We'll be moving into the manor house at The Slopes in a couple of weeks. Did anybody buy our poor little farm yet?

Love,

Eliza'

She includes a separate letter for Polly, and draws some spring flowers on the bottom for her to colour in.

CHAPTER 34

M*istress of* T*he* S*lopes*

The move to the Slopes goes very smoothly. Eliza pays the final rent on Linden and closes her bank account in Emminster. As the house had been rented furnished, they only have to pack their personal belongings.

— I'm taking my old washtub with me, Eliza, as a reminder of the past. I might just get it bronzed!

The worst part for Eliza, which she doesn't expect, is having to leave the Reverend James behind, all alone, in the vicarage. She has a serious talk with him before they leave.

— I hate leaving you here, all alone.

— I have to admit it but I hate to see you go. I'll miss you, dear; and I'll miss your mother. A very resourceful woman, Mrs Durbeyfield.

— You know there's lots of room at The Slopes if you change your mind. Rose Cottage could be yours, and you could have your meals up at the house with us.

— I know. You're very thoughtful. I'll be retiring before too long. I'll think about it then. It's a much better option than the Old Clergymen's Home!

They laugh together.

It takes a couple of days for the youngsters to settle down; they all have to get used to the staff, and the staff have to get used to them. Eliza treats all the staff equally and fairly, and they give her their full effort. Joan has the propensity to address them off the cuff and engage them in conversation. When Eliza gently remonstrates with her, she replies.

— 'Do unto others as you would have them do unto you', Liza-Lu.

That's my motto. Servants should be treated as equals.

— Next you'll be showing them how to wash clothes.

— I most certainly will, if my things don't come back properly laundered. Everybody has their off days but there are standards that must be kept up.

The young leaves on the oak grow to their full potential, and the orchards are filled first with the busy hum of bees, and then the calls of birds and night insects as the breezes warm. The spring-born lambs grow fatter, bleat occasionally and munch contentedly in the long grass. Crows caw from the tall dark pines, and starlings fall sideways from the sky in unison and disappear in the fields of growing grain, only to rise again *en masse* and disappear in a rush of wings.

Eliza discovers the rose bushes planted along the front of the house are all shades of pink, from pale baby hues through to fuchsia. Spring slides into summer and the Durbeyfield family slide into their new style of living. A governess with some experience is hired for the girls. Joan doesn't want to send any of her children to boarding school, and Eliza makes sure all the children will have a firm grasp of English literature, good penmanship, and a thorough knowledge of geography and history.

Alec's stallion is sold ('that fateful horse' as Joan calls it, the one that was instrumental in poor Tess' downfall). The two boys have new ponies and Eliza manages to find suitable riding horses for the rest of the family. The wind blows warm from the west, and they have their fair share of rain. It isn't until the end of July there is even the hint of a thunderstorm.

Joan has become interested in cooking and introduces exotic ingredients into their formerly plain and frugal diet. She's also been conferring with Old Spence, the gardener, about different types of vegetables that could be planted in the hothouses, such as tomatoes and Italian herbs. Eliza, too, consults him about what plants are already *in situ*, and which ones they might try in different beds for visual effects. She's particularly interested in having a garden bed in the shape of the D'Urberville crest and selecting the right flower colours to plant to represent the different sections of her floral crest.. They could develop this garden beyond the trellised courtyard that opens off the conservatory to the rear, with views of the pasture sloping upwards towards the Chase. She would have preferred to have her 'crest garden' in the oval out front but the shade cast by the huge oak and the pines makes it too difficult for annuals to thrive.

Modesty and the boys love climbing the old oak. Their mother is full of misgivings.

— They'll fall and break their necks. That tree's not safe. It's been weakened by lightning.

— It's perfectly safe, Mother. If we forbid them to climb it, they'll do it anyway; and if we catch them at it and call out, they'll be so nervous they'll likely lose their grip and fall. If we allow them but warn them to be cautious, their energy will be channelled into safe climbing and descending.

— I can see Trantridge from the top.

Joan draws in her breath. Eliza calls up.

—That's wonderful, John. Remember! Three points of contact at all times.

— I know. There's pigeons on the roof, Liza-Lu.

— There *are* pigeons on the roof.

— That's what I said. Lots of them.

*Making a silk purse out of a sow's ear. Is it possible to raise my young brothers as gentlemen when they weren't born gentlemen? And just because they weren't born gentlemen, do they have noble blood in their veins? Can they overcome a poor beginning and rise to their true potential, or do their parents have to be noble? Alec D'Urberville was born of wealthy parents and brought up in pretension but he met a sad end, and it didn't do him any good for all his father's efforts to buy a place for him in society. Will young John and Little Charlie turn out like Alec? What **does** it take to turn out happy, contented, responsible, (wise) men? More than money, it seems; and more than having a noble family.*

*These questions intrigue me. What about me? Can I be a lady? Can money buy me ladyship? I come from very humble origins. I like playing the lady, and money has certainly made lawyers, bankers and servants notice me and treat me with deference. It's a strange thing, Fortune. Fortune alone, the money, can lead to a positive change in fortune, opportunity or chance. Then one is called 'fortunate'. When 'fortunately' is used, it is always for the better, for improvement. Therefore, I am fortunate. And if I am fortunate, what can I do to improve or better not just my own life but my family's lives, or the lives of those with whom I come in contact? If it's only a case of enrichment by money, I could become poor again, by giving it all away (which I could do very fast and easily). Would that be a wise use of the money? Or would **increasing** the money be the best use: investing it, so I can earn more dividends? Money multiplication. Yes, I'll have to find out where Alexis has invested her money, learn all those aspects.*

I'll also have to find out if this farm pays, makes a profit; and become knowledgeable about the orchard, the sheep, the crops; how much it costs to keep up the house and outbuildings, to run the stables and vehicles, the servants' pay and the daily running of the house, food etc. That will be interesting. If it doesn't pay, I'll see if I can make it pay.

Eliza tries to set aside two days a week in London, 'learning to be an heiress', by visiting Mr Bailey, the bank manager, and others. She uses the library in Trantridge one day a week, and visits the one in Emminster another day, weekly, to do research on the family, but also to visit her father-in-law and keep him company at lunch.

— How's the family tree coming, Eliza?

— Very well. The Durbeyfields and Turvilles are connected about eight generations back, a couple of hundred years or more. That's when the original name, D'Urberville, began to disintegrate and change into other forms.

— My, my.

— I've been to the Public Record Office in Chancery Lane and researched some old wills there although I really need to see the parish registers in Kingsbere in order to trace the surnames. Would you like to go with me?

— It depends when it is, dear. I can't go on Tuesdays and Thursdays as that's when I visit my parishioners.

— How about next Wednesday?

— That will be fine.

Eliza enjoys every moment with Old Spence, the gardener. He had been with Alexis since they moved south, and he knows every tree and bush from a sprout. She learns where to place annuals and perennials, how to graft fruit trees, and how to assess a piece of ground by sun exposure, moisture and wind. Old Spence explains how to make compost with kitchen peelings and leaves, and how to propagate plants from cuttings. He teaches her about pruning and espaliering and what to use against earwigs, thrips, and aphids. She learns that he and Alexis had planned the garden so it will produce flowers and foliage almost year long. He brings cut flowers to the kitchen but that is as far as his jurisdiction goes. It is then up to Mrs Watley to teach Eliza all she knows about flower arrangement.

As far as the library at The Slopes is concerned, Eliza claims it as her own domain. She loves sitting at the writing desk with her back to the big glass windows so that light floods the room from behind. When she isn't involved in correspondence, she uses the comfortable couch. Tucked into a corner of it with her feet up and a fat cushion supporting her back, Eliza can see the shelves of books. *I'll be old and grey before I could ever finish reading all these even at the rate of one book a week. Maybe I can work from left to right, skim them, read the chapter headings, or the first sentence of each* paragraph for a couple of chapters. If I get caught up in one then I'll read it from beginning to end. If not, I'll put it back and go on to the next one.

Just look at the poetry Alexis collected! She has her reading material divided into categories, while she still could read, poor thing. The fiction is on the same shelf level all around the room, with authors whose names begin with 'A' starting at the windows, and proceeding in alphabetical order all around the room to the windows again. The non-fiction is similarly organized above it. If you want to look at Samuel Pepys' *Diary*, you look in the 'P's about two thirds of the way around the room.

Alexis has grouped similar subjects together on other shelves, such as history, both recent and ancient. Professor Maspero's master work on ancient Egypt is here; works on and by the British in the Indian subcontinent; Schliemann's accounts of Troy and Mycenae; and Pompeii. *Had Alexis been to any of these places or was she an avid armchair traveller?* There is also a section given over to travel journals: Marco Polo's travels to China via the Silk Road and his return to Venice mostly be sea; and Bernal Diaz' account of Cortez' encounter with Montezuma.

It becomes Eliza's habit to read to the children in the evening from the wonderful walls around her, and she keeps them wide awake, on the edge of the settee, two hundred years after William Dampier wrote about his adventures in his journals, the first Englishman to set foot on Australian soil. They listen eagerly as she reads how Dampier is a member of the rescue party who find Alexander Selkirk on the San Fernandez Islands off the coast of South America, whose privations over the four years he is stranded there form the inspiration for the fictional character, Robinson Crusoe. As she reads, Eliza is impressed how Dampier loses his entire ship through the absolute incompetence of the ship's carpenter when it springs a leak below the water line.

— The carpenter cut a bigger hole to match the board he's brought with him to patch the leak. Of course, all hands are manning the pumps but more water pours in through the bigger hole than they can pump out. The carpenter brings a bigger board, and begins to cut an even bigger hole. And guess what happens?

— More water comes in!

— Exactly! They are standing ankle deep in water and pumping, and pumping, and pumping. The water creeps up to their knees but they keep pumping. Finally the pressure is too great, and the sea water breaks through the hole. As it gushes in, Dampier gives the order to abandon ship.

— Abandon ship!

— That's right, Charlie. They did. And it sank!
She also reads them the voyages of Captain Cook.
— His ship, the *Endeavour*, had a big hole cut in it by sharp coral rock on the Great Barrier Reef but he saved his ship.
On a large revolving globe on a stand in the corner of the library, she gets the children to follow Captain Cook all over the Pacific Ocean, up to Alaska, and down to Hawaii.
— Tell us your story, Liza-Lu, about going on the ship.
— Yeah, Sewers Canal.
— Not sewers, John, Suez.
The boys giggle; but they become good at locating England, after the spinning stops.
— It's so little!
— Yet so mighty! 'Rule Britannia!'
They all shout out the chorus.

> Rule, Britannia!
> Britannia rules the waves!
> Britons never, never, never
> Shall be slaves!

The children can also follow the *Merrie Englande* and the *Orient* back and forth across the oceans of the world.
— Who can find where Abraham is?
— I can, Liza-Lu. He's *there*.
And a chubby finger strikes the Nullarbor Plain.
— You're pretty close, John.
Eliza also finds a chess set and draught board which she sets up, as well as a game of backgammon. *These thinking games will help develop their concentration.* Also Dominoes, a Ludo board, and the perennial favourite, Snakes and Ladders, which leads to riotous shouts: success or ruin in the throw of a die.

In former days, Joan had been in the habit of a drink or two at Rolliver's or the Dew Drop Inn. Eliza cannot imagine her mother arriving at the Trantridge pub in a carriage so she has Canning, the new butler, stock a small liquor cabinet in the spacious dining room with spirits, beer and wine both for guests and for their own use. Joan forms a pleasant habit of having a gin and tonic before meals.

May and June pass in this way, and all the time Eliza grows into her new role as mistress of The Slopes. *I need to realize the duties and responsibilities that come with wealth and privilege but at the same time I feel empty and unfulfilled, as if I'm lacking something. Did you feel this way, Alexis? That tragic line in your poem, which you probably wrote at the library desk in this splendid house of sorrows, keeps haunting me: 'There's not a moment I don't think of you'.*

The end of July and beginning of August are quite stormy. Black clouds often blow up quickly in the afternoon and lash the house just at tea time. It's been one of the warmest summers in years.

Eliza manages to travel to Kingsbere twice, visiting both the public library and the Church there, where she checks the Parish Registers as far back as 1610 when recording began in the parish. Occasionally there are a few lines, sometimes even a paragraph regarding the death of a parishioner beside the necessary short entry. While looking for 'D'Urberville' and its derivatives she reads of a young man who 'fell to his death from the ridge pole of the church, where he was walking while drunk'. Another entry reads: 'One of the Six Hundred". In the baptismal registers she finds the terms 'bastard' (son or daughter), and 'illegitimate' beside the child's name, who is always listed under the mother's surname. She starts from 1610 with the baptismal registers and writes down all the names that look or sound like 'D'Urberville'. Then she starts on the marriage registers. These are helpful as they always state if the bride or groom is 'of this parish' or is 'from the Parish of X'. These entries are more helpful in showing the dispersal of the name but it means more work for her. If she doesn't find any children of that marriage baptized in Kingsbere, it is more than likely the parents had moved to the wife's parish, or she had her baby in her mother's house, so she would have to follow these families in neighbouring parishes. The burial registers are useful because they confirm that the person she found in the baptisms and marriages actually lived out all their days in the parish of Kingsbere, and died there; and she can double check this by going outside and reading the 'monumental inscriptions' on the gravestones, or go down into the vaults where her long-dead ancestors lie.

These registers, kept for hundreds of years in churches all over England, are the primary sources. People like Parson Tringham can write their histories and can be right, or only partially right, but these registers are the evidence, the basic building blocks. Eliza becomes very energized and excited by what she finds. *I am actually tracing and following the change and spread of my own* *family name. I might be the **only** person ever to have systematically done this.* As with the library back in Emminster, time flies, and the driver has to find her, to get her home in time for dinner. Joan is resigned to Eliza's dedication but cannot understand her zeal.

— Liza-Lu, you're spending more time with the dead than with the living! What's the good of busting your head with all this old stuff? Where will it get you?

— The truth is, Mother, it's *my* line, not yours.

— I don't care where I come from or where I'm going. You gotta live for the here and now, Liza-Lu.

— Well, I find it very satisfying discovering the past, *my* past, and probably the Turville's past as well.

On some rose-edged notepaper she finds in Alexis' library desk drawer, Eliza officially invites Gabriel to visit The Slopes for Saturday dinner. In his reply he states he's written to Jack but hasn't heard back. She also invites her father-in-law, the Reverend Clare and is glad she is able to bring these two old friends together after so many years. Saturday arrives. James and Gabriel are very pleased to see one another after such a long time. Joan, of course, coddles the two of them, and they all laugh at her down-to-earth practical humour. After dinner, they are sitting in the courtyard.

— Are you getting used to your new life, Mrs Durbeyfield?

— Now, Squire, there's no 'Mrs Durbeyfield's from you. I haven't known you long enough for you to call me by my first name but you can call me what the Reverend does.

— I call her, 'Mrs D'.

— Mrs D it is, then.

— As for getting used to the life, Squire: it's not hard, I can tell you. Funny thing is, though, I have to find things to do. Liza-Lu won't let me wash and she won't let me cook; and I'm too old to learn ladies' arts, like playin' the pianoforte, although I like a good song.

— You've earned your life of leisure, Mother; although the servants still can't make her out, Squire.

— They're too stuffy. I like to throw them off, be spontaneous.

— You mentioned in your invitation you've found more Turville connections?

— Yes, come into the billiard room, Squire, and I'll show you the chart so far.

— I think we'll soon have to go inside. The wind's coming up.

Eliza leads the way and unrolls the family tree she's made in the form of a long scroll right down the billiard table. She has the different Kingsbere families descending in generations, and has painted the spelling variations of the names in different colours. The D'Urbervilles are black, the Durbeyfields are orange, the Durbeyvilles green, the Turvilles blue, and so on.

Gabriel pores over the various sections, moving up and down the billiard table.

— That's very impressive, Eliza.

— It's only the beginning. I've just begun to branch out. I'll have to come down to Harrowford and trace your surname through the parish registers there.

— You're more than welcome to stay, my dear. A few days, perhaps? An old man could use the company.

— You're not old, Squire.

— It gets pretty lonely, roaming around in that big old Hall. I've been thinking about what you said. Perhaps I was too hard on Jack. I wanted to mold him but he had his own ideas.

— That's what enterprising young people do, you realize. I'm sure the bright ones grate the most on their parents.

— How is it that you are so wise, Eliza, for such a young woman? And your name. I notice your family all call you 'Liza-Lu'.

— They always have. I felt it was rather a babyish name when I married Angel. My full name is Eliza Louisa so I decided to be called by my first name.

— It suits you; and I want you to call me by my first name, Gabriel.

— But, Squire.

— Forget the title. I haven't heard my name enough. When James was addressing me earlier I realized I had to reclaim it. I don't think your mother ever will, but will you?

— I like your name, too, …Gabriel. What I'm going to say might sound silly. I 'speak' to Alexis sometimes.

— Spiritualism?

— No, no. When I'm in the library, for instance, I say to her, 'Did you really read all these books, Alexis?' Things like that.

— Does she answer you?

— No! But I get a really good feeling about her, you know what I mean?

— She has, or rather, had, that effect on people.

— You haven't been here before; of course not. She designed this whole house, the farm, the conservatory, the colour scheme, the furniture. Let me show you the house, her house; and her room, where I found your picture.

You're part of this house too, you know. 'There's not a moment I don't think of you'. Isn't that beautiful?

When she repeats Alexis' line, her eyes well with more tears of empathy for the missing part in her own life, and something more. She quickly turns and points out some feature of the house. *This man looks too much like Jack!*

The wind begins to freshen, and Gabriel and James decide to head home.

— I can drop you in Emminster, James. It's on my way.

— Thank you, my friend. That's very kind of you.

The children join Eliza and Joan out the front, and wave them goodbye. Gabriel calls from the carriage.

— You come soon, Eliza.

— Yes, Gabriel, I will.

— Ooh, we're on a first name basis now, are we?

— Mother, the generations don't mean a thing if you're linked by a common bond.

— So he calls you 'Eliza' too. What's wrong with 'Liza Lu'? You'll always be 'Liza-Lu' to me.

— Do you think you might be able to drop the 'Lu' part, and call me 'Eliza'? After all, I'm going on twenty-one. Don't eye me like that, Mother.

— I'm just summing you up. I think you're right. You are a bit old for the 'Lu'. Yes. 'Eliza' it will be.

There's a crash from inside.

— Them windows!

— The servants will close them, Mother.

— I gotta go and oversee. If you want things done right, you hafta do them yourself.

— They'll close them, Mother.

— Any servant worth his salt needs overseein', and I'm the one to do it.

Eliza hurries in after her mother. It's getting quite menacing.

CHAPTER 35

*M*ARY

The Monday after James' and Gabriel's visit dawns calm and bright and the scent of hundreds of roses wafts in through the open windows of Eliza's room as she lies sleepily in bed with sunbeams slanting across her covers. She has a leisurely wash, dresses, and goes in to breakfast. It's hard to have a family breakfast in the summer. The two boys are already out on the oval having a mock fight with fallen pine cones. Hope and Modesty are still at the table with their mother but almost finished.

— Can we leave the table, Mother?

— *May* we leave the table. Yes, you may. 'Morning Liza-Lu, er, Eliza. It's going to take me a while to get used to this. Good sleep?

— Wonderful sleep. I think I'll have bacon and eggs this morning, Canning.

— Very good, Ma'am. Do you prefer muffins or toast?

— Muffins this morning, thank you.

She settles into a relaxed breakfast. Joan is having another cup of tea.

— That there marmalade, Eliza, is made from our very own oranges from that tree.

She points through the inner glass wall of the conservatory where the sun has risen high enough to glint off the peaked glass ceiling.

— It's from Seville. Old Spence told me. The postman came early today. The letters are in the front hall.

— Mmm. I'll deal with them later.

— There's one for you, a personal one.

— There is?

Eliza goes out into the hall and brings the letter back, and picks up a clean knife to slit the envelope. There are two or three pages and she looks at the last page to see who it's from. She gasps.

— What is it?

— It's from Jack — Turville. I wonder why Mary didn't write.

She starts to read.

— Oh no, Mary's very ill. They've come home.

She scans the letter, giving her mother the highlights.

— Consumption! She was coughing before I left. She thought it was bronchitis, a stubborn cold. She was coughing up blood at a picnic we went to but said it had happened before. She promised me she'd go to see the doctor and when she did he said it was 'galloping consumption', very rapid. Jack says she's too weak to write. She must be really sick. When she was told she didn't have much time to live, she wanted to return to England to see her folks. They packed up then and there and have just arrived in Millcroft. Jack writes, 'We left almost as suddenly as you did. I leased my properties but kept my shares in the gas company, the mine and the dairy. Polly and I did the packing and we all left on the first ship out of Sydney and made Plymouth in seven weeks.'

Eliza checks the postmark.

— Yes, Millcroft. Mary's asking for me. If I can spare the time, she'd love to see me. Mother, I have to go! She's the one who took care of me all across the ocean. I have to go and look after her, now. It's the least I can do; and I want to. Jack says she's getting weaker by the day: they didn't even know if she would make it home. I have to pack a bag quickly and leave for the station.

— I'm sorry to hear it, Eliza. She sounds like a really nice girl, a caring human being. And the poor little child.

— Yes, Polly. Poor little pet. I'll take some bread and cheese for the journey and a pot of that marmalade for Mary. Is there anything else I can take her?

— I think it's you she wants, not gifts. How long do you think you'll be gone?

— I don't know. It sounds like she's sinking fast.

— The Lord giveth and the Lord taketh away.

— But why take Mary? So young. A lovely person who's never done anything mean to anyone. She's not capable of it: she doesn't have a mean streak in her body. Why would God choose to take *her* and leave a little child motherless? Is that the act of a loving God? It doesn't make sense. There's no rhyme or reason. Life is so unfair.

— The old must die and the young may die. When you've lived as long as I have you see things in a more practical way.

— Life is just plain unfair.

Eliza arrives at Millcroft station that afternoon and realizes she doesn't know Mary's parents' surname. She asks the station master if he knows where they live.

— Their daughter and her family have just returned from Australia. She's very ill.

— Yes, Ma'am, I know just who you mean. If you go up that street two, three, four …take the fourth street on your right. There's a butcher shop on the corner. You can't miss it. You'll be looking for a house with a courtyard behind a wrought iron fence. Do you want me to send your bag up later?

— No, I think I can manage, thank you. It's quite light.

She hurries away, not noticing any of the shops in the high street until she turns right at the butcher's. The houses are all of brick and set on their long narrow blocks with tall paling fences running back, separating them. She finds the one with the courtyard and rings the bell. A tired, overwrought woman in her fifties answers, Mary's mother. Eliza introduces herself and explains she has come to help care for Mary, much to the older woman's relief. The dark patches under her eyes and the strain etched on her face are obvious.

— It doesn't seem fair.

— I know, dear, but at least she made it home and for that I'm very thankful. She's out the back resting. We've brought her bed down to the parlour as she's too weak to go up and down the stairs; and Jack sleeps beside her on the sofa. Little Poll sleeps upstairs with us. I don't think it's healthy for a child to be too close to someone who is coughing all the time. Mary doesn't want to stay in bed so we dress her and she lies on the summer couch with a coverlet over her on the back porch where she can see the garden. It's terrible how fast she's gone down, even since she arrived home, and there's nothing they can do for her. Just waiting to die.

Eliza catches a glimpse of her friend from the front door before Mary sees her, and catches her breath. Mary's face is pinched and flushed. Her flesh seems to have wasted on her slender frame and the sprightliness gone out of her. Beyond, Polly is running after butterflies on the narrow lawn. Mary's face is transformed when she looks up and sees Eliza.

— You've come! Eliza, I'm so glad to see you.

Brave face, Eliza. I mustn't show Mary how shocked I am. She's shrunk to nothing, and looks so weak.

— Wild horses wouldn't keep me away.

She gives her friend a gentle embrace.

— No, don't even try to get up. Sit back there and tell me about your trip home.

— It was very tiring, this time. Jack wrote to you about my condition? Apparently I've had it for a long while, the cough you know, and it suddenly got worse. Looking back, I was getting tireder and tireder but I wouldn't admit it to myself; and I was breathless too.

— Your voice sounds hoarse.

— Yes, that's another aspect of it. Consumption. It really does consume you. We only got back last week. Jack's gone to Harrowford to see his father and will be back in a couple of days. Oh, Eliza, I'm so glad you've come. How much time can you spare?

— As long as you need. You helped support me when I was low. Now it's my turn to reciprocate.

— You're a true friend.

— Now don't go getting soppy on me.

Mary smiles. *Now that's what I want to see.*

— All right, Eliza. Stiff upper lip and all that, eh? Why don't you call Polly for tea?

Squeals from the garden. A whirlwind of skirts and hair as Polly makes a flying leap into Eliza's embrace.

It doesn't take Eliza long to size up the situation. Her friend is failing rapidly. She can even see a change in her condition the next day. Mary is only able to eat and drink very little and is wracked by fits of coughing which leave her exhausted. Eliza tries to brighten what she now believes are Mary's last days. She and Polly go around the garden and Polly picks the prettiest flowers for Mama, the ones with the most delicate scent or the softest petals. Eliza busies herself in the kitchen preparing small tasty helpings of Mary's favourite foods like fish fillets poached in milk and little cup custards; and goes up to the butcher's on the high street and buys the best cuts of meat to make beef tea, light but nourishing. She takes over the nursing from Mary's mother who is too emotionally involved to be left in charge, and even makes extra portions for her. She sponge bathes Mary with her favourite soap, lavender; and insists she spend some time outdoors when it is fine.

— You can feel the sun doing you good.

She also does Mary's washing and hangs out the clothes and bedding in the sun so they all have that deep fresh wholesome smell.

— My travelling days are over, Eliza, but I'd love to see the trees out in the street; how they meet in a great green arch overhead.

— I can arrange that. Are you game?

— I'm game for anything. Do your worst.

— I'll do better than that. I'll do my best.

That is where Jack finds them when he comes back two days later on the train. He is walking down Mary's street when he stops and bursts out laughing.

— What are you ladies doing?

— Jack, you're back! Eliza is taking me on an 'outing'.

Polly dances around them.

— It's Aunty 'Liza's idea. She gave me a turn, too.

Eliza had found an old bed quilt and some cushions and lined a wheelbarrow with them. Mary is now relaxing in this chariot even if she is a little cramped for space.

— Isn't she ingenious, Jack?

— Certainly is. Hello, my girl, you got here quickly.

He kisses Mary and Polly, and puts his arm around Eliza's shoulder, giving her a welcoming squeeze. *Oh, the strength of his arm! I'd forgotten. His confidence; his warmth; his touch! I've been so busy looking after my dear friend I didn't expect to feel that thrill, that shiver again. I mustn't let it show.* She smiles up at Jack

— She's spoiling me, Jack.

— She's spoiling me too, Daddy.

— Thank you, Eliza, thank you

He didn't notice. That's good.

— At last I have a chance to pay you back for all your kindness to me.

— Here, Eliza, allow me to ferry the queen back to the palace.

Eliza had been prepared to spend two, three weeks, maybe a month ministering to Mary but the end comes much sooner. In the wee hours a few nights later Jack calls upstairs for everyone to come. Mary is having several bouts of coughing which exhaust her, and is finding it hard to get her breath. Her pulse is racing, she is sweating profusely and has to sit up in bed leaning against Jack who is sitting behind her.

— Oh, Love, I can't go on. I …

— Hush, Mary, rest. You're safe here in my arms.

He wraps her in his arms. She looks over at her anxious parents.

— Don't worry, Mum. I thought it would be you who'd go first.
Her mother's voice catches.
— So did I, dear.
Polly is very sleepy and lays her head on Mary's lap. Mary whispers as she strokes Polly's head, her hand lingering on the thick hair.
— Mummy's going for a long sleep now, pet. I'll always be dreaming of you, little Poll.
The sleepy child murmurs.
— And I'll always dream of you, Mama.
Mary looks up at Eliza.
— You'll look after her for me now, won't you, Eliza? Promise?
Eliza nods, tears running down her face.
— You know I will. She's like my own.
Mary smiles, a satisfied contented smile, and lets out a big sigh which brings on another coughing fit. She sinks back against Jack and he brings his cheek down against hers. He holds a hanky over her mouth which slowly turns red in his hand. She has no more strength left for coughing, and slips from this world into the great unknown. Eliza lifts Polly off her mother's lap while Jack gently lays Mary down and then carries his daughter back upstairs to bed.

Mary is laid to rest in the graveyard beside the church where she had been baptized, among her ancestors, to the gentle weeping of those who care about her most, to the short and practical Church of England Service of Burial, to the phrases of her favourite psalm falling like petals into the grave: 'he leadeth be beside the still waters; he restoreth my soul'. Jack is sadly strong for all of them. He has seen this coming for some time, and after he and Mary had accepted the inevitable they were determined to be as practical and positive as they could. It was Polly Mary had worried about the most as she tried to explain to her uncomprehending daughter that she would be going to sleep far away in heaven but would always be in Polly's heart as she grew up.
— I want Mama!
The adults turn their attention to comforting the distraught child.

Later that evening Jack recounts to Eliza the details of their departure from Wollongong: how the doctor had diagnosed phthisis when Mary had finally gone to see him after her promise to Eliza. He advised her to return home at the earliest opportunity, if she wished to go, as her condition was progressing rapidly. She had begun to lose her appetite and was getting thinner and weaker.

— The coughing really took it out of her but she bore up like a trooper. She never complained, never whined, never regretted. Always positive.

— That's her nature.

— That's what I loved her for.

— What are you and Polly going to do now?

— When I was home I talked with The Squire, that's what we always called the old man. I'm surprised how easy-going he is now. Maybe you mellowed him, Eliza. He thinks pretty highly of you, you know. Perhaps he's learned his lesson; or maybe thinks I've learned mine. He wants me to stay in England and take over the estate; and particularly wants to get to know his granddaughter. I think she'll set him back a pace or two, don't you?

— Well, she is a *little* precocious. I described Polly to him in detail when I visited him. Gabriel is crusty. He won't admit to sentimentality but he has a soft centre, really. He insists I call him 'Gabriel', and he calls me 'Eliza'. Even Mother calls me 'Eliza' now unless she's really worked up.

— I have something I have to discuss with you. When Mary and I were talking about Polly's future, she wanted you to be part of her life as well. She meant it when she asked you to look after little Poll.

*Stop jumping, heart! He's thinking only of Polly; or did Mary have an idea that I would become a type of governess-mentor? What did she mean when she said, 'You'll look after Polly for me, won't you, Eliza?' Did she mean like a godmother? Or maybe a mother? Did she have some plan in mind for Jack and me like Tess did for Angel and me? A second wife for a second time? Is that a wise step? Or would it be different this time? Anyway, Jack hasn't given the slightest hint of anything except genuine friendship. How did **he** interpret Mary's question to me? How could I possibly look after Polly if I'm far away from him? He'll not be separated from his daughter. I wish he would stop looking into my eyes so keenly: he'll be able to read my soul.*

— After a while, Eliza, would you be free to make a visit and spend a little time at Harrowford Hall?

— I could. Or Polly could come and stay with us for a while at The Slopes. It would be a lot more lively for her.

— True. We'll see how it goes. I'm sure it will be rough on her at first without her mother. I have to see how The Squire and I make out as a team, and I'll also have to return to Wollongong periodically to look after my business affairs there. Maybe that's when you could be a surrogate parent to her. I can't keep taking the child back and forth across the world.

— Whenever you need me. We'll see how it goes, Jack.

He gives her arm a little squeeze.

— Thanks a lot, Eliza. That puts my mind at rest.

He touched me again! I can feel it run all through me. Is that significant? A surrogate parent. That's closer than a friend. It's almost intimate! I mustn't think of the possibility of ever marrying Jack. There's that codicil to Alexis' will that says something about giving up the whole inheritance, The Slopes, everything, if I ever remarry. It didn't seem that important when I agreed to it but now it could overshadow everything. Dear Mary's gone, and, 'O, the difference to me!'

CHAPTER 36

Eliza's Choice

Eliza returns to The Slopes in a pensive mood.
— You look like you've grown years older, Eliza, in just a couple of weeks.
— A lot has happened to wisen me, Mother.
And she fills her mother in about the sad events. The implications of the sad events she ponders alone.

Three weeks later a letter arrives not from Jack, as she expects and hopes. It's from Gabriel. He writes he is really taken with his little granddaughter but she is pining for her mother and seems inconsolable. She reads the letter with more and more anguish.

'Polly cries and cries, "I want Mama, I want Mama!" and no matter how much Jack explains to her, she doesn't understand what it means that her mother has gone to heaven and won't be coming back. "Everyone I love goes away and won't come back. Aunty 'Liza went away and won't come back. Mama's gone away and won't come back. Why won't they come back, Daddy?" That's what spurred me to write to you, Eliza. I know Jack would like you to come and stay for a while but he is hesitant about asking you. He thinks a decent amount of time has not yet passed since his wife's death to be inviting you to stay at the Hall. In normal circumstances he is right. This, however, is not normal, for a little child to be so upset. I asked her, "What if your Aunty 'Liza came and stayed with us?" Her eyes brightened for the first time, and she said, "She could be my new Mama, couldn't she, Grandpa? Oh, please, please bring her back!" That's when I realized, "Out of the mouths of babes and sucklings …." Polly has come up with the obvious solution that we thick men couldn't see. I haven't broached it with

Jack. It's a very delicate topic, and so soon. I also realize it might be a very delicate subject for you, too. Polly needs a mother and I think you and Jack would get along very well. You have done me a service by uncovering my past with Alexis. I realize now that sometimes we hurt others by our actions (as I well may be by being an interfering old fool), and we sometimes hurt others by our inactions (if I failed to point out to the two of you what to me is the obvious solution) and I would never forgive myself if I let this opportunity slip by. That's what compels me to beg you to let this idea grow: give it a chance. Please say "yes" and come.

Affectionately,
Gabriel Turville.'

— What's the matter, Eliza?

I can't tell Mother at this stage what Gabriel is proposing. It would really upset the apple cart and I'm upset enough as it is.

— It's Polly. She's taking her mother's death very hard.

— It's hard on children, and that's the truth. It's hard on you, too, by the look of 'e. I think you need a stiff drink.

— At this hour?

— Bad news has to be bolstered.

— Maybe I'll have a glass of port. I'll take it into the library and read the letter again.

— Misery needs company?

— No thanks. I don't feel like talking right now.

What am I going to do? What is Gabriel asking of me? This has to come from Jack, not him. Oh Jack, I do want you! I can't keep you out of my thoughts. 'There's not a moment I don't think of you!' My whole body yearns for you but if I gratify my own desires I'll wreck the lives of all my family. Do you want to marry me? Is it too soon? And if you don't get along with The Squire, I could never cross that ocean again. I'd want to but I just couldn't. Jack! She finishes her port and starts to pace back and forth across the library, murmuring to herself, trying to sort out her thoughts. *I'm beginning to act like Angel.* The library is too confining and she goes outside to pace on the oval, under the shade of the pines and the big oak. *I'll just let nature be my guide.*

Oh, what is the right thing to do? Polly wants me to be her mother, and I want to be her mother, too. Aaagh! It's too hot a topic. I can't make a decision right now. I'll let it simmer and cool a bit, wait a little, deal with it when it's cooled down. I don't have to write a reply tonight. I'll think it over. I can't ask Gabriel to help me make a decision as he has a considerable stake in my answer. I can't ask Mother, either, as she has too much tied up in The Slopes *and wouldn't be able to see things clearly from my point of view. She would only make me feel responsible, or guilty, even if I was only **thinking** about marrying Jack. Maybe I'll ask Father Clare for his advice. I'll sleep on it. Things might be clearer in the morning.*

Eliza puts off replying to Gabriel for over a week. She's thought about involving the Reverend Clare but hasn't got around to it. *It's come down to deciding between Jack and my family.* Again, she puts off the inevitable and postpones writing. That evening they are all in the parlour playing table games, or reading, and Joan is doing her fancywork, when another summer squall comes up.

— I'm glad my family's all safe inside.

— I can hardly hear you, Mother.

— Deafening, isn't it? Good thing we're all doing non-talking activities.

— What's that noise?

— What noise?

— It sounds like wheels on the pebbles.

— It's the D'Urberville coach. You're hearing things, Eliza. It's all in your head. Bad luck's a-coming.

— No, it really is a coach, or something. Listen!

— I don't hear it. I just hear the rain.

— It's stopped.

— Just as I was saying. It's all in your ....

They hear a distant gong: the front door bell.

— Ghosts have come calling in the middle of a storm. I'm going to see what it's all about.

— Sit down, Mother. If it's for us, Mrs Watley will announce the visitor.

— You've been reading up the etiquette book again, haven't you?

— Well, there's a certain way of doing things, Mother, and we have to learn it as befits our new station in life.

— Well, the wheels have left.

— See, you hear them too. It's not the D'Urberville coach after all.

Mrs Watley appears at the parlour door.

— Pardon me, Ma'am, there's a young lady in the hall.

— A young lady! Well, show her in.

— She's a — *very* young lady.

This sentence piques everyone's interest.

Mrs Watley appears again.

— She won't come in, Ma'am. She won't budge from the mat.

— Won't budge?

They are all on their feet at the same time wanting to see the mysterious stranger who has arrived in a coach in the middle of a storm and who now refuses to come into the parlour. They pour into the hall. And stop, astounded.

There, on the rug, with rain staining through her thin brown coat, stands a child holding all her worldly goods in a large kerchief tied in a knot, like Dick Whittington but without the pole. She can't be more than five years old, and stares at the patterns on the rug with a grim look of defiance on her square little face. Masses of black ringlets cover her head and shoulders, the kind that tighten their natural curliness in wet weather. Joan goes forward.

— What have we here? What's your name, child?

The urchin neither replies nor looks up; just stands there, staring down at her worn little black boots.

— Cat got yer tongue, eh?

The children are ready to rush forward. Eliza puts her hand out and motions them to stay back.

— Why, she's frightened, the poor little thing. My goodness, darling, you're all wet!

She goes across the hall and kneels down in front of her.

— You have a note pinned on your collar. Will it tell me who you are?

The child nods without lifting her head.

Eliza unpins the note and opens it. She reads it in stunned silence. Then she takes the little girl's chin in her hands, and tilts her head until she is looking into those coal-black eyes. She smiles.

— Angelique?

— '*Ong*elique'.

The child corrects her, using the French pronunciation. Her chin begins to quiver, and tears spick from her eyes. Eliza murmurs.'Alexis'.

— No, Angelique. Angelique Claire Russell.

— Yes, darling. That's what the note says. Let's get you out of these wet clothes, shall we? Mrs Watley? Would you heat some water and run a bath for this young lady?

— She's staying, Ma'am?

— Yes, she's staying.

— I don't want to go with *her*, I want *you*. What's your name?

She speaks with a slight French accent.

— My name's Aunty 'Liza.

— Liza, exactly what is going on, and who is this ragamuffin?

— Children, all go back into the parlour. There are too many new people for this little girl to cope with. Come to think of it, it's bed time for you boys.

— Do we have to? Can't we stay up?

— Angelique will still be here in the morning. Now, off you go. Modesty, would you go and get one of your nighties? I know it will be too big but we'll sort out her clothing tomorrow.

— Eliza! *What* is going on?

Eliza hands the note up to her mother as she starts to unbutton Angelique's coat.

— What do you have in your kerchief?

— My things.

— Mind if we have a look? Do you have any clothes?

— Yeth.

Joan finishes reading the note.

— Liza-Lu!

— I know! Isn't it incredible?

— Do you really think that's who she is?

— I'm pretty sure. Look at the hair and the shape of the face, Let's untie the knot, darling. Ooh, it's really tight.

The child nods. Soon, all the worldly possessions of Angelique Claire Russell are visible in a four square foot heap on the carpet, and pitiful they are: one pair of bloomers, an undershirt, a hard slice of bread, two red ribbons and a lucky rabbit's foot.

— Are you hungry, dear?

Angelique begins to cry. Dirty as she is, Eliza puts her arms around the frail little frame and lifts the sobbing child, who clings to her as if she will never let her go.

— Eliza! Put her down! She's probably covered in lice and fleas and Lord knows what.

— We'll wash all those nasties away, won't we, pet? We'll get you something to eat and drink first, and then you can have a lovely warm bath.

— Make sure you wash her hair good, and go over it with a fine tooth comb.

Eliza nods, and carries Angelique into the kitchen.

— Who is she, Mother?

Joan has gone back into the parlour.

— She might be staying for a while, Hope.

— For how long?

— Quite a while, if your sister has her way, I would think.

— Who *is* she?

— She's a distant relative we knew nothing about. She has no one in the world to look after her.

To herself, Joan thinks, 'She's a fly in the ointment; that's who she really is.'

— Where are her parents?

— They both died.

— Where's she going to sleep?

— As she won't let Eliza out of her sight, I suppose she'll be sleeping in her room for the time being.

Much later, when the children have gone to bed, and Angelique is settled and asleep on the sofa made up into a bed in Eliza's room, mother and daughter convene in the parlour.

— Well! Did you ever? Do you think the friend of that child's mother, who wrote the note, is telling the truth, Eliza?

— I don't know. What would she gain by making it up? Let's take a look at the note again.

— 'The sins of the father'. That's what it says in the Bible: 'the sins of the father'.

— It's signed by an 'Alicia' who says that Angelique's mother was 'in the trade', and that Angelique was born after she 'slipped up' by not taking proper precautions with a customer whose name was Angel Claire. She remembered his name because he was different from her regulars, and she'd never met anyone with a name like 'Angel'. And he had a French surname, Claire. Angelique's mother was French, Monique Rousel, or Russell. When Monique became ill, she made her friend promise to send Angelique (named after Angel) to the child's father in the West Country. That's all she knew about him. When Monique died, Alicia packed up the child's things and pinned a note on her collar addressed, like a common parcel, 'To Angel Claire, West Country', and shipped her off in the mail coach. The only 'Angel Claire' now is me, Mrs Angel Clare, so the child was deposited on our doorstep. Thank heaven for the efficient British Postal Service!

— That child will bring nothing but trouble. You mark my words. That coach you heard has brought bad news. She ought to be shipped off to an orphanage at first light.

— I couldn't do that, poor little mite. She couldn't help being born any more than you or I.

— You don't know for certain she's even who they say she is. People read the papers, Eliza, and take advantage. Her mother might still be alive. You know what a mess that D'Urberville got poor Tess into. Angel's name was in the papers, and everything. That child's mother might realize an advantage for her daughter, and claim she is Angel's child. I might be country born, but I wasn't born yesterday. People get up to all kinds of tricks when huge amounts of money are involved. Lord knows, we might have a line-up of urchins at the door before we can turn around!

— Tess told me, Mother, that Angel had a liaison in London with a French prostitute. He confessed to Tess about it on their wedding night, and she forgave him. After Angel confessed, Tess told him about Alec D'Urberville and the baby, and that's what precipitated the whole thing. That's when he left her, and is precisely why he left her. He also confessed it to me on our wedding night.

— My, my, my. Doesn't life have strange turnings?

— Mother, that child looks exactly like descriptions of Alexis, especially the black ringlets. I'm *sure* she's Angel's child.

— We have to get the facts, Eliza, to prove it. It has pretty far-reaching repercussions if it's true.

— If she's Angel's child then she's Gabriel's grand-daughter; and the Reverend's grand-niece or adopted grand-daughter. I'd be her step-mother, and you'd be her step-grandmother!

— Now hold on, Eliza. Don't get carried away. You still have to prove it.

— The Registry of Births! I could check next time I go up to London; and the Deaths for her mother.

— Monique mayn't have put Angel's name as the father.

— Well, it's worth a try, Mother. Anyway, it now looks like we have a new charge to look after. If she's not a relative then she's certainly a ward. There seems to be nobody else to take care of her. I'll talk to Mr Bailey about it. In the meantime, we have to get her some clothes. I suppose I could make her some.

— You're far too busy to do that. Now you can afford it, get her some that are ready-made.

It's time we both got some shut-eye. Good-night, dear.

— Good-night, Mother. I'm going to have my cocoa, then go to bed.

I can't sleep. My body's tired but my mind is riling. All the things that have happened in the last few weeks! Gabriel's letter; Mary's death; James and Gabriel coming to dinner; and now Angelique. Is there a pattern in this? So much decision-making all at once, and such far-reaching consequences! Polly wants me to be her mother. Mother and the children need to continue in the life that I can provide them. Now Angelique has a claim? Is the Wheel of Fortune turning upside down again? Is this God's plan for my life? If it is, it's very confusing. If things were all laid out, and happened sequentially, I could understand it's God's plan, and accept it. It seems, though, that I'm being forced to make choices, and the choices all have very different results.

If I say 'Yes' to Jack (Down, Heart! I only said 'if'), and follow my heart, my Great Desire, then I forfeit the house and the fortune, and my family will be destitute again. If I go against my own desires by spurning Jack and Polly, and choose my family's security, I won't be fulfilling my true purpose in life. I want **both**: *Jack* **and** *The Slopes. And now there's Angelique. It will take weeks to find out who she really is, and Gabriel needs an answer* **now**. *Oh Jack! My Jack! I feel so close to you. Do you to me?*

Maybe things are not laid out for us, predestined. Maybe we don't follow a path of action: we create it as we go. Maybe life is nothing but chance and opportunity. Decisions have repercussions, but they're **our** *making, not God's. What can I think of to help me solve this? "The Rubáiyát"?*

> 'The moving finger writes; and having writ,
> Moves on; nor all thy Piety nor Wit
> Shall lure it back to cancel half a Line,
> Nor all thy Tears wash out a Word of it.'

That moving finger could quite well be my own. Maybe we make our own fate. I can't change what's happened in the past but my decisions can and will change what happens in the future.

Turn off your mind, Eliza, and get some rest!

Angelique's sudden arrival has a profound effect on the family. She is instantly attached to Eliza, follows her around like a puppy, clutches her hand, sits on her lap, falls asleep in her arms, and does everything Eliza tells her. Little Charlie and John are more her own age but much too rough and tumble for her. She bonds fairly fast to Hope and Modesty; and remains quite wary of Joan.

Eliza has to let the two grandfathers know. *I can't just turn up on their* *doorsteps with her, if indeed she **is** legitimate (or legitimately illegitimate). I'll write to them: Father Clare first, and then the big one because I have to answer Gabriel's question as well as introduce his new grandchild. They may not accept her.*

She plans to go up to London as soon as she can. However, Angelique is very clinging. She talks it over with Joan.

— Maybe I should take her with me. Mr Bailey might see a similarity to Alexis to prove the note is true.

— Take a young child like that to London? You're the only one in the family to have ever been to London.

— Mother, she's *from* London.

When Eliza is ushered into Bailey's office with Angelique's little hand in hers, he rises from his seat to greet her then immediately sits down again.

— Alexis!

— No! My name is Angelique.

— Good Lord! Where did you find her?

— She found me.

— I went in a big coach all over England to find Aunty 'Liza, didn't I, Aunty 'Liza?

— Yes, darling, you found me. This note was pinned on her collar, Mr Bailey. I believe it's true because I knew that Angel had a relationship with a French woman in London before he married the first time. He told me. I know that you knew Alexis so I thought you may be able to substantiate Angelique's identity.

— She has the same hair. Mrs Stoke had unforgettable hair.

— And Angelique has Angel's face shape *(which is more Turville than Clare)*.

— We can do a search for you, Mrs Clare, at St Catherine's House. That's what we're trained to do. Our lawyers are repeatedly searching the birth registers. We know the surnames of both her supposed parents so it should be routine. We'll see if the paper evidence is in those records.

Angelique is getting fidgety.

— We're going now, dear.

— There's one more thing, Mrs Clare.

— Yes?

— If proof is found that this child is the daughter of Angel Clare ….

— Wouldn't that be wonderful?

— Wonderful for the child, let me assure you. Do you remember the codicil in Mrs Stoke's will that I pointed out to you on our first meeting?

— About re-marrying?

— Yes. That was only one of the provisos. However, overriding that is the possibility of this child, Angelique, inheriting The Slopes and the whole Stoke fortune, and not you, if it can be proved that she is indeed Angel Clare's natural daughter and Mrs Stoke's granddaughter.

Eliza looks up, amazed. The solicitor continues.

— I said, *if* it can be proved.

— Does that mean I would lose everything?

— Don't let's worry about that until we find the evidence one way or another.

Good thing I didn't broach the subject of Jack. That would really complicate things. She thanks Bailey, trying to keep her composure.

— Come along, darling. Take Aunty 'Liza's hand.

And she hurries out the door. After visiting a ready-to-wear store for children, and outfitting Angelique with a presentable array of clothing: frocks, pinnies, camisoles, pantaloons, socks and shoes, as well as a new pair of boots, the highlight (in Angelique's eyes) being a red plaid coat and a beret to match, they have some lunch and head back to The Slopes. The rocking motion of the train puts Angelique asleep in Eliza's right arm; and for the first time since her arrival back in England, Eliza has an unforced opportunity to think of Jack, and a future with her and Jack — Jack.

Joan is watching for them to come from the station. She has one eye on the sky and one on the road.

— You made it back before the weather changed.

— You don't think we're in for another storm, do you?

— That's what Old Spence says. He only has to take one look at the sky and know what the weather will be for the next two days. Mutters things like, 'mackerel sky' and 'high cirrhus'.

— I suppose it proves useful in protecting the plants.

— What did you find out, Eliza?

— Give me time to take my hat off. Run along, Angelique. See if cook has a nice apple for you. Mother, I think you'd better sit down.

— It's not *that* bad, is it?

— Mr Bailey's firm is going to search the records to prove Angelique's birth, and her mother's death. The birth registration may state who the father is but more often than not, it doesn't. If nothing can be found, I continue as Angel's heir and keep The Slopes and the fortune. If there is proof that Angelique is his child, then she inherits the lot. It isn't stated in Alexis' will but implied, because she named Angel.

— Good thing I'm sitting down. Let me ring for Canning. I need a gin and tonic, right now. Let me get this straight, Eliza. That means we could be uprooted again? That little thing could turf us out?

— Don't despair yet, Mother. They're unlikely to find a connection. We'll just have to wait and see. Even if they can't *legally* prove it, I'm convinced she's Angel's daughter.

After dinner the wind picks up. The pines bend before it. The boys are playing trains under the billiard table, and the younger girls are in the parlour with Joan, playing 'I Spy' and 'Animal, Vegetable, or Mineral'. Eliza's glad to see that Angelique and Joan are beginning to warm to one another. She's told the family she needs the library to write letters and cannot concentrate when there are intermittent comments and occasional squeals of laughter.

She sits at the desk with her back to the now dark wall of windows with their burgundy drapes tied like low hourglasses, with the black reflections from the windows between each. First she takes Abraham's latest letter from the desk drawer. Dreams: 'I'll see you all again when I strike it rich'. *I have a sinking feeling I won't be seeing him for a very long time. What's that stanza from* "The West Wind"?

> 'Will ye not come home, brother?
> Ye have been long away.
> It's April, and blossom time, and white is the May;
> And bright is the sun, brother; and warm is the rain —
> Will ye not come home brother, home to us again?'

I can't beg him to come: he has his own path to cut in life; but I can always tell him how welcome he'd be. She also tells him about Mary, and about Angelique, and how their hold on The Slopes is in jeopardy; but all the while thinking of Jack, and of the letter yet to be written to Gabriel, which can't be put off any longer. Still, she writes to James, telling him about Angelique, and her visit to Govett and Bailey. She props the photograph of Mary, Jack and Polly in front of her then takes out some sheaves of onion skin, and begins.

'The Slopes,
Via Trantridge,
West Country.
and the date,

Dear Gabriel, …'

She looks at the photo. Jack exudes confidence, a kind of protective surety, from his glance and by the way he stands behind his family. The way he looks still thrills her, even from the sepia image. Eliza blinks faster now. Tears start rolling down her cheeks and splash onto the paper. The wind moans in the pines, occasionally howling as the gusts grow stronger. *Jack, I want you. I need you. Now and forever.* 'Since I received your letter certain momentous things have happened. First, though, give Polly hugs and kisses from me. I know, I can hear you saying, "Why don't you come yourself? Then you can hug and kiss her in person". What can I write as an answer to you? The fates of many lives depend on my response to your suggestion. There's a codicil in Alexis' will which says if I remarry, I will lose The Slopes and the Stoke fortune. What would Mother and the children do then? Yet when you mention my dear little Polly, my heart yearns to be with her (and yes, I'll acknowledge it, with Jack and you at Harrowford Hall). Now, we have another complication. A little waif about Polly's age was delivered, yes, actually delivered, to our door with a note pinned on her collar saying she is Angel's child. Unbelievable, isn't it? Mr Bailey, the lawyer, thinks she is the living image of Alexis. She has your face, Angel's face, the square Turville jaw. Alexis apparently had 'unforgettable' black curly hair, which this little one also has in abundance.'

The wind is constant now and heavy rain is driving against the windows. Lightning and thunder reflect Eliza's raw emotions as she wrestles with and tries to sort out her thoughts in this very significant reply. *Should I fly to Jack's side where I know I belong, and help little Polly? Do I really have a duty to Mother and the children? I'm not the head of the family. Mother is. I could remain rich or end up penniless. Do I have an obligation to look after that other child (real or imposter)? Why me? Why does it all fall on **me**?* Alexis must have gone through the same anguish. I remember how one of her poems ends.

> I drain the last dreg in the crucible
> Of truth, whose mystic tangles can't be taught
> But only learned by doing
> And by being burned.

Experience, the great teacher!

'The bird of Time has but a little way
To fly — and Lo! The bird is on the Wing.'

Intense, consumed, she writes and cries, and writes and wipes the tears as they drop onto the page, now a blur of words and emotions. Lightning is now coming forked and fierce but she doesn't notice. Nerved up, she's too concentrated on her letter to hear a change in the wind, and wheels crunching on the drive. The roaring now sounds like a steam engine and the old oak out on the oval finally succumbs to the battering gale. With a creaking tear it is violently uprooted, and snaps, crashing with a rush of leaves against the library windows, breaking them in. The glass rains down on Eliza and one large bough crushes her as she sits at the writing desk. Her head hits the table. The pen flies out of her hand and the burgundy curtains billow inwards like sails, filled with shards of glass.

— Liza-Lu! Liza-Lu!

Footsteps come running. Her mother bursts into the room followed by the others. They all stop dead in their tracks. A figure pushes past them and forces his way towards Eliza, half climbing through the boughs, crunching on glass,. He tries to lift the branch pinning her to the desk but cannot move it; then casts around for something to give him leverage. Books! Three hard-covered volumes under the branch where it touches the wide table top and he is just able to slide her lifeless body out of the chair.

He carries Eliza gently to a sofa away from the windows and slowly lays her limp form down, then kneels beside her and kisses those lifeless lips, whispering in wrenched tones.

— Eliza! Eliza!

The wind gusts in strongly, and the full-length curtains billow and flap while the rug shimmers with a million pieces of shattered window glass. The tree protrudes towards them, and there, in the light of the only lamp left burning is Eliza on the red velvet sofa, her alabaster face highlighted by the auburn in her hair; and a strange man kneeling, cradling her head. Joan cries out indignantly.

— Pardon me but who the Dickens are *you*? You arrive on our doorstep in the middle of the night and push right past us.

He slowly comes to the realization he is not alone. He turns, blinks, then gets to his feet.

— Excuse me, allow me to introduce myself. My name is Jack Turville. Eliza needs a doctor. I think I felt her breath on my face.

— Are you Liza-Lu's husband?

— No, but I'm going to be.

— Where's your shining armour?

— Charlie, enough of that. Mrs Watley, go for the doctor! Quick!

— Are you going to take Liza-Lu away from us again?

*So this is dying. I always thought dying would be painful but I feel nothing at all, just airy and light, as if I'm floating; it's so very bright; peaceful too. I smell sunshine, and roses. It's **so** peaceful. I thought my loved ones were supposed to meet me but Tess and Father haven't come. Maybe they don't know I've arrived yet. It's so calm here, lying still, bathed in this soft bright light, holding God's hand: someone to lead and look after me; someone to take the weight and worry of decisions off my shoulders. Now I feel a wind, and whispering voices, and the cry of swallows. I never realized there are birds in heaven. They must be the angels singing, wings come to earth. Now God is bending over me, stroking my cheek. He's whispering my name, my name.*

— Eliza. Eliza.

I'll squeeze His hand to let Him know I hear.

— Eliza.

— …yessss …

— Wake up, Eliza. It's me, Jack.

— Jack?

— Wake up, Eliza.

— Are you in heaven, too, Jack?

— No, no, I'm here on earth with you. Open your eyes and see.

She turns towards the voice, and forces her eyes to open.

— You're here?

— Yes, at The Slopes. I came for you.

— I'm so sleepy. I'm glad you're in my dreams, Jack. You're always in my dreams.

She closes her eyes again. Jack lets go of the limp hand he's been holding since last night, stretches, and goes to the door of Eliza's bedroom.

— Mrs Durbeyfield! She woke up briefly. I think we should send for the doctor once again.

He hears a moan and turns back into the room. Again, sitting on her bed, he takes her hand and calls softly.

— Eliza.

— Jack? You here? Wha …What happened?

— Last night in the storm, the big oak out the front of the house blew over and snapped, and fell against the front of the house, the library windows in particular, and through the windows of the room where you were writing. You were knocked senseless, pinned down by the tree. First Abraham, then you. You Durbeyfields must have hard noggins.

— Where do you come in?

Jack laughs at the double meaning.

— I love to hear you laugh, Jack.

She squeezes his hand.

— So you are waking up?

— Yes.

— You asked, where do I come in? I must say I arrived last night just at the right moment. You never replied to The Squire's letter so I came for an answer in person. I realized after dear Mary left us, it is you who Polly wants and needs; and — so do I.

— Where *is* Polly?

— She's at Harrowford Hall with my father. You made quite an impression on him, are you aware? He told me that you'd made him realize he'd perhaps taken too hard a line by forcing my older brother onto the land when he really wanted to join the Navy and travel the world. New strains of corn, tree grafting and lambing problems were not his cup of tea. After you were reticent in replying I thought you were having doubts but The Squire put the boot to me, and when I finally got up the courage to come for my answer, I never expected I'd have to rescue you again. Do you have an answer for me, Eliza?

— Are you going back to Wollongong, Jack? I couldn't face that ocean again.

— Not if you don't want to. Do you have an answer, dear?

— Oh, Jack. I'm torn between what I want and what I ought to do.

Just then come little running footsteps and a black-haired moppet pushes open the door.

— You can't hold her hand. I'm the only one who can hold her hand. Get away!

Jack raises an eyebrow at Eliza.

— One of your little sisters?

— No, not quite. Come round this side of the bed, pet. You can hold my other hand. Angelique, say hello to your Uncle Jack.

Jack looks from Angelique to Eliza, and back again. Eliza smiles.

— Hullo, Uncle Jack. You gunna stay wiv us?

Jack breaks into a big Turville grin.

—That all depends on your Aunty 'Liza.

The doctor tells them it's a miracle she was not killed outright. There is just bruising and concussion. He looks in her eyes and asks her to follow his fingers back and forth, and taps her knees, ankles and elbows. Has her touch her nose, then his finger, faster and faster, and pronounces her on the mend. It is nearly noon by this time and Eliza is propped up by big pillows, and tended by Angelique whom Hope and Modesty have dressed like Florence Nightingale in a white nightie with a belt, and a white table napkin tied in a triangle over her head. Canning even lets her carry a tray of broth and toast to her patient.

Jack sends a note to the Squire to come the next day and bring Polly. Joan says she'll find room for them, one way or another. Meanwhile, Jack meets the four other children, and there is simply no time available to have personal time with the person he'd come to have it with. Eliza wants to be up and about as normally as possible and Jack takes advantage of her concussion to walk arm in arm, 'to steady her', he explains. A good excuse. She doesn't mind a bit.

At 9 p.m. Joan leaves Jack and Eliza in the parlour, and goes out to play Patience on the dining room table.

— I trust ya, Jack Turville.

They are alone for the first time in twenty-four hours. He moves closer on the sofa and puts his arm around her; then she lays her head back on his shoulder with a contented smile and looks up into his strong face.

She explains all about Angelique and Alexis' will. Jack shakes his head.

— I didn't know old Angel had it in him. That would have been a shock for him, wouldn't it?

— It was before he went to Brazil where he caught the fever that wore him down physically and mentally. These are my greatest worries, Jack. My torments. I haven't told anyone else about them. I want to accept your offer; I would marry you tomorrow but I feel responsible for Mother and the children, and now also for Angelique. I'd lose everything if I marry you; and I might lose everything, anyway, if Angelique is really Angel's child.

His enfolding arm squeezes her shoulder.

— 'Grow old with me!
The best is yet to be …'

— That's beautiful!

— That's Browning, Robert. First, I'll only accept a definite 'Yes'. And now that you are going to marry me, consider the repercussions of that: I need for nothing. What's mine is yours. Your family will never want for anything, even if they don't live here. And there would be plenty left over for little Angelique.

— Isn't she a caution? She just clings to me.

— That's because you're a natural mother. Look how Polly took to you. Angelique will become more independent as she gets used to her new surroundings. Now, what other worries do you have?

— Something that worries me is the possibility that Angelique will inherit the blindness that runs in the Clare family. If so, she'll need to be looked after when she's older. I can't help feeling responsible for her.

— If she really is Angel's daughter and inherits The Slopes, she'll have nothing to worry about. If she isn't, I will make sure she has nothing to worry about. Any more worries?

— I think you've solved them all.

— See! Things always work out. Too many people spend too much time on needless worrying.

— I still can't believe you're here, Mr Rochester! Are you sure you'll still be here when I wake up in the morning?

— Oh yes. You can be very sure of that. I'm like Alfred Noyes' highwayman: 'I'll come to thee by moonlight, though hell should bar the way!'

— It nearly did.

— I have a little something for you, Eliza, from Polly and me.

Jack reaches into his coat pocket and brings out an oblong leather jewellery case.

— Open it.

Eliza takes the light brown case and opens it.

— Oh, Jack, it's just like the bracelet in Orchard's window.

— It *is* the bracelet from Orchard's window.

— How did you know?

— Mary told me. I felt sorry that Angel didn't get it for you so we bought it as a gift for you.

— It's beautiful. Help me put it on. It's difficult with one hand.

— Only if you'll accept it as a sign of our engagement.

He fiddles with the catch on the wide gold band of the bracelet inlaid with rubies and sapphires then slides it along her slender white wrist.

She gives him a radiant smile.

— I do. Now kiss me, Jack Turville. I've waited a long time.

There never was a more tender moment.

— I now pronounce you the future Mrs Jack Turville.

— Perhaps you should have asked Mother, first, for my hand in marriage.

— Dear girl, I already have your hand. Let's go and *announce* to your mother that we intend to marry, and this lovely bracelet is the symbol of our intentions.

— No need to, chicks. I heard it all, and I approve.

— Mother! You were listening at the door!

— And glad I was, too. Here, Eliza, I brought your cocoa. She always has cocoa before she goes to bed, and dunks arrowroots in it until they swell up big and soft.

— Sometimes I'm not quick enough and end up with a soggy chest.

How can I sleep after all that's happened? I'm too thrilled! Anyway, I slept half the day. Funny how someone else's perspective can change the whole way you look at things. Last night I was an emotional wreck wrestling with all these decisions. Tonight I'm as peaceful as a saint. Life really is serendipitous. In the end, though, I think it is we, as individuals, who bring about change. We each put our stamp not only on our own lives but on other people's lives as well because we act from our own free will. Life doesn't just happen to us. We **make** *it happen. And we can only make the best decisions if we understand ourselves. Polonius is right when he says, 'To thine own self be true … Thou canst not then be false to any man'. If we are true to ourselves then we can't make a wrong decision. Sounds a bit like heresy! Turn off your mind, Eliza: the angst is over. Time to slide into sleep.*

Next morning the youngest and oldest Turvilles arrive. Polly practically tumbles out of the carriage when she sees Eliza standing in the porch.

— Aunty 'Liza! Aunty 'Liza!

She runs straight to Eliza who sweeps her up in a big swirling hug.

— Oh, Aunty 'Liza, I missed you.

— I missed you, too, Polly.

— Mama's gone to Heaven.

— Yes, darling, I know.

Her little arms cling around Eliza's neck and then she notices the bracelet on Eliza's wrist as she snuggles and wriggles in Eliza's grasp, still hugging.

— You're wearing the bracelet! So you *are* going to be my new mama.

— What do you mean, darling?

— Daddy said if you wear it, you'll be my new mama.

— It's beautiful: look how it sparkles in the sunlight. Yes, I told Daddy that we'd all be one happy family.

— Goody! Today?

Eliza smiles. *How open and honest children are.*

— Not today, no; but in a little while.

— I really miss the beach, Aunty 'Liza. I used to go down and play in the waves every day.

— Who knows? When you're a big girl you might go back to Wollongong with Daddy when he goes on business, and see Muriel again.

— It'll be ages before I'm a big girl, and there aren't any beaches here.

— I wouldn't be so sure about that. Big breakers, maybe not, but I know a lovely beach we can visit near here with just the right sand for sandcastles.

— Aunty 'Liza, I love you.

And she nuzzles into Eliza's neck and gives her a big kiss.

What have I done to deserve this? The best man; the dearest little girl; and the nicest father-in-law to be, on top of my already nicest father-in-law. In giving up worldly advantage for love, I'm repaid with incalculable riches. It's the reverse of the Bible, where it says, 'For what doth it profit a man if he gaineth the whole world but loseth his own soul?' I've found my soul **and** *gained the world.* The little body in her arms stiffens.

— Who's that?

— Lift me up too, Aunty 'Liza!

— She's not *your* Aunty 'Liza, she's *my* Aunty 'Liza!

Eliza stoops and sets Polly down.

— Your Aunty 'Liza's still a bit tired from the bonk on the head the other night. Polly, this is Angelique. Angelique, this is Uncle Jack's little girl. I've known her a lot longer than I've known you so that's why she got such a long hug.

The two children eye one another. Both the same height and age, Polly's thick blond hair contrasts with Angelique's black curls. Two sets of searing blue eyes, Turville eyes, observe very similar features in the other. Angelique puts out her hand and takes Polly's.

— We've got a tree house. Come an' I'll show you.

Gabriel's turn now to give Eliza a hug. He shakes his head.

— You certainly have a way with them.

He surveys the mess. The branches have been cut off where they went through the windows and the boughs and glass have been cleared away. The gaping hole is covered by bed sheets.

— My goodness, Eliza, my girl. You survived that?

— It was Jack who saved me; or rather, Gibbon's *Rise and Fall* …. He grabbed the first books he could lay his hands on to prize me loose, so they tell me. Well, what do you think of your granddaughter?

— Eliza, I only have you to thank. She's such a joy. What a waste! But for my pride I could have known her growing up. I should never have been so hard on Jack. I'm sure his wife was a good woman. I only wish I'd had the pleasure of their company all along.

— It's no use being regretful, Gabriel. It'll just eat you away. The past is past, and nothing can bring it back. 'Nor all your piety nor wit can lure it back to cancel half a line, nor all your tears wash out a word of it.'

— True, true. Wisdom from one so young.

— I know you can more than make up for lost time, Gabriel. Did you catch sight of the little dark-haired one?

— Only a glimpse but as God is my witness, Alexis' blood runs in her veins.

— Jack tells me your property needs a bit of work and you want him to take it on, on a day to day basis.

— I hate to admit it but Jack really knows his farming, and he's wonderful with the people, the hands.

— It looks like I'll be joining you at the Hall.

— You said 'Yes'? You brave girl! There's no one I'd be prouder to welcome into the family. Give me a kiss, daughter.

Two weeks later a letter arrives from Govett and Bailey requesting Eliza to visit their chambers. She wants Jack to go up to London with her the next day.

— Mr Bailey, I'd like you to meet my fiancé, Jack Turville.

Bailey stops what he is about to do. He looks hard at Eliza, then at the man extending his hand.

— How do you do, Mr Turville. Do sit down. I gather, Mrs Clare, that you have thought it over very carefully before accepting Mr Turville's proposal?

— Mr Bailey, it was the easiest decision I've ever had to make. I cannot live without him. It's as simple as that.

— I commend you for your sentiment but do you realize what you are giving up by marrying, in accordance with the terms of the codicil to Mrs Stoke's will?

— I do, Mr Bailey: my right to The Slopes, its contents, and the Stoke fortune.

— Precisely. A *huge* fortune.
— Mr Bailey, my father is Squire Turville of …
— Harrowford Hall.
— Why, yes. Have you heard of him?
— He's one of our clients. He was in here only a few days ago to alter his will. I doubt that you will ever want for anything, Mr Turville.
— I was going to tell you that, Mr Bailey. I'm independent in my own right through properties and investments in Australia, so neither Eliza nor her family will ever want, either.
— Well done, Mr Turville. You see, the other piece of information, the real reason I called you here, Mrs Clare, is to show you these.

He pushes two documents across the desk for their perusal. 'Name of child: Angelique Claire Rousel; date born; place of birth; registered by mother (one week after birth); maiden name of mother: Monique Marie Rousel; age: 25; name of father: Angel Claire; age unknown; station: gent.' The other is Monique Rousel's death certificate.

— Which proves what we all suspected, that the child, Angelique, presently in your care, Mrs Clare, is indeed Angel Clare's daughter, and thereby the legal heir to the Stoke fortune. We also searched the marriage registers for Angel Claire or Clare but found nothing until his marriage to a Tess Durbeyfield.

He looks sharply at Eliza.

— And a second marriage to Eliza Louisa Durbeyfield. That would be you, Mrs Clare. Are you related in any way to this Tess Durbeyfield?

Eliza goes all weak. She whispers.

— Yes.
— You never mentioned the connection before.
— Will it compromise things in any way?
— No. I just find it strange that you never owned up to the relationship.
— Tess was my sister. It was very painful. And public.
— I understand. This search proves there was no polygamy, and clears the way for easy inheritance. Alexis, Mrs Stoke, did not spell out how and when such a child would come into its inheritance, and who would be the guardian. Angelique will not have access to her fortune until she attains the age of twenty-one years. You, Mrs Clare, will be her official step-mother and guardian until that time.
— But Squire Turville is her grandfather. He is Angel's father.
— Unfortunately that is not stated on any legal document. Alexis never

named him as the father of her child..

— She did in her poetry.

— Lines written by an unwitnessed hand are not considered proof. Strong circumstantial evidence but not solidly legal. Therefore, I appoint you Angelique Clare's legal guardian until she attains the age of majority. In effect, you have *carte blanche* in how she is raised for the next sixteen years. You are her Power of Attorney, and you can live at The Slopes if you wish. Instead of being the inheritee, you are now the trustee of your daughter's estate, Alexis' estate, and all names should be changed to 'Angelique Clare, in trust'.

— Oh my goodness.

— I know you'll carry out your responsibilities wisely and well. Mr Turville, congratulations. You have a very capable young woman here who has made, and will make, a positive difference to many lives.

— Thank you, Mr Bailey. I take it that Govett and Bailey will undertake to look after my affairs regarding the West Country estate?

As they leave the building, Eliza comments.

— Every time I go down the steps of these premises, I'm a different woman. I go in as one person and come out changed.

— You'll always be the same to me.

— I think we need to have a big family conference, now that we really are one big family. We need to appraise the Reverend James of developments. We should go and see him, Jack, and take the children. Angelique's his grandchild, too. Then we can bring him back with us to The Slopes to talk about future arrangements. It's certainly time for him to retire and be with his family.

— If anyone can talk him around, you can.

The big confab takes place around the dining table at The Slopes the following Sunday afternoon. Everyone present is in a new relationship with everyone else. The six children leave the table early. They've been invited to participate but it's way too far over their heads. Joan is trying to get used to having two step granddaughters. Gabriel is pleased and amused to be related to James as well as to Mrs D. The four Durbeyfield children will soon have a new brother-in-law; and James and his new granddaughter are getting along famously.

— 'Step-granddaughter' James.

— No, 'adopted granddaughter', Gabriel. Well, not exactly. Maybe we're grandfathers-in-law!

— What's it matter? We're all relatives, and we like each other! And that's rare.

They all laugh.

— Mrs D, *you* are rare.

— Now, Squire, don't nonplus me.

— James, you've reached retirement age. Why don't you come and live with me at Harrowford Hall?

— What's going to happen to the little lass?

— Angelique?

— Yes. I'd like to be near her.

It seems at last the D'Urberville curse has been broken. Hearing the coach that brought Angelique turned out to be a good omen, not a bad one. Look at the change in Father Clare: he has a spring in his step, and someone to live for. Angelique has bewitched Gabriel, as well. The 'sins of the fathers' in her case has resulted in the betterment of these two lives at least, and who knows how many more as she grows older? It's not a case of making the best of a bad thing: she's enriched us all.

— The Slopes is now technically hers and I think it best she grow up here. Mother, you and the children should stay on here, and Angelique should live with you. A good governess will knock her rough edges off in time.

— She doesn't think as much of me as she does of you, Eliza.

— Don't be silly. You're a wonderful mother. You sing and play games with the children, and now you don't have to work from dawn until sunset.

— She was helping me pick roses yesterday. Poor little thing — never saw a flower in London. Didn't even know they smelled. She loves the garden, and Old Spence is teaching her the flowers' names. She can be my little helper.

— She reminds me of the child in that poem of Tennyson's, "The Town Child" or "The City Child", or something like that.

— "City Child"

— Thanks, Jack. *He knows everything.*

> 'Dainty little maiden, whither would you wander? …
> Far and far away, said the dainty little maiden,
> All among the gardens, auriculas, anemones,
> Roses and lilies and Canterbury bells.'

— Jack and Polly and I will live at Harrowford Hall with Gabriel. In fact, I'm returning with them today.

— What about my little dark haired miss?

— Angelique will come back and stay with us for a short period but eventually she will settle here with Mother and the children. We'll do a lot of visiting back and forth. I want the two little cousins to see both their grandfathers often.

— Reverend, why don't you move into Rose Cottage? That way you will be able to see Angelique every day, and you can have your meals here.

— Mrs D, that is a suggestion worth considering.

— And *now*, Liza-Lu, it's time for you to set the date. I've missed out on two weddings and I'm determined not to miss this one, come hell or high water. How soon before these two can become legal, Reverend?

— The banns will have to be read in both parishes, here and at Harrowford, on three successive Sundays and then they can be married during the Sunday service. What do you say, Jack?

— Three weeks will give us enough time to get all suited up. What do you think, love, the Harrowford church?

— Your roots are there, Jack, and mine soon will be. That's the best place. I suppose I'll have to plan on several bridesmaids: my sisters, and your sisters, Jack? As well as two flower girls, the little ones. Father Clare, will you give me away? I suppose John could be a best man and Little Charlie could be the ring-bearer.

— And I'm going to sit there in a big hat and bawl my eyes out. Isn't that what the mother of the bride is supposed to do?

— Mother, you can do whatever you like. Would you also be in charge of the flowers? Do you think you and Spence could see to that?

Three Sundays later the congregation of Harrowford is witness to the marriage of one of their own, the Squire's son, no less. They all crane to catch a glimpse of the bride, a tall, slim girl in a copper coloured gown carrying a bouquet of huge white peonies (to honour Mary, who picked white peonies in the garden for her when she had married the first time). Their perfume wafts up and surrounds Eliza, and she smiles as she fulfils Mary's dying wish. She steps up beside Jack. The thrill is still there. She looks up at him and their eyes lock, smile, love. *I'm Home!*

CHAPTER 37

Harrowford

Harrowford Hall a year later.

It is Gabriel's birthday. Eliza has insisted the cousins see each other often, and there is a lot of coming and going both at The Slopes and at the Hall. Today, Joan, James, Angelique and the children have come to the Hall for Sunday dinner accompanied by a tall young stranger who seems to know everyone very well.

Two little girls, hand in hand, come up from the shady river with bunches of bluebells and wild daisies clasped in their free hands. They look remarkably alike. Polly's light straw-coloured hair, like her father's, is braided into two thick plaits while Angelique's dark curls defy capture and dance over her shoulders. They both have rectangular faces with large blue eyes under straight eyebrows.

— Grandpa! Grandpa! Look what we found!

They race up the back lawn, nearly tripping on their grass-stained pinafores, with the exuberant Rover at their heels. Gabriel looks up, delighted.

— What, my girls? What have you found now?

They reach his side.

— Flowers for Aunty 'Liza.

— You'd better get washed up for dinner. I heard them calling.

They rush into the house, nearly knocking cook off her feet, their boots clattering on the stone flags of the kitchen.

— Easy, now. Easy!

A breathless governess follows them into the main hall and up two storeys to the play room where they begin to wash and get bits of grass out of their hair.

The high-timbered ceiling of the ancient dining hall rings with chatter. The Young Squire sits at one end of the table and the Old Squire, his father, Gabriel, crowned by a paper birthday hat, sits at the other end as chief carver of the roast. The long table needs all its leaves as it hosts the extended family. Eliza sits on Jack's right and Polly on his left. Angelique is blissfully seated between her two grandfathers, James and Gabriel, with the stranger next to Joan. Hope, Modesty, John and Charlie make up the middle of the table.

— Tell us how you found the gold, Abraham.

— Hush, Charlie. The Reverend James is about to give the blessing.

Immediately after "Amen' …

— Tell us, Abraham.

— You'd better satisfy him, Abe. I want to hear, too. It's been a long time since Polly and I waved you and your sister off in Sydney.

— It was quite by accident. I was at the point where I was getting down a bit. I'd started a claim, and panned it every chance I got — weekends and after work; but …nothing. Other chaps found little beads of gold in the sand and grit, and the fellow on the next claim found one the size of a raspberry. It wasn't fair. They call it a 'gold rush'. There was a rush all right but there was no gold. One Saturday I was really fed up. I'd worked until noon at the store and my back was sore. By four o'clock out on the claim I'd had it. I was even considering giving the whole thing up and coming back to England. I was pacing up and down on the claim thinking about my options and kicking the stones around when I stubbed my toe on a rock that I couldn't kick out of the ground. It wasn't orange like the other stones in the desert. It was duller, more yellow, and smoother. And what do you know? It was a nugget. A gold nugget! Big as my fist. It didn't take me long to scratch the dirt away, I can tell you. I forgot all about my sore back. And heavy! That nugget bought me my freedom. Bit like you, Liza. All of a sudden I could be, and do, anything I wanted.

— That's going to be me some day too.

— John, let Abraham finish his story.

— It boiled down to: Do I want to live in England? Or do I want to live in Australia? I like it there. It might be hot and barren on the plains but I've learned to like it a lot. Big sky. Blue sky and orange desert. It's grown on me. The people are self-reliant and very friendly. (He tells Jack afterwards that he's known as 'Paddy Hannan' or 'the Pommy bastard'. Jack slaps him on the back and says. 'In that case, Mate, you're in like Flynn.') I took my gold nugget to the bank and had it weighed, and they put the equivalent in an account for me. I'd never had a bank account. I never had any money, not more than I could put in the toe of a sock. Besides the bank, I didn't tell anyone. I kept working in the store until one day another general store in Kalgoorlie came up for sale. The owner had struck it rich and left town. I bought the place at noon the very next day and gave my notice when I went back after lunch. You know who always makes their fortune in gold rushes? The general store keepers, and that especially applies to Kalgoorlie. Out there, we supply the gold fossickers with wheelbarrows and flour, picks, shovels, clothes, sugar, tea, hurricane lamps, boards and nails, cooking oil, everything they need (or think they need) and we get paid in gold dust, or sometimes the small odd nugget. My store just happens to be opposite the Pub so I can always drum up business over there while I'm having a quencher.

— I'm going to Kalgoorlie when I grow up, Abe.

— Me too!

— Eat your vegetables, boys.

— I hate peas.

— Me too.

— Think of the thousands of starving Chinese and be grateful for good wholesome food.

— Yes, Reverend James.

— And there'll be no Queen Pudding unless you clean your plates.

The boys exchange glances.

— Yes, Mother.

Joan looks round the table at all her children.

— Well, lookit here. We're all one big happy family come together to celebrate your birthday, Squire.

— My dear Mrs D, in my experience big families are seldom happy. Nevertheless, here's to us all. Let us hope that all we adults from diverse backgrounds and experiences gathered here today due to the life and actions of one person, Alexis, can give these young people a strong sense of worth and a firm base to achieve their dreams and ambitions in life.

He raises his wine glass and the others all raise theirs, filled with various liquids.

— To Alexis!

The penetrating wail of an infant floats over to them from the double bassinet in the corner and Eliza follows the noise with her eyes. She looks over at the new Member of Parliament for the West Country and their eyes light up as Jack smiles back. Joan gives some grandmotherly advice.

— You should have left the twins upstairs in the nursery, Eliza. It's too noisy for babies down here.

— They're part of our family, too, Mother. I wanted us all to be together when we sing "Happy Birthday".

Eliza puts her hand up to her heart and feels for a double-sided locket hanging around her neck which holds two locks of babies' hair. Inside one half of the locket, inscribed 'Gabriel', is a swatch of straight blond hair; while in the other, hidden from that of her twin, is an auburn curl behind the inscription 'Alexis'.

ISBN 1425140246